ALIHAHD . .

To most of the k
without a face, a
name.

But luck and disguises had finally given out, and a
Na'id squadron was in fast-closing pursuit of his
ship, *Liberation*.

He was staring out the viewport without really
seeing, when a pattern of lights appeared out of an
unexpected quadrant. And a slow sick horror
penetrated the blank space inside him.

> *Na'id?*
> Could he possibly be *surrounded* by Na'id ships?
> But it was not a Na'id ship.
> It was worse. . . .

R M MELUCH

Jerusalem Fire

Futura

An Orbit Book

Copyright © 1985 by R M Meluch

This edition published in Great Britain in 1986
by Futura Publications, a Division of
Macdonald & Co (Publishers) Ltd
London & Sydney

*All characters in this publication are fictitious and any
resemblance to real persons, living or dead, is purely
coincidental.*

ISBN 0 7088 8202 1

Reproduced, printed and bound in Great Britain by
Hazell Watson & Viney Limited,
Member of the BPCC Group,
Aylesbury, Bucks

Futura Publications
A Division of
Macdonald & Co (Publishers) Ltd
Greater London House
Hampstead Road
London NW1 7QX
A BPCC plc Company

Acknowledgements

Quotations from *The Koran*, tr. by N J Dawood (Penguin
Classics, Fourth Revised Edition, 1974), © N J Dawood,
1936, 1959, 1966, 1968, 1974; and from *The Bhagavad Gita*,
tr. by Juan Mascaro (Penguin Classics, 1962), © Juan
Mascaro, 1962, reprinted by permission of Penguin Books
Ltd.

Does Jerusalem stand?
>   —Traveler's question

I don't understand Jews.
>   —Shad Iliya

Christians, Mohammedans, and Jews, peoples who placed
revelation before reason . . .
>   —T. E. Lawrence, *Seven Pillars of Wisdom*

Idolatry is worse than carnage.
>   —*Koran*

Thou shalt have no strange gods before me.
>   —*Decalogue*

To whatever name you pray, God hears and answers.
>   —Na'id tenet, adapted from
>   the *Bhagavad Gita*

The human Deity hath many names. No god ever told us
a name to call. Perhaps we are being snubbed?
>   —Roniva

I don't understand Jews at all.
>   —Shad Iliya

PART ONE

ALIHAHD

I. No Blaze of Glory

The captain was a notorious rebel runner. He was called Alihahd. This was his last run.

He had no real name, only a Chesite word, *alihahd*, which meant "he left." He had no country, no planet, though several including Chesa claimed him. To most of the known galaxy he was a legend without a face, and to the rest a face without a name.

He was very tall, lank. Long arms, left bare below short sleeves, were gnarled like the ancient olive trees of Earth. Big-boned, loose-jointed, and spare of flesh, he had the punished look of one at war too long. A dignity of bearing saved him from being gangly.

His eyes were splendid, expressive in their depth. His features were strong and regular, but he was too drawn to be deemed handsome anymore.

He had lived over half his natural life span, which was much older than he had ever expected to get. He was not surprised that it was to end now.

Luck and disguises had finally given out, and a Na'id squadron was in fast-closing pursuit of his runner ship *Liberation*. Alihahd had begun loading his refugees into the *Liberation*'s twelve emergency shuttles; they would have to make the rest of the journey to the free planet New Triton without him. Alihahd and a handful of volunteers would stay in the mothership to lead the Na'id on a chase in a false direction until overtaken and destroyed. Or, should the Na'id try to board the *Liberation*, she would self-destruct to cover the absence of her passengers and shuttles.

Alihahd stood motionless on the command deck, one large knobby hand at his belt, one fist on the console, knuckles down as if he'd punched it and frozen there. He could overhear sounds of orderly flight drifting up from below where refugees spoke in whispers and shuffled in steadily moving lines onto the emergency craft.

He heard an airlock close, lock. The life bay thumped open. A shuttle detached and moved silently to the port side of the mothership, where four other loaded shuttles grouped in the bright oasis of the *Liberation*'s docking lights, waiting to depart all together in a convoy when the last of the shuttles was boarded.

Another airlock closed. Locked.

That was six.

The mind counted without passion. Alihahd hadn't thought that the end would feel like this. He was feeling nothing.

He had planned for this contingency a long time, down to the clockwork details. The actual crisis was so like the countless times he had run it in his mind that this seemed just one more exercise.

He was fundamentally alone in this, without friends or lovers; he had been so for years. He had only votaries and dependents. There was no one aboard who honestly knew him as a man. To his passengers, and even to his crew, he was a distant, unfailing protector come from nowhere without selfish motive to spirit discontented subjects away from Na'id rule. His history was a blank but for a hint in a beautiful and correct voice; he would slip into high prose at times, betraying a cultured, important birth, and everyone supposed he was fugitive royalty, but his cosmopolitan accent defied anyone to say from *where*.

He had kept himself always remote, but he had a personal diffidence that made it obvious that were he ever to meet another human being on an intimate level, he would be rather shy. And there was the too-gentle way he moved his hands, suggesting a tender nature—or hiding a violence that dreaded all but the lightest touch lest he destroy.

He was staring straight out the viewport without really seeing, when a pattern of lights appeared out of an unexpected quadrant; and a slow sick horror penetrated the blank space inside him.

Na'id?

Could he possibly be, he wondered, *surrounded* by Na'id ships?

But it was not a Na'id ship.

It was worse.

A ghostly white image of a derelict sailing ship glided into view on the waves of a nonexistent sea. Misty at first, the frosty glow took the shape of an ancient brigantine, a plague ship, a fighting sail, in sharp-edged lucent detail, its shredded jibs straining from the bowsprit on fraying ropes, its topsail a fluttering rag on the splintered yard, whipped by a vacuum wind. This ship was the last sight of many a Na'id crew. "Marauder," Alihahd breathed without voice. The *Flying Dutchman* of the stars.

A chill ran up Alihahd's back, pricking at the hair along his spine and his arms. His thick lips twitched, then he resumed his habitual stone face.

The Marauder had once been only a legend, for centuries the terror of superstitious travelers. Someone in recent years had made the Marauder real and used it to destroy ships of the Na'id empire.

Its long tradition had fixed the Marauder in popular memory as a childhood fear that never went away. On sight it was instantly recognized and instantly feared. The Marauder could scare a victim to death before firing a shot.

But the eerie brigantine was only a projection. The real ship was nearby; it hovered outside the periphery of the *Liberation*'s sphere of light, painted black and difficult to see, its surface albedo nil, giving the impression of something *not* there. The backdrop of stars allowed only glimpses of a spidery silhouette of clawlike angles. It looked like a nightmare.

The spectral hologram was the announcement: *You are next*. The ship had the guns.

A good many horrified people fired at the hologram.

Alihahd would not be thrown by the unreal—though he had in the distant past been accused of the tendency. He kept his eyes on the black ship.

He should have been relieved to meet the archfoe of his enemy—

—except that his own ship bore Na'id markings. *Liberation* was disguised to travel in Na'id space as a Na'id vessel, so how could the Marauder know the truth?

The command deck had become abruptly still; those of his

crew who were there looked at Alihahd the way they always looked at him—as if he could perform miracles. He could see a ghost of his own reflection in the viewport—rangy, under-fed, and old beyond his years—and he wondered what it was they saw.

He was conscious still of the unwary shuffling of refugees below deck.

On the Marauder's blank surface appeared the ragged out-line of mandibles opening to reveal a red furnace within. The thing was about to open fire.

Alihahd moved to his ship's transmitter, intending to get out an order for the six waiting shuttles to scatter and run, so that at least one might escape, but he froze at the switch—not from fear or indecision, but from instinct.

He drew his hand away from the switch and braced for the fire when instinct proved wrong.

But the Marauder held its position and observed, as if sensing something not right, something different, perhaps curious as to why a sound vessel was being evacuated. Or maybe the Marauder had instincts too.

An airlock closed. Locked. A shuttle detached, oblivious to the threat. Shuttles had no viewports.

Still the Marauder watched.

Alihahd moved his hand back to the transmitter, masked out the shuttle channel, and opened all others. In what code did one attempt contact with the Marauder?

He decided on a voice message. "Alihahd," he said. He did not know if the Marauder understood the Universal tongue, but maybe he would recognize the name of his enemy's enemy if nothing else. "This is Alihahd. We are not—*not*—Na'id."

He paused.

There was no movement on the command platform but the silent shifting of panel lights that washed pale red and green across bloodless faces, some of them terribly young.

There was no acknowledgment from the Marauder. But neither was there an attack.

The phantom ship menaced with its red maw agape, a ticking bomb to be defused before the caprice of a moment turned the decision. There had to be a way to get through.

Every next second the Marauder could imagine deception in a blinking bow light and open fire.

Without taking his eyes from the viewport, Alihahd spoke to his bridge crew in a quietly urgent whisper. "Close that hatch."

They scuttled across the deck to obey, sealing off the hatch to the shuttle bay before someone could come up and spy the shimmering sails of the ancient derelict and scream its name.

The command console had lighted up all over with hailing signals from perplexed shuttles which could detect but not see or identify the presence of an extra ship near them. They could only tell that the configuration was not Na'id.

Alihahd clicked off all the demanding lights with his long fingers, and he glanced at the chronometer. The Na'id would be closing in soon. Six minutes.

He leaned straight-armed over the console, glowering at the black ship, his mouth drawn taut, speculative. His dusky face darkened. He lowered his chin and glared, gaunt muscles of his arms standing out in high relief as he grew angry over a sudden suspicion. An instinct.

The bomb was not ticking; it was chuckling.

He touched the transmitter again. "I think you are reading me, Marauder," he said in a sharp voice that made his crew gasp and cringe and brace for explosions. "I also think you know Universal. So understand *this*: A Na'id squadron is due here to destroy us in five minutes Earth standard. Now I have to assume, since you are playing the *Dutchman*, that you also mean to destroy us, but if you want me to grovel for my passengers' lives you will have to inform me soon or forfeit the pleasure to the Na'id; but then you would have to break your precious silence, would you not?

"For myself, by you or by them, I will be equally dead. I don't very much care. So please either shoot, talk, or go away. Or you may go to hell, where I am bound with or without you." Then he added crisply, "Do you want me to repeat any of that?"

Again the Marauder gave no acknowledgment—except to pull away and vanish.

The crew stared at Alihahd with reverent, startled wonder. He had pulled off the required miracle.

No miracle, thought Alihahd. He had lived long enough to know the smell of a player of deadly games.

An airlock closed. Locked.

That was eight.

There was still time. The boarding continued smoothly, the refugees unaware that the ghost ship had brushed so close and passed them by.

The last shuttle was loaded but not launched when Alihahd saw glances and nods pass between the muscular crewmen to either side of him. Alihahd backed out from his spot between them to look at them, one then the other, straight into their guilty eyes. The rest of the bridge crew froze like dogs caught chewing the carpet. There were too many people on the command platform.

"What? What is this?" Alihahd spoke levelly, even gently. "Is this a mutiny?"

There was another exchange of glances—many. Whatever it was, they were *all* in on it. If they had turned against him, he was alone.

The handsome crewman to Alihahd's left shifted his weight, pushed an auburn curl off his forehead, cleared his throat. "Please, sir," he said. "Get on the shuttle. You don't have to die. Let us take the ship by ourselves."

After a grim, intimidating pause, Alihahd shook his head and said gravely, "You know better."

"We intended to force you," the crewman said softly.

For a moment Alihahd was too surprised to react. Not that they should conceive of such a plot—his crew were addicted to dreams of daring valor—but that they still, even faced with his disapproval, seriously intended to go through with it.

The mind assimilated this new development without the body giving sign of the incipient panic quailing at his core. Alihahd maintained his perfect outer calm—it maintained itself out of habit—while inside he had been struck very close to a vital point and was struggling to hold his guts in. Only his fragile dignity was still keeping his crew at bay. There was really nothing else to keep them from laying hands on him and ingloriously dragging him down to the loading platform, depositing him in the last lifecraft, and shuttling him away to safety.

There was not one of them he could best if it came down to physical pull, grab, and wrestle. They had chosen their beef for this task, knowing he would object for all he was worth. He was taller than the tallest and had the bone structure to match the strongest, but he hadn't the flesh; and age and abuse had taken much from him. He felt suddenly exposed and powerless in their midst, nothing within his grasp, clad in a pocketless red tunic, a holsterless belt, and rubbery-soled deck boots that would not even let him deliver a convincing kick.

And his mutinous worshipers were determined to save him against his will, at the cost of their own lives. They would stumble over each other to be first in selfless heroism—they had learned it from him. They wanted to be like him. Now he had to confront these heroic monsters of his own creation.

But in their bright-eyed enthusiasm—which they had *not* imitated from him—they oversimplified, overstepped, and overlooked, and did not realize that even selflessness had its selfish reasons, and Alihahd would not be turned.

He preserved his quiet poise, making no quick desperate motion that would bring them all lunging toward him at once. Liquid eyes cast a spell, and he cloaked himself in his lordly mystique—which they thought he radiated and he thought they built around him—and stood too stately to be touched.

But awe was a feeble barrier against a dwindling count-down. The chronometer read three minutes. Someone needed to act quickly or every one of them would fall to the Na'id.

With deceptive casualness, all his apprehension contained, Alihahd walked across the deck—ten steps was suddenly an eternal length—passed naturally between two mutineers, reached under the command console and took out a gun hidden there, pointed it to his own temple, and said, "Very well, then. Force me."

By the time any of them even thought about stopping him it was too late to do anything. The crew continued to stare—now completely stumped.

Alihahd gave them a few long seconds to realize defeat, then said, "Move. We are running out of time. You will jeopardize everyone with your ill-timed heroics. The thought is not unappreciated but remains very foolish."

The crewman who had spoken for the others moved first, backing off. And because there was nothing else to do the rest returned to the duties of the original plan of evacuation—Alihahd's plan.

Alone, Alihahd held the gun close across his chest, one

hand around its barrel, trying not to shake, and trying to hold inside what must remain inside.

They were going to admire him to death, his crew. They wanted him to live; but at what cost? He imagined himself aboard the shuttle, staying apart like a leper, meeting no one's eyes, reaching haven, and answering the question, "Where is your crew?" He felt sick. He knew this feeling. He breathed with his mouth open as if there were no air left in the ship. A slickness filmed palms that never sweated. He did not relinquish the gun until the last shuttle was launched.

The little fleet of twelve shuttles separated from the mothership, moved off, and disappeared. Alihahd turned off the bright docking lights and leaned back against the bulkhead, his head back, hands loose at his sides. From here there were few decisions, and few mistakes that could bring worse results than success.

An odd elation had come over him along with the first peace of mind he could remember.

He put on his spacesuit, secured himself into his seat at the ship's controls, and waited. One minute.

The countdown was still at thirty seconds when blips appeared on the computer tracker with simultaneous visual contact. Six ships of metallic blue sublighted for attack, their hulls ablaze with red twin symbols of Galactic Dominion/ Human Supremacy.

The computer pilot engaged, and the *Liberation* shot away past the Na'id ships, and the stars disappeared.

Before leaving the squadron behind in the sublight universe, Alihahd had recognized the flagship, *Jerusalem*.

I am being chased by Jerusalem. He found that thought horribly funny. Horribly.

Alihahd knew who commanded the flagship; and he was not a mindless destroyer. General Atta"id would try to catch Alihahd if he could. A high price had been put on Alihahd's head—something the Na'id did not do as a rule, but how else to combat someone they could not recognize on sight and who left no tracks and tripped no alarms? And in the end the price had done it; Alihahd's fall had come through no mistake of his own. He had been betrayed.

How fitting.

Six ships they sent after him. They had greatly overestimated him, the reputation grown bigger than the man. They thought him capable of anything.

At length the pursuit ships became visible again, gradually closing the million-mile gap their second's hesitation had made, and they came into range for weapons. None of the ships flew directly behind the *Liberation*, fearing what might be dropped back in its wake. They never guessed that the ship could possibly be unarmed. Their caution threw off the accuracy of their fire, and the runner ship was able to lure them farther and farther away from the shuttle convoy.

That much had been hoped for. Atta"id was a general, not an admiral, and ship-to-ship combat was not his forte.

Neither was it Alihahd's. He had made no pretense to his volunteers of having the slimmest hope of getting away. If he could have done without his crew he would have. He wished they were not with him. Did they expect another miracle?

I told you this was suicide. And—do you guess?

I want it.

The first close salvo came from the flagship. The next would find its target.

Alihahd touched the intersuit com switch at his throat and gave an order. "Brake."

There was a click in his headset. "Braking, sir."

The engines reversed. The chase ships overshot and disappeared, and the stars returned as the *Liberation* dropped back into sublight.

Before the ships could change direction, the end came in an instant.

Lights, sound, pressure, gravity, even the vibration of the ship's engines suddenly ceased. Arms and legs flailed with the outrush of air. Heart, stomach jumped; muscles contracted, Alihahd felt himself come off his seat, pulling against the straps in this abrupt weightless black silent limbo, and he hit the self-destruct in the dark. Nothing happened. He clutched the console with both hands, swallowed, his eyes wide and sightless. He wondered if he had been blinded.

In a moment, when everything was absolutely still again, he reached down, unlocked a catch, and swiveled his seat around.

And he saw stars where the hatch and most of the deck should have been.

No.

He turned on his headlamp. The command platform, with him on it, had been sheared clean off. The great bulk of the ship, with the engines, was gone.

One by one the crewmembers who remained switched on their headlamps. They were three. They stared at each other in shock, waiting for the circling sharks to board.

To Alihahd it was a nightmare of nightmares—one of the few things that could go wrong. The thought of facing Na'id mortally terrified him, and he knew they wanted him very badly. The only alternative now was suicide by vacuum, which also terrified him or he would have done it long before this.

But the Na'id did not board; they were not circling. They were, in fact, nowhere to be seen, and it took some moments to realize that when the *Liberation* had broken in two, the Na'id had chased after the other part.

There came a blue-white flash in the distance like a quick nova. That would be the *Liberation*'s engines exploding.

Minutes passed, half an hour, and the Na'id did not come back, and the surviving rebels knew they had been overlooked— left alone, without power, light-years from anywhere.

This was not what they had expected at all. They were supposed to have been in that nova, making a statement for the Resistance. The ship had made the statement without them.

Here was no end in a blaze of glory. Rather a slow and cold grave.

A creeping feeling of smallness grew in the quiet, nothing between the four small human beings and the inconceivable vastness of space. The gaping breach in the deck let the emptiness in.

Alihahd did not look at the others—knew they were looking at him.

Till at last, because he had to, he steeled himself to turn and face them. He nodded. He held out no hope to them. They accepted their fate. All they wanted was his approval.

He turned away.

He could not tell if their scrap of ship was moving. The stars did not appear to move. Nothing did. At least they were not spinning.

After a time the crew began to talk in short, muted murmurs through the suit intercoms. A voice, click, silence.

Answer, click, silence. An attempted joke, click, silence. A long pause. A voice, click, silence.

And then they fell asleep.

Alihahd was still mercilessly alert. It would be a while yet until air ran out. And in the silence his thoughts moved in on him. He was aware of what was left to him: endless dark, endless void, a floating tomb, the stars' indifferent steady light.

There was some comfort in knowing that he had made his last mistake. He had discovered he had a tremendous capacity for being wrong.

And he was never in a position to be wrong. He was one of those who always rose to the top. Leadership came easily to him; power fell into his hands. He need only stand somewhere and a line grew behind him.

The problem with power was that one's mistakes became catastrophic. Alihahd lived in perpetual fear of a false step, perpetual regret of past false steps, and he wondered if he would be better off blind drunk in an alley.

There was an alley in old Cairo on Earth he knew. He never should have left.

He found himself in vacillating prayer to a God he did not rationally believe existed, first asking to live, then, realizing he did not actually want to go on living, he would recant and start over—not that Anyone was paying attention either way. The idea of a benevolent, prayer-answering deity chafed against logic. Alihahd usually avoided thinking about it. But adrift in the eternity between the stars, it seemed a natural thing. The line between logic and illogic thinned and snapped.

He thought seriously of all the nonsensical religions, impossible to believe; they even found each other absurd.

The Na'id were much more sensible on that score. They combined rational and humanistic bits of many religions—which of course was unacceptable to *all* of them. The devout still died by the millions for their dogmatic and antiquated doctrines.

Alihahd had read their books—a few used the same one—in vain effort to understand their people. He found words now in one, words spoken in a garden.

It was easier to pray in borrowed words. Alihahd was not adept at talking to God in his own—he did not know what to say—and these fit his changing mind.

He remembered the garden. There had been much blood, none of it his.

Old skeletons rise. A lot of blood. Flame and billow. A summer day. A woman in a boat. God was suddenly very near, very Real, and it scared him.

Reality unhinging, time uprooted, space frayed and folded. He was going to panic.

Scared as never scared in his life. All-engulfing panic. Why had he picked those words, connected with that place?

Galloping heart shook his whole body. The others were sleeping and he was alone. With God.

Stop.

He held on to the armrests of his seat, hard and substantial. Only the ship and the stars are real. And all this nothing but panic, pure panic. A man going mad inside his spacesuit. He tasted salty beads on his upper lip.

Stop thinking. Hallucinations lurked around the edges of the light of his wavering headlamp.

Circulating air in his suit cooled the sweat on his heaving sides. At this rate his oxygen would run out first of the survivors.

Trembling hands uncoiled his suit's life cable, hooked it to his seat. He unstrapped himself and made a floating prowl through the remains of the bridge and found a stashed container of wine. He returned to his seat and drank himself into a stupor—so that he would not notice when he passed out for want of air.

II. Iry

When Alihahd awoke he was in a strange place—a spaceship—and he was no longer in his spacesuit. The air pressure was less than he'd kept *Liberation*'s but still safe.

He was lying on a deep-colored carpet spread over a hardwood deck. There were straps around his head, his shoulders, and between his legs, and for a terrible moment he thought he had been captured and bound. But he sat up and found that his limbs were free, his movement unrestricted, and that the ship was not of standard Na'id design. The strap around his head held to his face a tubed mask through which he was breathing pure oxygen. He lifted the mask and sniffed the ship's atmosphere. It was depleted of free oxygen, poisoned with carbon dioxide, and unbreathable. He fitted the mask back in place.

The other straps made up a harness that did not fit at all well with Alihahd's tunic. He fumbled at the buckle and was going to take it off as soon as he figured out how, but his wine-dulled mind was easily distracted and shifted to something else.

What caught his attention was the damage. The ship had been in an accident. Or battle. There were signs of fire and buckling in what he hoped was not the outer hull. The overhead lights were flickering, cold, blue-cast. Electrical burns, scorched metal, and ozone censed the cabin, whose mahogany fittings were charred, and frostily tinted lamp covers lay shattered in pieces on the black-fringed carpet.

Beside Alihahd on the deck his three crew members lay sleeping—or drugged. Closest to him was the athletic spokesman of the mutineers, his muscles smoothed in unconsciousness. Long lashes grazed his youthful cheek. His name was Neal. Alihahd lightly brushed an auburn curl out of his face with the back of his hand. *I could kill you for what you tried to do to me.*

Next to him was the *Liberation*'s engineer, Yuko, her petite form curled up like a puppy, her little mouth drawn down into a frown as in a bad dream. Her black hair was clipped so short it stood on end, and bleached into it behind one ear blazed a white pentagram. She was a witch, she said, but Alihahd had never seen her magic work. She was a better engineer.

Beside her was a pale slip of a youth whose name Alihahd did not remember offhand. He was also fitted into a harness.

And there was a fourth person. Alihahd had not noticed him immediately because he stood apart in the semidark unmoving and had looked at first like an empty spacesuit stood ceremonially to one side like a suit of armor. The viewplate was opaque one-way glass and Alihahd could not see the face. This would be the owner of the ship.

The stranger was tall, very tall, clearing even Alihahd's height. He—Alihahd assumed it was a man from his imposing frame—stood dead still, observing in silence, arms at his sides.

Alihahd rose to his feet and stood up straight—the oxygen tube barely reached—and he faced the stranger equally still and unspeaking. Alihahd was not accustomed to looking up at people, and he hadn't realized that it could make such a difference. The dimensions of the ship were slightly big as well and gave Alihahd the vague, uncomfortable impression of being a child again at the control and beck of others.

Behind the visor he sensed a familiar stranger—someone he had never met but knew as if he'd always known him. He was an adversary.

Alihahd did not try to communicate. If the ship's master wanted to talk, he could talk first, and he could say who he was and why he had taken the *Liberation*'s survivors aboard. Did he know whom he rescued? Was this a rescue at all? The man could be a jackal of war, a slave trader picking up Na'id leavings. He could be a Na'id private citizen who had found what apppared to be a Na'id wreck and had rescued what he thought were compatriots. He could be a neutral from uncharted space.

Or was this the Marauder?

How to know?

The ship spoke much but answered little. Its large dimensions were either a custom design for a tall man, or the standard of a tall race. It was an expensive craft, fitted out and detailed with somber luxury in colors of wine and gold, rose, wood, amber, and black. There were no nationality or planet markers anywhere in sight, and the man himself was totally obscured in his steely gray suit.

Alihahd held his stinging eyes steady on the smoky visor, trying not to look as weak as he felt. His head throbbed. He tasted stale wine.

At last the mysterious savior turned away and beckoned with a slow wave of his hand for Alihahd to come.

Alihahd hesitated, limited by his oxygen tube. But as the tall figure retreated down the corridor without looking back and disappeared through a hatchway, Alihahd took a deep breath, held it, dropped his mask, and followed.

Through the hatch Alihahd stepped into the control room.

Two great iris-apertured viewports were wide open on either side.

Stars. There were stars. The ship was traveling sublight.

The pearly white river of the Milky Way cascaded across one port; the vast glowing aureola of the galactic hub filled the other, a thick scatter of dust intervening to dim the light many magnitudes so that surrounding space still looked black.

Bright in the foreground shone a single yellow sun.

Alihahd drew closer to the port and looked down.

The ship was orbiting a moonless planet of muddy-green continents and blue seas, its equator wreathed in thick white clouds that spiraled and thinned to the north and south. Even from this distance Alihahd could see mountains. They would have to be gargantuan, though only the arctic ones were snow-capped. The world must be hot. Alihahd gave a second dubious look at the white-belted equator. The oceans were too deep actually to boil, but a permanent haze of vapor steamed off the water's surface in the tropics.

The ship's master drew Alihahd's attention to the control console, where he traced slowly on the smooth surface with his forefinger in Roman characters—symbols used by many languages, including Universal—a single word and question:

IRY?

A thrill of discovery awakened in a mind Alihahd had thought too jaded for wonder.

Iry was one of the lost worlds. There were many places known in the First Historical Age that had been lost after the Collapse and not yet rediscovered. But this one was a fantastic place; not everybody was convinced that Iry had ever existed—like Atlantis.

Yet here was a living planet, beyond recivilized space, its yellow sun hidden in the Great Rift where it was supposed to be, and it *looked* right.

The Eyes of Iry stared back at him, two impact craters peeking clear of the shroud of clouds. He could not see the encircling River Ocean, but the computer diagram on the ship's screen said it was there beneath the clouds and continuing around the dark side of the planet.

The computer diagram also revealed this to be a peculiar little solar system in keeping with the myth of one sun, one planet, and no moons.

This last was the telling point. In Alihahd's experience,

one was an extraordinarily odd number of planets for a normal yellow star, and there were few sizable worlds anywhere orbited by no moon at all.

Alihahd looked up to the ship's master and answered with a nod down, which would tell him *yes* if this man understood nods; then Alihahd left the cabin to return to the makeshift contraption that was his oxygen mask. This ship was not designed for guests or for emergencies.

Nor was it a slaver. Slavers did not pick up merchandise they could not sell. This ship could not even get itself to a familiar port. They would all be taking their chances on the strange world below.

Iry. The name summoned visions of Itiri warrior-priests, witches and warlocks attended by familiars in wondrous shapes, living on mountain tops, flying on wings with the eagles of Iry, journeying on quests between the stars, armed with their magical double-curved swords that never dulled. Legends always had their special weapons; it was required of them. For the Itiri it was the double-curved sword.

The mythic, fairy-tale quality pervaded all the stories, so of course the Itiri were beautiful, humanlike, tall and fair, golden-haired and emerald-eyed—a distinctively un-Na'id concept of beauty.

The legend was popular outside Na'id circles, for it dealt with what the Na'id dreaded and insisted could not exist—a superior sapient species.

But if the Itiri were anywhere near as prodigious as their reputation, where were they now and where had they been hiding for the two thousand years of the human Dark Age? Truth was that when Earthling ships had ceased to fly, so did the Itiri, which told Alihahd where the stories were coming from—human imaginations. He did not believe in the Itiri's superhuman exploits any more than he believed that Atlantis had developed atomic power.

For him the great significance of the stories about Iry's natives was not that they gave any insight into Itiri nature—Alihahd believed they did not—but that they suggested the planet itself—the core of the myth—was habitable.

And for the first time he realized that he was going to live. He was too numbed to know how he felt about it.

He held his breath and rejoined the ship's captain in the control room.

They had started a slow descent. Alihahd felt the added tug of the planet's gravity and the ship's resistance as the brakes cut in. He could tell by the way the ship was going down that she was not an in-atmosphere vehicle.

They were entering twilight, descending on the night side of the world. The creepingly slow landing would use all the ship's reserves, but the battered vessel was not going to take anyone anywhere again. When Alihahd left this world it would be in another ship, or never.

He glanced at the stats on the computer screen; they read in Scientific, a specialized language even more universal than Universal. The figures told him the planet was smaller than Earth, heavier, its density 7.19. It was .9 astronomical unit from a sun whose spectrum was strong with heavy elements. The planet's atmosphere was oxygen-rich and contained more inert gases than Earth's, but not enough to be of consequence as far as breathing was concerned. Pressure at sea level was three Earth atmospheres.

Already Alihahd felt hot and heavy and crowded. He started again to take off his harness, but a silvery-suited hand closed on his wrist and stopped him.

Contact startled Alihahd, and he looked up at the opaque faceplate in surprise.

The stranger patted the flat pack strapped to Alihahd's back as if that was an answer. Because it would mean speaking first, Alihahd did not argue, and only hoped that he would understand later.

The strong hand slowly let go his wrist. The grip had not been tight but it had been powerful, and Alihahd was not at all sure he could have pulled free had he tried.

He retreated from the control room, paused at his oxygen mask to breathe, then went searching for and found the head. The ship's owner *was* male. He also owned a cat or a ferret or some small pet. There was no one else aboard—no room for anyone else. For all the sense of space in the moody corridors, it was a small ship.

Everything on board was indicative of one man, one soul— rich, heavy, and dark with gilded borders, all custom-worked and, so, untraceable to any place or any period. It was disconcerting, the ambient strength, even arrogance of the place, its autocracy, and enigma—all impression and no facts.

Alihahd returned to his mask and sat on the deck. Had he

been alone he would have risked provoking the wrath of his formidable host and stolen into the engine room to see what kind of equipment the generators were loaded for. The number of exterior leads would tell quicker than anything what this ship was about. He suspected he knew. He wanted to look for a lead to an exterior hologramic projector.

But laws dissolved in outer space, and a ship's master was its god. There was nothing to say that the dark stranger could not put Alihahd and his companions right back where he found them.

For the crew's sake Alihahd remained where he was—where the ship's master had semiconfined him with a short leash of an oxygen tube.

He stayed awake awhile, watching his dozing comrades, becoming convinced that they were drugged. He heard the engines complain, more and more as hours dragged by. Then tension gave way to tedium and at last he slept.

A star fell out of the sky.

Five tall slender figures stood with the sentinel, silhouetted against the starfield out on the eagle ridge, gazing up.

It was a new star. It had not been in the sky the night before. At twilight it gleamed in the Red Geese like a nova, but then it slowly slipped out of the Ring of constellations and down toward the River Ocean beyond the horizon.

The Fendi Roniva turned to the younger aghara beside her with a wave of her night-colored hand, a black glitter of onyx flashing on her forefinger. "Go thou. Take thy fire kin and see. And take thou one from the fire clan of the carnelian snake. Take Arilla."

She met a quizzical look in eyes like moss agates. "Fendi?"

"Someone who knows of humankind. Thou may need." Roniva turned away, her thin, hard arms crossed. Naedenal, the night wind, moaned down the cliff face in a cold gust to become lost and voiceless in the deep ocean of air in the valley. "I sense. I sense."

"Humans?"

Roniva murmured assent. Her black eyes swept over the wide heavens. "After such a long time . . ."

Alihahd was still asleep when he heard a crashing. The deck heaved beneath him and he was catapulted into empty air.

He woke falling. He gasped in air, icy cold and sharp, not pure oxygen. He opened his eyes to bright blue all around him. The ship was gone. He was in Iry's atmosphere.

And dropping like a rock, head first, eight kilometers up, the air so cold it burned and sliced like knives. His tunic flapped wildly in the wind. His heart galloped, skin prickled. There was a sweet-sour taste of fear in his mouth, a roaring in his ears, nauseous terror in his throat. The oxygen mask was still strapped to his face, its disconnected tube whipping madly at his ear. He saw the dizzily closing ocean far below tracked with white, saw sky and white clouds and morning sun until his eyes teared shut. And he went down, faster and faster, trying to scream.

Then he felt a yank at the harness straps as if grabbed from behind and above, and he was righted, swinging suspended under an expansive white canopy, floating down at a gentle speed. Had there been anything at all in his stomach he would have thrown up.

The pounding of his heart subsided slowly till he was left with only the ashes of fear, a dull lump in his stomach, flat taste in his mouth. His skin was icy. He took off his useless mask and let it drop.

He looked up at his parachute. He had never seen one before. It seemed a primitive thing. He wondered what had triggered it to open and guessed it had to be his speed. His hands sought the harness straps and gripped them, trembling involuntarily.

He looked down. A silvery glint on the water still four kilometers below had to be the ship. He was drifting quickly away from it. Seeking a way to steer, he tugged at the risers and managed to guide himself back without setting himself into a spin.

Another parachute blossomed below him and to the windward. He looked for others, but remembered with sinking sickness that only one of his companions had been harnessed.

The ship had not been equipped for guests or for emergencies.

Then he caught sight of a long thin line plummeting straight down. At least one other person had acquired a parachute while Alihahd had slept.

A bad one. Alihahd watched, mentally screaming as it hurled down and out of sight. It never opened.

The only other things in the sky were the circling birds,

enormous creatures already clustering around where the fouled
parachute had gone, while others glided down in lazy arcs on
broad wings.

Scavengers.

Alihahd looked up again and clutched the risers, this time
in anger and horror. If only he had known.

Where is your crew?

He closed his eyes hard, grimaced, and tensed back his
neck, the feeling of someone driving nails into his skull.

Does it never never stop?

He opened his eyes and looked down at the blue ocean,
much closer now. The air had become very warm, then hot,
and the wind was heavy like a current of water. He could
now make out some definition in the craft on the water. It
was not the Marauder. And, closer, he could see it was not
even a spaceship. It was a seaplane. He could not find the
spaceship anywhere.

Surface winds across the sea swept him swiftly away from
the sea craft so he could not see more. He was aware of the
dark moving shadow of a bird above his chute, and he wished
he were armed.

Descent seemed very fast the last few meters. He hit the
water hard and plunged under. The parachute billowed down
over him a wide compass on the water's surface. He bobbed
up, but the parachute draped over his head and clung closely
without space for air. He tried to breathe through it but it
drew in, impermeable as plastic, suffocating him. He pushed
up on the fabric, but it only formed a vacuum and sucked up
the water with it.

Head ringing, lungs hurting, he fought to get out from
under the canopy, but there seemed no end. He felt heat
behind his eyes, saw black and red. He thrashed, tried to
breathe, took in water, coughed on reflex and gasped in
water.

Strength and even fear left him at once and he began to
sink in a druglike torpor. Thought he was dying. Thought he
was dead.

Suddenly there was light above as the chute ripped up and
off. There was a splash and a column of bubbles from
someone plunging into the water beside him, going down and
shooting up. A myth closed powerful hands under his arms
and heaved him up. His head broke surface. A fist pressed

under his ribcage. He expelled water, coughed, choked, spat, and finally drew air.

When the swirl of bright-dark colors blinked clear, Alihahd was staring into the green, kohl-smeared eyes of an Itiri warrior-priest.

III. Itiri

Alihahd could not speak. He opened his mouth, squeaked, then coughed.

Unconcerned with its own improbability, the myth disengaged Alihahd from the harness with agile hands and pulled him clear. The Itiri encircled Alihahd's upper body with a long hard white arm and swam toward the ship. Dazed and weakened, Alihahd let himself be dragged. Salt water and the heat of the air hurt his eyes. Steam was rising from the painfully bright glittering water, searing his brine-inflamed lungs as he inhaled.

The ship was the one he had seen from the air, an aluminum seaplane afloat on pontoons. Alihahd smelled fossil fuel, tasted it on the water, the back of his mind making note that this was not the product of a space-age civilization.

As they drew near the plane a wave came over Alihahd's head and set him coughing and gasping again. From above, two hands seized his armpits hard enough to hurt, heaved him out of the water, and sat him down heavily, a dead weight on the hot pontoon.

On the plane were a few more aliens, climbing over the wings and fuselage, and two wet humans on the pontoons—a boy spitting up, and a man.

When Alihahd could breathe again he grabbed one of the tall lithe humanoid aliens before he stopped to consider it might be taken as an attack. Green eyes turned to him, and Alihahd raised two fingers, gestured at the humans, then to the ocean, and croaked out, "Two more. There are two more of us."

The alien did not take offense. Green eyes registered comprehension, and the Itiri parted from him. Alihahd continued to speak after him as if the alien could understand, "I saw one go down with a parachute that did not open."

A voice behind Alihahd said in Universal, "That was mine."

Alihahd turned. A trickle of water followed down a strand of hair plastered to his forehead and ran down into his eyes. He brushed his bangs off his lofty brow and blinked.

"It opened, then?" said Alihahd.

The parachute must have opened. Obviously. The man was alive, not smashed into the water's surface at terminal velocity.

But the man said, "No," and pointed up.

There was an eagle.

Alihahd shaded his eyes and squinted up at the bird. From below it appeared dark until it passed out of cloudshadow and the sun struck its back, and its plumage burst into all the shades of fire.

It was fully large enough to carry off a man.

Alihahd remembered the shadow over his parachute and the Itiri dropping out of the air to rescue him. The immense birds were not scavengers after all.

Alihahd looked again at the humanoids. They looked like the impossible, creamy white with golden hair and brilliant green eyes as the stories said. All six of them were two meters tall with long, lean, hairless bodies, and they moved with a grace Alihahd considered the province of the animal kingdom. But then these were not humans. They had the physical fascination of big cats and fine Arabian stallions, beautiful, powerful, and frightening like cats, creatures that could prey on human beings.

Their eyes were elaborately lined with antimony as in Egyptian tomb paintings. The single female was squatting atop the plane, balanced on the balls of her feet, her arms crossed on her knees, her face into the wind, the image of a hawk ready to take flight. Gold tassels bobbed from a wide gold band across her forehead and dangled alongside the evenly spaced scars burned into her fair cheeks. In a sheath at her side she wore a long double-curved sword.

Alihahd looked away with a start.

At least they did not have wings.

The seaplane rose high on a swell, then settled into a horizon-swallowing trough as the wave rolled under. The sea had looked so calm from the air.

Alihahd groggily regarded the Itiri warrior-priest on the pontoon with him, and he spoke, rhetorically as much as anything, as some people talked to their cats or some drunkards to their pink elephants. "What men are you? What woman is this?" he said.

He was astounded to get an answer in kind. "We are such as thou see."

Alihahd jerked back. The elephants were not only pink, they were talking to him in his language.

The warrior crouched down before him, beads of water dripping from his coarse hair and his soaking, bright, jeweled clothes. His was an inhuman beauty. He hardly looked real, his smooth damask-flushed face made barbarous by the savage red deliberate scars high on his cheeks. There was intelligence in his green eyes smeared around with running kohl. His expression, if Alihahd could read alien faces like human faces, was benign, a little whimsical, and Alihahd sensed that his pink-cheeked elephant was laughing at him.

Alihahd spoke again with a feeling of the High Absurd. "Then I am dead, for Itiri warrior-priests are nothing more than the dreams and hopes of despairing souls."

The Itiri cocked his head quizzically, then replied with an equal sense of absurdity, "If I were born of thy desperation I could not say. Though I could swear I remember existing before I found thee drowning. All the same, we *are* now."

Alihahd raised his brows, paused to take in the dialect. He had read enough of the old histories to decipher it. He nodded. He had to admit this was all real—the planet, the eagles, the swords, and the warrior-priests speaking archaic Universal as it was spoken before the Collapse some two thousand years ago.

His head felt very thick, his ears caving in. The atmosphere was oppressive, too much pressure, too much oxygen. He was dizzy, hot and sick.

The Itiri started to rise. Alihahd caught his arm. "Others," he said. "There were two others."

"We continue to look," said the Itiri and nodded up at the soaring eagles.

The birds wheeled high over the water with slow turns on the heavy sea breeze.

The warrior-priest climbed atop the plane's wing and waved the eagles farther downwind.

Alihahd turned to see who had already been rescued.

The boy was standing on the pontoon, grasping the airplane strut in both white-knuckled fists and staring out to sea. He was very slender, clad in light-blue space coveralls. Alihahd could not think of his name.

"Are you hurt?" said Alihahd.

"N-n-no," said the youth, trembling in delayed horror at his near death. His brown face had paled; far-spaced brown eyes were wide and white-ringed. His appearance was unremarkable except that there was nothing particularly Negroid or Oriental about him. Even his skin color was still within the confines of the broad spectrum known as White. He looked suspiciously pure-blooded Caucasian. It might explain what made him a rebel.

The Na'id Empire espoused a doctrine of dissolution of all barriers that could splinter the unity of humankind, be they cultural, religious, or, most visibly, racial. The Na'id despised persons having a preponderance of recessive genetic traits, since the persistence of recessive traits indicated an isolation from the general gene pool. Such traits needed to be reinforced in order to perpetuate. If individuals of all kinds mingled freely, recessive characteristics would diminish and die out. People like Vaslav were symbols of elitist rebellion and disunion.

"Vaslav," said Alihahd, remembering.

The youth perked up at the sound of his name in Alihahd's voice, and he beamed to be known by his leader.

Alihahd had a memory for names, but this young man was not memorable, and, in truth, Alihahd could not say whether the name was first, middle, or last. He could not for the life of him recall the lad's other name or names, so henceforth he was simply Vaslav.

The other survivor was more mixed-blooded, older, striking. He was also wet, the eagle having slowed but not completely stopped his fall to the sea. He was sitting on the pontoon on the other side of the strut from Alihahd, emptying water from his rawhide boots one at a time.

He was of strapping build, wasp-waisted, his dark red-bronze skin stretched taut over a lean but imposing frame. His features were implicitly masculine but very fine. Wedge-shaped face narrowed toward his chin. His cheekbones, very high, seemed to crowd his eyes and give the effect of a permanent squint when actually he did not squint at all. His brows slanted up sharply and arched sharply over almond-shaped, tawny eyes. The eyes were really very beautiful—like of one of those angels who was asked to leave heaven—the whole face astonishingly demonic. Soft lips beneath a thick neat mustache bespoke a certain sensitivity, but that could be reading in too much.

Wiry graying copper hair was pulled back and tied at the nape of his neck, and he wore a russet bandanna twisted into a headband across his brow. Two bright gold loop earrings pierced through one ear, making him look like a pirate or a gypsy.

Gentleman pirate, it would seem. He wore a kid leather vest lined with gold, and a rawhide redingote that fell to midway down his thighs. He possessed the air of one unrepentantly self-confident as if he were someone of importance. Even sitting down he moved with a kind of swagger-unforced, second nature, not put on for anyone else's benefit. For the opinion of others he could not care less. There might have been no one else aboard the seaplane; all his attention was given to pulling on his sodden leather boots, nothing whatsoever amiss except that his clothes were wet.

Everything of his was uniquely his. His gun was a self-customized, crazy-looking thing with a wood handle and a long stabilizer that jutted out like the barrel of an old projectile weapon. He wore the gun at his belt toward his right side, grip forward, as a right-handed person would wear a sword.

Once finished emptying his boots, he drew from his waistcoat a white-gray meerschaum pipe with amber mouthpiece, its bowl carved into the figure of a fox head. Then he fished out the mess that used to be tobacco from his coat pocket. At this Alihahd had to crack a smile.

Tawny eyes slid sideways to Alihahd, and the man returned a slow, wan smile.

Alihahd's thickened brain realized this was not one of his volunteers. For one, Alihahd would have remembered if he had *ever* seen this man before. For another, he was too tall.

Their eyes met and held. Even without the mask of the dark visor the stranger was not afraid to hold a direct gaze. Menace and amusement lurked in the orange-brown tigerlike eyes.

This was the ship's master, and Alihahd was still wondering: friend or foe?

The man had spoken in Universal. That in itself was inconclusive. It meant he *might* be Na'id. He was dressed civilian but looked old enough to have been retired from military service if he was Na'id. He was obviously a private citizen, but of where? From his style of clothing he was possibly a native of Eridani. But Eridani was a Na'id possession now, had been for fifteen years. Whose side was he on?

Alihahd could not ask him to fly his colors without giving his own first. These were cautious days, and the correct answer to a stranger's inquiry of "Who are you?" was either "Why?" or "Who are *you*?" And Alihahd could not know if it was safe to speak his own volatile name. At its very mention that crazy weapon with the notched handle could come whipping out and shoot through his heart.

There were worse fates.

Alihahd could not bear to stay in ignorance and wait for the man to drop a clue. He felt a need to know *now*.

He looked dead into the tiger eyes. "Alihahd," he introduced himself. "Captain of the late runner ship *Liberation*."

"Hall," said the tall stranger. "Harrison White Fox Hall of the late ship *Nemo*."

And Alihahd knew hardly more than he had before. The name was not Na'id. But if Hall had been a conscript from Eridani he would not have an honorific name. He hadn't reacted one way or the other to the name Alihahd, remaining very cool and unimpressed.

Then what *did* the ship's name signify? "What is Nemo?" said Alihahd.

"In Latin it means *no one*," Hall said like a beginning, as if there was more to be said.

Alihahd was already alarmed. He knew what Latin was—a dead Earth language from the First Historical Age, the time before the Collapse. The Na'id were peerless in the knowledge of mankind's ancient history. A Latin name was a Na'id enough thing. Alihahd braced himself should the second half of Harrison White Fox Hall's answer be accompanied by the draw of his weapon and arrest in the name of the Na'id Empire.

Hall continued, "In Greek it means *I allot*."

That was curious. "Allot?" *Allot what*?

"Nemesis," said Hall. "What is deserved." He glanced away toward the horizon, his voice changed pitch, and he tossed the last line away as if unimportant: "Revenge, if you will."

He looked back to Alihahd, and understanding passed between them. Alihahd knew enough. Nothing more need be said.

"Mr. Hall," Alihahd finally nodded in greeting.

"Captain," Harrison White Fox Hall returned the nod, conspicuously avoiding the false name Alihahd.

Alihahd saw the wary tawny eyes taking another hard look at him.

Alihahd cut a fine figure, rangy, thin as though from dissipation, dark red tunic stuck to his gaunt frame. He spoke and carried himself like aristocracy—profoundly weary aristocracy, at once proud and sorry as a tattered flag.

He knew what it was Hall watched with those long stares and intensity bordering on venom. Alihahd's "name," his tunic, and his swarthy coloring were all appropriate to the planet Chesa. But his features were wrong; tall flat forehead, straight Nordic nose, fine hair—they were pure Caucasian. The mixture made him look very very Na'id.

Their gazes had locked again, and they tried to stare each other down. The boy Vaslav, standing over them, looked from one to the other, aware that something was going on beyond what he could see. Neither man was going to break away.

Till an eagle alighted on the aircraft, its great wings and tail fanned in braking, its talons outstretched. It screamed.

Its landing rocked the plane on the water, and Alihahd grasped for a strut to catch himself. As he pitched far over the edge of the pontoon, a whalelike head rose up from the sea, and Alihahd was suddenly face to face with a black-and-white sea creature sounding a barrage of delphine clicks and squeals from its blowhole. When the plane settled, a warrior-priest came to crouch beside Alihahd and listen to the whale as if the noises were truly intelligible. Then the fair Itiri turned to

Alihahd and said, "Two, didst thou say?" He held up two nailless fingers. "This many? Thy companions are dead."

· Alihahd hung his head, his arms slack at his sides, feet dangling into the water. He had already known. "Very well then," he said to the warrior. "We are in your hands."

The Itiri waved the whale away. The eagle launched itself with a push that bobbed the plane like a toy, and the warriors shouted and whistled to one another, climbing into the fuselage to depart this place.

Eyes downcast, Alihahd became aware of rawhide-booted feet standing at his side. He looked up. Hall had risen and was offering down a hand. Alihahd hesitated. He didn't want it. The unease he'd first felt on meeting the spacesuited stranger returned. He could stand up by himself.

But in some parts of the galaxy to refuse a man's hand was grounds for murder.

Alihahd took the offered hand, and Hall pulled him easily to his feet.

Hall climbed inside the plane with the Itiri. Alihahd started to follow, but noticed Vaslav hanging back, staring forlornly at the waves, distressed at their failure to retrieve the dead. He appealed to Alihahd. "But . . ." he stammered.

Neal and Yuko, thought Alihahd.

He put a hand on the youth's shoulder. "It's as good a resting place as any," he said with comfort and sureness he did not feel.

And to soothe the boy's mind he spoke a few words over the souls beneath the waters, though he was certain they could find their way to their God without him.

Then he and the boy boarded the plane and were taken on a journey to a place of legends.

IV. The Village

It was the first of the Red Geese when Alihahd, Harrison White Fox Hall, and Vaslav came to the Aerie. The journey took several hours in the slow way of primitives aboard a noisy vibrating craft powered by propellers and piloted without a computer. The hulking machine lurched into flight and climbed slowly, shuddering. The heat and pressure of the air lessened with altitude, and Alihahd felt better, though still plagued with the mistrust of a starman staking his life on an antediluvian transport that felt and sounded as if it would rattle apart.

The Itiri spent the entire journey in a separate compartment, leaving the humans in the cargo hold.

Fine by Alihahd. He had never liked aliens.

Harrison White Fox Hall had taken off his wet coat and had rolled up one of his shirtsleeves. He had drawn his notched-handled gun and inspected it for saltwater damage.

Alihahd was not going to ask if the notches represented humans or aliens. He had noticed the pattern of calluses on Hall's large elegantly shaped hands—thickened pads on the first two knuckles of each hand and along the outside edge of his palms.

Now Hall was sitting on the deck by a porthole, one elbow resting on one knee. He seemed to be enjoying the view.

A man who decides who lives and who dies. Not even a *pretense of regret*. His ship in danger, Hall had placed the available parachutes on himself and the other captain, the last people who should have been saved, and he stayed cavalier through the entire harrowing ordeal.

Alihahd felt anger. And envy.

The plane hit an air pocket, and it jumped and dipped. Alihahd closed his eyes and waited for the crash he thought was coming.

When it did not happen he opened his eyes. Hall was looking at him.

A ghost of a smile glided beneath the graying mustache. "Not afraid, are you, Captain?"

That was provocation. Hall wanted a fight. And he wanted it with Alihahd. The boy Vaslav did not interest him.

Alihahd would not have it. He would take a fall before he would be baited into defending himself. Self-respect he had none. Honor was long gone. There was nothing to defend; Hall ought to know that about men without names.

He swallowed the insult. "Maybe I am."

He could tell that Hall was unsure if he had won the confrontation or not.

Hall distractedly drew his pipe, took it between his teeth and reached into his pocket for tobacco. Finding his pocket empty he suddenly became conscious of what he was doing and he put the pipe away.

Alihahd had disturbed Hall's perfect understanding of the universe.

Avoiding a challenge was not a thing to do where Hall was from. It was cowardly. Yet Hall could not call Alihahd a coward—not under the circumstances in which he had found him. However, Alihahd had admitted fear outright. On Eridani a man did not back down from challenge like that.

Unless he was very very sure of himself.

And it occurred to Hall that Alihahd simply did not care what Hall thought of him. The accepted insult was not surrender. It was a slam at Hall. Alihahd's regard for Hall was so slight as to nullify anything Alihahd might say to him. Alihahd's words were empty appeasement as one might mouth to a bothersome child to shut him up. Alihahd knew who Alihahd was and to hell with Hall and his opinions. Alihahd probably did not even realize what he was doing, the insult more complete for being sincere and uncalculated.

Hall had never been so thoroughly put down in his adult life.

Hall was amazed, about to be angry, then a slow hunter's smile of intrigue crept onto his lips. He laughed, a low crumbly sound.

Alihahd looked at him. Hall winked a stalking tiger's eye.

The captain was an enigma, a maze of diametric leads, brave and frightened, strong and weak, assured and uncertain, serene and haunted. Nothing about him was clear or unopposed by some other trait.

And Hall realized it could only be that his elusive captain was two people. And one was not real.

The one without a real name.

The plane had abandoned the coast and gone inland to cross a mountain range.

"Good," Hall remarked on it. "I can't swim."

"I suppose I cannot either," said Alihahd. "I drowned once before."

"Only nearly, it looks like," said Hall.

Alihahd did not elaborate. He gazed out a porthole.

The land was stark and impassable save by air. The plane weaved between mountains, unable to clear the towering peaks.

Vaslav watched the austere terrain, his one hand clapped across his mouth, his eyes round with dread. He hadn't stopped trembling. He lowered his hand; it fluttered like an indecisive butterfly. "Will we be here the rest of our lives?" he said weakly.

"I do not know," said Alihahd, his words slow and distinct, for the boy was new to the langauge. "The natives did not learn Universal in total isolation. That much is certain."

Vaslav craned back his head, perplexed. "They are speaking Universal?"

Alihahd smiled. "Of a sort."

The plane stopped once to refuel on a lonely plateau, then continued over the rugged land on its solitary winding way. They had lost the eagles long ago.

At last the jagged peaks gave way to a sudden, startling cradle of relative flatness, a wide fertile plain in an open valley ringed by high mountains where eagles flew. Squares of green and gold cultivations checkered the fields and crept up the feet of the enclosing mountains on terraced slopes. A long thin veil of a waterfall spilled from one of the massifs and fed a meandering river that twisted through the valley in a lazy course lined with willowlike trees and neat, pretty little houses of broad woody reeds carved and shaped, perched on stilts, and roofed with varicolored reeds upcurved at the eaves.

The plane landed in a warm dusty meadow of brown

grasses. The warrior-priestess named Arilla came back to the humans' compartment and let them out to the summer village of Kaletani Mai.

Alihahd dropped down from the plane and took a few unsteady steps on the first solid ground he'd trod in a long time. It was summertime here. It was always summery in the village. The sky was clear blue. The smell of ripening fields drifted to him on a mild breeze.

The villagers came running out of the fields at the aircraft's arrival, and Alihahd backed up against the plane in the face of the noisy, barefoot onslaught of short stocky aliens panting like dogs and chattering in a strange tongue. But it was a benign rush, aimed at the warrior-priests more than the humans, who were a mere passing curiosity.

The villagers were short and bulky like big gnomes—as draft ponies to racehorses next to the six tall slender warrior-priests. A leathery smell exuded from their dusty skin, skin that was brown or white, changing as they stood in full sunlight or shadow. All of them had light red hair and black eyes. Their kind was called ranga. The tall fair warrior kind was called aghara. They looked like two different breeds.

Looks deceived.

The babbling, smiling ranga surrounded the laconic warrior-priests, who answered them tersely in the ranga's incomprehensible language. There was a lot of talk—questions, answers, directions, arrangements, acknowledgments. Vaslav listened closely, as if he could actually pick out patterns in the inchoate noise.

Alihahd eased away from the throng, retreated to the far side of the airplane under the shade of the wing, and leaned on the pontoon, his head on his arms.

Harrison Hall had taken off on his own, exploring.

Vaslav came under the plane wing with Alihahd. Alihahd lifted his head and rubbed his brow. "Yes, Vaslav."

Vaslav's eyes were darting this way and that, taking in the alien trees and crops, the charming village, the blue sky. He was furtively smiling but unsure if he ought. He looked to his captain for the proper reaction. Alihahd did not look happy.

"Are—are we safe?" said Vaslav.

"I see no evidence for alarm," said Alihahd reassuringly. "Go walk with Mr. Hall. I swallowed too much brine is all." He motioned the boy away with a weak wave of his hand.

Vaslav's smile spread to an open beaming grin, and he bounded away to catch up with Harrison Hall.

Alihahd covered his eyes with his hand. It was the mark of a great leader to be a consummate liar. Alihahd was scared to death. But why ruin the boy's image of an idyll—especially when he just might be right? Alihahd kept the worry to himself; that was what leaders were for.

The complete alienness of his surroundings weighed o' him. He felt ill. He needed distance.

He stooped, crawled underneath the body of the plane, sat with his head leaning against the rough treads of the tail wheel, and shut his eyes.

He found comforting familiarity in the sound of wind in leaves, the smell of chlorophyll and dry grain fiber, and the rubberlike tire at his back. He could almost imagine this to be one of Earth's far-flung colonies, and the alien voices to be but the chatter of slaves.

Yet darker visions invaded his illusion. He knew what experiments the Na'id performed on live aliens, on parts of them or with removed strips of their skin and bone.

And humans were the aliens here.

He bided an indeterminate while beneath the plane, and began to think he'd been forgotten. The day grew hot, and he had no ambition to move. The sun was directly overhead. This place, Kaletani Mai, was in the tropics. The planet was near its solstice.

He listened to the buzz and chirp of reptilian birds, dozed off and on, studied his sheltering plane with its wheels and pontoons, and decided it was a stupid design for an aircraft.

Harrison White Fox Hall returned from his prowl, his dark red-bronze face burned a deeper red, and he eased himself under the plane with Alihahd. Vaslav crawled in after him.

"Didn't get too far," said Hall. He took off his bandanna, loosed the knot, and retied it around his head. "Some industry behind the hill where the river curves round. Hardly impressive. This seems to be state-of-the-art technology." He patted the metal belly of the ungainly amphibious craft above their heads.

Alihahd groaned, his hopes of ever getting off-world fading. But he hadn't realistically expected more.

Hall stretched out his long legs. "My dear Captain, there are worse places you could be marooned."

Alihahd turned to look at him directly with deep liquid eyes. "With worse company?" he asked sincerely. He did not mean the aliens.

Hall grinned, took Alihahd's head in his hands, and kissed him on the mouth. "Possibly not," he said.

"I thought as much," said Alihahd. Many cultures sent people to the grave with kisses. And as Hall lowered his hands Alihahd grasped one of his wrists—the one with the sleeve not rolled up. Alihahd's fingertips touched something hard, the hilt of a hidden dagger strapped to Hall's forearm.

Both men froze, the same question on their minds: Should they decide to attempt it, which of them could draw and use one of Hall's weapons first.

Vaslav coughed nervously.

Alihahd turned his head to him. Vaslav was confused. Vaslav could not see the dagger, could not see Alihahd's and Hall's thoughts, which were so transparent to each other. He could not reconcile their actions with any antecedent action, their words with their silken tones. He could only figure he was having a severe translation problem.

"Poor Vaslav," said Alihahd and let go Hall's wrist.

Arilla came again, bearing thin-skinned fruit, green leafy stalks, and coarse flat bread. She placed them in the grass under the airplane. "For thee and thee and thee."

She saw their hesitation. "Not to worry," she said. "It is safe for humankind." She did not say how she knew.

Alihahd took a bite of the bread without appetite, then pushed everything away with an unsteady hand.

Arilla told him he was bony. Alihahd could not be persuaded.

Finally Arilla beckoned, her bracelets jingling and sliding up to her elbow. "Come, if thou wilt not eat. We are not home yet. This is only the Lower Aerie."

Lower Aerie? They were three and a half miles above sea level. "There is an Upper Aerie?" said Alihahd, climbing from under the plane to join Arilla in the open sunlight.

"There." She pointed up.

V.   Island in the Sky

High above the plain towered the forbidding peaks of a great mountain, its twin summits separated by a deep narrow crevasse as if a god had taken a cleaver and wedged the single mountain in two.

Alihahd could see in the misty distance, where the two peaks slanted away from each other, tiers of stone arches on both sides of the fissure.

"There is a footbridge," said Arilla. "On one side stands the Aerie. On the other Haven. Both together are also called Aerie."

The mountain was block-faulted, its south face a barren granite palisade with the Aerie an inaccessible citadel at the top of the sheer rise. Itiri planes did not fly that high. Even Iry's heavy atmosphere thinned at such heights. It was six miles above the sea.

"How can anyone possibly get up there?" said Alihahd.

"We are going to walk," said Arilla.

"We are?"

"You are going to fly." She guided the humans across the golden field to the foot of the twin mountain where a balloon was prepared.

Alihahd liked it less than he did the seaplane.

The plane had no computer; this vehicle did not have a motor. It was not even sophisticated as balloons went.

It rose slowly, smooth and soundless on a warm anabatic current, the wind the Itiri named eaninala, the day wind.

Then a sudden gust swept the balloon toward the cliff face. The mountain loomed very large and filled the view. A glitter of quartz. A rock wall with their shadow growing on it. And the shadow of an eagle.

There came a tug and a change of direction.

An eagle had seized a ring at the end of a long rope

attached to the balloon and towed it back into a rising air current.

There were more eagles just above them, traveling in vanguard, scouting the winds to find where the eddies flowed.

Vaslav leaned over the edge of the basket to gaze up at the birds. "Are they yours?" he asked the warrior Stasa-yxan, who had come with them in the balloon.

"The talassairi belong to no one," said the warrior.

The boy was abashed. He did not talk well—he had only been using Universal for a few weeks—and he was sorry he had tried to say anything.

Harrison Hall was relaxed and merrily sinister—even as they had been swept toward the rocks—the only one of the humans untroubled.

It began to grow cold, and Stasa-yxan gave the three humans black cloaks to wear.

The air was thinning; the balloon spread out. The country-side diminished into a sunny haphazard checkerboard whose straight rigid boundaries had been forced to curve with a winding river and to scallop the rising ground into flat stepped concentric levels outlined with blue-gray stone retaining walls, so that the whole scene looked as if an orderly pattern of red and brown and green and gold squares had melted and run together.

Stasa-yxan frowned at some part and murmured as if making a note for himself, "Blight."

The others saw nothing. The fields looked healthy.

Alihahd had been silent this journey, lost in a brooding sulk, until Vaslav glanced his way, did a double-take, and pointed, his mouth open but lacking words to say.

Alihahd blinked back to awareness and he looked down at himself. His cloak had turned from black to white. "Is this thing alive?"

"Thou mindest not the cold as much as thy companions," said Stasa-yxan. "Thy thoughts are elsewhere."

Alihahd pulled the now-white cloak around him, and huddled bleakly in the bottom of the woven-reed basket. "How appropriate."

The balloon rose to a level jut not far below the bald pate of the western summit. Alihahd climbed woodenly out of the creaking basket and jumped down to the rock shelf, landing weightily on his feet to find himself standing on an island in the sky.

High. So high. Above was nothing but cold sky and bright sun. The air was dry and thin, and everything appeared distinct in the harsh desertlike light.

Low furry plant life crept all the way to the tops of the mountains. Even on the nearly barren rock summits some life still clung, a tatter of grass, a patch of lichen. Permanent snowcaps were none at this altitude.

Stasa-yxan led the way on a twisty path footworn through moss and creepers to the colonnades of Haven. The path leveled and straightened to a paved walkway called the Ledge Path, from whose base the five stories of Haven rose up in columned tiers, each higher level set in farther on the slope. The little city in the sky gleamed in the bare light, the columns, arched doorways, and lancet windows intricately carved, latticed, fretted, and inlaid with gemstones and leafed with metal.

Across the narrow crevasse which separated the twin peaks, Haven's twin, Aerie, glittered in near mirror image, so that the terraced hollow between the summits formed a titanic natural amphitheater split down the middle.

Curious red-haired ranga poked their heads from the archways of Havenside to peer at the human strangers. There was no movement, no curiosity from Aerieside.

A bridge spanned the crevasse where it narrowed to twenty feet across. It was a single-person footbridge made of wooden planks and rope, with knotted handrails. At its moorings Stasa-yxan stepped aside for Alihahd. "Thou first."

A wind moaned up the fissure and the bridge swayed.

Alihahd watched it swing.

Stasa-yxan fastened a safety line to Alihahd, but it gave no feeling of security. If anything it made him feel worse.

For being six miles above sea level the winds were very calm here. They should have been roaring through the abyss as through a wind tunnel. They could always change.

Stasa-yxan nudged Alihahd. The short span was suddenly very very wide, becoming wider the longer Alihahd stared at the knotted fiber ropes and the wooden planks.

Somewhere beyond the sheltered hollow a wind howled.

Because there were no choices, Alihahd grasped the rope guides and stepped out, not looking down. He was midway across, poised over empty space, when a voice sounded from behind him on Havenside, calling long and tonal, a muezzin sound of repeated ritual.

"Erika! Ameeeeerrrrika!"

Alihahd turned his head with a start. He could not have heard what he had heard.

Sudden and startling as a splash of water, a child appeared, running down a mountain path like a hardy little goat. "Coming!"

A human child.

She was bundled in a long heavy dress, wide-legged trousers, thick cloak, and leather boots. Black hair spilled down her back to her hips. Baby-fat cheeks were red and round. Her black eyes had lights within.

Alihahd felt his interest spark, and was so shocked by it he had to clutch for the bridge ropes and catch his balance. He was not sure how old the girl was, but knew she was not old enough for *any* man to be looking at her the way he was—especially him.

And you, he was thinking to his prick. *Never mind that.*

It had a mind of its own, and its timing was awful. He considered himself too old. It should by rights be dead. He'd honestly thought it was. He just wanted it to leave him alone.

When is the last time you rose to any good occasion?

This had less to do with the girl than it did his present danger. It was a sad state of affairs when it took proximity to death to excite him. He held his white cloak fast around him and growled inwardly. He continued across the bridge, disdainful of the long drop—courting it, in fact.

Safe on the other side, he turned to look again, but the girl Amerika had disappeared into one of Haven's many rock chambers.

Did I dream her?

Human. His emotions raced. Not for the girl this time, but for what she implied.

Space travel.

Trying not to hope too much, Alihahd unhooked his safety line and let it drop back to Havenside so the others could cross.

As he waited, slowly, subtly, the aura of this side took on life and strength and pressed itself into his consciousness. He knew without being told that this side of the Aerie was home to the warrior-priests.

The Aerie was silent, in repose. Like a monastery, it breathed feelings of age, space, and power, as if God were actually more manifest here than other places. Mosques, temples, and cathedrals gave Alihahd the same impression and always left him uneasy—places built for the God of the People of the Book.

The sun had passed its zenith, and the first direct light of day was arriving now on Aerieside. The warm rays lifted steam from the shade-dank rock, and furtive vapors trailed low across the cold blue-gray stones and spilled out between the pillars of the shadowy arcade, then faded in the thirsty air.

The priestess first appeared like a vision, at the end of the colonnade. Backed in the sunlit frame of the farthest arch, she came striding up the columned arcade through alternate light and shadow, sunbeams catching on clouds of rising mist that swirled around her feet with her advance and rolled out in her wake. She moved with a purpose, flow and force in her walk, sharp as an arrow in flight.

As she neared she took on lines of reality. A sheer blue kaftan billowed out after her, its long full sleeves slit from shoulder to cuff so her arms showed through thin and cabled with sharply defined muscles. Her tough weathered skin was blue-black. Her coarse black hair swung down long, straight, and thick from a glossy topknot and was knotted again at the end. She wore a white flower behind her ear and a double-curved sword at her side.

She turned and passed under an ornate archway aglitter with topaz and chrysoberyl to an inner chamber.

And when Alihahd's companions had crossed the bridge, Stasa-yxan led them to the same monumental archway.

Alihahd paused at the entrance, then walked in.

The chamber was a great nine-sided room with polished wood floor and lofty domed ceiling of gold. Mirrors set in the tall window jambs shot sunlight up to the ceiling, where it diffused and spread softly, and the chamber glowed in warm golden light.

The golden dome unsettled Alihahd.

Two more warrior-priests flanked the inner doorway. Tall and strong as the others, they seemed smaller in this chamber, not so sure, not so proud. And Stasa-yxan changed as he passed under the arch. He seemed to shrink and become meek in this place.

But it was not the chamber itself that affected the warriors. It was the figure at the far end.

Enthroned in a wide ceremonial seat on a dais behind a low lattice barrier was the dark warrior-priestess. Her eyes, trained on the doorway, were black, bottomless, fierce/benign. Her daunting presence filled the room.

She was jet, head to toe, a melano color phase, like a panther. Broken red scars blazed on her sharp cheekbones. She sat with one elbow propped on the armrest, her body curved to the side like a serpent, one bare foot folded underneath her on the seat. A great snowy owl perched on the tall carved back of her throne.

Stasa-yxan bowed in the universal gesture of respect. "Azo! Fendi!"

The Fendi returned a slight nod.

"It was a starship that fell out of the sky," said Stasa-yxan. "These survive."

"Are they human?" said the Fendi. Her voice glided like a honed razor. Her dialect was clear—almost modern.

"They are," said Stasa-yxan.

The Fendi raised hairless brows. "Human starships fly to Iry again. How long has it been?"

"Fendi, I know not."

The Fendi smiled at Alihahd, taking him for the leader of the group. She spoke, eyes on him, words directed at Stasa-yxan. "It has been a while."

Two thousand years it had been.

Alihahd spoke. "So long we forgot you were real and not a dream of ours."

The warrior-priestess smiled wider, baring white, even teeth without canines.

Alihahd was puzzled. It had been two thousand years since an Earth ship came to Iry, yet . . .

He heard pattering feet on the path outside. Amerika. He knew her step already. She was no dream.

"Fendi," Alihahd dared address the priestess monarch. "Was that not a human girl I saw?"

The Fendi nodded to Stasa-yxan. He answered for her.

"It was," said the warrior. "We have all manner of guests

here. But she did not come on her own ship. We brought her."

Then they do have interstellar capabilities! Hope leapt to full life.

The Fendi spoke again, musing to no one in particular. Not to the humans. Not directly. "So Earth finally decides to remember us." Her tone was nonjudgmental. She considered the development neither good news nor bad news, only interesting fact.

Birds were flying in the chamber's spacious dome, flitting in and out of the tall windows. They were little black birds like swallows. One winged near the Fendi, and she absently snatched it out of the air with lightning grasp without even turning her head, nothing moving but her arm. She petted its head with one long finger, then tossed it back into the air, unhurt—all as effortless and unthinking as a person might bite his nails.

The snowy owl blinked a slow blink.

At last the Fendi said, "They are not of these new humans— the Na'id, they are named?"

New? Comparatively, Alihahd supposed. The Na'id had surfaced onto the interstellar scene only in the last century and a half—and had conquered a large part of the known galaxy in that time.

"No, we are not," said Alihahd. The question was for him even though directed at Stasa-yxan.

"They are not here to assert human supremacy and—what is the other slogan—galactic dominion?"

"No," said Alihahd. "We were shot down by Na'id." Then he remembered that he was not actually certain of what had befallen Harrison White Fox Hall's ship and realized he'd been answering for the man. He rephrased, "The boy and I were, anyway."

The Fendi's eyes slid to Hall. Stasa-yxan spoke for her. "And thou?"

"*We* were," Hall affirmed.

"Tell them to stay in peace, then," said the Fendi, finality in her voice. Alihahd sensed dismissal.

And he felt panic. *Stay?* He needed to get out of here, and soon. "Fendi," he said quickly. "I cannot stay. If you have a starship and could give me passage I will give you anything you ask. I can pledge a great deal. Only tell me what you want.''

The smile disappeared. The eyes flashed. Her head snapped toward Stasa-yxan. ''Say to him: 'Thou camest. We did not bring thee. We are not for hire.' '' Her dialect thickened in anger.

Alihahd immediately backed down and begged her pardon. ''I am sorry. I am already in your debt.''

She smiled again. ''Art thou a Fendi?''

Stasa-yxan made a noise in his throat, as she had forgotten to speak to the human through him. But the Fendi stood, pushed her warrior aside, and descended from the stepped dais and around the lattice barrier.

Alihahd was struck speechless for a moment. What a bedraggled thing he must look; he had just insulted her; and she asked if he was her equal. ''I was,'' he said.

''Thou hast a people to whom thou must return?''

''Yes, Fendi,'' said Alihahd.

She reconsidered—seemed to.

''When one of us next leaves Iry, thou mayest go also,'' she said. ''The physician may be next. Till then we can take you back to Lower Aerie. Most of our human guests are there. Winter drives them down. Only niaha—three—humans stay up here: Amerika, Layla, and Montserrat.''

''When will the next ship leave?'' said Alihahd. Why had she mentioned winter?

The Fendi frowned. The snowy owl clacked its hooked beak. ''It could be long. It could be tomorrow. Like death,'' she said.

Whether the last words were statement or analogy Alihahd could not say. The Fendi was displeased, and her warriors were frightened.

She rose to the dais again. ''My name is Roniva.''

That was a signal to go—for the second time—and they'd best obey. She did not want their names. She would learn them in time if she cared to.

The owl glowered with boring eyes from its perch on the back of the throne.

Stasa-yxan motioned the guests out. Alihahd started to leave, glanced back once, and forgot what he was going to say. His back hadn't been turned for more than two seconds.

The snowy owl was gone.

VI. The Turquoise Door

It was a long hall, its shadows very deep. Alihahd had parted ways with Harrison Hall and Vaslav, and had come this way still seeking an escape. The labyrinthine passageways of Aerie-side had led him up rock-hewn stairs spiraling up a mammoth newel like a ziggurat, and he was wheezing by the time he climbed to the top. There was oxygen enough in the air; he simply could not seem to draw it in. Blood pounded in his head.

At the end of the long hall shone a turquoise door. It was open. A shaft of sunlight fell into the dark corridor from the chamber.

A voice called to Alihahd from beyond the door. "Ave."

It was the girl Amerika.

Then came a male voice: "Peace be upon you."

"And upon you peace," Alihahd answered, curious. He ventured to the massive rounded door, its ancient, brilliant-hued mosaic paled from long standing in the dry air.

Inside he found a warrior-priest, the girl, and an eagle. The eagle cocked its head sideways and regarded Alihahd with one onyx eye, inhuman intelligence in its gaze.

The girl stole shy glances at him from beneath long black lashes, and her dark skin deepened color in a blush.

The elderly Itiri beckoned him farther into his chamber with a white, spidery hand, his drooping skin jiggling with his motions.

The cave with its stuccoed walls was small, clean and crowded, lined with racks and racks of herbs and delicate blown-glass vials of swirling colors. It was a physician's chamber. Even with the clutter the room was light and airy, its woven mats fresh. Swallows trilled at the tall windows, their nests crowding the eaves outside.

"Thou art ill," said the physician from his work table.

"No. No, I am not," said Alihahd.

The physician wrinkled his brow in doubt. He said to Amerika, "Healthy humans appear thus?"

"No," said Amerika.

"Thy temperature is high," the physician told Alihahd, and Alihahd wondered how he could tell.

"How is it you speak Universal?" said Alihahd, drawing attention from himself.

"It is the language between the stars," said the Itiri. "Is it not?"

The way you speak it? "Two thousand years ago," said Alihahd.

The physician made a motion with his head analogous to a shrug. "We knew you would be back." He rose from his work table. "Rest thou. Our air is thin to thee. Keep thee here and rest." He moved toward the door.

"What would be my chances of leaving Iry within the week?" said Alihahd quickly. "Seven days."

"Oh," said the physician without excitement as he was leaving. "None."

All in a wave, sickness rose in Alihahd's throat, his vision blurred and he reached for the wall, suddenly too dizzy to stand. There was no chair, so he sat on the floor.

When the spell passed, Amerika was kneeling at his side, biting her lower lip, afraid to touch him.

"It is nothing," said Alihahd. "The air."

Amerika sat back on her heels, unconvinced and unhappy. She was a lovely child, smelling clean of sunlit air, grass and leaves and the woolen scent of her cloak.

The eagle in its corner stretched out its neck and lifted one wing to peck at a bare patch of skin. Amerika snapped her head around briefly and cried, "Not to do that!" And the eagle stopped. Amerika turned back to Alihahd.

Alihahd gave a pale smile. The girl was a provincial. She spoke Universal in the peculiar dialect of the Itiri, having learned the language here, not on her backward homeworld, Solea.

Her necklace placed her. The necklace was a polished chain carved from a single block of petrified wood, each loop an unbroken circle. The chain had been placed on her as a baby and could no longer be taken over her head. The chains were customary to certain Solenese tribes. That Amerika still wore it meant she had never fallen into Na'id hands. The

Na'id habitually cut the repressive symbols from the necks of all the young Solenese girls. That she still wore it also meant she was a virgin.

"A Solenese healer?" said Alihahd. "Is that not unusual?" Solea had no medical technology.

Amerika tried to hide a bashful smile, but it glowed in her eyes and on her cheeks. "Who told thee I was of Solea?" she said playfully.

"You did." Alihahd looped his forefinger through the chain at her throat.

Amerika's skin warmed against the back of his hand, and she flushed very dark. Alihahd let the chain drop.

He got up and smoothed his tunic. He moved to the door.

Suddenly plaintive, Amerika said, "Why must thou leave in seven days? This place pleaseth thee not?"

The way she said it made him sound heartless and ungrateful for wanting to go. He turned at the door. "Do you know, child, only hours ago I believed I was dying, and I expected nothing else. I know I am fortunate to be alive and to be here. But now that I *am* here, alive, and I find these people have starships—"

"Thou wantest to go home," she finished for him with a downturn in her voice that was a litany of disappointment.

"No," said Alihahd. "I can never go home."

Amerika brightened. "Then stay thee here."

"I have no choice, it seems."

"Why so eager to go nowhere?" she demanded.

Alihahd could not explain, not without touching the past, and not without telling a child that the prospect of living could be infinitely more terrifying than dying. So he excused himself and left.

The warrior-priest Jinin-Ben-Tairre wrapped the felt cover around the ancient tungsten-plastic blade and replaced it in its scented wood chest, closed the lid, and fastened the polished brass catches. He had heard the eagles arrive earlier with Universal-speaking newcomers. Ben-Tairre had not gone out to look; it was his practice to avoid off-worlders. He preferred to maintain ignorance of things that lay beyond the planet he fiercely loved—or even of things beyond the Aerie—since the time he had first walked the fire and become a warrior-priest.

He stood, straightened his clothes, and secured his cloak with a short length of chain across his broad chest. Then he turned and bowed to his Elder. The hanina's hood was up; the old woman had ceased speaking for the day. The younger warrior withdrew and set off for his own chamber, muscles flowing in his powerful thighs with each stride, his winged familiar fluttering at his shoulder.

Long rays of the sinking sun had reached the far wall of the arcade. Ben-Tairre walked through the colonnade, stepped down to the Ledge Path, and came face to face with one of the newcomers. Thunderstruck eyes met his own, and both men stopped dead.

The newcomer was a tall gaunt human with straight Nordic nose and clear deep-set eyes in his swarthy, long face.

Jinin-Ben-Tairre's shock passed to fury. His eyes blazed and he walked swiftly past. Who had spat this being at him? Laws of hospitality forbade him striking the stranger's head off. The warrior's fury doubled at his own inability to choke down hatred. He did not go to his own chamber, but kept walking.

Alihahd turned to watch the retreating figure incredulously. If a hallucination, it was vivid.

The warrior was human.

VII. Jinin-Ben-Tairre

A swift breeze swayed the bridge unsettlingly as Alihahd crossed to Havenside.

He found Harrison White Fox Hall and Vaslav at dinner in the dwelling of the human woman Montserrat. The cave was large, warm, its walls hung with red and amber tapestries. A kettle bubbled on the hearth.

There were two women. The pale, nervous, petite woman in a red dress was Montserrat. She kept her rusty wiry hair cut very short except for long bangs that nearly obscured a red chevron tattooed on her brow. She gave up her cushion at the table as Alihahd came in, and she fetched another for herself, her brown eyes downcast all the while. Hall called her Serra.

The second woman was as small, tougher, wearing a hide jerkin and trousers. She was cleaning a jeweled dagger and scowling at Harrison Hall, her lightly freckled nose wrinkled in disdain. Straight brown hair was pulled off her heart-shaped face and braided back with a leather thong. Her brown eyes were lined black like an Itiri's. She wore a small beam gun holstered under her left arm but seemed to favor the dagger in her hand. She was Layla, a Nwerthan mercenary. Alihahd could spot those right away. Modern worlds custom-arily recruited and trained the primitive Nwerthans in warfare because they fought like the very devil and seldom asked why.

Both women were not much older than thirty years Earth standard.

Alihahd bid a proper Universal greeting to them, then spoke to Hall. "I saw—" And he stopped, doubting what he had seen—a powerfully built young warrior-priest with golden skin, brown-black slanted eyes, a heavy jaw, flat nose, and short black hair. He'd borne the things of a warrior-priest: the red broken scars on his broad cheeks; a white flower at his belt; a signet ring on his forefinger, though his was on his left hand. His right hand was gloved over in black and did not look real. His knife had been sheathed left-handed. Red rags were tied around the highly arched insteps of his small feet, which were scarred as if by fire.

A bird had ridden on his shoulder—a real bird, not an avian alien. It was a kestrel.

There was a power in the young warrior, and a horror-branded depth in his dark eyes that looked at Alihahd murder-ously. He had walked past Alihahd as if past an urn of ashes.

Alihahd decided that he was certain of what he had seen. "I saw a warrior-priest," he told Hall. "He was as human as you and I."

"Jinin-Ben-Tairre," said Layla. She sheathed her dagger at her belt and replaced eight dainty rings from the table onto the short, tapered fingers of her rough-lined and callused little hands.

"Is that a name?" said Alihahd.

Layla assented with a nod. "It means 'The Warrior's Feet Are Burned.' " She spoke Universal with the studied precision of a second language.

"The Fendi said there were three humans on the Aerie," said Alihahd. "Why am I counting four?"

"Because Roniva will not speak his name. And because Jinin-Ben-Tairre is not human anymore," said Layla.

Alihahd found the idea of a human trying to be alien offensive. "He pretends he is not human so that makes him not?" Acid had crept into his deep voice.

"If Ben-Tairre thinks something is so, it is so," said Layla with the simple-minded dogma of her people. "You will see. He has a familiar." Her pointed chin and lower lip jutted forward in a stubborn pout.

Alihahd remembered the warrior's kestrel and Roniva's disappearing owl. "What are they, the familiars?"

"I do not know," said Layla. She crossed one dun-booted foot across her opposite knee. "I do not think the Itiri know."

"Are they alive?"

"They do not eat," said Layla. "I do not think they breathe."

"They disappear from one place and appear somewhere else in an instant," Serra added haltingly in a low voice that went to breathiness and slight feminine gravel. "But they can't carry anything with them." Her hands fidgeted over her teacup. Serra's skin was pale brown, without sun, her eyes unlined. Her small nose had been once broken, and there were scars on her pretty face.

"From where did Jinin-Ben-Tairre come?" said Alihahd.

"He has no past," said Layla. "He killed it. He locked it in a box and burned it. It is dead."

Serra spoke in a near whisper. "Old ghosts have a way of catching up with you in the safest of places."

"I guess that bears keeping in mind," said Harrison White Fox Hall. He turned his eyes to Alihahd, who had nothing to say.

"And what are you?" Layla challenged him. "You looked like a Na'id."

Vaslav had been letting the others talk. Here he spoke up in defense, proud and indignant, "He is not a Na'id. He is Alihahd."

Layla's jaw dropped in surprise, showing crooked white

teeth. "I know you," she said. Alihahd flinched. Layla's attitude changed to deference. "You fight Na'id."

"I do not fight them. I run from them," said Alihahd.

"You are much too humble," Serra whispered. Layla had told her stories about the famous enemy of the Na'id.

"No. Point of fact I never met them in battle," said Alihahd. This point seemed important to him.

"But you are a great man," said Layla. "Everyone knows you made the Na'id leave Chesa."

The liberation of Chesa had been Alihahd's first and most notorious feat. It had made his "name." By means of false orders from nonexistent admirals and generals, false intelligence reports, bogus replacement troops, fabricated computer records, suspicions cast left and right so that no one talked to anyone else, and all manner of deceptions, Alihahd had systematically tricked the Na'id into abandoning an entire occupied planet. A full standard month passed before someone realized that anything was amiss.

"An exercise in vanity," said Alihahd. "They came back. There was no point to it beyond letting it be known that I could do it."

When the Na'id had reinvested Chesa and demanded of the natives who was responsible for this incredible plot, they replied, "Alihahd," which in their native tongue meant, "He left." And so he was known ever after, an elusive force with a formidable knowledge of the Na'id chain of command, codes, and way of doing things. He'd spent the rest of his shadowy career throwing the system into chaos and providing means of escape for unwilling subjects of the Empire.

"You are not eating," said Serra.

"We ate at Lower Aerie," said Alihahd. From the corner of his eye he saw Hall scowl at him. "Have you anything to drink?" said Alihahd. He'd barely touched his tea.

"If you mean alcohol, there is none." Serra shrugged. "The Itiri don't seem to make any."

Alihahd dismissed the thought with a pass of his hand. His head hurt.

The sun was setting. The light in the cave was from the hearth. It had been a long day—days. Alihahd had lost all sense of time since the *Liberation* had broken apart.

He stared futilely at the bowl of stew cooling in front of him. He could not eat.

Amerika had come to the door, and she peered in. Alihahd could see half of her, one bright black eye, half of a coy smile, one baby-fat hand hugging the doorjamb.

Hall was speaking to him, "Did you find a way off-planet, Captain?"

"No," said Alihahd and closed his eyes. "We are trapped here."

Layla uncoiled from her cushion. "Then let us find a place for you." She was looking at Hall. "You are not staying in *here*."

"There is a chamber," Amerika piped cheerfully from the threshold. "Sit thee down, Layla. I shall show them."

"Whose chamber?" said Alihahd.

"Thine," said Amerika.

Alihahd turned to Serra. "Why are we being given everything? Whose chamber am I taking, and who is giving it to me in return for what?"

Serra smiled for the first time, color in her pale brown cheeks. "It is the way of hospitality. Travelers must have what they need. If the cave is empty, you may have it. No one gives it. Nothing belongs to anyone anyway."

"Is this the Law?" said Alihahd.

"Not Law. Virtue."

"Then what consequence if you are not hospitable?" said Alihahd.

"Then you are a bad person," said Serra.

Alihahd did not understand the world. "I am all at sea." He had never been so lost, forced to conform to alien ways. "Is there anything I should be sure to do or not do? Am I likely to commit a crime in ignorance?"

"No there aren't any laws. Only for the warrior-priests. A guest would have to be very evil for harm to come to him. You're safe here," said Serra.

"From the Itiri," said Layla, her eyes on Hall.

No, I am not safe, thought Alihahd. *I must leave this place very very soon*.

"Come with me," Amerika sang and waved the men outside with her.

"And do something with their clothes," Layla called after the girl. "They stink."

The night was clear. There were no lamps on the paths, for

the starry sky was bright, shedding light equal to several full moons.

An albino Itiri sentinel crouched at his post on the dawn ridge, his face washed silvery blue in the cold light. Red eyes watched over the peaceful valley, while distant yellow fire-lights winked back from the little village far below.

Small black shapes darted through the air over the Aerie—swifts, catching winged bugs swept up the chasm on rising air currents.

Alihahd stopped on the windy path. Across the chasm a figure lurked in a dark archway. Starlight gleamed off a naked sword blade slanting down from a left-handed grip.

A man without a past was a dangerous sort, Alihahd knew. He stood out on the edge of the cliff path and faced the shadowed figure across the abyss, the wind in his hair, his long arms hanging at his sides from his wide straight shoulders in weaponless, tired readiness until the dark figure and the sword withdrew again into blackness; then he walked on.

The cave where Amerika led them was clean, with a fire already burning in its hearth, and three separate piles of bedcovers set on the expansive chaff-filled mattress that would have been big enough for six people. The girl had been busy. Amerika stirred the coals in the hearth, then she darted out again like a swift. "Good night. Good night."

Alihahd peeled off his tunic, pulled off his flat-bottomed deck boots, pounded out a place on the uneven mattress, and lay down.

Vaslav took a place against the wall behind which came the soft sound of water trickling down from a solar collector on the mountaintop. Vaslav huddled against the warm stone and was soon snoring softly.

Hall walked out to water a bush on the mountainside, then returned and undressed. His dirk he kept with him. That and his gun and his foxhead pipe. He gave up his other things to the little ranga male who came into the cave to collect their clothes and spirit them away.

Hall's trim body took on a burnished sheen in the firelight, muscular and taut for his age, deep-chested and wasp-waisted. A few age spots dotted across his shoulders. His hair, loosed from its tie, was streaked heavily with steel gray.

Hall settled under a pile of bedding on the other side of Alihahd from Vaslav.

The glowing coals in the hearth shifted and settled. Outside, night birds sang.

Alihahd shivered. This place was barbaric. He could have been in New Triton by now. His emergency shuttles should have arrived there by this time. He could hear them telling the other rebels, "Alihahd is dead."

Alihahd wishes he were.

He sensed Hall was still awake. Alihahd turned to him. One tiger eye was open and watching. "A touch xenophobic, aren't you, Captain," said Hall.

"I was never known for my love of aliens," said Alihahd shortly.

"The Na'id call rebels *alien-lovers,*" said Hall. And Alihahd was a notorious rebel indeed.

"Does not necessarily follow," said Alihahd.

They were speaking in near-whispers, reluctant to disturb the quiet. Except for the birds they seemed to be the only beings awake in the world.

Hall propped one bare arm behind his head, the brindle fur cover across his deep chest, his gaze directed toward the ceiling. Hearthlight picked up copper flecks of beard stubble on his cheek.

Hall was a hunter and a controller. The more elusive and powerful the quarry, the more interesting the capture and control. Alihahd was not about to abdicate any of his self-sovereignty, any of his private soul.

Hall sighed and went to sleep.

Alihahd was still shivering. He could not seem to put on enough covers. Alihahd had never felt the cold. This cold came from within.

He went to sleep shaking.

VIII. Circle Circle

Harrison White Fox Hall awoke the first morning, pushed the blankets from his face, and breathed in the cold sting of mountain air. The fire was dead. He reached out a bare arm from the warmth under the covers to rest atop the frosty outer blanket.

Some small light came from outside. It was almost dawn. The boy Vaslav was still asleep, quietly snoring. Alihahd had already risen and gone.

On the corner of the wide mattress Hall's clothes had been returned to him, neatly folded, clean, dry—and cold. He threw off the blankets and jumped out of bed onto the icy granite floor, naked and barefoot. He was quickly dressed.

A clay jug of water stood near the hearth. Hall broke the iced surface with a silver ladle and shaved the copper stubble from his face with the straight edge of his dagger, which was still warm from being sheathed against his forearm. He hadn't taken it off.

Vaslav, like most space travelers from more modern worlds than Hall's, showed no trace of a beard.

Outside the air was piercing fresh. Painted streaks were spreading in the eastern sky; a few bright stars still glimmered in the indigo west. Then a bright shaft of light spilled over the eastern mountains and splashed across the peaks, the valley below still in shadow. The sentinel on the dawn ridge opened his arms in salute to the sun as it climbed over the edge of the world.

There were no clouds anywhere, and Hall could see for miles—mountain after impassable mountain beyond the isolated terraced valley with its waterfall spitting rainbows into the air in the morning light. The day would be fair.

Hall stretched, feeling the mountain cold in his bones. He could see summer far below in the still-shaded village Kaletani Mai, but pride refused to let him go there. The air was only slightly thin to him, coming from Eridani as he did. He could survive.

The Aerie was already stirring. Hall watched the white ranga come out of their caves and turn dark in the sunlight. They were funny, cherubic little people, always cheerful, and a bit stupid. They were of one breed with the tall, slender, enigmatic aghara; so Serra had said. It was difficult to believe. Polymorphism in the extreme, Hall thought. The majestic aghara were actually the rare children of the chubby gnomes; and warrior-priests were what the aghara spent their lives training to become.

Hall watched a few warrior-priests summon aghara children from out of the ranga caves. Youthful scarless faces of the uninitiated appeared in answer to their masters' call, and the young cheelas crossed the bridge to Aerieside to run with their masters over the mountain.

Hall followed for a while, but he could not keep pace. So he dropped out of the running and walked alone along a swift-running brook where black birds with serrate beaks and oily feathers dove into the water seeking crustaceans under the rocks of the streambed. The winds were fast out here beyond the Aerie, and Hall's face was stung red. He unrolled his bandanna and tied it on his head to keep the buffeting from his ears.

He strayed from the beaten track through a stand of scrubby distorted would-be trees that fringed the sun-bleached rocks of the ridge. The hunter in him was drawn by a trail of footprints crushed into moss still exhaling strong fragrance as if recently done. Someone had strayed this way before him—someone who wore shoes. Possibilities were limited.

And in an isolated depression where the air was still, sheltered by a curving rock wall and carpeted with long low-lying grasses, he found Alihahd seated on a rock, his elbows on his knees, his head bowed, his hands trembling. At Hall's approach he looked up, pale, beads of sweat on his face: Then his watery gaze returned to his feet.

Hall jogged down the rocks into the low space and drew closer. He stood a moment in observation. This was not altitude sickness. "Alcoholic, Captain?"

Alihahd looked up in helpless self-surprise. He drew a wavering breath, licked his salty wet upper lip, and tried to steady his hands. "I would have said no." But his shaking hands held out before him defied him.

Hall watched curiously, weight on one foot, the other foot angled in. "You're not seeing snakes, are you?"

"No. No snakes."

Alihahd hung his head and closed his eyes. Hall climbed back out of the sunken area and left him alone with his misery.

Vaslav stumbled into Serra's cave late in the morning and squinted at the green breakfast Serra set before him.

A little while later Alihahd showed up, looking wounded and fragile. Serra took a separate kettle from the fire and poured an herbal brew for him. It smelled medicinal. Alihahd looked at Serra dubiously.

"Mr. Hall said you were sick," said Serra.

Alihahd's eyes shifted to Hall. "Mr. Hall said *that*, did he?"

Hall took his empty pipe from between his teeth and gestured with it to the cup of tea on the table. "It's a mild sedative."

Alihahd spoke stiffly with an edge in his voice; the words were, "Thank you, Mr. Hall." The tone said, *Back off, Mr. Hall*.

"You look pale," said Serra.

Alihahd's brows raised over deep-set watery eyes. "I imagine I will look much paler before long," he murmured.

Alihahd took to bed and stayed there, wretchedly ill. One by one his deadly secrets were beginning to slip away from him into open air for all to see, hard as he tried to lock them down.

He could not stop the Itiri physician from coming to examine him. The Itiri had to know if Alihahd had the plague.

Alihahd crouched back against the wall in drunken fear of the alien and in real fear of the examination—or rather the verdict of the examination. Alihahd had been afraid the alien would step back and declare, "He's a drunk." But the aged Itiri merely announced that he had never seen this particular malady before.

He rubbed his withered jowls in puzzlement and muttered about inoculations and quarantine.

A low chuckle at the door made him turn.

Harrison Hall rocked back on his heels, his eyes in merry crescents. ''Oh, it's not plague,'' said Hall.

From the bed, Alihahd's liquid eyes fixed accusingly on the tall satanic figure in the doorway, awaiting betrayal.

But Hall said to the physician, ''It's a poison.''

''Will he die?'' said the physician.

''I think not,'' said Hall.

''O God, why not?'' Alihahd moaned and tried to vomit.

He writhed at night with horrid dreaming and rasping breath, trying to draw in enough oxygen from the air that seared his throat raw as he gasped at it.

The ranga moved a mass of potted bushes and leafy plants into his cave to replenish the oxygen and moisture in the closed air.

Alihahd lost track of day and night. He knew only twilight and darkness and his own agony. Hall had moved out and sought shelter elsewhere.

From a nightmare Alihahd awoke, thrashing and sweating and shivering under the rough blanket. He turned over in the dark to someone there—Vaslav sitting on the edge of the wide bed keeping vigil, his youthful face angelic with devotion in the infinitesimal light.

Alihahd lay on his back, gasping, his hair a matted snarl, perspiration and tears beaded on his haggard face and trickling down its deep furrows. He reached up a feeble hand—he could only lift his arm from his elbow—and touched Vaslav's cheek with the back of his fingers. In deep, croaking voice, he said, ''Vaslav, do you love me?''

The boy's eyes flew wide. Pulse leapt. He sputtered, choked, stumbled over an aborted explanation, and stammered out, ''Yes.''

Alihahd's strengthless hand dropped back to the bed. ''Then please let me vomit in private.''

Abashed, the boy stuttered a flustered apology and left. Had he a tail it would have been between his legs.

Alihahd curled up and wrapped his arms around his abdomen.

He woke at late dawn to a cold waft of fresh air in his stuffy chamber. Long slanting sun rays streamed in from the doorway, its hide cover blown slightly agape. The bushes in their trough at the far wall of the shadowy cave leaned toward the light, stretching out their leafy branches. They seemed to be straining.

Then one pulled itself up by its bipartite roots and walked out.

Then all the rest of them save one unearthed themselves and pattered out in a herd.

The last one tugged itself free and ran out with a hasty *whap whap whap* of roots on the floor.

Alihahd pulled the covers over his head, delirious.

At midday, Alihahd woke again, lifted the covers, and peered out.

A trail of dirt was strewn across the floor from the empty planter at the far wall to the door.

Alihahd pulled the covers back over his head.

He swore the bushes would be back next time he looked.

He looked again when he heard Amerika's darting footsteps and sweet, scolding commands, "Get! Come back, you little monkey!"

And a stampede of slapping roots.

He lifted the blanket to see Amerika chasing a bunch of errant bushes back into the cave. They fled before her, dodged into the dark place, sank their roots into the trough, and became very still.

Amerika gave a single nod of satisfaction, wiping her hands on her skirts, and went out.

Alihahd laughed till he threw up.

And steadily, as days passed, he grew more pale—almost white—and his eyes became blue, and the roots of his hair emerged blond. When finally he sat up, washed, and dressed, he was perfectly fair.

Hall was surprised—and a little amused. "You're a nazi!"

"*Don't*—" Alihahd began too loudly, caught himself and finished softly, "—call me that, if you please."

Hall shrugged his big shoulders. "Isn't that the Na'id word for your kind?"

"It means more than blond-haired and blue-eyed. Do not call me that."

Hall shrugged.

The coloring was rare now, but not as rare as the Na'id would like. Still it was far too conspicuous for a man trying to move in Na'id circles without attracting attention. The way Alihahd looked now, he could not pass for a Chesite *or* a Na'id. The bogus Na'id captain was bogus indeed. "A white Na'id," Hall chuckled.

"Do not call me that either."

"Sorry," said Hall. He was aware of the full implications of that epithet and knew it was a bad one.

Serra stared at the new Alihahd. She did not say anything. She sat down on the bed, drew a skinning knife from its sheath in her boot, and proceeded to cut off his hair down to the blond.

Vaslav was thunderstruck by the change. "Are you really Alihahd?" he asked in distress.

A cut lock of black hair fell down Alihahd's face. He brushed it off his knee. "I am the only Alihahd there ever was," he said, changing the words slightly. "Alihahd was never quite for real."

The hero the boy believed in, he was not. There was no hero Alihahd.

White and shorn and still very weak, Alihahd ventured outside alone. Everything startled him, as if a filter had been lifted from his senses, and for the first time in over a decade he received the full assault of the world around him, so aware of life that it was painful.

He climbed the path on trembling legs just risen from sickbed, his hand out to steady himself on the cliff face, bracing against the winds.

Even his own hands were strange to him now—pallid, great bony things tracked with bulging blue veins. He was frowning at them and the blond hairs of his white forearms, when suddenly a warrior dropped down from the next level onto the path before him.

A flat and handsome yellow face with smoldering eyes. The blinding glare of sunlight on a naked blade. Jinin-Ben-Tairre.

Alihahd did not move as the sword turned, blade gliding in a silken pass from Ben's massive shoulder to another ready position. He was naked to the waist, and every clearly defined muscle in the warrior's arm and broad chest showed flexing and flowing as one with the weapon. Ben made no sound, not even the rustle of clothing, wearing only satiny black trousers, the red rags on his scarred feet, a carnelian ring, and a black glove over his right hand. He circled slowly.

Alihahd did not dare turn. He did not know what laws bound an Itiri but there was nothing to stay this bastard warrior from killing him here and now if he so chose. Alihahd waited for the sword to split his skull from behind, an old chant running through his brain:

> Circle circle, dance of death
> Once she cries, twice she lays
> A wreath about his youthful head
> Thrice she flies, for nothing stays.

Full circle, Ben stopped before Alihahd. Alihahd felt naked with his true face exposed. He was more gaunt and drawn than before, hollow cheeks deepened, marked crevices chiseled from his nostrils to the corners of his mouth, forceful bone structure manifest beneath emaciated flesh. But most revealed were the luminous blue eyes; sunken in their orbits their gaze penetrated with a daunting power that had been masked before by the darker pigment.

Ben's sword changed hands, left to right, and he reached out with his left hand—the ungloved one—to Alihahd's white face. Alihahd tightened, anticipating pain, but felt only the light brush of short fingers on his chin.

Ben withdrew his hand and left.

Alihahd stood, still frozen in place. Sun tingled his fair skin. The wind was cold on his short-sheared scalp. Finally Harrison White Fox Hall came and took his hand like a child. "Come on, Captain." Alihahd looked at the dark red hand, looked at Hall's laughing face.

"Are you laughing at me?" said Alihahd.

"Yes," said Hall.

And since there was no intelligent answer to that he said, "Oh," and let Hall guide him back to the cave—laughing.

Gunshots reported and echoed through the mountains in the early morning. Alihahd paused as he was dressing to listen for the pattern and tenor of the shots. It sounded like target practice. Or a skeet shoot.

That will be Mr. Hall.

Alihahd stepped out of his cave. Shadows were very long. He followed the sound, stopping every few hundred feet to rest and breathe in frosty clouds.

The gun's reports led him to Harrison Hall, poised on a mountain spur with his crazy-looking notch-handled rifle. He was shooting clay pigeons which Vaslav hurled out from a higher ledge.

Alihahd made his way to Hall's side, his approach loud enough, his tunic red enough that he would not surprise the gunman. Hall was hitting every bird, some several times when the fragments were large enough to bother with.

At last Vaslav called down, "That's it." The boy opened empty arms, having run out of clay birds.

Hall turned his head to Alihahd for comment.

"Impressive," said Alihahd.

Hall put one foot up on a rock and rested the butt of his gun on his sloping thigh. "Not my usual kind of target, but—" He finished with a shrug.

"What do you usually shoot?"

"Whatever's blue and glows in the dark."

Na'id uniforms and Na'id ships were electric blue with glowing red insignia of Human Supremacy/Galactic Dominion. Clay pigeons made feeble substitutes.

Earlier in the morning Hall had been target practicing on the little swifts that darted through the canyon before sunrise, but the Itir made him stop. "I *was* shooting the real birds," he told Alihahd. "Our hosts didn't like it."

"Do you ever miss?"

"Never."

Vaslav clambered down from his high ledge and came to them puffing, his cheeks and nose wind-bitten. He was looking healthy. A few days' primitive life had done him well, shedding him of his spaceship pallor.

Eight days. Alihahd had sensed the days were long here— 30.97 standard hours, said Vaslav, who wore a standard chronometer around his wrist. It seemed time for a tentative evaluation.

Alihahd propped his foot up on the same rock as Hall and leaned in, casually conspiratorial, one arm across his knee, a carefully magnetic gesture, and the other two men automatically leaned in for a private conference.

"What do you think of them?" Alihahd said quietly. "Our hosts." Himself he was not sure. He'd been in bed most of the eight days. These two had seen more than he.

"Too passive if you ask me," said Hall.

"That is bad?" said Alihahd.

"They have an army up here. I may be able to shoot the birds, but Roniva catches them in her bare hands without looking at them. I've seen their swords cut through tempered steel, and I hear you have to walk through fire to become a warrior. They're all crack shots, and from what I've seen it's not too much to guess that they could totally annihilate the Na'id's Great Human Army if they put their minds to it.''

Alihahd could not argue, even though he estimated only a thousand warriors on the Aerie by highest count. He wondered if there were many more. He shuddered at the words *totally annihilate*.

Given the proper technology—which, fortunately, they lacked—there was nothing the Itiri could not do.

"But what do they do?" Hall continued, then answered his own question, "Sit up here and protect the birds."

He raised his gun and centered a winging swift in his sights. He didn't pull the trigger, just said, "Bang." And Alihahd knew the bird had been spared—no luck or maybe about it.

Hall lowered the gun; his tawny eyes glittered with signal ferocity. His lips curved beneath gray mustache without a trace of softness.

Alihahd paused. "Whom did you lose?"

The eyes flickered to his, looked away to the sky.

"Everyone."

IX. Does Jerusalem Stand?

The date was the ninth day of the Red Geese, year of the Ship, in the Opal hexadecade. So said Vaslav. It was all mush to Alihahd. But, cast outside the stream of human events and beyond the relevance of human calendars, he ought to get used to it. Layla had been here on the Aerie seven Earth years; Vaslav had figured the conversion from the short Iry years. Serra had been here fifteen years, Ben seventeen. Alihahd best not let himself feel impatient; God knew when he would ever leave. He could die here. He was convinced that Ben-Tairre meant to kill him, though Amerika said not—it would not be virtuous. Alihahd did not place much faith in the human-turned-alien's virtue. The man hated him.

Alihahd heard the wind brass tapping in the swift gusts outside the cave where the humans had gathered.

"What is the date?" he asked Vaslav. "The real date."

Vaslav glanced at his wrist chronometer, "Tenthmonth ninth. It's 0935 hours on the meridian."

The year would have been 5856 C.E. were anyone still using the Gregorian calendar.

Earth's civilization had reached its height long ago, in the third Common millennium, with an interstellar technology and colonies flung across the Milky Way. At its peak the delicate balance had crashed and civilization itself imploded in a galaxy-wide political and economic collapse that threw humankind into a dark age for two thousand years, a time when no ships would fly. Colonies, cut off from each other and left to their own resources, lost their technology, their ties with Earth, their count of years. Many forgot Earth and each other altogether.

In their isolation—after the anarchy and struggle for bare survival was over—the colonies tried to piece together what they had lost. The old learning was reclaimed imperfectly and at different rates in different fields and in different places. Some worlds remained sunken in total savagery. One rebuilt to an atomic age and did not make it out. But most worlds progressed.

And finally a few tentative starships traveled out again at the middle of the fifth millennium. The Dark Age was over. But the travelers were hardly Earthlings anymore. They had their own worlds, their own cultures; Earth was some faraway cradle of civilization—if remembered at all.

Except on one colony which remembered well where it came from and why. The planet was Mat Tanatti—Land of Praise, Land of Glory.

The colonists of Mat Tanatti had begun as a large group of discontented idealists on Earth in the third millennium. They had gone forth in self-exile to an uninhabited world to start a new culture on a base of equality, undivided by artificial boundaries of nations and languages and antique faiths which the modern world had left behind and which turned brother against brother against sister.

The pilgrims named themselves Na'id, which meant

praiseworthy or *alert* in the dead Earth language they took for their tongue of naming names.

And since they had already isolated themselves before the Collapse came, they were not drawn down into it. No lifeline was cut; and Mat Tanatti was the one world that never fell. The Na'id kept their civilization, their history, and their purpose.

The end of the Dark Age found them successful beyond all prediction in creating a unified people. But the pessimists were justified in their insistence that Man must have his hatreds and prejudices, for the Na'id stressed their humanity—as opposed to aliens.

The end of the Dark Age also found the Na'id with the most advanced technology in the galaxy. They took it as a sign that their ideology was right and they were duty-bound to reunite their long-lost human brothers and sisters, and to free Earth from alien influence and wrong-thinking.

There had been no peace ever since. There was always fighting somewhere, and the biggest battles were not with aliens but with their own kind, the humans who did not *want* to be united—not after two thousand years—and *not* under Na'id domination.

For in professing tolerance of all human creations and culture, the Na'id encountered a big dilemma: Were they to tolerate intolerance? Most religions included more than one tenet which ran counter to Na'id thought, and the Na'id could not allow anyone's provincial ideas to infringe on the rights of others.

So they accepted all religions, with modifications, excising all portions that gave one segment of humanity superiority over another.

But the Word of God would not be picked apart so easily, and the Na'id movement met its major obstacle in the power of religion and the ferocity that met any attempted change.

Race was another sensitive point to the Na'id, but more quickly, if superficially, solved. The Na'id had never actually learned to live with and enjoy mankind's natural variations. There were always vague suspicions that one race was smarter, stronger, better than another, and vague terror that the suspicions might be right. So their method of eliminating prejudice against racial differences was to eliminate the racial differences—to mix all the races and make humankind into one homogeneous blob. Ethnic purity became equated with elitism, and the Na'id would not stand for it.

Altruism went insane. The Na'id fought their own kind to absorb them into the fold; they raped the pure races and stole the children to save them from narrow teachings. Brotherhood became assimilation, and supremacy leeched in besides. Forbidden to hate each other, the Na'id channeled all humans' hatred toward aliens. Humankind needed someone to dominate, someone on whom to blame the bloodshed, someone to be the common enemy against whom all humans could unite.

Thus began and continued the great crusade to save humanity and to liberate the homeworld Earth. The fighting had gone on for well over a hundred years.

"Does Jerusalem stand?" said Serra.

That was an old question. For a long time it had been the first question asked of any space traveler upon arriving anywhere.

The seat of the three major monotheistic religions, Jerusalem had become the most important city on Earth. To the Resistance it was a symbol of freedom that must never fall. The Na'id knew the value of symbols, and they were determined to have Jerusalem—for its impact on rebel morale and for its place in human history. The Mother City of Humankind, they called it.

The Holy City lay under siege for a hundred years, and humans everywhere, who had never seen Earth and never would, whether they belonged to one of the three faiths or not, asked of anyone who might know, "Does Jerusalem stand?"

The question was seldom heard anymore. Everyone knew the answer.

"You do not know?" said Alihahd.

"I had heard," said Serra. "Layla told me. I thought it was propaganda. Is it true then?"

"Thirteen years ago," said Alihahd.

The fall of Jerusalem had been a turning point in the war. The Bel had all but declared total dominion of the known galaxy in his Jerusalem Address, expecting the rest of the resistance to shrivel up and fall in quick succession to his unstoppable general, Shad Iliya, the White Na'id.

Shad Iliya's army had never lost a battle—though most of

the battles Shad Iliya ever fought were on backwater alien worlds. The general had been long kept a half-hidden embarrassment because of his un-Na'id coloring. He had only been brought into the open as a desperate last attempt to end the hundred-year siege of Jerusalem. Easy victory in the Holy City had made Shad Iliya's name and assured his infamy for a good part of forever. Instantly Shad Iliya was the greatest hero/villain in the universe next to the Bel himself. No one doubted that the rest of humanity would fall to the man who had taken Jerusalem. Na'id morale had never been higher, nor rebel prospects lower.

Except that Shad Iliya died soon after the victory. God/Jehovah/Allah consumed him in a pillar of fire, said the believers. The Na'id accused rebel agents. Rebels not of the faith said that the Na'id had gotten rid of the White Na'id themselves. The general's first lieutenant suggested suicide, but no one listened to him.

The uncanny timing of his death made Shad Iliya a convenient demon by whom rebels could summon curses and frighten childrᵉn. His was the face seen in the mirror in the dark. Being white helped to make him eerie. It also made his name a good insult for rebels to hurl at people who looked like Alihahd did now with his ghostly pale skin and white-golden fuzz of hair growing back on his shorn head.

But even with the death of the great general, the fall of Jerusalem remained a devastating blow. The mere speaking of it had dampened the spirit of all in Serra's cave.

Amerika turned on Hall and Alihahd as if they were negligent gods. "Could you not save it?" She beat the shoulder of the nearest one—Alihahd—with her little fists.

Alihahd rested his chin on his hand and looked forlornly heavenward with his large expressive blue eyes. He was still very thin from his illness. He drew in a breath as if to speak, then exhaled without saying anything. He changed expression and finally spoke one word, hard. "No."

"How was it taken?" said Layla, crouching on her hassock like a hunting animal, her hair braided back with leather thongs. Layla was the combat soldier of the group. "What strategy?"

Alihahd answered in dull, reciting voice, "Hand-to-hand. On the ground."

Amerika was confused. Hand-to-hand was the only kind of battle she had ever known. "Are not they all?"

"*No* battles are fought hand-to-hand these days," said Harrison Hall. "We have much more efficient ways of doing each other in."

Yet superior weapons and modern technology could not win the war, as the Na'id discovered. Shad Iliya had revolutionized modern warfare by taking it backward—to people with guns.

"Infantry will always win the war," said Alihahd quietly as if thinking aloud. "But it is a lost skill. The only way to beat a good infantry is to destroy their entire planet. Or come in with a better infantry."

There was a somber pause.

The distant eerie sound of the wind brass on the eagle ridge intruded into the quiet. The arrhythmic tapping of the whip ends kept the humans inside, warning them that the winds were fast.

"How goes the conflict now?" said Layla.

They'd had no new information at the Aerie in a long time. Even old information would be news.

"Not well," said Alihahd. "But we have had no crushing reverses since Jerusalem."

"The Na'id lost several of their best leaders," Hall added. "Besides Shad Iliya."

"Did you kill him?" said Layla.

The question startled Hall into a smile. He tilted his head and played at the two gold earrings in his one lobe. "Not I."

"I tried," said Alihahd.

Hall turned to Alihahd, his smile broader. "Did you really? I tried to kill the Bel."

"How is it you failed?" Layla demanded.

Alihahd leaned his head back against the wall, tired. "Diverse reasons. None of them good." He put his long knobby fingers to the bridge of his nose and closed his eyes. "It is in the nature of our side to be inefficient. When the ultimate goal is disunity, you cannot have an efficient organization. Our side has a seedy lot of heroes. Myself. The Marauder." He cracked his eyelids and stole a peek at Hall, who gave no reaction to the name; not a lash flickered out of place. Alihahd dropped his hand from his brow and sighed. "Decisive action is rather difficult when all factions of the Resis-

tance are at cross-purposes. For my part I am not trying to
overthrow the Na'id empire, only loosen its grip on the
unwilling. I haven't the right to decide how Humankind shall
or shall not be governed simply because it might be within
my power to do so.''

Hall laughed.

Alihahd frowned. ''Did I say something funny?''

''Your flights of eloquence are precious, Captain.''

''I am glad I keep you amused, Mr. Hall,'' said Alihahd.
He was, he thought, not good for much else at the moment.

Talk of the past had made him introspective—something he
liked to avoid—thinking of who he was, what he had become, and what was left to him now. He wanted to get back
into space and do his work as Alihahd the rebel runner.

Or, now that he thought of it, did he actually want to return
to that life—ever? The possibility of not wanting shocked
him. He was conscience-bound to want it. But it was out of
reach. Running from responsibility was one thing. Being thrown
from it was new.

The disturbing thought pulled him to his feet, and he
walked to the doorway, leaned against the rock jamb, and
gazed across to Aerieside pinkened in sunset.

He could not leave. The old way of life was far away.

Hall's shadow fell across him, came to his side, and he
breathed, ''Can I possibly be free at last? Can the albatross
have fallen from my neck and I be truly allowed to forget?''

Hall took his empty pipe from between his teeth. ''You
can't hide from the past, and there's no permanent haven.
The past will come looking.''

Alihahd turned from the door, the import ominous.

The opal eyes of the foxhead pipe glittered unevenly; one
was cracked.

Alihahd should have known Hall would champion the past.
Those who lived for revenge never forgot.

''What are you thinking of?'' said Hall.

Alihahd leaned back against the rock, his eyes wide, hands
gently, too gently, tracing the grooves in the wall behind
him. ''My death,'' he said darkly.

Then he looked up; his face changed; eyes became clear
and his voice all blithe explanation. ''I was to have been
taken alive by the Na'id. I was imagining General Atta"id
explaining my death to the Bel. That is all.''

Hall gave a wicked smile that was not a smile. "I fear the honored general Atta"id will explain nothing. The honored general is recently deceased."

"Ah," said Alihahd, a lament. He scowled at Hall. *Marauder*. That was never spoken between them. "I regret. He was a good man."

"You mourn your enemies, Captain?"

"I would mourn any good human."

"You've been impersonating the Na'id so long you're beginning to smell like one," said Hall.

"Not everything the Na'id believe in is wrong," said Alihahd. "Part evil is not necessarily all evil. People who hate cannot see that." He was looking squarely at Hall.

Hall smiled and appealed to the others as his jury. "What is one to make of this? One of the Na'id's most devastating adversaries does not hate them."

"Make of it what you wish," said Alihahd wearily, fingertips to his forehead. "I don't hate anyone. I am so very tired. .   "

X. Hunting

In the muted light before sunrise, in the hour of the eagles, a warrior-priest wearing a yellow robe stepped outside and swept away the dust and debris that had collected in the windpockets on the path overnight. The dawn was the last of the Red Geese. The sun would move into the house of the Twins at the solstice later in the day.

Alihahd sat in a thicket of leatherferns. His eyes were shut, his nostrils catching faint scents of dark green alpine growth, dusty rock, and dry earth in the thin air.

Earth?

Soil, he corrected himself.

The last of the fog had lifted from his mind, and his thoughts ran swift and clear. The heartsick weariness that had hung on him for so long was leaving him tentatively—as if he were afraid to give it up. It had so long been a part of him that it did not seem natural to be without it.

When you are who I am there is no such thing as a safe place. He needed to keep that in mind.

A flutter of wings very close made him open his eyes. A bird lighted on his bent knee.

Its heavy, seed-cracking beak parted. *Cheep.*

Alihahd watched it without moving, not quite sure how he felt about being perched on. It cocked its scaled head sideways, robin-style, to see him out of the eye on the side of its head.

Cheep.

"Alien," Alihahd croaked at it like an insult.

Cheep.

The bird refolded its wings and shrugged its little shoulders like a man adjusting his coat.

Alihahd guessed he had been deemed an adequate perch.

Chireet! The bird took flight with a flurry of wings and a rattling scolding *trrrr* as Amerika came bounding up the path, holding up her long skirts with one hand above the grass-stained knees of her wide trousers. An empty basket swung on her arm; burrs clung to her woven cloak striped in wide bands of blue and violet. She gave Alihahd a radiant smile as he sighted her, her cheeks and nose rosily wind-bitten.

She told him that Ben-Tairre was inviting him on a hunting expedition with his party today.

She took Alihahd's hard gnarled arm in hers and took him to where the hunters were gathering. Harrison White Fox Hall was there. He had words for Alihahd's tunic as Alihahd strode down the slope with Amerika trotting to stay at his side.

"If my knees were that bony I wouldn't wear a dress."

Alihahd smiled wryly. "I do not wear it for you to admire my legs. Who invited you?"

"I invited myself," said Hall. He had also invited Vaslav, who stood behind him like a small pale shadow. "Should be great sport."

Alihahd lowered his voice. "Though I am not sure of the game here." It was folly to take up this challenge, like following a predator into its lair. Ben-Tairre did not carry himself like a man making peace.

Ben equipped Alihahd with an Itiri weapon, a beam gun

called a taeben, "warrior's eye." Like the never-dulled tungsten-plastic swords, the taebens were products of a technology far beyond Iry's. The taeben Alihahd was given was a ronin's; it could be triggered by any hand, whereas the warrior-priests' weapons were keyed to their owner's use alone. Alihahd was told about the animals of the mountain, what to watch for, what to watch out for.

Alihahd was going to watch his back.

The hunting party was Ben-Tairre's fire clan of the carnelian serpent, and five young warrior-priests of the opal sword. They started out on foot down the green-cloaked north slope of the mountain and descended all the way to the timberline, where wind-tortured half-trees grew along the ground. Far in the distance ahead loomed the next taller peak, the Guardian.

Alihahd shot at nothing. It was all he could do to keep up and pretend it was easy. And when the hunters stopped to reorganize their movements Alihahd went apart to rest behind an escarpment of unweathered crag that cut like coral at the careless brush of a hand. There he could hang his head, bending over, hands on his knees, breathing hard.

Harrison Hall found him there. He leaned carefully against the glittering scarp, crossed one leg over the other at the ankles, and regarded Alihahd curiously. "Captain?"

Alihahd spoke very quietly. "I am not doing well, Harry." It was the first and last time he spoke the man's given name.

Hall looked down at the bowed blond head. "Unhealthy posture," he said. "Your lungs can't expand."

"If I stand up I shall pass out," said Alihahd.

His watery eyes focused on the contorted timberline trees. He began to feel like one of these stunted shapes twisted along the ground. He could see the direction of the prevailing winds from the trees' eastward flagging, though anything broken broke southward; there was a violence that came from the north.

Loud crunching footsteps made Alihahd straighten up cautiously. Vaslav had come searching for them, and he joined Hall and Alihahd along the scarp. "They say there are berinxes in the area," said the boy.

"Berinxes?" Alihahd looked to Hall. "Those have the teeth?"

Hall nodded.

And at that moment there was a noise from above, high on

the rocks, and a trickle of dislodged sand and pebbles. All three spun with weapons raised, but Alihahd immediately pulled back his own and reached over to hold Vaslav's hand from his trigger.

It *was* a predator up on the rocky outpost—one with slanted coal-dark eyes and a small mouth twisted into a hard contemptuous line in his flat-boned, coldly handsome face. "We are moving again," Ben-Tairre informed them and moved away.

Vaslav drew in a wavering breath and rejoined the hunters.

Hall waited for Alihahd. An insinuating smile crept beneath the mustache, as if he had caught some secret of Alihahd's revealed.

"What?" said Alihahd to the smugly knowing look.

"I don't care what you say, Captain; you've been in combat."

Alihahd was much too quick at turning and aiming—as a thing done so often it became reflex—and he was much too good at *not* shooting never to have seen battle.

Alihahd frowned at the weapon in his hands. "Not against Na'id," he repeated, and he hiked after the Itiri hunting party.

By the time they started home again in the face of the shortening shadows, Alihahd was lagging behind, the dwindling reserves of his strength nearly spent. He stumbled, skinned his knees on the gravel slope, and did not get up.

"Shall I carry thee?" said Ben.

Alihahd stiffened. "No. That is all right, thank you very much," he said with such a tone of offended aristocracy that it made Harrison Hall laugh.

Ben-Tairre made a pointed gesture of looking at the sun. At this pace they would not reach the Aerie in time. The noonday sun was lethal. Nothing stirred at midday, not even the cretinous lizards with reflective scales. The Itiri were anxious to beat the sun.

So Alihahd was left behind. The hunters found him a sheltering cave where he could stay to wait out the noon hour and continue the journey alone after the deadly time was past.

A lizard crawled off its sunny ledge and went slinking into a dark crevice in the rocks.

The croaking of a reptilian crow.

Burr of insects in the heat.

Then there was no sound of anything that was living. Nothing moved.

Shadows shrank to nothing.

Air sizzled. Brown grasses withered.

Outside a blistering glare—like the sun on a Mediterranean strand.

Sky boils. Rocks hiss.

Drip, drip, drip of water in a subterranean pool.

Alihahd could almost hear the perspiration beads thread down through the short hairs on his scalp. He should have worn some cover on his shorn head. His skin felt tight, burned. Higher up the mountain where they had started the air was cold; there the sun was deceptive.

His large red hands trembled. Spring water in the cave tasted stale. He wondered if he would be sick.

He remembered the sun on the Mediterranean Sea. Thought back farther to the last time he had been completely sober. Thought clearly about things best not remembered.

He curled his knobby thin legs up to him and hugged his skinned knees as if he were cold. His mind was clear and there was nowhere to hide.

Vaslav paced the north ridge, waiting for Alihahd's return. Hall came out once to stand at his side, coat drawn back from his wasp waist, fists on his narrow hips, empty pipe between his teeth, earrings glistening against his deep red-bronze skin.

The weather had changed. There was no sign of the captain.

The red flags were out, warning that the winds were picking up and it was ill-advised to go beyond the Aerie's sheltered amphitheater. The shadows had lengthened before the clouds cast them over. The Itiri were flocking home.

Pack beasts honked and gurgled. Itiri voices hushed; birds stopped singing. The beasts sniffed the air.

Broadside, a pack beast was an ungainly bulk. Face on, its enormous body was an aerodynamic wedge that could withstand a three-hundred-mile-per-hour gale.

All over the mountain the beasts stood aligned toward the north, facing the mountain Guardian.

A cloud. A shadow. A cool breath.

Alihahd woke from a dreaming half-sleep. He wandered

from the cave. He had lost track of time and he could see no shadows. The sky was a white slate.

High, high above came the faint echoes of the clashing wind brass and voices that carried even to this distance: "Off the bridge! Shandee!"

Alihahd climbed up a rocky prominence and gazed up toward the sound, curious.

From over the lofty mountain peaks a swelling cloud loomed and rushed down. A swift wall of gray darkness, seeming fast even far away, it must be moving in a torrent.

Alihahd was mesmerized by it, like the black cloud over Jerusalem that had come and engulfed him and blotted out the light, everything.

So, frozen dull and disbelieving, he stared at this storm that roared like a rocket train, advancing on him. Its speed was unreal, like a jet stream.

Or *was* it a jet stream? He was five miles above sea level.

And then it occurred to him he ought to be running back for cover. But—as at Jerusalem—it was too late for him to go anywhere. The winds were here.

He started for the cave in the last seconds, jumped from the rocks with a cold spray of sand and grit from the storm's vanguard, fell hard, pain exploding in his shoulder and shooting in fiery spikes through his body, into his guts and behind his eyes, and he rolled.

He stopped rolling, opened his eyes to search for the cave, but saw a figure over him, cloaked in storm clouds.

Jinin-Ben-Tairre.

XI. Stormwind

A yank on both arms, a blaze of pain. Picked up like a rag doll as if he had no weight. Falling against Ben's firm body almost too hard to be flesh. A blast of wind like a truck. Thrown. Flying into sudden still darkness and folding over in pain on the rock floor of the cave as Shandee roared past.

At length Alihahd lifted himself on his knees, looked up.

A moving wall of gray wind thundered by the cave entrance, looking like the single open window of a speeding vehicle. All outside was a blur. Inside was quiet.

And Ben was there, snorting, shaking debris from his hair, his face burned, broad flat cheeks scored by flying grit. He stopped on catching blue eyes directed fixedly his way.

Alihahd simply watched, tired, cornered, his long limbs drawn in and folded to fit the cramped space without Itiri grace, his big frame ill accustomed to bending into unaccommodating places. He was not without his dignity; it never failed him.

He held his one shoulder at an odd slope. His thick lips turned down, furrowing deep frowning lines into his long face, his brow pinched.

Ben moved smoothly to his side and grabbed Alihahd's arm with a twist and a hit and a flash of blinding pain. Alihahd roared and turned to strike with his other hand but realized that the pain had suddenly abated as quickly at it had come, down to an aching throb, and he could move his right arm in its socket again.

He was not grateful. Anyone who pushed him into a den of lions could damn well pull him out and not expect thanks for it.

He withdrew as far as he could within the shallow natural grotto to wait out the storm, squared off opposite Ben-Tairre, both of them wary.

Why not simply lose me to the wind? thought Alihahd. It would have been a human enough thing to do.

But this being was trying very hard not to be human. He'd been born among humankind, had once answered to a human name. It was not what he wanted to be.

Alihahd could see the struggle inside—a man who was two people—and he knew the feeling well.

He slumped back against the dank rock wall, rueful at the situation—caught here, prisoners of the storm, hating one another—*all four of us.*

Ben spied the corners of a sardonic smile, and his head turned a quick hawklike fraction in suspicion. He did not like to think himself a source of humor.

Dark eyes bored into Alihahd's, but did not penetrate through. Alihahd was well practiced at being opaque.

I am older than you. My armor is thicker, thought Alihahd. *Though you are not doing badly for yourself, warrior-priest. I still see a human boy. You hate me.*

Alihahd coughed, deep honking spasms that shook his aching shoulder. Then he sat back again, blue eyes heavy-lidded, drained, guarded.

You hate me. Hatred is fear. But I really cannot see what you fear.

Alihahd was two meters tall, fair and blond like a warrior-priest, with a warrior's composed reserve, but haggard, bone-weary, old, the ruin of a once great man, his calm bearing a vestige of the power he once had. He let his head tilt to one side.

You fear me? he smiled again. *I am the one defeated here.*

When the winds lifted, Alihahd could not walk. He was sick, and weakness forced a humiliating ride up the mountain on the back of a shaggy pack beast.

His illness went on for days, and this time he could not recover. Already drawn, with sickness his face became skull-like, long, hollowed, his eyes sunken below lofty brow in wide orbits, a mask of wasted grandeur.

His breath rattled. He did not want to leave the lordly inhospitable heights of the Aerie as most humans did, but he realized this place was going to kill him, and finally he asked to be taken down to the summer village Kaletani Mai, and Lower Aerie.

With a cloak wrapped around his emaciated figure, Alihahd retraced the twisting trail to the waiting balloon and climbed into the woven reed basket, subdued and unhappy.

Harrison Hall had come to see him off at the ledge, the place where they had first landed on the Aerie, seemingly a long time ago. He faced into the wind, his redingote open to the breezes that tugged at the moored balloon. He clenched his empty pipe between his white teeth, all the sinuous lines in his dark red face molded into one of those lovely demonic smiles that revealed absolutely nothing. He was sorry to see his adversary get away from him, fallen to another opponent.

Alihahd looked back, bitter. "I don't lose well," he said quietly.

Hall nodded imperceptibly.

Two ranga unfastened the balloon's ropes and threw them to the pilot. Eagles guided the balloon as it lifted off the rocks.

Hall took his pipe from between his teeth, nodded. "Captain."

"Mr. Hall," said Alihahd.

Jinin-Ben-Tairre was alone in the training hall. Its great wide windows were flooded with sunlight reflected in honey glow on the butterwood panels. The worn wooden floor was pitted and scarred with sword grooves. Ben knelt, sitting back on his bare feet, his head bowed on his heavily thewed neck, his eyes shut, trying to clear his mind, think of nothing. He would not talk to anyone. He let no one near him.

His even breaths deepened, but not to the calm of sleep—deep in anger. He tried to calm his thoughts. Darkness kept stealing into his mind, angry suppressed thoughts rising into the clear space. He needed to banish them altogether, the dragons he had never really slain, merely forgotten for a time.

He opened his eyes, stood, crossed to the sword chest, and took up his blade, Da'iku. He glided it through all its possible moves, then began to visualize attackers and cut them apart. They came by twos; he killed by twos. More moved in, all sides. His ivory-gold skin glistened; black hair matted to his head; mechanical hand whirred. Invisible necks severed and heads tumbled. Ben rolled, stood, kicked, slashed. Attackers reeled back. He drove straight down with the blade, kicked straight back, wheeled, cut the air. Movement became random, precision muddied in savagery.

"Careless, careless, careless," said Roniva from the archway.

Ben came to a standstill in the center of the chamber, perspiration streaming down his labored sides, sword in hand, its blade crossed before him, its point a hair's width above the floor. His face was wet. He blinked sweat from his eyes. He was upset. He hadn't even heard her come in. His training, his awareness, failed him. Did she see it?

Had to.

Such slips could be fatal when one had powerful enemies waiting.

Ben spoke without intonation. "How may I serve thee, Fendi."

"Thou hast hurt my guest," said Roniva.

There was danger when a Fendi spoke face to face. Direct speech from the monarch was reserved for certain messages which brooked no intermediary. Roniva had not spoken to Ben-Tairre since the day she had become Fendi of the Aerie. This moment had been a long time coming, long dreaded. Ben knew what this meeting meant. Time had come. Setkaza, the inevitable deadly conflict; legend called it dance of death. It was an ancient right to be invoked when there were no more options. Declaration gave one leave to kill at any time—and opened oneself to being killed at any time by his intended.

"Thou hast killed my cheela. Thou hast killed my son. Thou hast driven away my guest," said Roniva, whites of her eyes flashing lightning in her ebony face. She wore a long flowing tunic of shimmering green; it left bare and free her thin whipcord-sinewed arms. Her hand was on her sword hilt.

"He is evil," said Ben-Tairre.

"I wanted him *here!*" Roniva cried as she drew her sword in a furious arc and jabbed its point into the floor. She stepped back from it, her fists at her sides, her voice a strained tremulous quiet. "From this moment we are bound in setkaza, thou and I. Look to thine own resources, Wolf, for thy days are numbered from today."

PART TWO

BEN

I. Wolf at the Door

Gregorian Year 5839 C.E.
In the year of the Topaz Gateway, in the days before Roniva became Fendi of the Aerie, a small stowaway was found aboard Xanthan's spaceship when the young warrior returned to Iry after a year's journey among the stars.

"Azo! What hast thou brought to us, Xanthan?" said the Elder Roniva as her warrior cheela stepped from his ship into the yellow grass of Lower Aerie.

"What have I . . . ?" Xanthan echoed in puzzlement and turned back to his ship.

A starved, wild-eyed boy stared out through the hatchway at the sunlit village Kaletani Mai and the towering mountains of the alien world.

"By the fire of my making!" Xanthan exclaimed, and the boy pulled back with a start.

Roniva advanced to him. Her linked electrum swordbelt jingled with her stride. Sun lit a blue sheen on her hair. She leaned in and sniffed at the boy, who drew down into a wolfish crouch. He smelled bad. "What *is* it?" said Roniva.

Xanthan stammered. "I—I meant not to bring him. He is a human being. One of the Earth breed."

The boy emerged from the ship cautiously to crouch in the warm sunshine. His ribs stood out in high relief under translucent sickly yellow skin. Coal-dark eyes smoldered deep in his skull-like head. He snarled at Roniva and ran past her to Xanthan, threw his stick arms around the young warrior's waist and locked his talon fingers together. Xanthan placed his hand gently on the boy's dirty black hair.

Xanthan was lovely, his tender eyes soft green like the sea, flaxen hair braided into a crown, creamy skin smooth and unaged. The boy was in love.

Roniva pressed the back of her forefinger to her lips speculatively. Her onyx signet left a fleeting imprint of a sword there when she took it away again. "What doth it call itself for a name?" she said.

"I know not. I found him in a trash heap. I fed him and let him go," said Xanthan. He *thought* he had let the child go. He bowed his head to meet the oddly shaped dark eyes at his waist. "What is thy name?"

Sunlight glistening on the bright edges of Xanthan's clean golden hair cast a shining corona around his angelic face. The boy simply gazed up at the face and clung fast to his silence.

"Doth it speak?" said Roniva.

"He hath a voice. I have not heard him to speak." He had heard the boy yowl and snarl and screech.

"Perhaps it hath no mind," Roniva suggested. Her arms jangled with enameled bracelets, and she reached out to touch the boy's head. He snarled and bit her hand.

Roniva jerked back, flashed anger, and smacked him down his nose with her open palm.

His face turned up cold and twisted into a vindictive mockery of a smile. He had known she was going to hit him. But he'd gotten her first.

The Elders who had come behind Roniva agreed they had never seen anything that untamed, that dangerous.

"Shalt thou kill it, Xanthan?" said one. "It is distorted."

Roniva licked her punctured hand. "I will kill him."

The boy, without letting go of Xanthan's waist, skittered around behind the warrior and peered out with pinched glowering face.

"Ah, it understands," said Roniva. "It doth have a mind, if not a name."

One of the other Elders spoke. "Then we cannot kill it."

"It is a *guest?*" Roniva cried.

"How can it be else? Xanthan brought it."

The stinking little creature protruded the lower lip of his small mouth at them angrily.

Roniva leaned forward, her hands on her knees so her eyes were level with his. "Thou art vicious, and I shall call thee Wolf for lack of a name."

"What is to be done with it?" said an Elder.

Xanthan reddened, chagrined. "I brought him. I shall take care of him," he declared shakily.

"It will die on the mountain," said Roniva.

Said another, "Leave it here with the ranga. They will feed it. The rest is for its own devices."

The other Elders agreed. And that was to be the final word on the human boy, Wolf.

No one counted on him following Xanthan up the mountain.

When the hungry, frenzied, mangy-haired thing peered over the rock at the top of the snake path, a ranga woman screamed and dropped her water jug. Clay shattered, water splashed, and the ranga woman ran on stubby legs, shrieking that she had seen a monster.

A crowd gathered to see the monster. Xanthan pushed through because he had an awful feeling that he knew what he would find.

He halted in dismay to watch his skinny foundling, hands and feet torn and bleeding from the climb, crawl over the last step onto the Ledge Path. The boy searched the staring faces and picked out his ivory-and-gold god Xanthan from the crowd, his dark eyes wide with abandonment and asking why. He could not understand what he had done to have been left behind.

And the boy did not know why all these other Itiri had come out onto the terraces to look at him. They were gazing at him in hushed awe. He did not know what he had done.

What he had done was to begin turning into a warrior-priest.

Aghara children came to the mountain by instinct. Drawn to the Aerie like spawning salmon, they answered an impulse to be with their own kind. From all parts of the world they hunted the hidden valley and climbed the mountain to become warrior-priests. Or die trying.

Xanthan blurted out before thinking, "I want to make him a warrior-priest."

"*That?*" The voice was Roniva's.

The boy scratched his runny nose. His hand left a smear of blood there.

Xanthan looked up to the second level where Roniva stood. "He hath the heart."

"Thou mistakest madness for courage," said Roniva more gently.

An Elder's hand came to rest on the nape of Xanthan's neck. "A human child, Xanthan? He will die."

"He doth not want to die. I will not let him," said Xanthan.

"He will endure not the ordeals. At best he will bore."

"Then let him bore," said Xanthan, defying his Elders and feeling utterly alone. He thought his was a natural decision. What great foolishness did the others see that he did not? "Let him fail for himself and return to his own kind of his own choice. He came here like a warrior cheela."

As he was speaking, everyone turned away, and Xanthan's blood turned cold, knowing who approached. His soft green eyes fluttered for a moment, seeking inward for courage. The crowd parted.

The berinx padded through the parted way on heavy paws with lowered head, fanged jaws agape and drooling. It stopped in front of the Earth boy, shook its brindle mane, yawned wide, and sat with a *woof* like a real berinx.

"Where is thy master, Chaulin?" said Xanthan in weary ritual.

The berinx snarled thrice: *Thy master also.*

The Fendi came slowly in his familiar's wake. He wore his naxa cloak thrown over one straight shoulder, its chain passing under his sword arm. His cloak always black now. His wispy hair was too thin to be bound. He held himself strictly erect as one who begins to feel gravity too much.

Eyes like hard green glass chips fastened upon Xanthan, then upon the little Earthling.

The monarch extended his blue-tinged, fragile-looking hand. The boy made to bite it, but, quick as a katalin's wingbeat, the aged Fendi closed his grip on the boy's lower jaw and held it unyieldingly.

He turned the child's head first to one side, then the other, examining his face, his yellow skin, his exotic slanted eyes sunk deep in his hunger-stark skull and burning with mistrust.

Finally the Fendi released the Earthchild's jaw with a slight firm push that prevented the creature from snapping at his withdrawing hand.

The Fendi turned slowly to pat the head of his fanged berinx. He talked to it. "If he climbed up the mountain, then he can climb back down in his own time. Yes?'' The Fendi's hard glittering green eyes slid to his youngest warrior-priest. ''Xanthan, he is thy cheela.''

Xanthan, left without words, first stared blankly for a long moment, then smiled and looked to his new cheela in joy.

The boy knew the meaning of smiles. Something good had happened: lovely Xanthan was happy. The boy started to return a wan grin gapped with missing baby teeth.

Then his eyes rolled back and he crumpled to the path in a dead faint.

II.   Wolf by the Hearth

5839-5850 C.E.

Xanthan came to the bedside in the ranga cave and watched his sick cheela. Asleep the child looked even younger than he actually was. His closed eyes were smoky-ringed in his starved face. He took up such a tiny corner of the wide mattress.

Then the eyes, dark like a ranga's and slanted like no other creature's in the world, opened and blinked sleepily.

''How is it with thee, Earthchild?'' said Xanthan.

The boy's black brows lowered at the name Earthchild. His tiny bow mouth curved down so hard his chin puckered; little fists balled, and he sat up and spat in hatred of his own kind. He made it clear that he was not an Earthchild. He bit his upper lip and glowered at Xanthan.

''Be thou then no more an Earthling,'' said Xanthan. ''Only let go thy hatred.''

The boy fell back on the bed, exhausted.

''I have something for thee,'' said Xanthan and held up a closed hand.

The boy uncurled his scrawny, claw fingers to receive the blue gemstone Xanthan dropped into his palm. The boy brought it right up close under his eyes and watched the stone move with his pulse.

"Lapis is thy courage and thy will," said Xanthan. "That is one. There are eight. When thou hast eight, thou wilt walk the fire."

The boy grabbed Xanthan's ring hand and pulled it to him to inspect the warrior's carved signet stone. "That comes ninth." Xanthan smiled. "Not till thou art a warrior. That is for my clan—the topaz twins. We walked only two years ago. I am a very new warrior."

As he was speaking, a white bird appeared from nowhere and alighted on Xanthan's shoulder. The boy gave a startled cry. Unperturbed, the dove preened a snowy wing, puffed up its ruff, and rearranged its long plumed tail. "My familiar," Xanthan told the frightened child. "That comes tenth—I know not from where." The boy frowned dubiously. "This thing I have named Asha," said Xanthan. "What is thy name, my cheela? I need something to call thee."

But the boy would not speak. His hand clamped shut over his gemstone and retreated under the covers.

"Please tell me," said Xanthan. "Or they will call thee Wolf."

The boy nodded, his native gesture of approval. His lips were pursed, his brow knit, but not unhappily. Wolf was fine.

The first thing Wolf needed to learn, if he was to be mute, was the way of silent speech. There were many signs and attitudes in use, so he could go a long way without speaking. And it was well that he spurned the chatter of little birds and ranga. Eagles and warrior-priests soared silent and alone. A warrior-priest did not disturb the silence without a reason.

Wolf was soon healthy again. Flesh covered his ribs, and his skin turned from sickly yellow to an odd but vital sun-darkened brown-gold.

And once Wolf was fit, Xanthan began to tap on his door in the mornings.

"Sae duun. Sae duun, cheela."

The boy was always outside on the first tap. Then Xanthan never needed to tap at all. Wolf was awake ahead of the dawn and listening for Xanthan's footsteps. Xanthan would approach with soundless tread, and still the boy was outside.

For the first year he did no fighting, but learned to fall and jump and listen and feel and see and breathe. He had already had a great deal of martial training among humans; it was obvious in the way he used his inner strength and the way he moved—not sticklike and unnatural in the usual human fashion.

In the first year, Xanthan was learning as well, discovering the oddities of his small charge.

Xanthan woke, first time of many times, in the dead of night in his solitary cave on Aerieside to find Wolf curled under the blanket at the foot of his bed asleep.

Xanthan lifted him by his narrow shoulders to face him.

Sleepy eyes blinked back.

Xanthan's white skin was smoothed cold like marble in the dim starshine that spilled into the cave. His warrior's gem-stones gleamed darkly in the polished rock wall. Xanthan told the boy his place was across the way at Haven with the ranga.

The boy shared a cave with eight male ranga, as most aghara children did. The ranga lived in heaps. Warriors lived alone. Wolf cared for neither arrangement. He did not care for the ranga, but he was terrified of being alone. He wanted to be with Xanthan.

Xanthan would wrap a cloak around the skinny form and send Wolf back to Havenside, except when the wind brass sounded. Then Xanthan would either carry him across the swinging bridge himself, or let him stay, breathing softly at the foot of the bed.

The next surprise came on a cool and breezy day in what passed for summer on the mountain when Xanthan took his cheela hunting runner-birds.

Xanthan soon spotted a trail, and he trotted over the ridges and down the gullies and inclines in pursuit, his cheela dogging him faithfully.

Then the trail split—a bird and mate. Xanthan told Wolf to take the low trail; Xanthan would climb the steep rocks. And Xanthan bounded up the treacherous rise.

The boy just stood in the ragged brown grass, bewildered.

Xanthan stopped on his rocky perch, perplexed and an-noyed. "Follow thou, before it fades!"

The boy turned a complete circle, searching for something fading.

Xanthan became cross. "Art thou *blind*?"

As soon as the words were out the young warrior recalled

something spoken once of humans being blind. He leapt down the rocks and rolled in the grass at Wolf's feet. He jumped up. "Come thou with me."

They abandoned the hunt and returned to the Aerie. Xanthan sought his own master, Roniva.

"Azo!" Xanthan saluted the Elder with his sword fist on his left palm. "Hanina, knowest thou of humankind?"

"I know some small thing." She strolled across the cave and ran her fingers through Wolf's hair; it was coarse and black like her own. Wolf had learned by now not to bite everyone who tried to touch him. "Ask thou," she bid her warrior.

"Are humans somehow blind?" said Xanthan.

"Heat-blind," said Roniva and shook back the chained loops of electrum strung through her long hair. "Infrared they cannot see. They see one octave only. The lower frequencies are invisible to them. To thy Wolf this cave is dark."

Xanthan was numb with shock.

"Knowest thou wherefore I opposed thee, cheela-nu?" said Roniva as Xanthan began to realize how difficult a task he had taken upon himself in this human cheela. A cheela needed every sense and every strength and skill he had to become a warrior-priest. "I wanted not to see thee break thy heart." Roniva drew her saffron shawl around her and stepped out of the cave into the wind.

Xanthan turned to his cheela and took his glowing hot face in his hands. The boy must have some other strengths somewhere, something only humans had. Xanthan sensed it pulsing between his hands, knew it as he knew some part of his spirit would transcend death, knew it without having any reason to believe. The boy had to have something *else*. He must.

Because Xanthan, like all warriors, could not fail and live.

It was Roniva who taught Wolf to write and to count in the Itiri way. "It uses its left hand," she said to Xanthan. "Mark thou on that?"

Xanthan had noticed. The boy would carry a sword in his left hand. "It—" Xanthan began, then caught himself. *It*.

Roniva smiled with white teeth and admonished, "I trapped thee in my circle, Xanthan. Be thou more careful."

"Yes, hanina."

"And feed it." She squeezed the boy's arm. "It needs to be fatter."

"I fear for the winter," Xanthan admitted.

Roniva demurred. "Not so. Not if it be fat. I wish I were built like thy creature. Its stock cometh from mountains. Look thou at it. How short its fingers and toes. How flat its face. How thin and small its lips. How short it is. Its blood has less a journey from its heart and will not cool. See the fold of fat over its eyelids. Those eyes will never freeze, nor that flat nose. Its stature looks as if it will broaden if he grows. I would spend my winters easier had I that build and those fingers and toes.' The tall, lithe warrior-priestess felt the cold quickly in her long, tapered extremities if she did not bid her heart to work faster. "He hath mountain eyes like mine. Dark eyes burn not in the light at these heights where the air is too thin to blunt light's cutting edge."

Xanthan blinked his antimony-lined green eyes. "He."

"Cheela?"

"Thou said *he*."

"Ah." Roniva spread her long spidery fingers. "For I am weary of thy savage. Take it with thee and go."

Wolf survived the winters well, and in the year of the Topaz Beacon, Xanthan began to teach him to fight with his open hands.

Days were idyllic on the mountain, and, with no other humans around him to remind him, Wolf started to forget, truly forget what he was.

Then, in the year of the Topaz Serpent a ship of humans was brought to the Aerie. They had been found drifting in space without power, victims of a war humankind was waging across the stars.

Wolf hated them.

"But they are thy kind," said Roniva.

Wolf motioned negative. He would not be human.

"The girl perhaps," said Xanthan. "Thou wilt need a mate someday."

No. No. No.

And to Wolf's bitter glee, the humans could not bear the cold winds on the rugged mountaintop, and all but one retreated to the mild climate of the Lower Aerie, so Wolf did not have to look at them.

Only the one named Montserrat stayed, a timid woman who kept to herself on Havenside.

Wolf would not hurt her; such would violate his emerald. He would take out the stone and gaze into its clear green crystal when the hatred boiled up inside him. The emerald was for kindness. Wolf had been given the gemstone for his generosity to the eagles. The boy had an affinity for the talassairi.

He still did not talk. He would howl if he was hurt or left alone, savage as a dog wolf and as wily. He still came to the foot of Xanthan's bed at night—so stealthily that the warrior sometimes did not waken. All those practices came to an end in the winter of the Topaz Serpent.

Wolf was given his own cheela-cave on Havenside. It was a small solitary chamber, a proper home for a warrior in training.

Wolf hated it worse than he hated the cave full of ranga males. At the best of times he hated it, and he spent little time in it.

But he no choice come winter, when, on the eighth of the River, Shandee returned for its annual maraud, and all activity came to a standstill and everyone took to his home as the deadly jet wind raged through the mountain peaks nonstop for twenty days.

Wolf had never spent the twenty days alone.

The forsaken pleading in his slanted eyes when Xanthan shut the door on him to seal his shelter haunted Xanthan back to his own winter prison.

Shandee howled. Or was it the boy? Sometimes Xanthan could hear both and thought his heart would break.

After five days he heard only Shandee.

At the end of twenty days, in the abrupt silence of the winter wind's leaving, Xanthan burst from his cave in a flurry of snow and sailed across the bridgeless crevasse with a running cat's leap to dig out his cheela from the piles of blown snow.

The cave door opened with the cracking of ice.

Xanthan's glare-blinded green eyes saw nothing at first in the dark cave, then perceived the heat aura of the solitary figure in the corner. Wolf was alive. But he did not move, or whimper, or fly into Xanthan's arms. The boy was silent, his eyes open. He was there, but not there, lost somewhere inside himself.

Xanthan hugged him and cried, "Come back. Come thee back."

But Wolf stayed rigid through nightfall, and Xanthan carried him back to Aerieside on the new bridge, set him at the foot of his own bed, and waited. The boy did not curl up there. He had always curled up. He stared at the ceiling.

Xanthan caught him up, held his stiff unyielding form, and cried on his black hair. "Oh, little Wolf, what hast thou done to me? Who ever had such a stupid cheela?"

"I am not stupid."

Xanthan was shocked out of tears. "What sayest thou?" he whispered.

Calm eyes riveted to his, and Wolf spoke distinctly. "I am not stupid."

Xanthan could not speak. The boy was perfectly composed. "I will drink now," he said, and Xanthan gave him water. Then Wolf said, "I will eat now."

And when he was fed he returned to his lonely cave and slept.

He never came to crawl into Xanthan's bed again to sleep at his master's feet, and Xanthan was very sorry for that, the last gentleness gone from the child. Wolf had been taught to stay by himself, and Xanthan wondered if it had not been a mistake.

Wolf now cherished his solitude with a vicious fervor. Patience he had also acquired. It was a weird and unworldly kind of patience, not like turquoise at all, and he took hurt without sound. This was not the peace of eagles. This was fire in the mountain.

He was a different Wolf ever after, grown, with an Itiri warrior's reserve and dignity, transformed by the winter wind. The ranga said Shandee was still on the mountain and it lurked within him. They sensed something odd in his brand of quietude.

And the eagles were afraid of him.

In the year of the Topaz River, Wolf was taught his first weapon. It was a sword, the tungsten-plastic kind. "When thou wilt walk the fire, this will be thine," said Xanthan.

Wolf ran his palm along the flat of the ancient blade, his dark eyes alight.

Xanthan's white bird trilled on its perch over the lintel by an inset ruby rose.

"Why do we not teach a sword to wield itself?" said Xanthan.

Wolf scowled. He pulled at the cuffs of his rough-woven cheela's tunic; he had outgrown another one. "Because it is impossible," he said.

"No," said Xanthan. "Had we want, we would find a way. Thy answer shows a want of thought. Topaz is wisdom. Thou hast it not."

"Then I do not know why we do not teach swords to wield themselves," said Wolf.

"Because a sword hath no virtue," said Xanthan.

Wolf wore his virtues on a leather thong around his right wrist. He had four: lapis for courage, beryl for kindness, diamond for honor, zircon for modesty. Xanthan closed his hand over the bracelet and squeezed his wrist. The stones bit into his brown flesh.

"Keep these little stones in mind when thou hast thine own sword," said Xanthan.

He showed Wolf a few simple moves with the sword and let him practice until his wrist and forearm tired. Then Xanthan brought the felt cover to wrap the sword and replace it in its scented wood chest. Wolf's eyes fluttered uneasily to the disappearing blade. "The Gurkha never sheaths his kukri unblooded."

Said Xanthan, "Art thou one of these Gurkha?"

"There is one in my ancestry," said Wolf. "My brother owns a kukri. There is much blood on the blade."

"It is a foolish custom," said Xanthan, covering the tungsten-plastic sword in red felt. "How is one to practice with one's actual weapon? Thy Gurkha brother must have many scars."

Wolf was about to speak and suddenly frowned, as if catching himself at something forbidden. "I forget," he said.

In the year of the Topaz Veil, Wolf was taught his last weapon, the taeben. The Itiri called the beam guns "eyes" because they were useful and powerful, and they lured their users into letting their other talents atrophy. Relying solely on a taeben was seductively easy.

"A gun is a coward's weapon," said Xanthan. "Any child can kill with a gun. It is also thy most powerful weapon, not thy sword. The sword is art; the sword is discipline; the gun is life and death."

Wolf had handled guns before and was quickly expert. He was also quick to put the taeben aside and polish his other skills. He did not like the weapon. Guns were too human.

As the short years passed, Wolf was becoming a young man. His frame broadened as Roniva had predicted, and his muscles filled out with great strength and un-Itiri bulk. He stretched hard to keep his form sleek. Bulging thews were for Earthmen.

And toward the close of the Topaz hexadecade, more Earthlings were brought to the Aerie, refugees of the human war. They were surprised to find a human cheela among the legendary warrior-priests; and the young women thought him breathtaking. Wolf was disturbed and confused, and he kept his distance, which made him all the more attractive.

He stood on the highest level of Aerieside, glowering across the crevasse, his head held high, only his disdainful slanted eyes directed downward. He wore only dark trousers, a sash, and a wide red band across his forehead, tied over one ear, to keep his human sweat from his eyes. His arms he crossed defensively over his bare chest; and the girls peered up at him from lower-level Haven and giggled.

"What is *wrong* with them?" said Wolf.

Xanthan was crouched beside him on one knee, his sword planted point down before him like a staff. "What is wrong with *thee*, cheela-nu?" he said. "Thou art bright as plague fever."

Wolf's heat aura glowed vividly about him to Itiri eyes.

"Be this something human?"

Wolf burned more brightly still; and scarlet blushed down his neck and chest. "I am not human," he said.

Xanthan considered the young females across the way. They were a varied group in color and size. Xanthan did not know what was the desirable standard for humans. Itiri came in two basic types only—the tall, slender, blond, green-eyed aghara, and the short, stocky, red-haired, black-eyed ranga. Humans came in all sorts. "Thou findest none of them an acceptable mother for thy child?"

"No. I am Itiri."

"Thou canst not give child to an Itiri woman," said Xanthan.

"Then I will have no mate," said Wolf. "I need no children."

"Thy choice," said Xanthan.

In the year of the Carnelian Sword, to begin the new hexadecade, Xanthan embarked on a trek with his cheela on foot across the mountains to visit outlying ranga villages and show Wolf there was more to Iry than one mountain and one valley. They were gone four years.

When they returned, Wolf would have been twenty-one years old by Earth count. By Iry count he was thirty-four. Onto his leather bracelet Wolf had added turquoise, which was patience, topaz, which was wisdom, and sapphire, which was control and strength.

At nightfall Xanthan came to Wolf's chamber and sat at the foot of his bed. Wolf rose in puzzlement.

A cold wind of coming winter moaned outside.

In the almost dark Wolf could see beloved face, soft eyes, and golden hair in a braided crown—angels looked so in the dim early memory of gentle times when Wolf was still a baby and bore a human name.

Xanthan pressed a pebble into his hand in the dark. Wolf held it up to see fiery-colored flecks within milky white blaze and shift in the hearthlight. An opal, which was integrity, soundness, wholeness. The gem was his eighth. The last. His training as a cheela was over.

Xanthan bowed his beautiful head, his face happy, sad, proud, and troubled. "When the spring cometh, the fire is for thee."

III.   Wolf in the Fire

5851 C.E.

The place of fire was open to the sky. Its hearthstones had been laid into a level breezeless garden court where its flame burned upright, though the slopes beyond were basted by stiff winds, baring the rocks. Their sharp crags isolated the fire garden; it was a difficult approach from whichever way one tried.

Wide flat squares of marble checkered the courtyard alternate red and black; and leafy plants circled round about the sanctuary, or trailed inside on tendriled vines. At one side of the square an ancient spring still bubbled to life from time to time, and a carved stone basin was inset where the marbled tile had been worn down by the slow trickle. The tiles at the center were discolored where flames licked from the pit and sooty feet had trod.

In the year of the Carnelian Beacon, on the first of the Sword, only one cheela was walking. That was not proper. But he was expected to fail. Not to taint the fire for others, Wolf would go alone.

The Elders ringed the court with vibrant dress and somber eyes, antimony lines extended in flowing curves and drawn lashes to the broken red scars on their cheeks. They wore eight jewels in their hair with their Elder's stars. Their swords lay unsheathed across their knees as they sat cross-legged on the marble, their familiars crouched, perched, or lying to their left. The warrior-priests who were not Elders sat with their fire clans. There were no ranga here. This was the one place ranga could not go. But no fretful mother and father would be hovering at the sanctuary boundaries this time.

Wolf gazed into the flames, his trousers rolled up and tied below his knees, around his neck a thin leather strip which he would untie on the far side of the firepit.

A walk through the fire. Easily done if done at all.

Xanthan waited on the far side with his clan of the topaz twins. He was angrier than Wolf had ever seen him, upset that his cheela's walk was to be solo, that no celebration was prepared, that everyone was already trying to forget this day.

Wolf tried to catch his eye. *Watch this*. But Xanthan could not see through the wall of heat.

Wolf tossed back his head. *I am Itiri. I shall not burn*. And he stepped into the fire.

He smelled it before he felt it. Pain and utter shock arrived at once.

Wolf leapt from the firepit and fell to the cold marble tiles hard on his knees and over onto his side, writhing in pain, digging his fingers into his thighs as if to cut himself off from his charred, oozing black-and-red feet.

Repulsed and embarrassed faces were turning away.

Wolf ran, scrambled, from the place of fire, out of their sight and into the snow. He tumbled down a jagged embankment and landed in a drift. He buried his feet in the snow, eyes rolling, breathing fast, the pain inside greater than the searing throb of his burns that wracked his body and made him tremble and sweat in the cold.

All his agony and shame could not change what had happened. And it happened over and over with every blink of his eyes, branded into his mind.

Ice melted on his feverish skin. With a will born of extremity he blotted out the physical pain—ignored it. It was not there so he gave it no mind. No mind at all. Nerves brought pain pulses to tap at his brain and found the gates locked fast.

He rested, breathing, trying not to think. There was only one thought.

Clouds moved in, closing up the sky. The snows would return.

At last Wolf tore his red headband in two and wrapped his ravaged feet in the rags, and he hiked the tortuous blowing path back to Aerie.

On the high terrace he caught sight of a tall slender figure dressed in plain brown, hooded, arms folded into wide sleeves. All Wolf could see of her was her blue-black feet. Roniva was in mourning.

Wolf was puzzled. She would not be mourning him, so who? Who was dear to Roniva?

Wolf's heart caught.

No. What had to be could not be. Wolf forbade. *No! NO!*

Roniva's hooded form moved like a shadow, retreating from his sight. Wolf stumbled to her at a hobbling run. She did not stop for him. One did not speak to the hooded, but Wolf fell to his knees as he reached her and he cried, "Where is my master?"

Roniva's eyes were hidden, the hood pulled far forward and drooping down, casting evening-deepened shadows over her ebon face. She continued away, soundless.

Wolf clutched at the hem of her long sleeve and held fast. "Where is Xanthan?" he screamed.

The hooded figure stopped, withdrew a spidery hand from her opposite sleeve, and pointed a long black finger to the bridge, where a ranga woman was weeping and yanking out tufts of her red hair and tossing flowers, gems, and pretty things into the crevasse. Wolf knew her. She was Xanthan's mother.

Roniva pulled her cloak from Wolf's numbed grip and walked away with specter steps.

Wolf crawled down the terraces to the bridge. A whining snarl squeezed from his tightening throat as he grasped the ropes, and Xanthan's mother fled in terror.

Wolf dragged himself onto the bridge and clutched at the scattered flowers she had left. He whined at the pretty flowers, tears coursing down his cheeks, "Why? Why? Why?" He collapsed in sobs.

He could not see downward; tears blurred everything. He tried to look over the edge where Xanthan had gone, where he was supposed to go. He was expected to jump.

Just as he'd been *expected* to fail.

In sudden fury he was on his feet, crushed blossoms falling from his clothes. He ran from the bridge and away from the Aerie on wounds that felt nothing as the spring snow began to fall.

Warmth came ever late to the Aerie. The snows quit the mountains and true spring came at last, without Xanthan, and without Wolf. It was assumed that Wolf had gone off alone to kill himself in his own way. The season passed in fleeting brilliance.

The valley was still cloaked in summer while autumn crept quickly over the mountain. Seasonal grasses turned red and gold. Desiccated plants crumbled to ash. Keys and grain and clouds of tufted seeds drifted and tumbled in the brittle wind. Eaglets flew. The berinxes left the high slopes, and a sharp burned-wood smell hung in the air when it was still. Burrowers went into hibernation, and Itiri stocked their caves; soon Shandee would be upon them again.

He appeared over the summit on scarred feet after a cold rain, come like a dark spirit, changed, fearless of the lightning; bolts only made each other brighter.

He was a fraction taller, his chest deeper, the youth fully a man. The leather thong of a fire walker was still tied around his thick neck. He gazed down at the Aerie.

The berinx padded up the high trail, its thick brindle coat catching burrs, its long tongue hanging from the side of its heavy jaws. It woofed at the rogue cheela.

"Where is thy master, Chaulin?" said Wolf.

The berinx could not snarl its ritual answer: *Thy master also.* The rogue cheela had no master. He ought not be here. He ought to have been dead. The berinx knew not what to say. It scratched at its mane in distracted confusion, then disappeared. The burrs from its fur fell to the ground.

The Fendi came slowly up the path the berinx had taken. His glass-green eyes were narrowed to slivers against the drying air; moisture came hard to old eyes. Withered hands held thick cloaks around his slight, once-powerful body.

Wolf crouched before the monarch in attitude of humble favor and asked to walk the fire again.

"Never done."

The answer was not the Fendi's. It was the Elder Roniva who had spoken. She stood behind the Fendi and placed another cloak over his head and shoulders.

"Never done because never tried," said the Fendi, his thin voice a whisper in the thin air. "No one ever lived to try. It was not because of a law."

"Natural law," said Roniva.

"If a natural law be broken, it is the law, not the violation, that is wrong," said the Fendi. He beckoned his berinx. It appeared at his side out of the air. The old man scratched the beast's ruff. "I must consult the archives," he told his familiar. "Something must govern this matter."

*   *   *

The Great Chamber had once housed the Fendi's throne. It was a nine-sided chamber with a great gray stone dome; tall lancet windows, fluted pilasters of colored granite, and opalescent white alabaster fittings. A fire blazed in the hexagonal firepit set into the floor of honeycombed red flagstones; and black smoke sooted the high dome.

A second attempt to become a warrior-priest—requirements were three. For the first the cheela must combat a full warrior-priest, and win. The volunteer for combat was Sentalla of the fireclan topaz twins.

Smell of death threat hung close and tense in the wide chamber. Wolf tested his grip on his sword. He crouched on a black hexagonal tile across the Great Hall from his warrior foe. Wolf's black hair was cut short, out of his eyes and off his ears. His wrists and right forearm were wrapped in leather, the soles of his feet resined. The floor had been polished to a glassy sheen.

Wolf had nothing to lose here. He was, to his own mind, already dead. All from now was gain, and he was free. There was only to let himself do what his self knew to do. Anger he had locked away in some deep part of him. An angry warrior defeats himself in combat, Xanthan had said. Sentalla had a personal grudge in this battle; the more *his* burden.

At the command to begin, Wolf swung up his sword and sprang across the floor with a screech, but Sentalla had already fled his place on an oblique and turned to slash at Wolf's flank. Swords met with a dull clash, then strained crossbar to crossbar. Both pushed and sprang back out of sword reach to circle more warily now, failing at first-shock tactics.

They stalked, feinted, shifted feet. Sentalla's sword switched hands. Wolf charged in with a yell. Sentalla parried, countered, was blocked, danced away.

Wolf screamed again, leapt, slashed.

Sentalla sidestepped, put out his blade in Wolf's flying path.

Wolf batted the sword away with his own, turned in the air, landed facing Sentalla.

Sentalla danced lightly back, circled. He had done really nothing yet, watching. He was nearly ready. He had seen enough. Jade eyes took in all of his opponent at once.

Xanthan had always said that his fire brother used his eyes too much.

Wolf circled behind the blazing firepit and disappeared from Sentalla's view behind its rising curtain of heat.

Sentalla approached the pit cautiously, eyes darting both ways, ready for whichever direction Wolf might reappear. Sentalla circled the firepit silently to his left, but Wolf circled also, staying exactly opposite him across the pillar of heat.

Among the spectators, Roniva bolted to her feet and stood a rigid, quaking statue. She could see that Sentalla did not know—Xanthan had never told him—that Xanthan's cheela was half-blind. Heat-blind.

The odd thing with this blindness was that it left no veils before Wolf's eyes. The opaque heat barrier over the fire worked only one way.

Roniva wanted to shriek a warning: Sentalla, *he can see you!*

The fire crackled and spat up sparks.

Wolf crouched to leap, neither left nor right but straight over the firepit. Few warriors would risk a blind attack. For Wolf it was not blind.

Wolf came flying through the fire, silent and suddenly *there*, blade slicing—and turning at the last instant to smack Sentalla across the midriff with the flat of the sword hard enough to stagger the warrior.

"Stop!" cried the Fendi, and his berinx appeared between the combatants to divide them. "That is a victory."

Sentalla was winded and scratched with two long curving red lines across his belly. Had the blade not turned he could easily have been sliced in two.

Wolf blinked soot from his eyes, slightly dazed, victorious. He did not move from his place.

Someone came to take the sword that was not yet his from him. Wolf's short fingers uncurled slowly from the grip, reluctantly.

"Thy mercy does thee credit," said an Elder, wrapping the sword in felt and taking it away. It was the first thing anyone had deigned to say to him directly since his return.

Wolf lowered his eyes and bowed his head.

His hair was singed, the edges curled up in thin frazzled coils that broke off with a touch and stank. A black hand reached over to brush him off. It was Roniva. She sniffed at the burned stench. "Very resourceful, my cheela's cheela. Virtue of liability."

"Hanina," said Wolf.

Roniva was dressed all in black bedizened with diamonds. She ran her hand across the shimmering stones. "But where are thine?"

His diamonds, she was asking, his honor. She meant that he should have suicided for honor's sake instead of subjecting everyone to this insanity when he should know he could not succeed.

"Mine honor is that I cannot know defeat," said Wolf.

Roniva clamped her teeth and lips tight. The thought, the possibility was awesome—the existence of a thing that never breaks, that could come crawling out of the lowest gutter.

The Itiri had never conceived of the Phoenix. Such a creature did not exist even in dreams. It was too much like impossible. Too close to divinity.

And Wolf was a third of the way there.

Wolf took a plane to the primitive side of the planet where rain forests grew thick and ranga had not bred an aghara in so long that the idea of tall blond warrior-priests was not in their memory.

For his second trial Wolf had been given a labor. All the Elders had conferred and at last bid him bring the claw of the leopard of Ma-pall-mo.

So he had come to the village Ma-pall-mo, the Springs, where the chameleon-skinned ranga were dark most of the day in the bright equatorial sun and white at sundown. They were afraid to venture into the jungle anymore day or night. They gathered where Wolf came to land, awed by the flying machine and its pilot—a tall man who remained dark in the dark.

They said the gods sent him to kill the leopard.

Silly, superstitious ranga.

They told him, "We black our skin with coal in the dark so it does not see us; it smells us. We mask ourselves with jungle herbs so it does not smell us; it hears us. Now the gods send you dark and odd-smelling and silent as the leopard itself."

"I was sent to kill the leopard," said Wolf in their own tongue. "But not by the gods."

But the ranga insisted.

"I do not even know what it *is*," said Wolf. "Tell me about the leopard."

"The Claw! Watch out for the Claw!" one cried.

"What claw?" said Wolf.

"Silent it comes," said another. "It comes in the dark with its claw. Sometimes you smell it come. You cannot hear it until it is upon you, then it paralyzes with its voice and claws you to death. In a big group maybe one of you will escape and tell the same tale."

"The Claw! The Claw! Look out for the Claw!" a ranga cried, and everyone made him be quiet.

"What does it look like?" said Wolf. "Was it ever seen?"

"No," they said.

"This is not helping." Wolf's small mouth curled in exasperation, but he could not be angry with the villagers. They were like children. Nervous ranga plucked at their red hair, seeing him displeased. There were some very thin-haired villagers in Ma-pall-mo. *I must slay this leopard or they will all be bald.*

"What does it smell like?" said Wolf.

Someone dashed away at a waddling run and came back bearing a torn rag on the end of a stick so not to contaminate it with his own musky smell. "It smells like this."

The scent on the rag was very faint. The short hairs rose on the back of Wolf's neck.

He knew the smell.

The jungle was black as sundown without stars, a verdant hell, dripping heat. Darkness training let Wolf move without sight, silent and loud at intervals. He wanted the leopard to come to him.

He heard the leopard at a distance—not its footfalls nor its passage through dense spongy vine nets of the rain forest, but its quiet panting in the heat. The leopard could not sweat.

Wolf had become still. The leopard fell silent. It could neither see nor hear him but had caught his scent, and Wolf could tell it was puzzled. It had never smelled an Earthman.

Wolf crouched in an acania thicket, ready to move, holding a dagger in his left hand, waiting for the leopard to attack or flee.

Then it came, screaming an Itiri death cry, with the whistling through the air of a slashing double-curved sword that tore into the acania thicket.

Wolf was no longer there.

The leopard had not been expecting one of his own. He was not prepared for any skill, any threat to himself. He had been very reckless. There was a dagger in his gut, thrusting up through his diaphragm, and he knew too late that this strange-smelling creature was an Itiri too.

Wolf buried the warrior's body in the jungle so the villagers could not do anything abominable to it, and he took the tungsten-plastic Claw back to the Aerie.

He threw the double-curved sword at the feet of the Elders.

"What would it have cost thee to tell me what I was hunting?"

The Fendi picked up the sword and passed it to Roniva, who bowed her head. "No one told him what was hunting him," she said.

Wolf bristled. "Was that not neat and clever—to have one distort kill another. It matters not which wins. Maybe they will kill each other if you are very lucky. You must have been very proud and pleased with that idea!"

"No joy. No satisfaction. And not lightly decided," said Roniva, holding the flat of Claw's blade to her cheek.

The tender gesture was alarming. Wolf's mouth was suddenly too dry. He tried to swallow. "Who was he?" he said in dread.

"No concern of thine."

Another cheela of hers? Or—but that was hardly possible. Aghara women were almost always sterile. Aghara children were rare enough—one out of one hundred thousand births— but an aghara born of an aghara? Wolf had never heard of such a thing.

Yet Roniva wore an eternity flower at her belt; she had a mate. Sterile women did not mate.

Someone say I did not kill her child! thought Wolf. But no one was answering him. "Thou hoped I would lose," he said.

"I hoped he would not lose," said Roniva with altered emphasis. "Thy losing was merely the other edge of the same sword." She passed Claw back to the Fendi—it was no longer anyone's weapon—and she sadly walked away.

*   *   *

And so Wolf had come to the last trial—as ever, a walk through fire.

"There is a full clan this year," the objection was raised. "He must wait."

A fire clan should be two, three, five, or seven. There were five for the carnelian serpent.

Then one died; his cave was opened after the twenty days of Shandee passed, and the cheela was found frozen, nine days gone.

The time of fire was thirteen days hence. A decision needed to be made. The would-be clan was now one short or one too many, and Wolf was waiting.

"This could be a destined thing," said the Fendi. "Ask of the carnelian serpent if they will take him; otherwise which of them will stay behind."

The four cheelas said they would take Wolf as their fire brother.

"He could taint your fire," they were warned. "He hath already failed. You may yet be a clan of four."

"We will be five," said the girl cheela at that time known as Mardeia. "Let him walk."

Wolf at the edge of the firepit gazed through the wavering heated air and smoke to the hooded figure cloaked in brown waiting for him on the far side with a bare sword. Failure a second time meant death, not by choice but by law, and Roniva would see the law fulfilled—as she had made certain that Wolf did not bathe his feet in ice before coming to this place of fire.

The other four cheelas had already walked. Now they looked back for him to come through the firepit and join them, four nameless warrior-priests of the carnelian serpent. They had shed their cheela names in the fire and had not yet been given new ones. They untied the leather thongs from around their necks and waited for Wolf to make them whole.

Go to them.

He relinquished conscious control, released everything—

Let go. Let go. To win, let go.

—and cast his fate to an inner voice, years of conditioning, faith. The body is limited, Xanth   had said, the mind hath no limits.

Wolf stepped one foot in the fire.

The ring of Elders and warrior-priests rustled uncomfortably. This would be painful to watch. They had seen it before. A cheela ought to have the grace to spare them from pain. This one was putting them through it twice. The Fendi should forbid.

Wolf stepped with the other foot onto the coals and became lost to their sight, shrouded in heat.

Into the forge. To be burned or created.

Heartbeats paced off creeping moments. Smoke curled to the sky.

He reappeared on the other side as from a mist, face visible first where the heat dissipated, a demon in hell, icily serene and belonging there. He came striding over the coals and out of the pit, unscathed.

The mountaintop erupted into a clamor of war cries, crashing wind bronzes, rattling daggers, and stamping, all the warriors on their feet at once, and the ranga echoed from Haven with jubilant shrieking and beating metal.

The new warrior joined his brothers and sister, and he turned, not smiling, no happiness on his face, not even pride—only vindication, some kind of revenge.

He tore off the old leather circlet from his neck and threw it into the fire.

It was a clean fire, and others danced through it.

The brown-cloaked figure remained isolated amidst the crowd in the fire court. She tore back her hood, eyes flashing, thin nostrils flaring; the sword trembled in her tight grip. Unhooded, she still did not speak.

The rest of the mountain was in uproar, the din reaching to Kaletani Mai. Only Roniva and one new warrior were silent—until white hands gently tugged on broad yellow-brown shoulders and beckoned him from his dark visions. "Dance, fire brother."

The words, like an enchantment, charmed away some of the black spell that loomed about him, and he danced with the others.

A wayward breeze blew smoke through Roniva's hair spilling from its hood, and she wished she were ranga to believe in protective spirits and to make a warding sign. She felt need of them. And she wondered what name would be given this being that had just been made from the fire. She was shaking.

What have we wrought here today?

IV. Wolf on the Ramparts

5851-5856 C.E.

Jinin-Ben-Tairre they called him, the Feet of the Warrior Are Burned. A point of awe, the name carried a sense of overcoming the insurmountable. To a strong people with a stony will there came a point where they would break instead of springing back. This warrior had no such limit. The name was who he was.

Roniva approved of the reference to his burn scars; but Ben was a rare name, conferred on few—*Warrior*. There was only one other Ben alive on the mountain. This great honor seemed to her a mistake.

The girl Mardeia became known as Arilla, named for corundum, the virtuestone of strength. The other warrior-priests of the fire clan were given good names also, and the ranga foretold that one of these five would be Fendi one day.

With the glowing red tip of a firebrand they burned the dotted warrior's lines into each other's cheeks and pressed herbal ash into the wounds so they would heal red. A ranga artisan fashioned their signet rings, serpent intaglios carved into polished carnelians set in platinum. The artisan chattered about Ben-Tairre's "ranga hand," broad and stubby-fingered next to long, tapered aghara hands. No one had ever made such a wide signet band for a warrior-priest.

Ben was given a book of law and philosophy. He vowed never to take a life without a cause, to fight only his own battles and those of his allies, which were his fire kin; the talassairi, the eagles; and the mandesairi, the whales.

And he was given his sword. Ben christened his Da'iku.

He shed his drab cheela garb for warrior's finery. Warrior-priests were peacocks except during the days of restraint, the somber days between the leaving of Shandee and the New Year's fire.

He climbed to the top level Aerieside to stand on the high

cold ramparts with his fire kin, the wounds on their cheeks yet unhealed, a pride of young lions, flush with the newness of their arrival. Jinin-Ben-Tairre took his place with them as a warrior-priest, once a wolf that had come to the door for warmth.

A thin layer of cloud brushed the top of the mountain with gray gauze. It meant the winds were very calm.

Jinin-Ben-Tairre looked to his fire kin. Two familiars had appeared while his head had been turned: a white binaya for Arilla, and a red snake for Kaliathan. Ben muffled his own pain. He had resigned himself a long time ago to the fact that he could not have one, any more than he could ever hope to have heat vision or green eyes. Everything he could control he had won. He had walked the fire. He had a sword, a fire clan, and a name. That would have to do.

Not to be unhappy in his brothers' and sister's joy, he started down the terraced slope of the Aerieside settlement.

Suddenly there was a keening *screee* and a burst of talons and feathers in his face. He ducked down, and Da'iku flashed a cutting sweep through the air.

The bird disappeared at the advancing sword's edge, then blinked back into view as the blade whistled through its completed arc.

A familiar. Ben-Tairre stood up from his crouch and sheathed his sword. The little brown hawk fluttered around his head and screamed at him. *Whose?*

The familiar alighted on his shoulder and squawked in his ear.

Comprehension arrived with a rush of surprise and emotion. *Mine.*

''What is that supposed to be?''

Roniva blocked Ben's path in the arcade, appearing severe, hard, and angular as an eagle. Her black hair was pulled back and hanging straight from its topknot. Her whip-thin body was robed in plain beige but for all her bright enameled bracelets, anklets, and toques. Black eyes critically regarded the bird perched on Ben-Tairre's shoulder. ''Well?''

''My familiar,'' Ben answered.

Roniva's expression soured as if to say, *I know that; what is it supposed to* be?

''It is a kestrel,'' said Ben.

"An *Earth* creature?" she said as if it were the ultimate insult.

Ben remained undisturbed. He did not mind the form of the creature, which at one time would have upset him horribly. Enough that it was a familiar and it was his. It was an indelible stamp of legitimacy. No one had expected a familiar to appear for him. Now there was no doubt that he truly was a warrior-priest. "It only appears so," he said.

"My Xanthan's familiar had not talons and a hooked beak," said Roniva.

The kestrel was screeching in Ben's ear. "Knowest thou what it sayeth?" Ben asked.

"Thou wilt have to decipher its noises for thyself," said Roniva. She had meant to be short with him, then decided to say more. "It is a primitive language. The first sound out of it will be a verb; the mode and tense thou knowest not and it will tell thee not—but I can tell thee it will be almost always a command. They are not informative. Thy familiar will spend most of its time giving thee orders."

Screee, said the kestrel.

"Another thing," said Roniva as the bird batted Ben's face with its wing. "They are not known for their patience."

Ben pursed his lower lip over his upper lip and furled his brow a thoughtful moment. At last he said, "Can I give him back?"

It was the first time he'd expressed anything like humor.

"Certainly," said Roniva, taking her leave of him. "Discover from where he came and thou mayest return him." That was a no. No one knew where familiars came from.

The familiars were once assumed to be manifestations of the fully trained aghara mind, since they seemed to take their shapes from their owner's thoughts. But the kestrel's appearance to a human destroyed that theory.

What was left then?

Ben drew his sword, turned it in the light that came streaming in shafts through the pillars of the arcade.

A blade that would cut stone, handed down for countless generations and still fine-honed.

And a creature companion that came from nowhere.

"Thou art not my familiar," said Ben to the hawk.

The kestrel squawked.

"Thou belongest to my sword."

The bird turned its head from him and preened its wings, noncommittal.

Ben sheathed Da'iku. He moved swiftly to the outer edge of the arcade, leapt lightly, barefoot, upon the balustrade, hugged a jewel-encrusted pillar, and leaned out, gazing down into the chasm cleft into the mountain between Aerie and Haven. Xanthan's grave.

"One can teach virtue to swords, Xanthan," he whispered.

The kestrel bit his ear.

"Rather swords will teach," said Ben.

His eyes burned, staring into the crevasse. He shrugged off a ruby-inlaid armband and hurled it down the void. He swallowed the thickness rising in his throat, made a fist, and swung impotently at vacant space. "Wherefore is it too late to tell thee anything!" he hissed without voice. His voice failed him entirely. "Couldst thou not wait? Thou didst not know thine cheela."

Tiny claws were digging into his shoulder. A trickle that could have been blood or sweat traced down his back.

Ben dropped into a sorrowful crouch on the stone rail, his forehead on his knees. He pointed down the abyss without looking. "Get thee down there. Get thee down and tell him."

Piercing talons released their hold without a rush of wingbeats. The kestrel was simply gone and Ben was alone.

He doubted the kestrel would give any message to Xanthan.

He raised his eyes, peered over his own knees, and spoke, muffled. "Would that thou wert alive to forgive me. . . ."

The evening brought afresh the festive air that started with the vernal equinox and lasted through the first days of the Sword, a time of beginnings, plantings, and things new. All the Aerie stayed awake late into the night. Torches blazed in sconces along the terrace paths and arcades; and all the doorways glowed with warm yellow hearthlight from inside where sounded drums and the rap of poles for the dancers, singing, and cheerful voices. The engineers had thrown bridge hooks across the chasm and made a second temporary bridge; and through the night people wove back and forth across the crevasse, talking, wearing flowers in their hair.

Ben walked away from the light until the way was illumined only by stars, visible in their uncounted multitudes out here away from the torchfire. A desire for solitude took him this way. He had never fitted well in big merry groups.

The healing wounds on his face itched. A wreath of winter flowers looped lopsidedly across his brow. He took it off and let the chain of white blossoms trail from his curved fingers at his side and flutter with the random gusts of allato-bei, the winds that are.

He wandered off the main path on a twisting foot trail crushed through moss and brush. Had he heat vision or had he been more aware he would not have gone this way.

In the tall wind grass he nearly stumbled over a warrior and his ranga mate coupling in the private darkness.

Ben spun off in another direction and ran, hot and flushed, disturbed and more embarrassed than the incident called for. And more than that, he was frightened.

Here was something alien he could not assimilate or even understand. The way they did it—so calm, like passing water, without drive. As conscious and purely mental a decision as adopting an orphan. No imperative. No physical intensity.

Thought of flesh moving on flesh did not leave a young Earth man calm. The blood quickened, heat rose, and the body burned. Ben knew what sexual heat was, not from his memory of life as a human—he'd been ten years old when he'd left their company—but from the mountain animals that howled and danced and puffed up fur ruffs and bit and scratched. He had seen rutting males chase a female, seize her, and pound themselves into her. That was physical desire, and that was well for mountain animals, but not for a warrior.

Ben could kill the passion with a concentrated effort of will. But that also killed the physical reaction. He could not mate passionlessly like the Itiri. So he would not. He had resolved long before this to forgo a mate and children if it meant returning to humanity.

Humanity from its side found Ben-Tairre fascinating. Reserved, with an unconscious, touch-me-not sexuality, Ben gave only disdain and was answered with fawning. Winter never came back soon enough to drive all but the most rugged humans off the mountaintop. Ben was accustomed to the quiet perennial presence of the former slave woman Montserrat on Havenside and her recently arrived companion, the

mercenary named Layla. They ignored Ben. There was room
for them in Ben's world. The others he could not abide.

He returned to his cave one night at the height of summer—
the cave that had once been Xanthan's—his virtuestones set
into the wall glittering darkly together with Xanthan's in the
starlight that chanced through the wide-flung windows, and
he sensed in the dim light that he was not alone. He blinked,
waited for night sight to sharpen.

There was a human woman in his bed.

He smelled sweet oil, saw glossy brown arms, a tumble of
wild dark hair, a thin cover draping a curving form and fallen
from one full breast, its rose-brown nipple standing out pointed
and hard.

Ben took a step back, his handsome face a hard stoic mask
chiseled in ivory. He fought down revulsion.

He had no conception of himself,- his appearance, soft
black bangs fallen across the brow of his still-boyish face,
his taut, virile body, animal strength—and half-alien mind.
The woman's eyes traveled slowly the length of his figure,
then returned with bright excitement to his slanted eyes.

"Hast thou not a place to stay?" said Ben.

"I would rather stay here," she said. It came out more
gently hopeful than sultry—but Ben could not read human
expressions anymore. A quiver rippled through the woman's
body as she inhaled and arched her back to make the thin
blanket fall from her other breast. There was fear in the
gesture behind the seduction.

Ben could still recognize fear in any creature. He did not
know why she was afraid. He would not let himself know
why she was here. He turned to go.

"Warrior," she said.

He paused, his broad back outlined in the starlit doorway.
His breath deepened in tried patience. He turned.

"I am cold," said the woman. She moved over in the bed
with serpentine motion of her rounded hips, and she opened
her arms. The pulse in her smooth throat was quick.

Ben strode to the bed, stripping his cloak from his shoulders with the twist and flowing power of a big cat.

He draped the cloak over the woman and strode out.

He found an empty cave, lay down on his back, and closed
his eyes to sleep on the floor of cold stone.

*   *   *

In the year of the Topaz Triquetra, the Fendi sent Jinin-Ben-Tairre starward in an ancient ship called *Singalai* to live awhile in the world outside.

"I shall not revert to my blood," Ben vowed, anticipating the reason for this quest.

The Fendi patted the head of his shaggy berinx and echoed Ben's claim. "He will not go back to them." Its certainty suddenly sounded boastful to Ben's own ears, and the Fendi answered him in the next breath, "Then he shall know—for certain."

The Fendi read hearts and minds as most people read the stars and the seasons.

The hard, glass-chip eyes of brilliant green shone with eternal fire within the mortal confines of their papery translucent lids. Wispy white hair wreathed an eggshell skull so brittle and frail it could not be of this world much longer, the monarch's husk of a stately form become ethereal as if one day soon it was to be spirited away on a dry autumn wind with the rest of the season's ashes of transitory life.

A ghostly figure of awe and wisdom, the Fendi was not one to whom brash declarations should be made. Ben backed down to a humble silence.

The Fendi scratched the brindle ruff behind his berinx's ears. "Let my warrior stay because he is an Itiri, not because he knoweth humankind not."

Ben dropped to one knee and touched his forehead to the floor in final acceptance and farewell. "Yes, Fendi."

Two years abroad revealed nothing to sway Ben's already fixed mind, nothing to endear humanity to his estranged soul. He found confirmation of his judgment in the human war still raging, just as he had left it, in the name of supremacy of a savage, vulgar race. If any change had occurred, it was but a widening of the already enormous gulf between professed human ideals and their actual deeds. There were good people incompetent to reach the goals naively set far beyond their abilities; and there were evil people perverting the ideals to their own ends. Bungling and avarice took their toll in equal measure of suffering among humanity and everyone they touched. Good intentions did not an empire make.

Human greed was especially stunning to Ben, coming from a place where the concept of ownership was loose. Things were *used* on Iry; to *own* a thing was an oddity and a rare privilege.

And among humankind Ben lost one of his only possessions. His sword.

Contempt had made him careless. The idea that someone would actually take Da'iku from him was inconceivable. He could not believe it was gone.

The blade was shipped to another planet, sold at a bazaar, and was in the hands of a new owner by the time Ben caught up with it, led by his shrieking kestrel.

The sword's buyer watched in mute astonishment as first a hawk appeared in an instant from out of the air and scared his prize rare white Arabian mare, then a young man with almond eyes and scarred feet walked into his garden and seized the reins of the gold-caparisoned horse, and made her stand still. The mare came to a stamping halt, her sides, under her heavy ornaments, panting with noisy breaths in the damp oasis heat.

The elderly man's bushy eyebrows rose and disappeared under is kaffiyeh as Ben unstrapped the newly purchased sword from the mare's saddle, drew the blade, and cast the gaily tasseled velvet sheath to the ground. The warrior turned the double-curved blade in the light before his exotic eyes, then whistled it through a helix in the air. Then he walked away with it.

The old man did not interfere. His leathery skin pinched in frowning crevices around a beaked nose and deep owl eyes. He picked up the discarded red velvet sheath, watched the warrior retreat barefoot through the white pillars of his oasis paradise, and he breathed a baffled oath: "Al*lah?*"

That night, asleep under the desert stars, a pinprick invaded Ben-Tairre's dreams. His mind sludged upward to thick consciousness, never clearing to alertness. His limbs moved as through water, and he knew he had been drugged.

He fought it—in the wild thrashing way of panic, not the calm methodical way of the Itiri. He hadn't the patience to learn that kind of control, so his fight was the charging of a wounded animal, without the concentrated power of thought to break down the evil inside him. He could only rage against it. He thought his simple *will* could force anything.

For the second time, it was not so.

He tried to turn back and learn—learn *now*—a systematic defense against the foreign substance in his veins. Too late.

Feebly he pushed at the ropes on his arm, at the heavy feet that stood on his other wrist and on his ankles, till he was pinned down on the sand and could not resist anymore, the drug sapping even his desire to fight. It was so easy just to rest and watch them, as if it were all happening to someone else's body and he was only an observer.

His right arm was held out straight and strapped down to a wooden board rough with splinters so that he could not move but to curl his fingers and make a fist around the biting woven hemp bond pulled tight across his palm.

A meat cleaver appeared before his stupidly curious and uncomprehending eyes—a heavy square blade with a keen edge and a black handle. The steel flashed in the lantern light, a harsh cutting glare—unlike the lustrous reflection of tungsten-plastic, was all Ben could think.

A great bear of a man with a woolly beard wet his fingers on his fat red lips, wiped them on his long striped coat of green, black, and gold, and gripped the cleaver's stout handle in both his hairy hands. He stepped up to stand over Ben, frowned down at him, and muttered a word. "Thief."

Ben followed the focus of his bloodshot brown eyes to his own wrist, and meaning penetrated his drugged thoughts. Fear returned. He yanked at his bonds with a sudden twist of his whole body. Wood and rope groaned. He shifted his pinned weight to try again, but a blue-smocked man sat on his chest.

The man with the woolly beard put one foot forward, swung the blade back and up, and with a grunt and a heave brought it chopping down through Ben's wrist and buried it in the wood.

Then the men cut his bonds, took his sword, and left him there spurting blood into the sand.

The kestrel brought a physician, who followed the bird like a messenger from God to where Ben lay in shock, holding his veins and arteries shut, and waiting out the drug's effects. He could do no more.

The physician sealed the wound, said his bone was not shattered and he was lucky. He had no blood to give the

warrior but said Ben was strong and thought he would recover—
inshallah—God willing.

Having come this far, Ben knew he would not die. When
he regained strength he walked back to the oasis and retrieved
his sword once again. He cut off no hands, though he
was tempted. He returned to his ship, *Singalai*, and went
home.

The ranga fashioned a new appendage for him of jointed
metal padded and gloved to look like a hand.

The kestrel hated it and would not alight on it.

"Where wert thou when they were firing drug darts at
me?" said Ben to its angry cries.

The new hand lacked dexterity and feeling. It was good for
clutching and holding fast and for striking with great force.
Ben adapted. It was useful.

But in the darkness, its faintly audible clicks and whirrs,
ignored in the daylight, became magnified, a loud and desolate song of loss, like the shifting sands of a desert in the
quiet of deep night.

The year of the Opal Sword began a new hexadecade. It
was the year the child Amerika came to stay on the Aerie.

It was also the winter the Fendi died.

Ben withdrew to a lonely ledge in the gray twilight to be
by himself. There was no order in the world. Ranga were
wailing in their caves.

It was a cold day when Ben-Tairre wore boots, a day when
breath froze in the lungs and eyes would coat over with ice.
All was bleak.

He could not find the sun.

He tried to bring to mind hard green eyes like glass, and
the voice of a monarch who had let a Wolf become a
warrior-priest.

The Fendi's dying words had been: "Not to make Ben
Fendi."

Jinin-Ben-Tairre thought it an incredibly odd thing to say.

There were two Bens on the Aerie. The Fendi must have
been referring to the other, for Jinin-Ben-Tairre did not think
anyone would even consider making him leader for the Fendi
to need to make a dying injunction against it. It was like
telling berinxes not to fly. Why?

"Knowest thou not?" his fire kin had said to him. "Because thou hast defeated defeat. Something none of us has ever done. And because thou art not a follower. And because no one is sure what else to do with thee."

He had not known there were so many on the Aerie who would call his name. The Fendi had known. Ben agreed it would not be a wise decision.

As it was, Roniva was chosen.

A small breeze cut like bitter knives. Ben covered his face with the edge of his brown mantle, the soft fabric feeling rough and hard in the dry cold.

A hooded figure wended the rocky approach to his isolated ledge with careful deliberate steps on brown-slippered feet. A thin figure set in regal resolve, her back erect but fluid, she was known to Ben even without a glimpse of her jet black skin.

Ben saluted as she arrived on the ledge, his sword fist over his gloved false hand. "Fendi."

Roniva lifted her hood from her face and her glossy black hair, which she wore low over her forehead and wrapped over her ears. "Not yet," she said. Breath froze to her lips. A white haze of drying skin chalked her high cheeks. "This is the last time I may speak to thee."

Wind picked up the edges of their mourning cloaks, billowed and snapped them like wind flags.

"What sayest thou, hanina?" said Ben, his brown-black eyes barely open within epicanthic folds.

"Thou murdered my Xanthan," said Roniva.

"I know."

"Thou art here and my son is not. A poor substitute."

Her son. She had never said as much. "Thy son was distort," said Ben very softly.

"So art thou. Shandee drives thee. Thou art nothing without thine anger. This is my Aerie."

Wintry gusts pierced through fabric like sharpened blades through flesh to bone marrow. "Is this setkaza?" said Ben. He hadn't expected to die today.

"No," said Roniva. "I shall not begin my reign with a bloodletting. I shall try, Wolf. If I cannot live with thee, I will have no choice. And have thee no doubt who will win."

"No, hanina." said Ben.

*   *   *

They held the peace for less than a year, until the coming of an Earthman in the year of the Opal Ship, the man who came to them under the name Alihahd.

Suddenly setkaza was here, intent to kill, and Ben lived now in perpetual readiness for his fatal combat. It could come at any time. Or he could make it happen, choose the time and place to his own advantage and readiness.

But it was said that he who moved first was lost. Setkaza was a waiting ordeal, a trial of nerves. The one who endured, who did not break to the pressure of death threat day after night after day, had always been victorious. Setkaza could go on for years. It could snap tomorrow.

Ben knelt on the floor of the training hall, touched his forefinger to the groove in the wood where Roniva's sword had stabbed, locking their fate.

Turns of life were an unaccountable whirl. Caprice and sudden death and tragedy, fortune, chance, destiny made vanity of expectation. There was but one certainty now. The death of a warrior.

PART THREE

ASHAR ARI

I. Virtue

It was still the first watch, the hour of the bells. The air was cold, sharp. The sky was clear and the stars shone in full array. Amerika stopped on the Ledge Path, gazed to the east, and sighed, "The Wellspring is rising already. Oh, Harry, I am not ready for winter."

The Wellspring was a cold-weather sign; it was at its zenith at midnight in the dead of winter. Amerika did not like to see it threaten on the horizon.

Summer was already gone. Amerika had picked a bunch of the season's last gay cerulean flowers and tucked them into the bandelette tied beneath her small breasts. She took Harrison Hall's arm and pointed up to show him a blue-white open cluster of stars which the Itiri had named for the flowers.

Iry had no moons, so no months. Instead the year was divided into sixteen signs, each named for a constellation in Iry's zodiac. The sentinels would announce the beginning of a new sign at whatever hour of day it occurred—the time varied, for the number of days in the year did not divide evenly by sixteen. There were 171.8 long days in the Iry year. Vaslav, who had a wrist chronometer that kept Earth standard time, said there were 30.97 Earth standard hours in an Iry day. It still made a short year, too short for summer to become actually warm, and, with any luck, too short for winter to grow killingly cold.

Just now it was autumn, the eighth of the Beacon, the sign of an eclipsing binary. Only the constellations on the ecliptic were named. They were the only stars of any use to the Itiri, except for a pole star, but from the Aerie the pole star was always hidden behind the towering mountain Guardian.

The names of the constellations were not as imaginative as Earth's constellations. Iry's were mostly literal, and, once upon a time, the stellar configurations looked like their names— Hexagon, Crown, Cross—but that had been ages ago. Since their ancient naming the signs had slipped along the ecliptic and the stars drifted in different directions, so that no sign looked like what it was supposed to be. The Red Birds used to form a spearhead and did not now; but then no real bird on the planet Iry actually flew in a V anyway, so it mattered not that the red stars formed a disorderly flock.

Harrison Hall sat on the balustrade of the arcade, his back against a stone column, and he gnawed on the mouthpiece of his empty pipe. Firelights were fluttering to life inside the ranga caves, warming the doorways. Voices carried more clearly in the night air. Music of two woodwinds in rippling cadences chased each other from two caves on Aerieside. Hall tried to hum along but could not predict the alien patterns.

He caught Amerika gazing at the valley. Alihahd had been down there all summer.

Rumors and reports made their way up the mountain upon occasion with messengers and deliveries of food from the valley. The rumors were not of Alihahd, but of Alan James. No one in Kaletani Mai had ever met an Alihahd. They knew a tall, white, blond man with blue eyes and a big voice; his name was Alan James.

So the captain had assumed another name, thought Hall. Well, Alihahd was not really Alihahd either.

By midsummer the stories that wended up to the mountain-top were of "the Earth Fendi." Hall roared with laughter. Earth Fendi, indeed. If Alihahd stayed down there much longer the villagers would have him deified.

Very good, Captain, very good.

Amerika hung on every word spoken about the man. She would grab every courier, every eagle, every traveler who came from Kaletani Mai, and squeeze every tale out of him. Her face was wistful now as she leaned over her forearms resting flat along the balustrade, and she gazed at the lights of the valley where he was. The little girl was missing him.

Then her black eyes shifted to a closer focus and she pointed down. "Harry, look."

Harrison Hall took his pipe from his mouth and squinted into the dark.

Starlight caught on a movement in the blackness, a figure coming up the steep snake path from the valley to the Aerie. Hall could see no details, just a long-limbed form climbing up with a dogged way of moving.

Only warrior-priests climbed the sheer torturous snake path. But this was not a warrior. Hall knew who this was.

Yet it was with a sense of disbelief that he beheld the lank, heavy-boned man appear over the top of the precipice to stand on the Aerieside Ledge Path. Harrison Hall thought of something he'd been told about legends—they always return.

Alihahd strode the path with a relaxed gait, tired but without exhaustion. He reached the narrow footbridge and began crossing to Haven.

He was halfway when Jinin-Ben-Tairre appeared from shadows and stepped onto the bridge from Havenside to cross in the opposite direction. Their gazes met, and they both stopped.

The bridge swayed.

Ben gripped the knotted ropes; muscles moved in his powerful shoulders. His small mouth drew down in a sharp tight frown that wrinkled his chin. Oriental eyes slanted even more steeply with the threatening cant of his brows. He took another step on the bridge, his intent clear without words; this *Earthling* would have to make way for him.

But a deep voice came from the bridge, very tired, short of temper, and unimpressed. "Move back. I shan't jump." And Alihahd looked away to the side as if annoyed and impatient. He knew what was rightfully his and was not about to be intimidated out of it.

Ben-Tairre blinked, slow to believe Alihahd could actually mean it. But Alihahd was not going anywhere—least of all backward—and slowly Ben-Tairre stepped down.

Alihahd completed his crossing. He walked past Ben without deigning to look at him. It was not a gesture of avoidance; it was nonacknowledgment. Ben might as well have been a bush for all Alihahd cared.

Amerika gave a joyful little shriek and ran along Havenside's Ledge Path to meet him, Harrison Hall following her at a casual walk. Hall stopped a few paces away, his weight on one foot, one hand in his redingote pocket, the other holding his pipe. "Captain."

"Mr. Hall," said Alihahd in his elegant voice. He hadn't changed; not in that.

Hall had to smile. "How did you get up here?"

Alihahd's glance shifted sideways toward Ben-Tairre, and he answered loudly, "I walked."

Amerika clapped her brown, baby-fat hands with a gleeful giggle.

Hall gave a small nod. "Bravo," he said softly.

Jinin-Ben-Tairre turned away from the bridge as if he had never wanted to cross it in the first place, and he mounted the stepped path to the higher terraces instead.

When he was gone, Alihahd let some starch from his proud stance, turned his head to Hall, and said, "Have you any conception of how far three miles straight up is?"

Hall chuckled. "Do you know what you just did to him?" He cocked his head in the direction in which Ben had retreated.

Alihahd did. Ben's first climb of the snake path was a village legend. "Purely intentional," said Alihahd.

"Are you going into warrior training next?" said Hall lightly.

"Are you mad?" Alihahd returned. He pictured himself a forty-eight-year-old cheela. The mind reeled. No, he hadn't climbed the snake path in answer to any calling. He'd climbed it to slap Ben's alien-posing face.

"You were saying, you don't lose well," said Hall, picking up the end of their last conversation as if Alihahd had never left and there had been no long summer intervening.

Alihahd nodded and spoke low, his voice tinged somehow with regret. "I don't lose."

He retired to the cave he had originally inhabited upon coming to Aerie. His pile of blankets and furs were still folded on the wide mattress waiting for him. Vaslav's were in a rumpled pile against the wall. Hall's were not there. Harrison Hall did not sleep here anymore. Alihahd was not going to ask.

Alihahd collapsed on the mattress without bothering to take off his boots. The boots were the same red leather ones he had brought with him, but the thick, flat white deck soles had been replaced. He stretched his arms above his head, gazed at the ceiling, and exhaled long, at ease in his reclaimed territory.

Hall stirred the fire that had been dying in the hearth. Warm light caught the red sunstreaks in his coppery hair and reflected a wet gleam off his tawny eyes and flashes of gold from his two earrings. His strong, graceful profile was outlined in an orange-red corona, the rounded slope of his brow, the curve of his nearly aquiline nose, the neat brush of his mustache, his full lips, and firm chin. He rose from his crouch at the hearth and sat next to Alihahd on the bed.

Alihahd was little changed from when he left, still gaunt, spare, but healthier, hardier, and his short-shorn hair had grown out to cover his tall brow, the tops of his ears, and the back of his neck. His skin was weathered but still fair; it would not hold the sun's color like Hall's. Harrison Hall was by now very dark.

They could hear music from outside, across the abyss. The woodwinds sang a new tune, sad, haunting, passionate, longing, the song of the abandoned or a captive spirit wanting wings. It disturbed, made its hearers restless, wanting to move, wanting, making one look toward the stars. It recalled to Alihahd what he had felt in the valley, dwelling in the shadow of the far-off peaks wrapped in clouds halfway to heaven—and he had been exiled from even halfway to heaven.

"Do you mind explaining to me, Captain, how you got to be 'the Earth Fendi'?" Hall said, scattering his thoughts.

"It was none of my doing, and all actually rather comical," said Alihahd. "I suppose the ranga started it. They assumed because I was tall and blond and lived alone that I must be the Earthling equivalent of a warrior-priest. It escalated from there. I was Fendi before I knew it."

Hall nodded. But Hall did not believe it was the ranga's doing. Wherever Alihahd went, no matter how many times displaced, Alihahd would always lead. He was set apart by the way he talked, the easy grandeur of his carriage, his lordly silences.

"I have something for you," Alihahd said. He unlaced a pouch from his belt. It was filled with dried leaves. "I am told these can be smoked."

Hall received the pouch as if it were treasure. "I thank you, Captain."

"Do not thank me. If I cannot breathe up here, neither shall you. I give you hypoxia, and may your night vision go to hell."

"Merrily," said Hall, laughing, a deep sound in his barrel chest. His lung capacity was enormous, and never mind that smoke added an equivalent of four thousand feet to the altitude, Harrison Hall would endure.

He withdrew his foxhead pipe from his vest. Both its fire-opal eyes were cracked now. Alihahd commented on it.

"Serra," said Hall. "She shied it at me."

"She does not like you," said Alihahd.

"She likes me fine."

Alihahd had already surmised that Hall was living with Serra. Hall's move was entirely expected. Eridanin lords were not known for their celibacy. It was only natural that Hall would be sleeping with *someone*. Just as it was natural that Alihahd be alone.

Alihahd pursed his lips, chagrined on the rare occasions when it occurred to him to think about it. He had always been a failure at human emotion. The ranga even reminded him of it . Ranga hugged each other at any excuse—something he could never do. Spontaneity for him was not there. He'd tried once, inspired by a child laughing. He beckoned; the child frowned and toddled away. Fitting. A face to frighten children. He did not try again. It was his way to be aloof. It was awkward and unnatural for him to be close. If he ever had to hug someone his arms were suddenly eight feet long and his body did not fit to anyone else's. He was not a person for embracing, and he usually liked his distance. There was no one he really wanted to embrace. At the same time he was envious of the ranga. He envied them their ability and their desire to be close. Alihahd had never been at ease where tenderness was expected of him, around pets, children, or women except his wife. His had been an arranged marriage. He would never have married if he'd had to go courting for himself. It was not worth the effort.

Now he was afraid to touch anyone.

He looked at his hands.

Harrison Hall picked up one of Alihahd's hands and laid it across his own open palm. The back of the big knotty hand was bruised purple, and the skin was split across the knuckles. "Rough climb," said Alihahd and took his hand back, too quickly.

Hall's lips twitched beneath his mustache. He withheld comment.

The palms of Alihahd's hands were unscathed.

"I have something else for you," said Alihahd. He gave

Hall a small felt bag. Something within clicked together like pebbles.

Hall emptied the glittering contents onto the bed.

"Surely that's a zircon," said Hall, pointing to one of the eight big gemstones.

"Which? No. The pink one is a zircon. The boulder *is* a diamond."

Hall picked up the diamond and held it to the firelight. "What do you think—five carats cut?"

Alihahd shrugged.

"You're worse than an Itiri," said Hall to Alihahd's total lack of avarice or even interest. Alihahd had handed them over as if the gems were pretty quartzes and cut glass.

Alihahd rolled onto his side and propped himself up on his elbow. "The ranga decided I needed these, since I was something like a warrior-priest. These are virtues."

"Is that what they are," said Hall.

"No warrior should be without them. The beryl is your hospitality, kindness, and mercy—'humanity' if you will," said Alihahd. "The diamond is honor, respect, and loyalty—there is a single Itiri word for all those, and a single stone."

"A single very large stone," said Hall.

"Turquoise is patience and serenity. Lapis is courage. Topaz is wisdom. Zircon is humility and modesty. Opal is integrity in the sense of soundness, wholeness, and the like. The ruby is self-control, or fulfillment of potential, or inner strength. The way they consider certain concepts as synonymous I find quite bizarre. At any rate, there you have them. Please take your virtues and let me go to sleep."

Hall scooped them off the bed in his fist. He held them each up to the light one more time before putting them in his pocket. He decided he might keep the diamond. The rest he would hock as soon as he was off-planet.

After all, of what use were serenity and modesty to a man who piloted a black ship?

II. The Gathering Storm

Harrison White Fox Hall and the Fendi Roniva crossed swords. The snowy owl observed from a high perch in the training hall, slowly rotating its round head to odd angles as if on a ball socket, so that sometimes its gaze was nearly straight upside down. Roniva never spoke a word to Hall. At times she would stop, point at Hall, and bark to her owl, "Again!" That was bidding for Hall to repeat a technique. Hall was not unfamiliar with swords, but the double curve was unusual—like a yataghan, which Hall never had used well. Hall preferred guns and short daggers—though he would have sold his soul for a blade of tungsten-plastic. The technology that had made the nearly indestructible tungsten-plastic swords no longer existed anywhere in the galaxy. Where the Itiri had come by their swords was a mystery.

Roniva demonstrated a series of passes and bade him repeat it. The dark woman's appearance was still very neat, her hair smooth and tied up, her skin dry. The Itiri did not sweat. Hall was shirtless and his skin was gleaming wet. The bandanna tied across his brow was drenched, and his hair coiled in dark, wiry curls stuck to the back of his neck. He repeated the series.

Alihahd stopped in the doorway to watch. He leaned the front of his shoulder on a column, his hands tucked under his belt, his head tilted to one side. Soft, clean blond hair kicked over his tall forehead. There was color in his usually sallow and drawn cheeks. The mountain was not killing him this time around.

Hall omitted the last move of the series, which was to flip the blade under his arm as he turned its edge away from him and hide it behind his back. Roniva snapped to the owl, "Tell him to finish."

"Fendi, if I do that I'll cut off my arm," said Hall. It was a tricky move to do the first time with a live blade.

Roniva let it pass and continued to something else.

Alihahd questioned the wisdom of teaching Hall anything. Someone who christened his ship *Nemo* did not need to know anything more about fighting. Alihahd did not advocate the training of terrorists. By the time Hall left Iry he would be twice as deadly as when he'd come. How could the professedly neutral Itiri possibly justify turning such a being loose on the galaxy?

Or did they ever intend to turn him loose? Alihahd had seen nothing sinister so far. The thought was a recurring paranoia.

He waited to speak until Roniva was not wielding her sword. "Fendi, you realize, do you not, you could be aiding and abetting an interstellar terrorist."

Roniva seemed to register the data with a momentary wrinkle of her hairless brows. She gave no comment and she did not quit sparring with Hall until she was ready and done. Then she took her leave without a word. The owl sailed out behind her in a sudden silent swoop and glide.

Hall picked up his shirt and slung it over his shoulder. He sauntered to Alihahd. "There's a burrower hunt today. You're not going?"

That was sarcasm. Alihahd did not answer it. "*You* are not going?" he asked. Hall never passed up a chance to hunt.

Hall shook his head. "Layla is. I don't trust Layla behind me with a club."

"I see." Alihahd's gaze dropped to the Itiri sword in Hall's grip. "You are getting to be a very dangerous man, Mr. Hall."

"I always was a dangerous man." He mopped the sweat from his body with his shirt, took off his sopping bandanna, and shook back his hair. "You, dear Captain, could be immeasurably dangerous if I could ever pull you from this Itiri-like pacifism of yours."

Itiri-like, I? That was a curious concept. "I'll not be pulled," said Alihahd.

"Wherefore?" said Hall, imitating Alihahd's high-style, sometimes archaic speech.

"Because I could be immeasurably dangerous."

Were he ever to anger, Hall was certain Alihahd would be lethal. But his flashes of glorious rage never lasted, quickly fading to contempt, pity, indifference, or plain weariness.

"Pity you won't budge," said Hall. "I'd have you with me."

"If it is all the same, Mr. Hall, I would not trust you behind me with a club," said Alihahd.

Hall laughed aloud. "Point taken."

Alihahd turned to go.

Jinin-Ben-Tairre was standing in the exit with a drawn sword.

Alihahd felt a ripple of surprise, and . . . *disappointment*. Alihahd was not much opposed to dying, but he would have liked some advance warning. This was too unexpected, like a bolt from the clear summer sky, just when he was feeling safe. It wasn't fair. The feeling of helplessness in the face of the caprice of the universe upset him more than the actual prospect of dying. *So here it is.* He waited.

Jinin-Ben-Tairre turned the sword hilt outward and tossed it to Alihahd.

Alihahd caught it by the hilt.

Hall raised both eyebrows and drew in his chin like a comment, to remark that Alihahd had held a sword before.

Ben's smooth face remained an unchanging mask. He had lost the ability to be surprised by anything Alihahd did.

Ben moved like a pacing cat to Harrison Hall and thrust out a broad demanding palm to the sword Hall held.

Hall surrendered the blade to the warrior-priest and stepped back to the periphery of the practice floor as Ben began to circle.

Alihahd turned slowly, keeping his face and his sword toward Ben. He made no circle himself, only pivoted guardedly.

Suddenly Ben charged in with a stomp of his foot and a shout, the sword whistling over his head and down. Tungsten-plastic blades met with a dull crack. Alihahd deflected the blow and dodged to the side.

Ben spun full around with another attack from the side, and Alihahd had only time to shift his sword to a vertical block, catching the blow straight on, and he staggered back with the force of it.

Would he kill me?

Ben's strokes felt real and unrestrained. But Alihahd sensed that the warrior-priest could kill him anytime he wished. This was nothing but cat-and-mouse here.

Alihahd did not counter either attack, or even attempt to counter. Time after time, Alihahd's moves remained strictly defensive. He had no desire to attack Ben. This was Ben's game and Alihahd did not want to play.

Then Ben backed away to a weapons chest. He put down his sword and brought out a dagger. Alihahd waited, uncertain.

"Captain." Hall's voice came from behind him, and Hall pressed the hilt of his own poniard into Alihahd's hand. Alihahd passed back the sword and squared off with Ben again to continue the match with new weapons.

Travesty of a match, thought Alihahd. Ben was trained to be a warrior of the galaxy's legendary killing force. To what purpose was this shadow show being staged?

Ben came at him with an underhand thrust. Alihahd dropped his own weapon and blocked downward on Ben's wrist with crossed hands as he jumped back, curving his lower body away from the blade. He seized and twisted Ben's thick wrist—like trying to throw a tree off balance—then abruptly shifted balance with a foot sweep. Ben rolled and came back up, still holding his dagger. Alihahd's was on the floor. Alihahd skidded it back to Hall with his foot. The blade was worse than useless to him. One did not use a knife to block a knife, and that was all Alihahd wanted to do. In this situation he was better off open-handed.

So Ben changed weapons again. Then again.

Alihahd had broken into a sweat all over his body. It became harder and harder not to attack. They were dueling with sabers now. Ben slashed fiercely, hit hard, left himself open for counter. Blows rained on Alihahd's blocking blade, jarred his wrists and arms. Crashing metal pounded at his eardrums. Ringing steel kept at him and at him and at him, like a goad. He could see the demand in Ben's fierce dark eyes, *Fight me, fight me, fight me!*

Alihahd was not even thinking anymore. He moved without conscious deliberation. In another part of his mind, above, serene and removed from all this, he heard a mocking chant:

> Circle, circle, dance of pain
> One is free. He remains
> Who cannot see our circle's edge
> Another circle, once again.

A crazy look glazed his eyes, blue with white all around.

A hunted way of standing made him the image of a wounded animal, cornered, about to turn and bite.

The spectator, Harrison Hall, straightened from his casual one-foot stance. He wondered if Ben knew what he was doing. He was going to make Alihahd turn on him, calling him a fraud, daring how deep the pacifism truly ran.

Alihahd was angry—or was a better word mad? His thick lips drew back from his teeth, and he watched Ben from the tops of his wild eyes. The saber trembled in his too tight grip. Ben pressed until Alihahd surely must crack.

Alihahd did not.

And at length, when Ben-Tairre himself was sweating and drawing ragged breaths, Ben stepped back, put up his weapon, and left the training hall with an air of satisfied curiosity.

With a shudder and a sighing moan that was half a cry, Alihahd dropped his saber as if it were a loathsome thing. He stared at his own hand.

Only when his breaths began to lengthen did normality return to his face, to his being; and all at once his strained muscles untensed and he looked simply tired.

Harrison Hall picked up the discarded saber, tested its balance in his hand. He nodded at Alihahd's proficiency with it and the other weapons. "You're better than you look, Captain," said Hall.

"I was not born this old," said Alihahd. He dropped to a squat, his back to the wall, his forearms on his knees, hands hanging loose.

"Careful what you call old," said Hall. "I believe I am your senior."

Alihahd lifted a hand at the wrist and pointed toward the door. "That man does not like me."

"Oh, I don't know," said Hall. It was hard to tell what Ben was thinking, what about Alihahd fascinated him. Hall was only glad that Ben was not interested in *him*. "I wouldn't worry anyway," he said. "Roniva is in your camp, and between the two of them, my money is on the Fendi."

Alihahd gave a shrug. "Hypothetical situation."

"I hear not," said Hall. He explained what he knew of the ancient rite of setkaza. Sooner or later Roniva and Ben would fight to the death.

Alihahd shook his head and gave a laugh that was helplessness rather than mirth. "Aliens," he said with a quixotic lilt.

He stood. Unfolding his long legs was painful. He took the saber from Hall and tossed it back into the weapons chest in distaste. "I used to be good with these toys of destruction," he said. He did not like them anymore, the swords and bola and archaic things no one really used but to play at war. He slammed the chest shut and turned away from it. "Too much blood under the bridge between then and now."

"Whose?" said Hall.

"Oh. I was speaking in general," said Alihahd.

Harrison Hall watched with a hunter's eye. Alihahd was a complex individual. The more he revealed the less he was known. He never spoke of his home, whether he had disowned it, was ashamed of it or protecting it. His accent and manner and knowledge told that he'd been just about everywhere. But his origin was a mystery, until one day Layla, who never had heard of tact or even of civilized rules of conduct, simply asked him point-blank, "Where are you from?"

Alihahd hesitated. The frankness of the inquiry precluded evasion, especially in front of Hall. Not to be too obviously secretive, he answered the question. "Earth."

The reply caused a stir among the humans. Although called Earthlings, none of them, Layla, Serra, Amerika, Vaslav, or Hall, was actually from the cradle of humankind, Earth. None of them had even *seen* it, and they all had questions about it.

Alihahd did not want to talk about it. "I hardly knew the place myself. The whole world is a perpetual Na'id battlefield. I left shortly after birth." And went where he did not specify. "Many places," he would say and change the subject.

He was certainly aristocracy. His lofty, occasionally tortured way of speaking was not affectation. Alihahd fell into it without thinking. There was something so *unassuming* in his elitism. And he had a voice that made those god-awful speeches sound right.

He did not possess Harrison White Fox Hall's cocksureness; rather the bearing of a man fallen from a great height, a vestige of pride that persisted like an afterimage once the reality was gone. Instinct for command also persisted, like breathing.

Harrison Hall was a lord but he was not a leader. Men and

women did not die for Harrison Hall. He inspired no trust, no desire to march into hell for him and breathe one's last gasp at his feet.

Alihahd could command that kind of loyalty if he cared to—and even if he did not. And it seemed he did not want it, from anyone. He did not want the attention, the bright focus; he did not want to be followed, watched, or known.

It was obvious he had a past—the kind one does not talk about. But the more secretive he was about it, the more apparent it became that he was not simply hiding from the past—he was running from it.

The rebel leader, so calm, mature, level, patient and wise—one could see the paragon, as everything that had stood too long, was wearing, and glimpse through the cracks severe emotion.

He had developed a series of quirky little mannerisms since his return to the mountain—unobtrusive patterns and rituals that appeared at first glance to be simple habits—a way of ordering objects on his night stand, layering his blankets in a certain order and going out of his way to maintain that order. He would clean his teeth with salt twice upon rising, his motions identical both times. He would take twelve steps to cross the bridge, no more, no less, starting always with his right foot. This was more than simply being methodical.

None of it went unnoticed. The weakening of a fleet animal did not escape the watchful eye of the tiger in the brush. Patterns were a snare. The greater the attempts to create order outside, the greater the chaos inside. Something was drastically wrong. Alihahd was trying to lock down the corners of an unpredictable universe that kept curling up at the edges.

But Alihahd was not absolutely patterned. He reserved enough flexibility and unpredictability to keep him elusive and unknowable. Out of all his patterns there was a wayward independence and disorder only in his time schedule—he *had* no schedule. None at all. Hall never knew when Alihahd would be anywhere, when he would sleep, when he would rise, none of which activity had anything to do with daylight hours and was never the same twice. It just did not fit the other obsessive patterns, and the waiting tiger was baffled—and wondered if he was being baited. He bided his time.

*   *   *

The red flags were out; the winds were fast and no one on the mountain ventured beyond the sheltered oasis of Aerie/Haven. No one climbed the peaks, for ele-ala, the wave, would sweep them away. They could see the eagles riding the undulating current, soaring over the valley without a wingbeat. A swirled puff of a cloud poised over the village, caught in a rotor; the eagles avoided it.

Harrison Hall took refuge in a small cave on the third level of Haven, where he stayed when Serra was bleeding and wanted to be alone. It was Alihahd's custom to retreat there at erratic times; Hall never knew when. On occasion, as today, their visits would coincide.

Hall had a fire burning brightly in the hearth when Alihahd came in. The cave was a small place, its decoration begun a long time ago and never finished. Crumbling stucco on the unornamented wall came off in dust at a touch. The worn design on the other walls was also faded, painted quatrefoils within squares, carved in relief and intaglio alternate squares.

Hall was in his shirtsleeves, sitting cross-legged on the bed, tinkering with a gadget retrieved from his ship, *Nemo*. The mandesairi, the whales, had found pieces of his broken ship on the ocean floor and had sent them back to him on the mountain with the eagles.

"Is it a transceiver?" said Alihahd.

Hall shook his head and tossed the black box aside. "Just a gadget." He picked up his pipe and, after a few tries, lit it and puffed clouds of gray smoke. "I take it there aren't any in the valley."

"Transceivers?" said Alihahd. "None that have the range to contact anyone in civilized spaceways—not within this century at any rate."

Hall waved some of the smoke away. "They really don't seem to give a damn about the Outside."

Now and then the Itiri sent scouts abroad to pick up pieces of someone else's technology, a ship, a weapon, and maybe rescue an alien in peril or two along the way, then return home, recluse again.

"I do see the purpose in hiding their existence from the Na'id," said Alihahd. "The notorious warrior-priests of Iry are sadly unprepared to fight a modern war. Yet they continue to stagnate. There is no effort to build for themselves. They are not *ignorant* exactly, but there is a decided lack of ambition and want of foresight here. Their folly if they think they can hide forever."

Hall was chuckling, gently, mockingly, fondly, his laughter indulgent as at a clever child. "What?" said Alihahd.

"The way you talk."

"So glad I keep you entertained."

"You know, of course, you're wrong, though."

"I know this?"

"The Itiri *could* hide forever," said Hall.

Alihahd had to nod. They were truly lost out here. Na'id ships never came this way, never would. Unless something were to draw them.

Hall set aside his pipe, the fire of which had gone out, and he picked up the piece of equipment from his ship again. "Have you noticed they count in hex?" he said.

"Hexadecimal?"

Hall pulled out a lens from the black box. "Yes."

Alihahd paused in thought. "I suppose I had noticed something odd." He'd never heard an Itiri count past nine in Universal.

"Vaslav figured it out," said Hall. He pulled out another lens.

"What kind of people use hex?" said Alihahd.

"People with sixteen fingers." The Itiri had ten. Logically they should have developed a base-ten number system. "Computers," Hall continued. "People who use binary."

"Which is to say high-tech," said Alihahd. "Which the Itiri are not. They are an odd people." He stopped talking. He'd caught himself, not for the first time, calling the Itiri *people*. He brooded in silence for a long time while Hall repositioned his lenses. Alihahd looked over his shoulder. "Is that anything that will help us escape from this planet?" said Alihahd without much hope.

Hall looked at Alihahd. He'd already said it was not a transceiver. The man was grasping at anything to get out. "No." He looked into Alihahd's eyes, lifted his hand, touched Alihahd's cheek with a hot, dry touch. "What an incredible color for eyes."

Blue eyes dropped away from Hall's gaze. Alihahd could not meet his eyes anymore. He left the cave with the restlessness of a caged beast.

Hall balanced his projector on his knee and slouched back

against the wall thoughtfully. He hitched his thumbs in the pockets of his gold-weave vest. Hall wanted to leave Iry too. He had a battle to fight. And if his need were not as desperate, at least his motive was clear, which was more than he could say for Alihahd.

There was no good reason why Alihahd should be so anxious to leave Iry and rejoin the crusade against the Na'id Empire. His heart was not in it. He was weary of the whole thing. Yet he was obsessed with return.

Hall's reason was simple: vengeance. But what made Alihahd go? It was not revenge. He espoused no specific ideology. He had no real cause, except perhaps freedom of choice. But what did that mean to *him*? He had nothing personal against the Na'id. He did not hate them. He opposed them but not for himself. Or maybe selflessness was very much for himself.

Hall sat up straight. He saw it in a flash. There was only one real motive for martyrdom, and it was not devotion; it was atonement.

You're doing penance.

For what? What had he done?

Evening passed into early night, the seventh of the Serpent. It was unnaturally mild on the mountain, becoming actually warmer after sundown. There was little movement in the air but for a gentle, pleasant breeze, soft and moisture-laden.

On the horizon could be seen a black mass blotting out the stars. Then distant lightning would light up the outline of a monstrous thunderhead, its top sheared off by a jet wind way up high. One did not perceive the bolts themselves—only the flashes of cold light from behind the massif and the muffled report of far-off thunder.

The Itiri were taking off their swordbelts and their metal jewelry.

Alihahd climbed to a ledge where two warrior-priests kept vigil. The towering thundercloud menaced in slow advance on the far side of the valley, its flat top miles above the mountains. The Itiri marked the ominous shape of the thing and muttered.

"How long?" said Alihahd.

"By morning," they said.

As they spoke there was a change in the air, cold, with a downdraft.

Alihahd was aware of another menace, in counterpoint, on either side of the great rift between the mountains. On the dawn ridge he could see Ben-Tairre backed by the turbulent sky. Always striking, he'd assumed a dynamic stance, in conscious or unconscious display of power and dominance. Loose clothing still showed the play of muscles in his thighs, his heavy shoulders, his hard abdomen. He carried an obsidian blade.

On the eagle ridge opposite, black, hard, and sharp as if fashioned of obsidian herself, crouched Roniva. Her long, thin limbs, tight-corded and agile, were folded beneath her catlike, her body hard as stone, fluid as water.

Over them the sky was about to break. The air was electric, charged with premonition so strong even Alihahd felt it. A storm that had been building long before he'd ever seen the Aerie mounted, boiled, about to be unleashed.

Alihahd spoke to the warrior-priests on the ledge with him. "What happened here? What is between Roniva and Ben?"

Emerald eyes exchanged hesitant glances as if the warriors were actually afraid.

And they told him there would be a death tonight.

III. Thunderhead

A strange sound rose over the Aerie, beginning softly, steadily gaining in strength. It was not a rain sound, but an odd rhythmic swelling of voices in an ever building chant, over and over.

Kaza, kaza, kaza.

Serra was drawn from her cave. She stepped to the rail of the arcade and looked out.

The sky was dark, starless. A few fluttering torches lit the paths of Havenside. The chant carried eerily from Aerieside, from within the Chamber of the Golden Dome.

Kaza, kaza, kaza.

Serra called in to the others. "Something's happening."

Alihahd joined her at the balustrade. An electric hiss of lightning tracked through the clouds. Then the whole sky lit up brighter than daylight. In the brief weird illumination, the landscape was surreal, blue-white, with jagged edges and black, black shadows.

Alihahd saw Arilla dash along the Ledge Path toward the Chamber of the Golden Dome, so fast she was but an impala-bodied white streak. The lightning flash caught her expression—fear, an odd thing to see on a warrior-priest.

Harrison Hall spoke from behind Alihahd. "Ben-Tairre's fire sister. This is it."

Arilla flew into the Chamber of the Golden Dome and broke through the ring of warriors, but at the inner edge she was caught in the arms of an Elder who lifted her off her feet and stopped her flight. There could be no physical intervention here. Her fire brother was alone in this.

In the center of the ring, Ben-Tairre and Roniva circled the floor, the surrounding crowd calling on them to break setkaza now, finish it.

It was said that he who made the first move lost. Neither would strike first. But the ring of warriors was intent on breaking one of them. They could not leave this chamber until one was dead.

Kaza, kaza, kaza.

Alihahd came to the jeweled arch. He shifted to see between the heads of the crowd of warrior-priests. Their chant surged like the incessant pounding of a heartbeat.

Kaza, kaza.

Suddenly Roniva's sword was out. She moved to the center of the chamber and stabbed the point of her sword into the floor.

The chant stopped. The ring widened as everyone moved back to the farthest boundaries of the chamber, onto the benches and the stone sills of the tall lancet windows.

Ben and Roniva circled the sword three times.

Someone gave Ben his sword. Roniva pulled hers from the floor, and the final battle began.

Blades flashed. The two swept across the inlaid floor like sidewinding serpents. Spectators fled from their approach. The players owned the space, pausing for no one. No one had the right to be in the way of their fatal dance, which Roniva, having begun it, was fated to lose.

Roniva's sword changed hands. Ben was limited to his left hand only; his right hand was a clumsy machine.

Roniva swung at him. With a ringing crash, Ben batted the flat of her sword away from him with his false hand, the awkward thing becoming for him an extra, secret weapon, and he lunged into Roniva with his sword.

The trick should have caught her, would have, but Roniva was quick and wise to Ben's way of turning his weaknesses. She parried, jumped away, and countered.

A wet sheen glowed on Ben's skin in the unheated chamber. The Itiri would see Ben in a shroud of heat. Exotic eyes that always looked angry narrowed in ferocity. Small, broad feet wrapped in strips of red rags were a burned reminder that Ben did not know defeat.

Roniva advanced on him, her sword a whistling blur before her, and she pursued him to the wall, where watchers divided and dove to either side. Her strike sheared the curtain from the window and shattered the mirrored jamb with a spray of glass. Ben had spun off to the side. He seized the offensive, beat Roniva into a retreat and backed her to the hearth.

Her sash ignited at the fire's edge. She sprang backward over the pit, arched like a cat, cut her sash from her waist, and wielded it as a flaming bola. It swished in a circle, searing the air, and Roniva released it.

Ben leaned far to the side as it flew at him, and before the bola was even on the floor, he was on immediate counter-offensive, swinging his sword at Roniva in a mighty arc.

Roniva's sword was down, Ben's blade driving at her head. In a swift deliberate move, as fast as a sword's sweep but with an eerie sense of slow motion, as if time itself were commanded to wait, Roniva raised her left hand in a gesture of *halt* and caught Ben's blade on her bare palm.

An edge that could sever tempered steel, the tungsten-plastic should have gone through with no more resistance than slicing air. The blade was stopped dead.

The look in her eyes reflected a power, a force to stop a starship. A faith to move mountains, a borrowed power of the universe, the myths of magic that surrounded the Itiri like rubbish, all were there, focused in the palm of her hand.

Ben took a step back in shock, looked at his blade for blood that was not there. In that moment he lost the battle.

It was quickly done after that. Ben's feet were swept from under him by a long, lashing kick. Roniva stepped on his sword hand and put her sword to his jugular. All motion came to a stop.

Arilla turned away and hid her face against the chest of the Elder Eren-Ben.

Jinin-Ben-Tairre did not breathe. He waited for Roniva to finish him.

Roniva spoke to him directly. He was next to dead and counted as no one. "He who breaks a setkaza first loses. Except that not for nothing was I made Fendi of this Aerie. I can break traditional bonds also. Thou wert someone before thou wert Itiri, Jinin-Ben-Tairre. That someone may live, if the Itiri agrees to die and never be seen on this Aerie again." Dark eyes met dark eyes and asked, "Art thou dead, Jinin-Ben-Tairre?"

Any Itiri would rather actual death to ritual death. But survival instinct would not leave him. "I am."

"Let all be gone," Roniva commanded. "Tell everyone that Jinin-Ben-Tairre has died."

As the warrior-priests were filing solemnly out, Eren-Ben knelt by the dead warrior, took his sword, and placed it in a wooden chest. He took his eternity flower from his belt and his signet ring of the carnelian serpent from his finger. The flower and the ring he gave to grieving Arilla.

Jinin-Ben-Tairre spoke softly from the floor at Roniva's feet for only her to hear: "The corpse requests to be buried with his book."

Roniva's visage was severe and scowling. She did not look down, but hissed through her teeth, "Ben, shut up."

Outside the sky had split open and rain poured down in torrents. Lightning flashed and roared. The smell of ozone scorched the air.

Jinin-Ben-Tairre stayed sprawled on the wooden floor where he'd died, until only he, Roniva, and the hanina Eren-Ben were left in the chamber.

And Alihahd. He had not gone out with the others and did not intend to unless he was told. He stayed in the background in the nine-sided chamber, behind the lattice barrier in front of the dais. No one paid him any attention, though he sensed they were aware of his presence.

Roniva took her sword from Ben's throat and melted from her regal statue pose. She seemed to sway for a moment, and she leaned against the sturdy figure of the Elder Eren-Ben, who was quietly there where she needed him. The only other living warrior to bear the name Ben, he was shorter than the other aghara, wider across the shoulders. Pacific eyes were a striking blue-green, wide and fathomless. His ageless face was mild, sad, serene. His hair, a flowing mane as long as Roniva's, was a silvery ashen blond different from the normal Itiri gold. He wore his eternity flower behind one ear, as Roniva did.

Roniva drew away from him as Jinin-Ben-Tairre rose to stand. "Thou art kind," he said to the Fendi.

"No, I am not," she said. "I will not have thy death on my sword to weaken my rule."

"Then may I say thou art wise," said Ben-Tairre.

"Thou mayest, and I am," said Roniva.

Ben-Tairre took a few steps as if moving in a body that was not his. It was strange to be dead. The reality was only now occurring to him. All that had been his life was gone. He did not know what was left. "Who am I?" he said, lost.

"I never wanted thee as an Itiri," said Roniva. "Because thy heart is in the wrong place. Thou wantest to be an Itiri so thou wilt not be human. But thou *art* human. Be thou human now."

Eren-Ben put his arm around Roniva's thin waist and escorted her to the archway, leaving Jinin-Ben-Tairre in the center of the domed chamber like a lonely ghost. He called after Roniva.

"May I have thy blessing?"

It had not been offered. It was impudent of him to ask. "I should flay thee, Ben-Tairre. Thou art too forward, not to mention *dead*. Be thou gone from my sight forever." She went out.

Ben blinked, shuddered. Thunder crashed.

He barely heard, for the loud rush of the driving rains, the voice of one leaning in through the mirrored jambs of one of the tall windows, barking:

"With my blessing!"

*   *   *

The weather changed several times in the days that followed. Snow came after the torrential rains, and the cold encased the mountain in ice. The morning brought a fog, and all about the Aerie was perfect white. No one could see past arm's reach, and no one could go outside unless he could walk the paths without sight. Pale eyes went quickly blind in the whiteness.

The sign of year turned to the Cross. The clouds lifted near midnight, and the high winds swept them away. The cold night grew colder.

Around the Aerie the air was still. Overhead the stars shone bright in a velvet field. Around the rocks a powdery white scattering of phosphorescent blossoms dotted the ground like more stars underfoot.

Alihahd walked alone in the starshine. It was the hour of the meteors, the beginning of the third watch.

Thin air made sounds fainter; snow muffled them. But the night quiet, the cold, seemed to tune Alihahd's senses very fine. He listened.

Jinin-Ben-Tairre was dead. Or at least gone. Alihahd had watched him descend the snake path toward the valley. Yet Alihahd still felt he was being watched.

At last he stopped on the path, and spoke without turning. "Layla, why do you follow me?"

All was silent, but for a distant wind. Alihahd waited. Then she appeared with the soft crunch of crushed ice underfoot. She dressed like a child set loose in a theater's costume storage, with no continuity of style. Her head was veiled like a Moslem lady so that only her brown eyes showed, and she wore a down jacket, hide trousers, her dun boots, a pair of gloves without fingers, and a gold-fringed shawl which she'd tied around her waist. Her jeweled dagger was sheathed in her boot. Her gun was no doubt tucked in her pocket. Always a soldier, Layla was never to be found unarmed.

She came to Alihahd's side, and looked up at him. Her head did not even come up to his shoulder. "Why does one move about at this hour and avoid the sentinels?" she said.

Alihahd smiled. He realized he'd been skirting the sentinels' vigilance. "Habit," he said. "Is that not a sorry comment on a way to live?"

The question was too nebulous for Layla, and she made no comment on it.

Alihahd admired and envied Layla, her strength, resolution, and unshakable conviction. Layla was also slightly stupid. Blessed with a simplistic bullheadedness, no profound dilemmas ever disturbed her dreams. She was right; her enemies were wrong; and that was the secret of the universe. There were no shades of gray.

Alihahd touched her chin through the Moslem veil. "Do you know what your name would mean in Jerusalem?" he said.

"No," said Layla.

"It means *night*," said Alihahd.

"I like that," said Layla.

"Better than mine," said Alihahd.

Layla took his arm and walked with him a while. She pressed close to his side, not sexually. She was cold and he was there. She did not mistrust or hate him as she did Harrison White Fox Hall.

Hall's name came up. Layla called him a "slave master."

"Men and women were not meant to be slaves," said Alihahd. "The Na'id are not without a point in that matter. The class system on Eridani was wrong. I think even Mr. Hall can see that."

"I think he sees nothing," said Layla. Hall was bad; therefore nothing about Hall could be right.

"I think I can understand Mr. Hall better than you can," said Alihahd. "We are both ruling class, he and I."

"You more," said Layla.

"I?" said Alihahd. She knew nothing about him. She did not even know whom he ruled.

"It justs sticks to you," said Layla. "Harry insists too much. You do not say anything. You do not need to."

"*His* empire fell," said Alihahd. "It makes a difference."

"Did not yours?" said Layla.

"No. Not yet." Alihahd gave a sad smile. "It is a tottering tower of cards. It will fall. I may even weep when it does."

"You think the Na'id will destroy it?" said Layla.

"Yes," said Alihahd. "The Na'id will destroy it in the end."

A sudden bright light flaring in the valley drew his gaze.

The roaring followed, lagging behind the light that had begun its ascent; it blazed toward the heavens, to the stars and gone.

Alihahd stared in disbelief. "Goddam," he breathed. His shoulders drew back, blue eyes flashed, and his voice became a rolling roar, "Goddam."

A starship. A starship had left Iry without him.

He pulled away from Layla with a growl." Where is Roniva?"

"Do not anger her," said Layla.

Alihahd cared nothing for the warning. He would not be treated so. Roniva had said he would leave on the next ship.

He parted from Layla and crossed the footbridge in twelve steps. Aerieside was black, without torches, soundless in its majestic repose. Alihahd filled his lungs, then into the imposing silence of the caverns and arcades Alihahd bellowed the Fendi's name.

The echoes of his wrath faded to the night quiet. The wind moaned in the crevasse, softly.

She would not come to him. Dammit, he was going to find her.

A single dim light glowed from within the Chamber of the Golden Dome, the place where Jinin-Ben-Tairre had died. Alihahd went inside, his footsteps loud in the cavernous space, ringing off the nine walls and the high metal dome. The snowy owl loomed over the throne; the rustle of its feathers startled, like a rat scurrying across the floor. Its round yellow eyes stared at Alihahd unblinking. Cold gusts blew in the windows and the arch, swirled leaves in the hollow emptiness. This place was deserted. But *she* was here, even when she was not here. She filled this chamber.

Alihahd met the preternatural yellow eyes; his voice trembled with rage. "Where is your master?"

The owl clacked its black beak.

Alihahd did not hear, but he perceived. He turned around. Roniva stood in the archway. "Here is the creature's master," she said.

Alihahd's big-boned frame appeared very large even in the yawning chamber. "Forgive me if I abuse your hospitality, Fendi," he said bitterly, "but your hospitality is not all you would have me believe."

"Explain." She was unhappy and short of words. Her brows were drawn together in a pained squint over her eyes.

" 'When one of us next leaves Iry, thou mayest go also.'
Whose words are those?" said Alihahd.

"Mine," said Roniva.

"Then what the hell was that?" Alihahd pointed skyward.

The Fendi's brow smoothed, squinted again, puzzled. "A
ship has left?" she said. She turned her head aside and held
up her fist. "*Eho!*"

The owl appeared on her fist.

"Find," she snapped, and threw the owl into the air. It
disappeared. Roniva folded her spidery black fingers in attitude of waiting. "We shall both know shortly."

The owl reappeared on the throne, crying three notes.

Roniva turned back to Alihahd. "No one left on that
ship," she said. She rubbed her temples and moved toward
the door.

No one? "Lie to me, Fendi?" said Alihahd.

Roniva halted short. A volatile word, *lie.* Alihahd was too
incensed to care if he angered a woman who could stop a
tungsten-plastic blade with her bare hand.

"It was Jinin-Ben-Tairre," said Roniva, her own anger
withheld. "He is dead. He is no one."

"I am no one with whom to try semantic tricks," said
Alihahd.

"Not semantics," said Roniva. "To us he truly is no one.
I am not accountable for the actions of the dead. When someone leaves Iry, I will know and thou wilt know. That is all."

Alihahd rumbled, "That is *not* all!"

"I become wroth,' Roniva warned softly. "Not easily
done."

"I had not noticed that particular fact," said Alihahd
acidly.

"Done!" Roniva cried.

"Easily," said Alihahd.

"Oh, thy tongue is a sharp sword and thou art evil. Ben
told me so. I should have let him kill thee. You would both
be gone from me now!"

Alihahd was shocked to wordlessness for several moments.
Then he continued in softer voice, "How does a neutral
nation justify aiding the Na'id Empire by holding one of the
opposition's leaders prisoner here and unable to lead?"

"I was aiding the opposition by saving said leader's life,"

Roniva countered. "Neutral, I should drop thee back in the ocean whence I dragged thee."

"Perhaps you should," said Alihahd quietly. "If I am to be your prisoner."

Roniva threw her arms wide in exasperation and cried, "Thou took exception to my aiding the opposition by training thy Harrison Hall. *Which side art thou on?*"

Alihahd looked around him, saw the walls, threw his head back, and gazed up at the tall ceiling that was suddenly too low for him. He cried in a helpless voice, "Humanity's. Trying to be!" He slapped his palm against a pillar behind him, and almost laughed at his own uselessness.

"As I am the Itiri's," said Roniva. "Remember thou who I am. May I go now?"

Alihahd gave a bark of pain, frustration, laughter, absurdity. "*Ili! Ili!*" he cried.

"What sayest thou?" said Roniva.

"I am saying, 'Go, I am sorry, dismiss everything I ever said,' " said Alihahd. "Why not? I am as no one, as Ben." And he ran from the chamber.

Serra listened to the rain falling outside. The fire in the hearth sputtered from drops straying down the chimney. Harrison Hall rose from the breakfast table and took his rain fur from the peg by the door. "Be careful," said Serra.

Hall navigated the slushy paths pitted with footprints, while on either side of the trail the rain pocked the untrodden snow with wet perforations. He came upon a moody Alihahd braving the elements. Blond hair was wind-tossed, his ears and fair face stung deep red, his blue eyes half closed in the cold wind. He was not dressed for the weather, either from self-torture or neglect. He must have been out here all night. He was deep in thought. Hall sensed anger.

They stepped around a spongy euglenoid colony creeping across the path, soaking up the rain.

Hall walked along in silence. When they had come at length to the entrance to Alihahd's cave, Hall asked for words. "Captain?"

Alihahd expelled a breath, shook his head, said nothing. He went in.

Hall returned to Serra's cave. Serra, Amerika, and Vaslav were at the table. Hall hung his rain fur on its peg and joined them. "Mad," he said. "Absolutely unpredictable. He's as regular as the damn weather."

"No," said Vaslav.

Hall frowned at the boy. "No? What do you mean, *no?*"

Vaslav proceeded to explain that Alihahd was not erratic at all. According to Vaslav's chronometer, Alihahd was perfectly predictable—unbelievably so. Alihahd, said Vaslav, kept a perfect twenty-four-hour Earth standard cycle.

Harrison Hall seized the boy's wrist and stared at his chronometer. "Are you sure?"

Vaslav swore it was so. He did not understand it, how Alihahd did it, but that was what he was doing. Alihahd rose every day at the same time—on Earth. He went to bed at the same time each Earth day. At any given Earth time, he was to be found in the exact same place. The schedule put him far out of rhythm with Iry's days and nights. Not to be regulated by an alien sun, Alihahd ignored it entirely, and he rose and slept as his inner clock bid, whatever time of day and the Iry sun said.

Hall's smile was slow and evil, breaking to an open grin. His gaze turned aside with glinting eyes, toward the door and the outside where the rain had turned to snow.

IV. A Winter Conversation

Alihahd woke at sunset, just as Vaslav was crawling into bed. Vaslav glanced at his wrist chronometer. The time was exactly 0735 on the Earth meridian.

How does he do it? Vaslav marveled. *I have the clock!*

Alihahd went through his waking ritual with seeming meticulousness, putting on his clothes in habitual order, remaking the bed just so—first the quilt, then the woven blanket, then the brown fur, then the silver fur. He brushed his teeth twice.

Then he went outside without his rain fur like a forgetful old man.

The cliff paths were slick with snow falling lightly from the high clouds. No one was about at this hour except the two sentinels, who were easy to avoid. Alihahd's walks had settled into a set pattern that kept him away from others as much as possible.

Alihahd wallowed in his solitude. He did not feel the cold.

Then a voice split the silence and dragged him out of his reverie. "Why art thou always elsewhere than thou art, Alihahd?"

He knew the voice and was shocked that it should address him directly.

Waiting in shadowed ambush on his accustomed path, alone and unattended, was the Fendi Roniva. Blending in with the black shadow, she was barely visible but for her white teeth, the whites of her glittering black eyes, and the broken red scars on her cheeks. She wore no jewels to catch the starlight. Alihahd was so amazed that he had nothing to say.

"Thou livest out of time," said the Fendi. "Be here now."

He wondered what she wanted.

She drew closer and passed a leathery hand over his wet hair. She shook the icy snow crystals from her hand. "Thou hast little regard for thyself," she said. "That is not good. Thy spirit is not well."

"How may I serve thee, Fendi?" Alihahd said at last.

"Dry thyself. Eat. Wear warm clothes and come to me." She turned sharply and glided across the bridge.

Alihahd had detected a subtle nervousness about her he'd never seen before—something in the stiffness of her shoulders, a thin edge to her voice. Nothing blatant, it was the held-back tension of the brave solemnly facing something dreadful.

Alihahd quickly complied with her wishes. He went to Hall and Serra's cave; the two of them were usually to be found up late.

"Good morning, Captain," said Hall, smiling.

Blue eyes darted outside to where it was dark. Alihahd frowned.

Serra fed him. Hall gave him warm dry clothes and his own fur-lined parka. Before Alihahd left, Serra slipped a packet of breadcakes into his pocket. "Take. It will be a long night."

Alihahd took her shoulder in his hand. "You know what that is about, Serra?"

Serra kept her eyes lowered as a good Eridanin woman to a strange man. "I think so." She tied the leather drawstring of the parka's hood under his chin. Her shoulders were as stiff as Roniva's. Her voice had gone husky.

"Am I in danger?" said Alihahd.

"No. You can walk away. She cannot."

Serra did not explain further. The topic was upsetting to her.

Alihahd left the warmth of the cave. Using the safety line, he crossed the bridge to Aerieside in twelve steps, starting with his right foot.

Roniva had not told him where to go, so he went where one always had audience with the Fendi, the Chamber of the Golden Dome.

Even as he approached he could see yellow beams pouring from its arched doorway and its tall windows, darkened by flitting shadows of people moving inside.

He stood at the entrance and witnessed an odd little ceremony in progress within.

Roniva was standing in the center of a ring of ma-hanina. She wore only a loose flowing ice-blue shift pinned at her shoulders. Her hair was loose. Bare arms were crossed over her flat chest. Without all her enameled toques Alihahd could see how very wrinkled was her neck.

A warrior-priest stepped into the circle and emptied a bucket of ashes over her neat, glossy head.

She did not move against him, only closed her eyes and frowned in revulsion. She uncrossed her arms, all her corded muscles taut. Her body was firm and thin and hard beneath the sheer shift that was no protection at all against the cold.

Alihahd was aghast to see the shift suddenly stripped from her and she driven out naked into the snow.

Alihahd lunged forward to help her.

Leathery black hands met his as she stumbled. Then her resigned face turned up to him and silenced anything he might have said.

All was happening as it was meant to be.

She spoke, smudges of white ashes on her black lips. "I

am of an age to demand a companion. Walk with me, Alihahd.'' She straightened herself and marched into the winter night.

Alihahd cast an appalled look back at the other warriors, now assembled in a row barring the cave entrance and the golden glow of warmth within, jewels sparkling on their thick robes, and he ran after the old woman with ashes in her hair.

Roniva's hairless blue-black skin was mottled in places with wrinkles and scars. Her sagging abdomen was corrugated with marks of childbirth.

Alihahd could not contain his wrath.'' What kind of sadistic and barbarous ritual is this that they should degrade a dignified, elderly woman in this way!''

Roniva gave him a dim smile and spoke to him directly, for she had no attendants anymore. Even her familiar was nowhere to be found. ''Too dignified,'' she answered. ''That is the issue. I am the single most powerful being on Iry. One begins to feel like deity.'' She spat the ashes from her lips. ''I am not.''

''And you are aware of it. This is not necessary.''

''For them too.'' She gestured backward. ''One's life is not entirely one's own up here.''

They hiked over a ridge. A blast of wind kicked up a swirl of glittering snow around them. Roniva threw back her head and howled.

Alihahd was puzzled that she could not overcome the cold. ''I have seen you step in fire and stop naked steel with your bare hand,'' he said.

''Ah. That was then. Now is now. I am naked and I am cold. How I hate this.''

Alihahd wanted to give her his coat. He knew she would not take it. Trying to lift her spirits, he reminded her of her own greatness.

''Not to flatter me,'' she said. ''I need to find some humbleness if I am to bear this. How beautiful the new-fallen snow.'' She frisked away like a colt.

Alihahd thrust his hands into the pockets of Hall's parka as he followed her. He felt pebbles in the bottom of one pocket and he drew them out to see. They were the eight gemstones he'd brought to Hall from the valley.

Roniva was delighted. ''Give thou to me. Hast thou a zircon? I am in need of a zircon.''

Zircon. Humility. Alihahd gave her all eight stones. She fingered them like prayer beads.

Silent a while, Alihahd's thoughts jumped. Then he blurted out, "Why did you kill Jinin-Ben-Tairre?"

Neither the question nor its abruptness surprised Roniva. "I am getting old," she said.

Alihahd foundered in puzzlement. Wind fluttered the fur lining of the hood wreathing his face.

Roniva continued, "I grow weary. An Elder is truly an elder, thou see. I am . . . what is the number . . . one hundred and sixty years old. I could die."

Alihahd was amazed and still confused. "What has that to do with Ben?"

"When I die they could make him Fendi."

"*What?*"

"Thou didst not know? He is a miracle among us. I had to kill him while I had strength. I'll not have him rule my Aerie. He belongs with humans. I sent him back."

"That could be difficult," said Alihahd.

"Thou meanest because of the Na'id?"

"Among other things," said Alihahd.

"Harrison White Fox Hall tells me much about the Empire," said Roniva.

"I know." Alihahd had told Hall to stop maligning the Empire to the Fendi; he endangered the better part of humanity should the Itiri ever decide to break their neutrality and go to arms. Hall had replied, "Don't use 'better' when you mean 'bigger.' "

"Alihahd, thou talkest not and thou art the one I would have talk," Roniva prompted.

Know thine enemy. She wanted to know the Na'id.

"In true conscience I cannot," said Alihahd.

Roniva made a questioning noise. She wanted to know why.

Alihahd admitted bluntly. "Because they are human and you are not."

The Fendi was not offended. Honesty did not offend.

"I am afraid you will have to rely on Mr. Hall for your information," said Alihahd.

"Thou art a worse threat to the Na'id than is Mr. Hall," said Roniva.

"How do you figure?" said Alihahd. Hall was set to

destroy the Na'id, Alihahd only to break their stranglehold
on free humanity and to avoid bloodshed.

"Thou knowest them best," said Roniva.

"I do," said Alihahd. "It *has* been a decided advantage."

'Harrison White Fox Hall tells me evil things about the
Na'id. Tell me something good, canst thou?"

Trapped. This woman always won what she sought. He
could hardly *not* answer her, and he ended up telling her
about the Na'id despite himself.

He explained to her the Na'id ideology, before it had run
afoul, and its lofty ideals to eliminate the barriers dividing
humankind.

Roniva countered, "They oppose color barriers yet they
despise thee for thy color. How is that?"

Who had told her about his color? Hall. *Damn him*.

Alihahd regarded his pale hands. He was sensitive about
his strange color. It was difficult to keep emotion from his
voice. "This is the color of a pure race. It is a symbol of
many evil practices in the past—"

"Thou art not a symbol. Thou art a man," said Roniva.
"Thou hast also been brainwashed by thine own enemy."

Alihahd wanted to protest, but he would have to tell too
much. He sighed. He could not even reason with human Jews
and Arabs; what made him think he was going to make an
alien hear sense?

It was comforting to know that all these irrational Itiri were
staunchly neutral and would not set out with their deadly
martial skills to threaten the Empire.

All but one dead one.

V. The Sunset Village

Ben strode down the old lake road toward the village Qiatte,
bare feet padding silently on pressed dirt. The kestrel followed at intervals, flying from tree to tree ahead of him, then
waiting in the boughs of the imported oaks for Ben to catch

up and pass under its perch. When there were no more oaks shadowing the road, the bird hovered high in the air and cried.

Ben broke stride, raised his right hand, and the kestrel floated down. It screamed as its talons clicked against the metal of the false hand, and it beat its wings in a flurry, climbed back skyward, and cried.

Ben raised his left hand. The kestrel came down and fastened its talons into his flesh, drawing blood. Ben lowered his familiar to eye level with dark resentment, close to tears, not that the wounds themselves were painful, but he was heartsick and this creature had all the compassion of the north wind.

"Knowest thou that thou hurt me?"

The kestrel cried.

The village was the kind where life goes on and on, little changed year to year, generation to generation. The spaceport far down the river had little to do with the oxen in the fields or the wagon-wheel ruts in the unpaved road. The level land nodded with grain; vineyards ripened up above the ridge; villagers still mined salt deep beneath the lake; and each house which hugged the slow rise along the southern shore had its own garden.

But something was wrong in the village. The warrior-priest sensed it as the road led him over the pine ridge to see the buildings below half-deserted and old.

The villagers who were left in Qiatte came to their windows and peered with wonder at the warrior up on the ridge above their town.

He was human, an Amerasian. His powerful body in stillness suggested fire in containment. His dark eyes seemed to burn. Red rags bound the high arches of his small, broad, badly scarred feet. He carried only the clothing he wore, a white flower, and his familiar—which was now on his shoulder, preening its feathers with its hooked beak—and his sword. There was blood on his hand.

He was a dangerous stranger, not one to go out and greet.

He descended to the shore of the lake, then left the road to climb the hill into the village itself. His muscles stood out in hard, molten definition across his broad shoulders and in his thighs, where his black trousers pulled against his striding legs.

The townspeople, those not too terrified, followed his movements at a respectful distance.

The building he came to was the schoolhouse. It was unused of late and in disrepair. The warrior stood before it, then with the bottom of his foot, kicked the door off its hinges. The door fell in with a swoop of dust. The warrior stalked inside and surveyed the empty hall. It was dry and musty, smelling of cobwebs and wood, warm from sunlight streaming through the dirty windows.

The warrior backed out of the schoolhouse, seeming more cautious of the emptiness within than of the villagers without. He climbed down the hill again to the shore road.

As he was passing an entrance to the salt mines that extended beneath the lake he stopped and stared down the cavernous hole for a very long time, as if it meant something to him.

He became very still. Then he whirled suddenly, drawing the long double-curved sword in a wide arc as he turned, bringing his free hand to grasp the hilt as well, and he raised the sword high. The blade flashed over his head, then stabbed down into the dirt road with all his force.

The village recoiled. Windows shut; shutters locked; curtains drew; all battened down for a storm.

The Itiri was angry.

He walked away from his sword and disappeared into the forest.

No one touched the abandoned sword—or even considered coming close. Some, on reflex, worried that the children might be tempted, then remembered that Qiatte had no children anymore.

In a while the windows opened and the village stirred again. People clustered in their usual groups where people always collected in Qiatte, and they asked each other questions none of them could answer.

In the darkened barroom of the town's single inn five old villagers half-sat on tall stools, smoked flavored tobacco, and talked over cups of resined brew.

"He wouldn't hurt us, would he? We've done nothing to him, have we?" said the nervous birdlike one—loudly, for he was nearly deaf from the guns of two years past.

"He wouldn't leave his sword in the street if he was going to hurt us," said the wizened salt miner before he broke off in a fit of tubercular coughing. He spat on the floor, and the innkeep cackled at him peevishly.

"It's a dare," said the horse breaker. "Broken horses we are." She shifted painfully on her stool and accidentally brushed her crutches, which were propped against the bar, and they clattered to the floor.

"He's angry," said the birdlike man. "Why is he angry? You saw him stab the ground. That's anger."

"That's how the Itiri declare war," said the gray-whiskered man who used to be the schoolmaster.

The innkeeper recited, her voice quavering thin like a witch woman's chant, "When the warrior E-Leel avenged her brother's death she stabbed the ground at Groden's feet and said, 'This is my battle.' "

"That's a story," said the horse breaker.

The innkeep pointed a gnarled, arthritic finger past them all, her other two fingers curled in like claws. "*That* is not a story." Her three-fingered hand wobbled in the air portentously.

Her customers bent over their cups and hunched their shoulders against a sudden chill.

No one was speaking when the door opened. The figure in the doorway was a dark blot against the day beyond the door of the dark tavern, and no one could make out his features, but the outline was unmistakable.

The Itiri crossed the wooden floor soundlessly and stopped three paces from the schoolmaster at the end of the bar. The warrior spoke quietly in Universal. "Where is everyone?"

The villagers mumbled among themselves in confusion.

Finding himself closest to the being, the schoolmaster was compelled to attempt the answer. "At home . . . here and there . . ."

The Itiri was shaking his head slowly, his eyes remaining fixed points never straying from them. No, the answer was not the one he wanted.

The innkeeper nodded in frowning comprehension. This stranger knew somehow that Qiatte was a town without most of its people and that the attrition had not been natural. "The Na'id," she answered.

The Itiri snapped his head sharply to the side at the sound. For a breath no one moved. The miner fell to a fit of deep-bubbling coughing and folded onto the bar, overcome for several moments. The others paid him no mind and kept their attention locked on the Itiri.

"Na'id," the Itiri repeated gravely. "When?"

"A year," said the horsetamer.

"More," shouted the deafened one.

"Not two years," said the horsetamer.

The schoolmaster, trying to be helpful, said, "Our year in relation to Earth standard is slightly long—"

"I know the length of a year," said the Itiri.

The schoolmaster stuttered an apology. He had been speaking in Universal. The horse breaker, seated next to him, muttered aside to him in the local tongue, "Don't volunteer anything. We don't know what he's here to do."

The Itiri did not demand translation. No notice crossed the dark eyes. He cared not at all for their whispers and private remarks.

"What company?" the warrior demanded.

"Sir?" said the schoolmaster.

"The Na'id. Which company?"

The villagers conferred quickly in their own language:

"What does he want?"

"Which Na'id were here."

"Do you know?"

"Jan might."

"Na'id are Na'id. What difference which company?"

"What does he want to know for? He doesn't look like a real Itiri. He looks like a Na'id."

"Speak up, I can't hear."

"Shhhhh."

"Jan," said the Itiri, and the villagers silenced, frightened.

How had he picked Jan's name out of their whispered jumble of foreign words? He could not be familiar with a language as provincial as theirs. Could he?

"Who is Jan?" said the warrior. "Samura?"

The villagers gasped. The miner wheezed, hawked and spat.

Jan Samura was Qiatte's local hero, maimed by the Na'id during their last invasion. Jan was famous in the immediate region; and certain of the Na'id knew him; but no one else from off-planet would have heard of Jan. Not an Itiri.

"Don't answer," the horse breaker hissed in thick dialect. "He'll hurt Jan."

The Itiri's focus narrowed hard to her, and he spoke full of indignation *in the local tongue:* "He will do no such thing."

They all pulled back as if he had hit them. A mug spilled over, ignored.

The Itiri turned his eyes to the gray-bearded schoolmaster. In a voice that may have had emotion in it, he said, "Master Brown, do you know who I am?"

The horse breaker clapped her hand over her mouth. The bent-over miner sat bolt upright.

The schoolmaster's bearded chin quivered. He reached out to touch Ben's arm, but epicanthic lids raised and thickly muscled neck tensed; the schoolmaster quickly withdrew his hand. There would be no welcoming the boy home. Wherever he had been had made him thoroughly strange to everything he once was.

Schoolmaster Brown had taught him to read.

"Where is Jan?" said Ben-Tairre. "The house is gone."

"He—he built a house in the woods—"

"Take me to Jan."

The door opened before the schoolmaster could raise his hand to knock. Jan had heard them coming up the forest path and recognized their approach: the schoolmaster's flat-footed tred, the miner's wheezing, the horsetamer's rhythmic crutches, and the birdman's halting shuffle. Jan knew who they were, but detected something unusual about them. Villagers were always ill at ease when they came to Jan, but missing this time were their furtive whispers. Someone was with them— someone who made no sound, detected only by his escort's frightened quietness. It would not be a villager. This stranger would be more than ordinary.

Still Jan was shocked when he opened the door.

The villagers scattered to either side to get themselves out from between the Itiri and their own war hero. Jan Samura came outside with lurching steps on unflexing feet, his mangled hands helping to support his muscular bulk on two canes. He was square-built like a wrestler with taurine neck, and arms thewed like horse's haunches. The pectorals on his massive chest were hard and flat as plates of armor. Even crippled he looked truly formidable. Was.

His long black hair was pulled back from a widow's peak and the deep-sculptured hollows of his temples to lie sleek against his head and leave unsoftened his severe, handsome face. His features were sharp. Large eyes were narrowed keenly by epicanthic folds but did not slant.

He did not look much like his brother.

Jan breathed, "Akio." He started forward, wanting to embrace him, but a small quick move of the warrior-priest's head—like a wary hawk—stopped him. The man was a stranger.

Don't presume upon the man simply because you knew the boy, thought Jan.

Or because he is your little brother.

Jan searched the cold warrior for a vestige of the child he'd known, who once upon a time looked up to him and adored him. But Jan might as well have been lookng at an alien.

You knew him once. You don't know him now.

Resigned, Jan granted the warrior his distance.

Jan was not afraid of the Itiri. Jan was the only person in Qiatte not disturbed by him. Not because of their relation, which counted for nothing. but because Jan was fearless.

He recognized that the Itiri had not come to his door as a brother. More likely the Itiri wanted to call upon a warrior leader of the village. Jan knew the townsfolk tended to gibber.

Jan stepped back and welcomed the Itiri into his home on the warrior's own terms, as a respected stranger, and Jan bid his wife make tea.

The villagers faded back from the door and returned to the village at a hobbling run.

Jan's tea room was spare and simple, warm with the light colors of maple, pine, and butternut. One wall was clear glass, letting in sunlight filtered through the evergreen forest. The door was full-sized.

Jan paused at the table, then began the humiliating, laborious process of sitting down. Balancing heavily with his canes he lowered himself with painful awkwardness into a crosslegged position at the low table. If he could avoid it he never did so when anyone else was in the room.

Once in place he regained his aura of power and dignity.

Jan made a striking figure. Like a living work in marble, the forceful structure of his heavy skull, his square jaw, square chin, and broad flat cheekbones suggested origins in a solid block of stone. His other features were fine and razor-etched—his narrow straight nose; thin lips of his wide straight mouth; and his black eyebrows, sharp, almost cruel, over brilliant eyes. There was no softness to the lines of his face, though there was grace.

He glanced up at Ben. The warrior glided into a cross-legged position on the cushion opposite Jan at the table.

Attempts at ceremony and polite conversation were met with curious bewilderment by the alien guest, so Jan ceased trying and told the Itiri what he wanted to know, which was what had happened to the village.

Ben already knew that the Na'id had been to Qiatte many years ago when Ben himself still lived there. As the villagers told the story, Jan had driven the Na'id out that time single-handedly.

"They came through again the winter before last," said Jan. "They weren't here to occupy this time. They had no use for our little mining town. They are hurting. They're not into expansion these days. They've been suffering heavy losses. They needed soldiers. So they took everyone. Not just their pick of the sturdy children like before. Anyone with a whole body."

Anyone except Jan himself, who had instead been nailed to a cross upside down. His hands had regained partial function since the ordeal; they still had great power but no dexterity, and he moved them with great pain. His feet were fused lumps of calcium. The local technology could not mend him. The Na'id could—and that was to be the telling blow. The Na'id had singled out Jan to be a symbol of the futility of resistance. Not without regret. Jan was a magnificent soldier, and the Empire could have used his like. But they recognized incorrigibility when they encountered it. Sometimes.

They would have slaughtered Jan and eaten him, but they wanted to break his spirit, not give him martyrdom. Besides, his unyielding muscles were probably inedible.

Jan mentioned his own experiences briefly and without emotion.

Then his wife brought out a steaming teapot and two china cups on an enameled tray, and Jan said to Ben-Tairre, "You remember Cathy?"

Cathy had been a skinny little girl in those days, Jan's

childhood sweetheart. She was still thin, but now hard and limber, her skin sun-weathered and freckled. Her gray eyes were wreathed in fine lines. Her hair was strawberry-blond, and she was thoroughly Caucasian, as were most of the people of Qiatte.

Ben's eyes moved to Cathy, then back to Jan, not to be sidetracked even by civility.

Cathy in turn regarded Ben with suspicion. She was afraid for her husband, seeing some kind of threat in his alien brother—as if Ben might possess Jan and make him alien too. She tried to keep overt hostility from showing in her face, and she maintained an unspeaking, forced courtesy.

She bent down and set the tray on the table. Ben slid his hand aside—the gloved mechanical one—and it clicked as it moved. Cathy jerked back as if there were a snake on the table. "What are you?" The words flew out without thought.

"Cathy!" Jan barked.

Cathy retreated from the room.

Jan said by way of apology, "How the woman can be shocked by that, I cannot imagine." He picked up the delicate teapot with his own crooked, ugly hands. The Na'id had not been precise with their hammer blows when they'd driven the nails through his palms.

Jan poured the tea, then carefully, precariously, his large eagle-claw hand took up the tiny green china cup embossed with an opalescent white dragon. He was left-handed.

Ben consented to drink. Strangers were served tea on the Aerie.

He lifted the cup with his left hand, which was dotted with red wheals and many small scars. The kestrel was nowhere to be seen.

"Are you an Itiri warrior-priest?" said Jan.

"I was. He died," said the stranger.

"Who are you now?"

Ben studied the talon marks on his hand. "I do not know." His small mouth drew into a petulant near-pout. "Where did they take everyone?"

Jan shook his head. "I don't know." He'd been upside down trying not to choke on his own vomit when his towns-men were being taken away. "They caved the mine in on my

Cathy. We couldn't dig her out until they left. I couldn't dig at all. She was buried for three days.''

"Were they the same soldiers?" Ben meant the same ones who had occupied Qiatte seventeen years earlier.

"The very ones," said Jan. "They knew my name."

"The same commander?" said Ben.

"Mushabriqu," Jan nodded.

Ben sank to an inward-turned silence.

Jan took one cane and rose with effort to balance himself on his short ill-proportioned legs, his thighs thick and muscular, the calves small and undeveloped. He slipped out of his black-and-gold silk robe and let it fall to the floor. Underneath it he wore a black sweater and trousers. "Come. Let us walk outside."

Ben flowed to his feet, a soundless panther.

"Cathy!" Jan called, his shod feet clumping loudly on the wooden floor with his ungainly steps.

Cathy peered in, saw that her husband was preparing to go out, and came to twist his long silky hair into a knot and fasten it with two long pins. She held the door open, and the Itiri stole out, Jan following, lurching from side to side with each step.

The forest and fields were autumn-fresh and cooling with the evening. A reddish cast of sunset tinged the pine ridge over the vineyards. Birds sang noisily at the close of the day.

Ben accompanied Jan down the hill to the lake road as a smooth, shifting shadow to the lumbering figure.

The other villagers kept their distance in fear. The village had learned to fear much.

On the road, Jan stopped and pointed with his cane. "Your feet, Akio."

Ben looked down at his rag-tied feet. Jan was pointing at the burn scars.

"Were you crucified like your brother?" said Jan.

Jinin-Ben-Tairre crouched down and touched his feet. The Warrior's Feet Are Burned. He touched the scars lightly with his fingertips, then his broad hand moved aside and clenched the black soil of Qiatte in the agony of something lost. "No," he said.

He stood, and the two of them walked up a green, grassy hill that was Qiatte's graveyard. Jan pointed again with his cane, this time to a stone marker. "Your grave."

Ben walked ahead of Jan to read the flat slab over the empty plot:

AKIO SAMURA 1198–1207 A.F.

Jan came to stand with him at the grave and rested both his hands on the walking cane planted in front of him. "Shall I have it removed?"

"No. Let it stay," said Ben, not looking up from the stone.

So the warrior wanted a total break with the past. It was what Jan wanted to know. It was why he'd brought his brother this way.

Just when Jan had accepted that Ben had erased his blood roots from his every thought, Ben asked, "Had you children?"

Since the question could not be idle, polite, or curious— Ben totally dispensed with those—his interest could only mean that he still cared something for his kin. Some tenuous tie still persisted.

"I have a daughter," said Jan. "She was away at a girls' school in the mountains when they came." She was one of the very few of Qiatte's children to escape Na'id conscription. Jan kept her away still so as not to grieve the otherwise childless town. Qiatte's hero should not be the only person so blessed. Also, his wife was jealous. The girl was an angel. But that was no one else's affair.

Jan was not bitter, in spite of what had been done to his village and to himself. He was still defiant, but he nursed no acid hate for an absent enemy. Let the Na'id return to his reach; then Jan would hate. Had he been younger and whole, he would have followed them to the sky and fought them. But he knew his limits. They had broken his body, and he would not torment himself longing for revenge he could not have. So he stayed here with his wife in the sunset village by the lake, an esteemed man of his townspeople.

Jan and Ben walked back down to the lake road and approached the place where the Itiri sword stuck into the dirt, lonely and untouched, naked blade catching the day's last light.

Ben stopped at the sword and gazed down the mine entrance again.

His familiar appeared in the sky, keening *ki ki ki ki*. It descended to light upon Ben's flesh hand.

"Is it a kestrel?" said Jan.

"It is an albatross," said Ben.

The bird screeched and hopped onto his shoulder.

Ben tugged his sword from the ground and sheathed it. "I shall leave now," he said.

They returned first to the house, where Jan collected his sturdy crutches and a cloak to walk his guest back to his ship. As they waited for Cathy, who decided she was walking too, Jan maneuvered around to face the warrior-priest. "Akio, I don't know what you have in mind or where you're going, but—" His eyes strayed to the window in the direction of the half-empty town. "The children. Could you bring back the children?"

"Adults, perhaps," said the Itiri. He had switched back to speaking Universal. He was very far away now. "Thy children are gone."

The severe lines of Jan's face hardened, stone-set. His finely drawn brows peaked and his thin lips pulled down into a deep, furrowed frown, giving him the look of a bird of prey.

"A year in Na'id hands and thou wouldst not know them," said Ben-Tairre. For a moment his small mouth softened like an unhappy child's. "Thou wouldst not want them."

Frustration welled. "If I could go after the dogs that did this to my village . . ." Jan's ruined fists clenched and unclenched impotently on the handles of his crutches.

"I am not crippled," said Ben.

Jan beheld him anew, hard, lithe, and dangerous. "No," Jan agreed. His frustration eased, settling into bittersweet solace of assured vengeance. Even to his missing hand, Jinin-Ben-Tairre was not crippled.

Cathy appeared at last, throwing an oversized knit sweater-jacket over her cotton dress, and then the three of them went outside. Cathy slid the door shut behind them to keep out the bugs and the sundown chill. There was no lock.

The night was innocent and unsinister, the cooler air revived. It was the kind of night that children—had there been children—begged to stay outside. Crickets trilled lively to the mildness of the night. The silhouettes of the trees, the moons on the lake, the gentle calling of the native waterfowl, the clean smell of green grass, clover, pine needles, and oak leaves all spoke of peace and home.

They walked over the ridge and out of the village, across open fields on paths the three of them used to walk a lifetime ago when Jan and Cathy strolled hand in hand dogged by a tagalong brother who talked too much. Jan recalled now that Little Brother had been constantly told to shut up. He wished he could take that back, and he wished his brother would say something.

Cathy walked with her arms crossed, her gait the long straight stride of a farm girl in flat-soled canvas shoes. Her mood was light, relieved that Ben was going.

Cathy had smacked Akio once for picking tomatoes from her garden. This thing was not Akio.

Ben's carbon-striated ship, *Singalai*, stood in an open meadow, an incongruous technological creation among the surrounding wildlife. Cathy, Jan, and Ben left the path and crossed to it. The grass was cold and felt slightly damp underfoot.

Singalai's hatch opened at Ben's approach.

"Where is your bird?" said Jan.

The kestrel had blinked out somewhere along the way.

"It will catch up," said Ben.

Faster than light? thought Jan.

Ben turned to face him and said abruptly and simply, "Farewell."

Crutches propped under his arms, Jan reached out and took the startled Itiri's head between his mutilated hands, pulled it to him, and kissed him. "Godspeed, my little brother."

He could tell that Ben was affronted, but Jan was undismayed. He had determined that he would do that regardless. Like it or not, what could Ben do about it?

Released, Ben pulled back and gave Jan an astounded stare of an offended stranger. He walked toward his ship's hatch, looked back, his brow furrowed. He reached his ship and looked again, a bewildered alien, as if he truly did not understand. The hatch closed on him that way, staring.

Cathy stepped up to Jan's side, her arms firmly folded. "He didn't know you at all." Her tone scolded him for daring to grab a stranger and kiss him.

Jan made a noncommittal noise. "Just in case he did," said Jan. He looked slyly sidelong at his wife and gave her a hint of a coaxing smile. She uttered an exasperated growl and rolled her eyes. She was trying to keep from smiling, but one teased at the corners of her mouth and she hid it behind her hand.

They returned to the path that led to the village and started back. The ship lifted off behind them with a flash and a roar. Jan turned back to watch, then faced the village again with his wife.

They would have held hands, but Jan could not free his hands and still walk. He pitched ahead on his crutches while his wife strode alongside, in no hurry on the beautiful clear night, sometimes pausing to gaze up at the peaceful-looking stars.

VI.   A Winter Conversation (Reprise)

Night turned to the hour of the meteors. The snow had stopped; the clouds were gone. Under the clear sky, the temperature plunged.

Alihahd warmed Roniva's long toes between his hands. It seemed to him that there was something terribly arbitrary about the physical characteristics of the Itiri and their purposeless dimorphism—the aghara too tall for the gravity and too fair for the irradiation on the mountaintop.

A meteor streaked across the icy sky. Snow on the ground glinted like quartz flecks, crusty cold underfoot. Starshadows were hard-edged and black. Roniva yawned.

Alihahd took her spider-monkey hands and held them inside his coat against his chest. "This is abominable," he growled.

"Thou mayest go in if thou art cold," said Roniva.

"No." The cold never bothered Alihahd much.

In the east the sign of the Mountain was rising, a random-looking jumble of stars that had not formed a double peak in 100,000 years. Dawn was still hours away.

Roniva started to walk again, one hand slipped into Alihahd's coat pocket as a human lover might do—as his wife used to do when they were young and still pretending to be in love for the public eye.

"Are you not afraid of falling ill?" said Alihahd. He worried about her in the wind.

"We do not sicken," said Roniva. "Most of us are immune to every disease on this world. Frostbite worries me." She flexed her long fingers and toes. "Disease doth not."

"That is incredible," said Alihahd. "How did your people develop such immunities?"

"We died by the thousands," said Roniva simply. "Those that survived passed down immunity."

"A harsh method," said Alihahd.

"Nature's method," said Roniva. "We try to be at one with Nature."

"Nature is cruel," said Alihahd. "Humanity is compassionate."

"Is it?" said Roniva.

"Kindness is a human trait," said Alihahd. "Which is not to say that all humans are kind."

"True enough that one does not find kindness growing wild," Roniva conceded.

And Alihahd became disturbed by something that had only gradually crept into his awareness since he had come to Iry—the total absence of physical and mental defectives in the population. He asked cautiously if there were any.

"Oh. Distorts. Of course they happen."

"Where are they?" said Alihahd.

"We kill them."

"That is inhuman," said Alihahd.

Onyx eyes flashed. "We are not human."

"I tend to forget," he said bitterly. "The level of a civilization is measured by how it cares for those unable."

"Very noble," said Roniva. "Very impractical at this point."

"Humans manage," said Alihahd.

"Is it true that human children are cruel to the deformed and the different?" said Roniva.

Alihahd's white face colored. "Yes, but—"

"Such treatment distorts the inside. The abused grow crooked. They carry much anger. That distorts others. They distort their own children. The spiral goes down."

"That is cold-blooded reasoning. These things can be overcome," said Alihahd.

"So who told thee we were perfect?" said Roniva. "You have your interstellar wars. Why dost thou begrudge us our private atrocities?"

And who *had* told him the Itiri were perfect? The legends. He of all people ought to know the frailty of legends.

"Is it true you have to kill someone to become a warriorpriest?" said Alihahd.

"No. That is not true," said Roniva. But before Alihahd could breathe relief, she said, "Thou must kill someone to become a hanina."

A noise like the beginning of gagging escaped Alihahd.

"Oh, one doth not go out and murder someone," said Roniva. "It is not a thing to strive for. It happens or it happens not. It is no one's goal to be a hanina. It is a burden. When one becomes an Elder one gains access to the Archives. I know thou thought we had no written records. We do. They are kept in a cave in the desert. One can read things one would rather not.

"Ours is not a shame culture, Captain Alihahd. We have no use whatsoever for guilt upon which some human cultures thrive. The Archives collect much dust."

"There is an ancient shame?" said Alihahd.

"There is. I shall not jump off the bridge for it."

"Your people do not fear death, do they, Fendi," Alihahd reflected.

"No. It comes to all sooner or later. Preferably later."

Alihahd gazed pensively at the sky. Another shooting star blazed across the Milky Way. "You must be formidable in war," he said.

"I suppose we would be," said Roniva. "But we have not seen war in several lifetimes."

Alihahd's brows drew together sharply. "How did you achieve that?"

"No nations," said Roniva. She crouched in the snow, tried to make a snowball, but the graupel would not stick together. "It is difficult to organize a war without nations. And thou knowest our attitude toward ownership. Humans kill each other for that handful of stones in thy pocket. We own nothing. So we have no property to protect. The ranga are docile. As for the aghara, we all become warrior-priests. We are strong. Only the weak and frightened must fight.''

"*All* the aghara become warriors?" said Alihahd.

"Or they die," said Roniva.

"They are killed," Alihahd interpreted.

"The same," Roniva agreed.

"Why *must* an aghara become a warrior-priest?"

"When aghara go their own way, war will return to Iry."

"Or when it comes from the stars," said Alihahd.

"Or that," said Roniva.

"You seem to be taking that possibility very lightly," said Alihahd. "A few thousand warriors and a handful of antique spaceships will not avail you against a modern fleet. Your people were introduced to high technology two thousand years ago and you've done nothing with it in all that time. Your science is stagnant."

"We have all we want," said Roniva. "Why art thou worried about us?"

"I swear I do not know. I should let you all go to the devil. And you will if the Na'id find out that Itiri warrior-priests actually do exist. You wanted me to tell you something about the Na'id; I shall tell you something; They will turn you back into a myth as fast as they can seed your sun with a nova core. Sooner or later."

"I should hate to have to deal with that," was Roniva's only comment.

When the eastern sky began to gray, Roniva climbed up the highest rise and waited with open arms for the coming of the sun.

Alihahd dropped to one knee a distance behind her to watch, smiling that the long night was past and she was still here to salute the morning fire. The winds picked up her hip-length hair and fanned it out behind her like a sail. Sun gleamed on her black arms thrown wide. She cried out in the ancient tongue, a sound of exultation, fittingly barbarous to Alihahd's ears. He expected nothing less or else from his savage warrior queen.

She turned to him, and he rose.

She returned to the Chamber of the Golden Dome. The

warriors who had driven her out were still there, waiting to envelope her in furs and a jeweled robe when she came in. They brought her to the fireside and brushed her hair and dressed it in gold and tapestry ribbons. Her colored toques were replaced around her neck, and her jingling swordbelt looped around her small waist. Lastly, a warrior brought her sword wrapped in felt. He bowed all the way to the floor at her feet, unwrapped the blade, and offered it up to her over his bowed head.

She took it in a solid grip, reassured by its comforting weight, and then sheathed it.

"Tell the Earthman the Fendi is grateful for his service," said Roniva to the air. "Tell the Earthman he may go."

No one needed to tell Alihahd to go. He had left the cave. This conversation was ended.

Alihahd sat on his neatly made bed, lost in thought. Vaslav came in, unwelcomely energetic and tried to talk to him. Alihahd changed his clothes, folded up the ones Hall had given him, and excused himself shortly. "I must return some things to Mr. Hall."

Vaslav scowled at him perplexedly as he went out.

Alihahd took the things not to Hall and Serra's cave, but to the private cave on the third level. Alihahd did not want to confront Hall. He wanted to return his clothes there and leave. He wanted to be alone, unseen.

He found a fire blazing in the hearth as if he'd been expected.

Alihahd let his bundle drop onto the bed, irritated. Of course he'd been expected.

The foxhead meerschaum pipe had been left behind on the yellowwood table. Alihahd was tempted to pitch it into the crevasse. What would Hall think of *that?*

Hall would laugh.

Alihahd paced to the fire, stopped, regarded the pipe, paced. Hall was so sure Alihahd would not touch it.

Hall was right.

Alihahd touched the yellowwood tabletop with an elegantly gentle hand. He ought to pitch *Hall* into the crevasse. That was the real matter here.

Alihahd lightly pressed his palms together and wove his

long fingers together as if praying, and he gazed hypnotically into the fire. Licking tongues of flame reflected in his pale eyes.

He saw his own setkaza.

VII.   Witch Wind

The time of year came when the wind Shandee would blow for twenty days straight, from the second of the River through the sign of the Wellspring to the seventh of the Veil—nearly half of the winter. Caves were stocked with food and water, and denizens of Haven banded together for the long season. All six humans gathered in Serra's chambers to weather the storm. They were sick of each other after a few hours, sick of the walls, sick of the howling wind.

Alihahd kept to his singular schedule and intensified all his little rituals, a pretense of control and order in this helpless confinement.

And he dreamed of being buried alive.

He woke in semidarkness, the edge of a dream fading from his mind.

The sentinel from within her cave on Aerieside was beating out the hour for all the prisoners of the wind. Alihahd counted the bronze clashes. Seven. The hour of the eagles. Predawn.

Alihahd sat up on the wide mattress, finally awake.

He pulled on his boots, first the left, then the right. He went to the back chamber to wash and pass water. Serra's back chamber with its nonporous refuse drain was the reason these caves had been chosen for the humans. Itiri excreted little water; neither did they sweat.

Alihahd rubbed salt on his teeth, did it twice, spat, and came back to his corner of the bed.

He put everything in its place. He owned four changes of clothes by now, and he stacked what he was not wearing in order under the pillow. He folded his quilt, the woven blanket, the brown fur, and the silver fur precisely, in four folds, and set them on his sleeping place.

There was also a mat on the floor which was not his but had to be aligned with the crack in the floor or Alihahd was not happy.

In this small area of this particular chamber, things were as Alihahd willed them to be. All the rest was as it fell to random human chance.

When all was arranged, Alihahd stepped back (with his left foot) to inspect his niche, and he saw that Amerika had hung her mirror on the wall.

It had been years since Alihahd had looked into a real mirror and seen more than a ghost image reflected in a glass or a polished metal surface. This was a real, merciless mirror. He saw that the skin of his neck had acquired the plucked-chicken texture of old age. Tiny broken blood vessels marked his nose, and rays of new lines etched his face. He had forgotten how truly unpleasant was the look of white skin on a face—the color ancient Caucasians in their infinite elitism had termed ''flesh tone''—not the smooth marble white of the aghara Itiri, but a sometimes ruddy, sometimes sallow translucency showing tracks of blue and purple veins.

Alihahd turned the mirror to the wall. It was to become part of his ritual.

On the wide mattress everyone used for a bed, Amerika was now sitting up, her face puffy and marked with lines from the pillow; her hip-length black hair had been laced into a single thick braid for the night. She had been sleeping right beside him. He hadn't noticed.

She was looking at her mirror turned to the wall.

''Is it an instrument of sin?'' she asked timidly, childish guilt in her lovely black eyes. ''I only use it to part my hair and paint my eyes. And I only paint my eyes against the sun. I swear.''

''No, it is not sinful,'' said Alihahd.

''Why didst thou turn it over? So the spirits cannot come out?''

''No,'' said Alihahd. ''Because some faces are better not faced at this hour.''

He gazed up at the coffered rock over his head, murmured that he could have been light-years away from here if Ben had not gotten off-planet without him.

"He was not to have taken that ship," said Amerika. "The Itiri were upset. He was not to have taken Da'iku either."

"*Da'iku?*" Alihahd cried loud enough to disturb the sleepers. Serra stirred under Hall's arm, then her breath evened again. Alihahd faced Amerika gravely and whispered, "Da'iku—is that what he calls his familiar?"

"No. His sword."

Alihahd was on his feet, up and to the battened door. He brought his fist against the stone jamb. The howling wind sounded very near on the other side. Alihahd truly felt the walls closing in on him. He needed to run, to find Ben, to stop him.

"Da'iku is a Na'id name, is it not?" said Amerika.

Alihahd nodded, his fist on stone.

"Thou knowest a meaning," Amerika whispered, pulling her blanket around her, feeling a chill grow within the rock walls.

Alihahd faced the door. "It means Killer," he said.

An evil in their midst. The Na'id conscription base locked in on itself in unknowing terror; brave soldiers feinted at drafts. A presence among them like a ghost, there but not there, had them cowering defenseless, because they did not know what it was—they, the arrogant members of the Na'id conscription force who with laughing pride called themselves Mushabriqu's Press Gang. No one was laughing now. Something was here. Dammit, something was here.

Without striking a blow, the evil in their midst reduced the entire base to grasping paranoia. Without striking a blow yet. A voice inside the evil told it to wait: *Thou art one. They are many. Yet they fear thee!*

The Na'id numbers were overwhelming. This conscription force had carried off the able-bodied population of a village by force. They must be reduced before they could be fought.

I am the attacker. They defend.

The advantage was in the role chosen. The Na'id could have been a hunting party stalking a lone cornered beast on their own ground. Instead they let themselves be frightened, be the defenders, shrinking from a killer in the house.

A night of fear. Slamming doors, heavy footsteps, a flutter of wings that was here and gone, the specter of a hawk, the shadow of a sword.

174   *R. M. Meluch*

Thou canst not slay them all at once.

One had to start somewhere. Strategically.

And, after the long night, just when the soldiers began to feel relieved and foolish, they flung the windows wide, and the gentle morning sun graced the courtyard where General Mushabriqu hung by his neck from the flagpole beneath the bloody Na'id flag.

And so it began.

Layla was absently passing her finger through a candleflame, collecting soot on her skin, the warm light flickering across her rough, impish face.

Serra was seated at the table, sewing a shirt for Harrison Hall, and refilling teacups as they emptied.

Alihahd's third cup of tea sat half full and growing cold. Alihahd never finished the third cup. He always drank two and a half cups at a time. Always.

On the floor, Amerika was teaching Vaslav a pebble game.

From the adjacent chamber, Harrison Hall was snoring.

Faintly from Aerieside Itiri music spun through Shandee's howling.

Layla lifted a pendant on a chain from around her neck and held it out to Alihahd across the table. "What is this symbol?"

Alihahd picked up the pendant from her small palm and rubbed his thumb over the metal face. It was a Na'id cuneiform symbol:

"Where did you get this, Layla?"

"From a dead Na'id."

"Did you kill him?"

"There were many dead on the field. I know not which of them I killed."

"I see."

Layla pointed with her soot-covered finger. "What do the markings mean? Amerika says you know Na'id."

"It is a DINGIR. In this case it means *God*." The Na'id had adopted the Jewish/Moslem custom of not depicting God. Christians had a tendency to make God a male Caucasian.

The Na'id preferred a deity without form, without color, intangible like the human soul. "This is a religious medal."

"In this case it means God?" said Layla. "What other case is there?"

"This mark can also represent a sound in a word—*an* or *il*," said Alihahd. He marked on the table with a piece of chalk:

"There it is pronounced *ili*—literally *gods*, but this is a name."

"This is confusing," said Layla, her cheek resting on her fist.

Alihahd pointed to one symbol at a time. "The first mark is pronounced *shad*. It means mountain. These middle two are your DINGIR and a plural sign. The last is pronounced *ya*; it means *my*. So *Mountain of my Gods*."

Serra put down her sewing. The red chevron on her forehead creased. Ignoring the translations, she strung the pronunciations together in order and said, "Shad Iliya."

Layla's brown eyes widened. She pointed at the chalk marks. "That is what this says?"

Layla scowled at the markings, then methodically wiped them away with the side of her hand. She regarded the resultant smear with satisfaction. In the primitive culture of her origin, to obliterate the infamous general's name was to obliterate the man himself.

Amerika came to the table and looked over Alihahd's shoulder. "Oh. I did not see it. Write it again."

"The same thing can be written a slightly different way—without the DINGIR," said Alihahd and marked on the table again:

"This language cannot make up its mind," said Layla.

"Shad-ili-ya," Alihahd voiced the symbols.

Serra pointed. "But the middle two marks are the same."

"NINI means *ili*," said Alihahd.

"That is stupid," said Layla, and she erased Shad Iliya from existence again.

"It is an ancient language. It went through several evolutions. Humankind was then only developing the concept of the written word," said Alihahd. He tossed the chalk over his shoulder. "Anyway, it was not my idea to use it."

"It is stupid," said Layla and fastened her pendant back around her neck.

Hall stopped snoring in the adjacent cave, and Serra brought him some strong tea.

Talk switched to other things, and Alihahd toyed with a nail, using it to scratch signs into the stone wall, until Layla noticed what he had written:

"What is that?"

"Ashar Ari. Place of Eagles," said Alihahd. "All Na'id planets are called Ashar something or Mat something—Place of this, Land of that."

"You gave us a Na'id name?"

Alihahd put down the nail. "In Na'id culture, to name a place—to give it a Na'id name—is to legitimize it. The name officially recognizes this planet as Place of Eagles—that is to say: place sovereign to nonhuman aliens."

"In that case, I like it," said Layla. "Ashar Ari."

"The Na'id would hate it," said Alihahd.

"The Na'id may go to hell."

Flames raked the sky over the recruiting station, consuming the myriad dead which littered the compound blackened with blood. Mushabriqu's charred body dangled a grim banner over the blaze until the flagpole melted and fell. Explosions eructed fireballs and roiling smoke with an outrush of heat that singed the leaves on trees far away.

Beyond the inferno, freed conscript children were running into the surrounding forest. They were not Qiatte's children; those had been sent on long ago—and the nameless killer knew to where. He had been this way before.

He boarded his ship, *Singalai*, flew over the flames, and set course for the nearest reloc center, to kill again.

The caves grew colder. Snow had covered some of the solar collectors outside, and the captives of the storm could only hope it would blow off again.

To make it worse, Layla and Serra were telling ghost stories. Inevitably they came to *Flying Dutchman* and Marauder stories. Hall just listened and smiled. He relit his pipe. One of its fire-opal eyes was missing, giving the fox a winking look.

"They say that at the battle for Jerusalem the whole galaxy came to the aid of the Holy City and all the ghosts of those buried in the hills rose and fought. And they say Shad Iliya saw the ghost of a brigantine ship sail over the city. He died right after that. They say that is what killed him."

"Truly?" said Amerika, breathless and enthralled.

"So they say" said Layla. "Something got him. It may as well have been the Marauder ship."

"I saw it," said Alihahd. He set aside his third, half-finished cup of tea and did not touch it again.

"You never struck me as a teller of tales," said Serra.

"I saw it," said Alihahd.

"I saw it too," said Vaslav.

Amerika's eyes were huge. "And you were shipwrecked!" she exclaimed in a whisper.

"Very shortly afterward, yes," said Alihahd. "Although I think I was equal bad luck for the Marauder. I believe he wrecked soon after I did."

"How can you wreck a ghost?" said Layla.

"Because my luck is very, very bad," said Alihahd. "And because this Marauder was not actually a ghost. It was a hologram that a pirate used to frighten Na'id ships before he destroyed them. Unfortunately we two curses crossed each other's paths and that was the end of us."

"Did you see the Marauder?" Serra asked Hall.

Alihahd sat forward. He was interested in how Hall would answer that question. Hall said only, "I was on another ship."

A neat evasion, that one—neither *yes I am the Marauder*, nor *no I am not*. The man would not be pinned down. He did, however, admit to garroting a Na'id captain with his own

hands. He went into graphic, relished detail about it. He had
no regret. He waved his hand at the cuneiform Alihahd had
engraved into the wall. "It is written in those ancient chicken
scratches somewhere, 'an eye for an eye.' " He looked to
Alihahd for verification. "True?"

"True," said Alihahd hesitantly.

*If a citizen has destroyed the eye of a citizen, his own eye
shall be destroyed. If he has injured the limb of a citizen, his
own limb shall be injured. If he has destroyed the eye of a
subordinate or injured the limb of a subordinate, he shall
weigh out a recompense in silver. If he has destroyed the eye
of a slave of a citizen or injured the limb of a slave of a
citizen, he shall weigh out half the slave's buying price.*

"The principle, I believe," said Alihahd, "behind the law
'an eye for an eye' was, at the time it was written, not that
the punishment be severe enough for the crime, but that the
punishment not exceed the crime, which was rampant practice in those days."

"You think me excessive?" Hall asked.

"I was not there."

"You think me excessive."

"I think you excessive."

Hall sat up and moved in closer. Low, so only Alihahd
could hear, he said, "You didn't tell me you beat a man to a
bloody pulp down in the valley."

"It slipped my mind," said Alihahd frostily.

"Why are you so cool toward the idea of vengeance,
Captain?" Hall said with oily insinuation.

He was surprised to receive straight out front with troubled
countenance the answer he sought.

"Lest it fall upon me."

The drill master enjoyed his work. He had survived yet
another summons before the review board on suspicion of
excessive and brutal disciplinary measures. He had said all
the right things, admitted he was often severe with his young
charges but only to train them to survive in the field in harsh
environments, combating aliens. He said he was strict out of
concern for his recruits and that most of them respected a
tough master; however, there were whiners in every group.
The board found his explanations acceptable. The drill master
always knew what to say.

In reality, he liked to beat children. Real torture and sexual abuse he reserved for those children already on record as compulsive liars and unwilling conscripts. He had worked hard to get where he was—to be commander and not the commanded, the abuser not the abused—and he knew how to preserve his position.

He had been master of the juvenile wing of training station Alpha 4 for twenty-five years. He could handle the squealers.

But the last little girl from Qiatte had come across as entirely too credible. She had been responsible for his latest trip before the review board. It was a pity that her class was gone on to *Omonia* Station and he was unable to get back at her.

That whole class had been trouble. Qiatte was a sleepy little mining village on a grade-four planet, yet it turned out some of the most recalcitrant hellions ever to come through this training station. The reloc center always sent them here. The reloc center had very recently met with a mysterious catastrophe that killed everyone on the base—may they all burn in hell, thought the drill master. He would get no more ungovernable conscripts from *that* place.

Still discomfited over the Qiatte girl, he soothed himself with food. He ate another honey roll with tearing bites. Then he swiveled in his office chair to the water fountain to rinse his fat, sticky fingers.

He turned on the fountain, and the water ran thick red. It looked like blood.

He shut it off, but continued to stare at the red splashes in the basin. Practical joke. Sick one. Someone would hear about this.

He reached back to his desk and patted around the messy piles of records, feeling for his transceiver.

Suddenly there was a movement and a bouncing clinking as the transceiver was tossed over the drill master's head into the fountain basin.

He grabbed for it, but before he could swivel his corpulent body around to see who had tossed it, a fist closed on his hair atop his head. There came a whistling swish and a current of air on his face. He blinked his eyes shut.

Instantly, he lost all feeling in his body—except for the damnedest dizzy sensation of rising.

Upon opening his eyes, he saw that he *was* rising, being pulled up, weightlessly, jiggling and bobbing, by his hair.

His eyes shifted down to an obese body falling from its chair and spurting blood from a sheared stump of a neck. He could not scream.

The severed head remained conscious only fifteen seconds.

It was a long fifteen seconds.

Nineteen days passed and time stopped. The last day of Shandee seemed to drag on forever. Layla rapped the hourglass on the table till it broke because she said it was not moving.

Alihahd still kept Earth time—as valid a schedule as any in this sunless prison. For him the days—Earth days—numbered twenty-four and a half so far. His rituals were rigid and changeless. His patience seemed limitless, his temper ever cool day after day. He was coping best of the group.

The heat was on again. Harrison Hall took off his coat. He pulled a gold thread from the frayed lining of his vest. Without his heavy rawhide redingote one could see how narrow was his tightly knit waist and lean flat stomach. He was a powerful man.

"'What country is Jerusalem in?'' Hall threw out the question casually, all his attention seemingly on the loose threads of his vest.

Alihahd laughed with more bitterness than he had ever let show. "God knows," he said; then, "Depends on whom you ask."

Hall knew that; it was why he had asked the question—to discover where Alihahd's loyalties lay. And he received his answer: nowhere. Alihahd was not radical *anything*. His sympathies were everywhere, allegiance nowhere.

"That little shred of land on the coast has always been a hotbed of violence and contention. Whoever has it is perpetually at war to keep it," said Alihahd.

Layla was listening while she combed her hair, ripping out the snarls rather than untangling them. "If the land is so hard to keep, why does not everyone move?" she said.

"Why, indeed?" Alihahd said with a sorrowful laugh, his blue eyes watery, bright, sad, mystified. "It is God's land, you see. Everyone's religion bids him fight to keep that land."

"And what are you?" said Hall. "Religion."

There was a hesitation. "Baha'i," said Alihahd.

"What is that?"

"A renegade branch of Islam, but rather similar to the Na'id without the imperialism and without the armies."

Hall did not believe it. Perhaps—just perhaps—Alihahd was a convert, but Hall was dead certain that Alihahd had not been born into that faith. Alihahd had been in an army. He had been disenchanted with something. Baha'i was a later choice. Or a lie. Hall did not think Alihahd believed in God at all.

Besides, there had been no Baha'i at Jerusalem.

Alihahd had finished drinking two cups of tea. Harrison Hall had poured the third round. Alihahd lifted his third cup to drink, looked inside it, and froze. The cup was half full.

All color drained from his face. His lips twitched. Nothing else moved. Some part of him was shredding away behind his glassy blue eyes.

Hall held the kettle with an expression of false innocence: Is something *wrong?*

Alihahd set the cup down clattering, spilling the tea. He pushed back from the table with quaking hands, stood woodenly, knocking his stool backward, and he stumbled over it to get away. He staggered toward the doorway to the bedchamber with sightless eyes. Long arms reached for the lintel to hold himself up and drag himself through.

The others thought he had been poisoned.

Layla did not know what had happened or how, but she knew who. She turned on Hall. "What did you do to him? You did something!"

Hall opened his arms with an exaggerated shrug to say, *Who, me?* But his crescent eyes were merry, the sinuous lines of his beautiful wedge-shaped face upswept in barely contained glee.

A guttural cry came from the next room, and a crash and sounds of things being thrown and broken.

Hall had rearranged the cave.

With a groan, Alihahd hurled all the reordered jars against the walls and threw the twice-folded covers onto the floor.

Amerika and Vaslav cringed together at the table in the other room like children whose father was not well. They stared about them, their round eyes begging someone to make everything all right again.

Hall sat himself at the table, satisfied, and he took up his pipe.

Alihahd returned, shaken, stiff, his face long and frowning, bloodless. He sat at the table without a word. He clasped his big hands on the table, knuckles white, his back erect, a muscle twisting over his jaw, standing out in high relief from clenched teeth, eyelids stretched white around staring eyes, looking at no one. A muscle under his eye twitched.

He did not speak again until the days of the Witch Shandee were over.

VIII.   A Slow-Falling Star

The days of restraint enshrouded the Aerie, a somber time when the splendid warrior-priests, like drab birds in molt, put away their beautiful clothes for the thirteen days from the leaving of Shandee until New Year's Day. The air was calm and becoming mild again. Warm breath still showed in frosty clouds, but the ice on the sunlit slopes was melting at last. Spring had already arrived on the middle slopes in a haze of blue buds on the trees.

Harrison Hall slogged along a path sodden with spring mud and snowmelt; leathery green shoots of the emerald spikes braved through the ice on either side. He felt a cold trickle on his instep and knew that his old boots were finally done for. He turned his foot to find the crack in the thinned sole.

He heard a strange sound. His ear was attuned to patterns by now, and this one was not usual. He straightened and drew his gun from his belt.

The noise was a shuffling as of a sick or injured animal. Nothing moved so blunderingly on the Aerie. Quietly Hall stole over the rise toward the sound.

Over the top he relaxed and lowered his gun upon meeting Alihahd coming up the path.

Alihahd was clad in his red Chesite tunic and red boots. Hall was about to comment blithely on Alihahd's bony knees being the first sure sign of spring, but he perceived something wrong. Alihahd was smiling, smiling wrong. He leaned against the rock face, shiny-eyed and wryly whimsical. His hands flopped strengthlessly. Footprints in the slushy snow behind him wove on and off the path.

Hall pushed his gun into his belt and stepped down to take Alihahd's head in his hands. He looked into his eyes, searching for signs of fever. "What is wrong with you?" he demanded. Then he got a whiff of his breath.

Alihahd smiled. His hands moved elegantly, almost in caricature. His eyes were pale, drowned sapphires. "Mr. Hall, I am drunk."

Hall's face darkened, and he pushed Alihahd's face aside—the motion was disgust—and he stalked past him in the direction Alihahd had come, looking left and right with the sharp motions of anger—and searching.

Alihahd scrambled after him in alarm. The blundering foot tracks blazoned a conspicuous trail, and Hall would surely find what he sought.

Alihahd drew himself up on a rocky bluff and thundered at Hall's back in the most commanding voice he could muster, "Mr. Hall!"

Alihahd had once been a magnificent man and could still summon power—even drunk. Most of the orders he'd given in the past ten years had been issued in varying states of insobriety, and still had the voice of absolute command.

"Stop! This is no concern of yours!"

With insistence, his dignity slipped a degree. He took a step forward from the rise and immediately felt his vulnerability increase. "Mr. Hall!"

Hall ignored him and strode away with an angry set to his shoulders. As he neared his hidden goal, Alihahd became shrill and frantic. He stumbled after Hall. "Mr. Hall! This is none of your affair!"

"I am my brother's keeper," said Hall. "As the Na'id would say."

Alihahd scowled blackly.

Hall found the distillery behind a thorn bush, and Alihahd lunged to put himself between Hall and his lifeline. He spoke in a deep, cultured, angry tremolo, each word precise if thick. "Leave. Me. Alone."

Hall started forward. Alihahd laid hands on him to restrain him. But at the height of his strength Alihahd had never been a match for Harrison White Fox Hall. Alihahd felt a shift of balance and a sudden helplessness. *Why is he doing this to me?*

Hall threw Alihahd to the ground. He marched up to the still, ripped out the condenser tube, and threw it at Alihahd as if onto a pile of rubbish. His driving heel came down on the soft copper still pot; and honey water gushed out over the coals. Hall kicked and scattered the painfully collected stack of firewood, and smashed all the clay jars of mead on the rocks.

Alihahd stood up, indignant. "Who do you presume to be? See the lord and master of Eridani. Thou art lord and master of nothing. And not of *me!*"

Hall rounded on Alihahd and gave him a slap that staggered him; his brain seemed to ricochet inside his skull. Alihahd tasted blood. And he fought, tried to. Alihahd's blows landed uselessly, or did not land at all. Then Hall's fist drove into Alihahd's solar plexus, knocking the wind out of him, and Alihahd crumpled to the ground. Hall picked him up and set him on his feet. Alihahd leaned on him, gasping. Alihahd lifted his head and in the next breath cursed Hall. Hall hit him again, harder, in the same place; Alihahd dropped, doubled over, sick and in pain up to his eyes. Hall stood over him, hands in fists at his sides, waiting for Alihahd to get up.

Alihahd crawled to his feet. Hall steadied him, then hit him with his open palm. And kept hitting him after Alihahd ceased to fight. The blows kept falling, and Alihahd could only wonder why.

And he cried, great drunken teardrops rolling down his sunken cheeks.

The blows stopped, and Hall hauled him to an icy stream and made him kneel. "Look at yourself." Hall forced his head down to face over a reflecting pool. Alihahd resisted with a groan, trying to turn away, but Hall's hands were like a vise holding him over the sotted, blubbering face in the pool.

Alihahd slapped the water with a cry, "I am trying *not* to!"

After a useless scuffle in the streamside mud, Alihahd was pulled to the rapids. Hall grabbed a fistful of blond hair and pushed Alihahd's head under the icy cataract.

Alihahd's hands scrabbled behind his head at Hall's fingers. Frigid water filled his ears, and sounds were suddenly muffled and singing, otherworldly, like death.

Alihahd was afraid that Hall was trying to drown him. It

had been on his mind, but Hall let him up for air, then pushed him under again.

After the fourth time, Hall pulled Alihahd up by the hair to a kneeling position and searched his beet-red face. Alihahd's eyes were shut and spilling hot tears. "Leave me alone. Leave me alone."

"Shut up and breathe or you'll be sorry."

Alihahd breathed.

Hall could tell when Alihahd began at length to sober—he stopped whimpering. Hall released him and crouched back on his heels.

Alihahd, on his hands and knees, hung his head forward, water streaming down his face from his hair. "I don't like you at all," he croaked.

Hall smiled.

Alihahd knelt up, teeth chattering, his face scarlet. A dark red wet swatch patched the front of his tunic. Water drained from his ears and he could hear clearly again, and he felt the cold air as if it were blowing through his head. He brought his fingers to his eyes too big for their sockets. "Oh."

"Have you never been in battle, Captain?" said Hall.

Alihahd answered shakily, "Of course."

"Jerusalem," said Hall.

Alihahd did not answer, and Hall seized his hair and pulled him toward the water. "Jerusalem."

"I was there," said Allihahd. "If you must know, I ran."

Hall let go of Alihahd and barked a single laugh in gleeful surprise. "You deserted!"

"I left," said Alihahd. He put his hand over his eyes. "You're a sadist."

"No, I'm not," said Hall; then, "Just a little." He helped Alihahd to his feet like a doll of wood and rags grimacing from ribs that were bruised or cracked. He brushed off pebbles embedded in his purpled knees.

Hall was looking at the sky. "I think it's time to get dried and presentable, Captain."

Alihahd lifted his head in mute *Why?*

Hall pointed up.

Alihahd narrowed his too-big eyes at the daylight sky, and emotion rushed with sober clarity.

A slow-falling star.

* * *

A spaceship descended and sank into the layer of cloud that hung over the valley, billowing up puffs of the white vapor that swallowed it from view of the watchers on the mountaintops.

Alihahd went to the Chamber of the Golden Dome to be there when Roniva received her returning warriors.

Alihahd's wayward blond hair, newly dried, kicked up in wispy cowlicks. He had changed clothes to a dry gray tunic and sandals. His eyes were red and puffed, his face bruised all colors.

"Are thou ill?" said Roniva.

"He's fine," said Harrison Hall.

Alihahd's teeth clamped tight, and he stood rigid in silence.

Roniva had spoken to him directly. She appeared a harsh figure without jewels or soft colors, wearing only a muted green robe, her hair confined atop her head. She beckoned Alihahd to her with a ringless hand, and he moved around the low lattice barrier onto the dais with her. She took his arm and made him stand beside her throne. "Stay thee here with me. I shall speak through thee."

And when her two warrior-priests entered and greeted her, she said to Alihahd, "Ask my warriors why they return after a single year. What is wrong?"

In answer, the travelers unfolded a long tale of a series of mysterious attacks on Na'id installations, reports they had gleaned of a man and a sword and a hawk—and many dead behind him. The warriors had begun to follow the deadly track but never caught up with the assassin.

As Roniva listened, her face smoothed in slow-growing shock and dread, then hardened into sharp, eaglelike planes, and her long fingers closed around her sword hilt and tightened until her midnight skin paled.

Her warriors opened their arms, powerless in the face of an inevitable and unacceptable conclusion. "An Itiri."

"A Wolf," said Roniva. "A wolf that walks like a man."

"We would stop him," said one warrior-priest. "But we know not where he is now or whither he will go."

"Has *Omonia* Station been hit?" said Alihahd.

Roniva's head shifted with a quick eaglelike turn to face him. His question was curious but it seemed to have meaning. Roniva looked again to her warriors and bid with voiceless command in her burning onyx eyes: *Answer that.*

The warriors exchanged doubtful looks. "*Omonia?* Not that we have heard."

Roniva tilted her dark head up to her intermediary who spoke with a mind of his own. "This is significant?" she said.

"I think so, Fendi," said Alihahd. "There *is* a pattern to these attacks."

"What pattern?"

"They follow a path that a conscript of the Na'id might take from first capture to assignment—first to a conscription force base for classification, then to a reloc and orientation camp, then to a training center like Alpha 4. All of Alpha 4's trainees begin service on *Omonia* Station. If the pattern holds, *Omonia* is where Ben will go next."

"Ben is dead," said Roniva.

"Call him what you like, he will attack *Omonia* Station," said Alihahd. He was peripherally aware of tawny eyes studying him from a shadowed corner of the great chamber— Harrison Hall watching him talk to Roniva as an equal, a contradiction of the sniveling human wreck at the streamside.

"Tell my warriors to take a ship and stop him," said Roniva. "Take *Topaz.* Thou shalt guide them." Her face softened and she gazed up from her throne at Alihahd's bruised face and red-shot blue eyes. She reached up to touch Alihahd's chest. "And I fear I shall lose thee once I let thee aboard one of my spaceships, thou so restless to be gone."

"I shall not return if I have any choice," Alihahd admitted.

"Then I bid thee, once thou art free, leave us lost to humankind, if thou carryest any memory from this Aerie. Bring us no human war."

"It may be too late for that, Fendi," said Alihahd, thinking of Ben-Tairre loose on the Empire, on his way to *Omonia* Station.

"This I fear," said Roniva. She did not look frightened. "Go now."

"Fendi." Alihahd bowed. He turned away in a forceful motion and took long strides to the archway, the blaze of a renewed fire on him—mission, freedom, and command—and the warriors fell into step behind him, his sinister shadow

Harrison Hall at his flank. He swept out of the nine-sided chamber into sunlight.

He could not believe he was free. He was actually leaving this alien world after all this time.

He found himself oddly reluctant.

PART FOUR

TRUE COLORS

I. Rogue Wolf

As the spaceship *Topaz* broke through the ceiling of clouds into bright sunlight, Alihahd glimpsed the twin mountain crests of the Aerie gleaming with ice-glazed brilliance in the snowy sea of vapor. The ship quickened its ascent, and the great mountain became small, then lost entirely. The atmosphere thinned, cleared to black, and the *Topaz* was in space.

With his hand pressed to the viewport, Alihahd watched the blue world dwindle; then, with the jump to faster-than-light, it was all gone.

He was overcome with sudden déjà vu—the depressing sameness of starships, the isolation of faster-than-light. The familiarity of it overwhelmed. He had, for so much of his life, been a nomad living onboard one ship or another, traveling between one star or another, that coming back to this life was like never leaving it. The short year on Iry was reduced to a dream, as if it had never happened.

Free at last. Then why feeling so ill?

He knew what was waiting for him. He wished to anyone's god that Hall had not destroyed his hard-made mead.

He glowered aside at Hall, who lounged easily in the next seat, his feet up on an unoccupied seat across from him. He was puffing Iry weeds in his eyeless foxhead pipe. He wore his bandanna gypsy-fashion. His teeth flashed very white in his dark bronze face.

Alihahd wore Na'id type clothing that Amerika had made for him at his instruction. She'd expressed liking for the design; Hall had told her to bite her tongue.

There were four Itiri warrior-priests aboard *Topaz* along

with Alihahd, Hall, Vaslav, and Layla. They had a plan to intercept Ben at *Omonia* Station, take him home, and leave Alihahd behind under one of his many Na'id guises. An elaborate plan, full of contingencies, it left all kinds of openings for things to go wrong.

Things went wrong before it had even begun.

Topaz sublighted for its approach to the space station and arrived to silence.

The great plastic triple torus of the station turned in the sunless void, dark as if deserted, without ships coming or going, without radio chatter, without signals of any kind.

There was no question as to what had happened. It was only left to wonder if anyone was yet alive on *Omonia* and if Ben was still there.

The Itiri ship *Topaz* attached itself to a station lock and sealed the passage. *Topaz*'s lock opened. *Omonia*'s lock remained closed against them. The Itiri were about to blast it with their taebens when Alihahd motioned them aside. "Don't do that."

"Canst thou open it?" the eldest warrior asked.

Alihahd moved to the manual access panel at the side of the lock, keyed in an imperative code, then crouched before the sensor and waited for his retina to be scanned. "I can open any lock in the Empire," he said. They were in Alihahd's milieu now. Na'id ships were a world he knew.

Harrison Hall came to crouch at his side, his gun drawn and resting across his muscular thighs. "How about the Bel's door?" said Hall ironically in what was supposed to be a joke.

"You want to see the Bel?" said Alihahd very softly and without humor. It was flat affirmative.

Surprise rippled Hall's perennial nonchalance. The level of infiltration of the Na'id security system implied in Alihahd's quiet answer was beyond belief. That kind of clearance simply did not fall into the hands of an impostor.

Omonia's lock spun in answer to the imperative, and it released. The outer iris dilated. The lead warrior gave the inner hatch a push with his bare foot, and it swung heavily open.

From the first moment of the lock's opening came the assault of wrongness, alarms blaring, miasma of death, smell of blood.

The Itiri bounded through the hatchway like hunting cats and fanned out, listening, looking.

Alihahd followed them aboard. He had originally intended to dye his pale, telltale skin, but there was probably no one left he need deceive.

Hall shadowed close behind him with ready weapon.

They came upon the first corpses right away. The slaughter was absolute, the station corridors splattered with blood as far as could be seen.

There was a squeak from Vaslav, who had crept out of the *Topaz* and tripped over a head torn from its body, which lay several paces away from it.

The neck was not severed; it was ripped. The head had come off in the hands of someone of great strength. The wide pools of blood were not yet dry. The killer *could* have simply choked this man, or broken his neck. This was overkill, tremendous force used out of no necessity, no reason. Fury ruled the moment. The lack of control, the madness of it, was un-Itiri. It was human. The kind of thing humans liked to call inhuman.

Alihahd had backed away and flattened himself against the bulkhead, sweating, paled to ash, lips bloodless. Something darker than fear haunted the white-ringed eyes. He was shaking, his neck stiff.

Then he steeled himself in a deliberate moment. His head lowered until he was staring out of the tops of eyes that had taken on a gravelike chill. The crevices in his face deepened, his breath came shallowly as if loathing the air, and he moved away from the wall, not talking, meeting no one's gaze, sickened, dangerous. Layla did not know him. Even Hall would not approach him when he looked like that.

The Itiri themselves gave him a wide berth. In search of Ben-Tairre—if he was still in the station—they divided and glided down the corridors where they saw the blood was warmest. Sounds of life—terrified life—could be heard retreating before them—children's whispered shrieks and a desperate scrambling in the air vents.

Alihahd was eerie, transformed into someone else altogether. He was clad in the dress of an abhorred people that made him appear so strikingly one of them that it was hard to see him otherwise. Na'id square shoulders with epaulets, a tapered waist, and full, cuffed sleeves and trousers—the clothes made a hated silhouette, and Alihahd carried himself differently in them.

He opened a wall panel, shut off the clangoring alarm, and turned up the air filters, all with the throwaway ease of one who has handled such controls many times. He was in his element, and he was angry. He swept down a corridor where the Itiri had not gone, stepping wide over the bodies in his path with little pause, wrath growing with each one, and he stalked out of view with the menacing military stride of a new master taking over.

Hall chose a different route, and Vaslav came with him, afraid of Alihahd. Layla struck out on a path of her own.

Claustrophobia and carnage.

Alihahd walked the ravaged corridors, the soft *stick, stick, stick* of blood on his bootsoles sounding loud in the dead quiet. He stepped over more bodies, human bodies, then paused to kneel beside one he thought was still alive. He touched his fingers to the neck.

Not.

He closed another's eyes, rose. The mode of death this time—all down the corridor—was a long blade.

That would be a double curved sword.

Menin aeide Thea . . . He remembered snatches of a song of slaughter. *Sing of the destructive wrath* . . . It ran through his mind in rhythmic chant as he stepped over oozing dead.

. . . *that hurled many brave souls of heroes to Hades and made their bodies a spoil for dogs and carrion birds* . . .

From time to time he heard the scurrying of children. There was only one child's body in the corridor—a little girl with a gun in her hand. The rest of the corpses were adults.

. . . *and so the will of God was done.*

A pain pushed itself into Alihahd's consciousness. His jaw hurt. His teeth were clenched and the muscles in his face had been tensed into a deep, immobile frown for a long time now.

He made his muscles relax. His face ached.

He continued down the passage, paused again to bend over a gibbering victim, not sure whether she was alive or this was rigor. An Itiri would have been able to tell at a glance if the body was still giving off heat.

He had just begun to crouch down when he heard heavy running footsteps from farther down the curved passage.

A Na'id engineer came stampeding around the bend, then skidded to a stop at the sight of a tall, blond figure bending over a bloody corpse. Alihahd looked up at him, showing his white face. The engineer screamed and fled.

Alihahd stood up. His chest felt tight, breath constricted. The Na'id at his feet—alive or dead—writhed ignored. Alihahd stepped away until his back was against a door.

There were adults alive in the section. Ben always killed all the adults. The butchery was not finished yet. Alihahd held his breath.

Ben was still here.

Suddenly the door slid open behind Alihahd and he spun.

There was a movement directly before his face—Jinin-Ben-Tairre spinning with raised sword—the sword striking down on the Na'id-clothed figure in the doorway.

II. Na'id

The blade deflected down Alihahd's side in last-instant recognition, slicing flesh and nicking the bone at the point of his wide shoulder, and slashing open the full sleeve of his Na'id shirt.

Ben coiled back with his sword, and both men froze.

Alihahd gazed into feral eyes—dark pits that went down and down forever—saw all the horror and hatred in them, and all the pain.

Less a man now than a maddened wild animal, Ben stared with half-sight. Consciousness did not register Alihahd, only a white face, a white man in Na'id dress, and the sight incensed him. His breath came audible, rough panting of rage. Then he blinked, his brows tightened together. True realization penetrated that this was Alihahd standing before him—

And Alihahd was not certain that Ben would not kill him anyway.

A trickle of blood weaved down from Alihahd's shoulder, prickling at the hair on his arm, the ragged flap of his sleeve hanging loose from his cuff. Alihahd could not move, could not talk, even to save his life.

A movement behind Ben broke Alihahd's trance—a man with a gun shouldering his way through the circulation vent and taking aim at Ben's back. Ben's Itiri awareness must have failed him, for it was Alihahd who sang out, "Behind you!"

Ben dropped into a spinning crouch, drawing and firing his taeben.

The Na'id gun clattered to the deck, and the dead man slid out of the vent and flopped on top of his weapon in a heap. From the narrow passage from which he'd come sounded the hasty scrambling of a companion retreating.

Ben did not chase the survivor. He turned back to Alihahd, all his weapons lowered, his dark eyes full of wonder, wordlessly asking why Alihahd had warned him.

"I do not know," Alihahd answered harshly as if the question had been spoken aloud. His voice was thick and he was shaking. "I will assume there is a reason for this." There had to be a reason. Alihahd gave him the benefit of a gigantic doubt, but let it be known he granted this grudgingly.

Only then did Alihahd look down to inspect his own wound. He touched his cut arm and shoulder with his opposite hand, assessing the extent of the damage, which turned out to be minor. It would leave a pitted scar in his shoulder.

Alihahd turned to go. The light touch of two fingers on his unhurt shoulder stopped him. Alihahd paused, startled by the contact. He turned his head to look back.

Ben sheathed his sword and holstered his taeben. He drew his dagger slowly as if it were painful to him and held it to his own leg. In his pause, Alihahd saw Ben fighting down great fear as if he intended to cut himself. But Ben slashed open his trouser leg, and he turned for Alihahd to see.

A blue tattooed number marked his thigh, the brand of a Na'id child conscript.

Bitterness rose in Alihahd's throat. He swallowed. The bitterness stayed.

Why hadn't he guessed? Aliens had not been the ones who had taught Ben to kill. They had merely perfected it.

Shock, hatred, and all the rest of it subsided into weary

sickness. Alihahd reached back his hand and bade Ben come. "Well, let us be on."

Ben put his bloody hand into Alihahd's and padded after him on silent feet. It was like leading a leopard from the kill, blood dripping from its jaws, leading him on a leash made for toy dogs. But the leopard had abandoned his rampage and meekly put himself under Alihahd's authority.

What made Ben think he could turn to Alihahd? He could, and knew it. *So you see that in me,* thought Alihahd.

Alihahd wished someone had been there to take *his* bloody hand.

He led Ben back to the *Topaz* and broadcast three words through the space station's public-address system: "I found him."

With that, the Itiri came gliding back like ghosts. Not one of them saluted Ben. One did not talk to the dead.

Layla did. She callously saluted with her dagger. "Good job," she said and boarded *Topaz*. Ben masked reaction if he felt any.

Alihahd took Ben inside the *Topaz* to a solitary compartment, a spartan, unlit cubicle. Neither of them wanted the light. Ben walked into the cabin slowly, then circled back and abruptly offered his sword to Alihahd, hilt first.

Alihahd regarded the sticky hilt in surprise and quiet distaste. "I do not want it," he said, almost chiding. What was *he* supposed to do with it?

Ben let it drop at Alihahd's feet, withdrew in the small space, sank to the deck, folded his legs under him, and shut his eyes.

Alihahd closed the door on him and left him there. It occurred to Alihahd only outside that maybe he was supposed to execute Ben. Maybe the Itiri expected it too.

They were all mistaken.

Alihahd went back through the lock to board *Omonia* Station.

Vaslav was returning to the lock, a green cast to his face, cringingly following Harrison Hall, who carried himself with the jaunty air of a man taking a stroll on the mountain, no more affected by the mass murder of the Na'id than Layla had been. He stepped over the bodies in his path. Vaslav skirted around them.

Corners of a smile disappeared into Hall's mustache on

seeing Alihahd. Whatever grim possession had held Alihahd in its grip earlier had released him now. Alihahd looked like Alihahd again.

Hall came to stand with him, his weight casually on one foot. He swept one side of his coat open and back and tucked his hand into his hip pocket. He glanced about him for something he did not actually expect to see. "Goddam," he said.

"Mr. Hall?" said Alihahd. He pushed back the sweaty bangs stuck to his forehead, and unfastened some of the buttons of his double-breasted shirt so that the outer flap fell open. Blood still oozed from his shoulder and wet the tattered edges of his torn sleeve.

"There isn't a damned ship on this station that's flight-worthy," said Hall. "The hangars are a mess. He's blown off half the locks. He hit all the ships—including his own. It seems this was the last stop. There is no way off this station, Captain, except the way we came." He nodded through the lock toward *Topaz*, which would take them straight back to Iry.

Ben had been appallingly thorough. He hadn't even left himself an out. What had he intended to do?

"It looks like I go back to Iry, Captain." Hall sighed. "What about you?"

Alihahd hardly heard him. He was still thinking of Ben. *He wants someone to kill him*. Ben had destroyed his own ship *Singalai* because he intended to die here. Dying was not so easy sometimes. *Now begins the real horror*. Alihahd looked down at his own hands, marked how easily the blood seemed to get under the nails and stay there. He could not seem to keep it off.

"Captain?"

"What?" said Alihahd, summoned out of his thoughts.

"You coming or staying?"

The Itiri pilot of *Topaz* had come to the hatch and was also waiting for Alihahd's answer.

Alihahd frowned, indecisive and chagrined. He was off-planet at last, on familiar if ravaged ground. He could not turn back, having come so far. It was only a matter of time before Na'id ships would come to *Omonia*. Alihahd might be able to blend into their ranks if . . . there were many ifs.

Alihahd beseeched the Itiri, "Give me a few minutes."

The pilot lifted his chin. "Be thou quick."

Alihahd gave a single nod and ran toward the station dispensary. Up ahead of him all along the way he heard the furtive whispers and scuttling of a flock of preteen girl conscripts taking cover at his approach. One made the wrong move and blundered square into him. She lurched to a flailing halt, a splay of gangly adolescent limbs and distended mouth and eyes. She screamed, "Nazi!" and she sprinted away on her long legs.

No matter who said it, the sound of that epithet never failed to cut like a dull blade.

Alihahd busied himself searching through the dispensary stores for melaninic. Vitiligo was a common malady among Na'id, and their installations always had a supply of the drug. Alihahd found it and seized up the bottle of pills in his fist with grim relief. Half of his problem was solved. He could melt into the Na'id ranks as a respectable color of brown. He was not going to be called a nazi again. It was not his fault he was born blond, blue-eyed, and pasty white.

He left the dispensary and quickly made his way over the stiffening bodies in the corridors to the com center. He lifted a corpse out of its chair and sat down at the controls. He switched on the transceiver without video, and immediately received a signal from a ship captain trying to make contact with the silent space station. "This is *Sharru Sennacherib*. Please acknowledge, *Omonia*. Where is your ID signal? What is your status?"

Alihahd transmitted a voice message: "Mayday. Mayday. This is *Omonia* Station. Acknowledge, anyone."

"*Omonia*!" the woman answered as if she had been hailing for a long time. "This is *Sharru Sennacherib*. Acknowledge. What is the nature of your emergency?"

"*Sharru Sennacherib*, this is *Omonia*," Alihahd answered. "It's a disaster." That statement carefully told nothing.

"*Omonia*, elaborate," said the captain. "Are you in immediate danger?" the woman's voice was familiar.

"*Sharru*, everyone is dead. When can you be here?" Alihahd infused some calculatedly disjointed panic into his too calm, too military voice—because he thought he knew the woman, and she might recognize him if he spoke too clearly. Wide as the galaxy was, clear, deep, and cultured voices with correct speech such as his were rare.

But even with the precaution the woman's reply was tainted with curiosity. "ETA twenty minutes, *Omonia*. . . . Who is this?"

And all at once Alihahd knew her. No mistake. *This will not work*.

Alihahd disconnected the transmitter and sat back in his seat, his thick lips pressed together in frustrated thought. He could not bring himself to retreat. Not now—actually on board a Na'id station, with melaninic in his hand.

But this captain knew him; no matter the disguise, he could not slip past her.

Having the woman eliminated did not even enter consideration. Alihahd would not kill another human being, not in defense, not in war. Never again. He had sworn. Or everything he lived for was nothing.

Harrison White Fox Hall came to the com center, paused to make sure Alihahd was not transmitting, then he said, "Time's up, Captain. They want a decision." They, the Itiri.

Alihahd put his hand over his eyes, chasing down every possibility and squeezing his brain for more. So close. The same answer returned again and again, adamant. He rose, tapped Hall's arm, too disappointed to speak a word, and they ran together back to the *Topaz*.

Alihahd slouched down low in his seat aboard the spaceship, the length of his wounded arm resting flat on the armrest, his other arm flung loosely across his abdomen. Emotions were several and jumbled, fear of the Na'id twined through everything.

Was it possible for the Na'id to unravel what had hit *Omonia* Station from the tangled evidence left behind? An ungodly hecatomb; the wreck of Ben's two-hundred-year-old ship, *Singalai*; a voice calling Mayday, sounding like someone it could not be; and Ben's footprints in blood—which could be identified by the Na'id computer if he was not listed as dead. Na'id were singularly negligent in checking the rolls of the deceased. They assumed a person could not act simply because the computer thought he was dead. Someday they would learn not to be so certain.

And on top of the physical remains at *Omonia* would be the stories stricken children told of a semihuman juggernaut, of Itiri warrior-priests, and of a nazi.

Alihahd remembered all the people who had encountered him and had seen his face. There would be other stories too.

Into his thoughts Harrison White Fox Hall strolled down the aisle of the spaceship that had once been a passenger craft, and he let himself fall into the seat across from Alihahd. He slung one leg over the armrest and took out his pipe. He glanced at Alihahd with his beautifully sinister orange eyes as he lit it.

Alihahd, Hall thought, had made an extremely convincing Na'id onboard *Omonia*. Gone for the moment had been the worn-out, pacifistic, sometimes wet rag of a man flagellated with self-doubt and guilt. Left had been a soldier to be feared. Hall admitted to being impressed, and even a little frightened—as near to frightened as Hall could feel. There was considerable strength left in Alihahd. And madness.

At this moment, Alihahd was some kind of hybrid creature. He had returned to his customary docile brooding, but was still in Na'id dress, and some vestige of the commander—the mad one—lurked just below the restored calm. Hall had seen the insanity before, but not its power. And still not its source, the horrible goad from the past that drove Alihahd to heroism and despair. Memory of cowardice? Something was not right with that image.

Hall spoke between languorous puffs on his foxhead pipe. "You're subdued, Captain."

Alihahd sat up. "Should I not be?"

Hall fanned away the gray billows wreathing his head. "Where's your righteous indignation?" Alihahd was always so piously magnanimous to any human foe. He ought to be saying something eloquent for the slaughtered Na'id.

Alihahd shook his head. "No."

Hall pointed at him with his pipe's mouthpiece. "You hate them after all."

"He has a number," Alihahd said tonelessly, his gaze directed down at the deck between them.

"What was that, Captain?" Hall cocked an ear, better to hear Alihahd's soft murmur.

Blue eyes lifted to Hall's. "Ben-Tairre. He has a number. A blue one."

"That's a boy soldier, isn't it?" said Hall.

"Yes."

This was interesting. "You've forgiven him already," said Hall.

Alihahd slumped back in his seat. His shoulder hurt. "I was thinking."

"Yes," Hall prompted.

"At his age and that number sequence, he would have to have been a trainee roughly sixteen years ago. In fact, he was most likely assigned back there at *Omonia*." Alihahd wondered what they'd done to him to make him come back at them like that. "Had he remained with the Na'id, he would have been assigned to an army—in all probability to one of the three armies that fought the Jerusalem campaign. He might have been butchering Jews and Arabs and Christians for Shad Iliya instead of butchering Na'id at *Omonia* today."

"Maybe he *was* in Shad Iliya's army," said Hall.

Alihahd felt a shock, then reason returned. "No."

"Why not?" said Hall. "Could be why he hates your looks." Alihahd was blond, blue-eyed, and fair, like the infamous general.

"He was not in Shad Iliya's army," said Alihahd, a little unsure, Hall thought.

"How is it you know?" said Hall. "You left."

Alihahd paused, treading around the edges of a nightmare. He answered deliberately, almost as if thinking up reasons as he spoke; he did not *want* Ben to be at Jerusalem. "There is no red suffix on his number. He left the Na'id army when he was still a child." Alihahd's voice dropped even lower. "What they do to child conscripts is rather harsh. It washes away their past and instills a rabid loyalty. The conscripts make more enthusiastic soldiers than Na'id native-born. But the methods are extreme. They backfire sometimes. . . ."

Ben had become a Na'id boomerang. Curious, thought Alihahd, that was one weapon the Itiri had never developed.

"Revenge, Mr. Hall, I understand. Emotion is a human thing. Blind hatred I understand. It is not my place to forgive or condemn. I simply recognize it. It does not horrify." And underneath the words his eyes spoke: *That is why I can endure you, Mr. Hall.*

Then his tone changed again, became distant. "Killing for an idea. Killing for justice. Killing for the Right. That is horrifying. And that is wrong."

And killing and liking it . . . . I don't know what that is . . .

III. Ghosts

Guilt. Alihahd felt worse and worse the nearer he came to
Aerie, bringing back Jinin-Ben-Tairre—or whatever the man
was supposed to be called since the Itiri had revoked his
name. Try as he might, Alihahd could not justify handing
over one of his own kind to a race which had made Ben what
he was, then disowned him, and now presumed to decide his
fate. And, upon arrival, Alihahd stopped trying.

The Fendi Roniva was waiting for the crew of the *Topaz*
and its "cargo"—that being Ben—within the Chamber of the
Golden Dome, her attendants around her, her sword drawn
and flashing in the light of the newly built fire which crackled
in the cold hearth. The Fendi was clothed in midnight colors
without ornament in these last somber days before the new
year, and the dull gleam of the tungsten-plastic blade seemed
very bright against her dark figure. In the frigid air her breath
barely showed a frosty cloud, having little moisture in it—
and little warmth, Alihahd thought.

Roniva stepped down from the raised dais and advanced,
barefoot on the icy tiled floor, toward the captive warrior
Ben. Her black knuckles paled to brown on the hilt of her
sword. Ben himself was motionless—and his stillness was not
the contained, stored energy before an explosion of movement; it was an inert kind of stillness, motionless and nothing
more. Someone had cleaned the blood off him. His eyes were
unfocused, unless they saw inward, and Alihahd was next to
certain that this man like a pale ivory carving was unaware of
what went on around him, unaware that Roniva meant to kill
him. And as Roniva drew close to him, her sword arm
beginning to lift, Alihahd stepped in between them, barring
the Fendi's way.

Ebony skin and crimson scars rippled with the movement
of facial muscles flowing into an expression of alien disbelief, puzzlement, and impending wrath.

Then Roniva's alien face, with its too keen lines, its hairless brows, its narrow sharp nose and hard, carved cheeks, abruptly snapped to the side and she barked at an attendant, "Tell this man he is to move aside."

"No," said Alihahd, unshaken, with a quiet force that gave even the powerful Fendi pause. And he heard himself continue, almost as if someone else were speaking using his body as an instrument, "It is not your battle."

Slowly Roniva's head pivoted back so that she was fully facing him once again, her expression more astonished by degrees. She could not even talk, astounded to have heard an Earth man—to have heard *Alihahd* speak Itiri law at her.

Alihahd was at least as surprised as she, but he pressed on. "Jinin-Ben-Tairre is dead; I heard the Fendi say so. This man is a human being, the Fendi made him so. Have the Itiri a war with humankind?"

Roniva struggled for words and someone to speak them to. She would not talk to Alihahd. She presented her back to him and gave her face to her snowy owl, which was perched on the monarch's throne upon the dais. She screamed at the owl, gesturing with her sword, her voice ringing off the domed metal ceiling, "It was not meant that this *dead* warrior take all that the Aerie taught him and use it in a war that is not of the Aerie. It was meant that he go *home*!"

"The Fendi neglected to consider that perhaps he does not have one," said Alihahd coldly—to the owl.

Roniva wheeled around, her sword hilt in both hands, eyes flashing rage.

Alihahd went on unwaveringly but speaking directly to Roniva again, "The Na'id were there. This home to which he was to return may not exist anymore. This is his battle, his and the Na'id's. I thought that was permitted even under *your* rules." His tone grew bitter and sarcastic. "But then who is bound by which law seems to change at the Fendi's convenience. Is this Itiri justice?"

"Justice?" said the Fendi. She turned her head away, adamantly addressing herself to her snowy owl. "I have told this one that there is no justice here."

"Yes, I can see that!" said Alihahd and stormed away, abandoning his stand between Roniva and her intended victim, making straight for the chamber's archway with long, angry strides.

Roniva drew herself erect as a rod, extended a pointing arm after the retreating man, and shrilled, "He is to hold!"

Alihahd did not stop. Even when two armed Itiri warrior-priests stepped into his path, blocking the bronze archway, he pushed through them, buoyant with the death threat.

He was surprised to make it outside to the snapping cold gray dawn. No one had used real force on him yet. The Itiri could afford their customary patience and caution. A thin, aging Earthman would not get far if Roniva invoked her true power. Alihahd kept walking.

Under the golden dome, Roniva stood in rigid, quaking rage.

Suddenly she dropped from her frozen pose, abandoned her attendants, her intermediaries, her victim, and bolted to the arch. Pushing between the same two warriors Alihahd had passed, she ran out onto the Ledge Path shrieking after him, *to* him, "No one is given what he deserves on the Aerie! *There is no one to decide!*"

Alihahd halted. The sharpest of all thorns had stabbed into his most vulnerable point. He who led, who decided so many fates, who was law, judge, and jury, and so often wrong, he had presumed to a wisdom which Roniva never pretended to possess—to be truly just.

Mollified, Alihahd turned back. He walked to her and spoke quietly in the chilling air. "You took everything from Ben and you turned him loose with nowhere to go. He is human; he fights a human war. The odds were one against the trained military personnel of four army installations. By any measure, how can you condemn him?" Blond hair kicked across his tall brow permanently etched with deep lines.

Roniva sighed. "Ah. I should have killed him at the first, truly killed him. This would never have come to pass. One cannot separate the dead Itiri from the live human as I tried. My mistake. I should have killed him."

"That is beside the point," said Alihahd. "What will the Fendi do now?"

Roniva brandished her sword. "Correct my mistake."

"He is human," said Alihahd. He raised his voice only slightly. "As I. You kill him and we are at war—*thou* and I."

Roniva stepped backward, her sword before her as if there

were real danger from such a dissipated being. For a while she did not speak.

Then she sheathed her sword. "O, by the sun, what *am* I to do with him?"

Alihahd wondered if there was actually anything to be done. They were arguing over a man who could very well decide his own fate. Guilt, Alihahd knew, was the greatest of crippling forces. He had watched Ben change from the moment Alihahd had found him in the space station. Alihahd recognized the sudden docility come down from ultimate rage, the abrupt dive, the mind's death leap, a plunge that went down as deep as life. This whole debate could be moot.

"I could resurrect Jinin-Ben-Tairre," said Roniva. "He would be mine again, not thine, and I could do with him as my will." She meant kill him. She tilted her head slyly at her human adversary, but then she let her hard shoulders sag and her eyes soften in uselessness. "But I really have not the strength." It had taken everything she had to defeat him the first time.

"You could resurrect Jinin-Ben-Tairre and let him live," said Alihahd.

"Tell me how I could do *that*, Fendi Alihahd," said Roniva ironically.

"Your original reason for killing him was . . .?" He lifted blond brows and paused to let her remember for herself before he answered. "You feared the Aerie would make him Fendi—or so you told me. Do you think anyone would choose him Fendi now?"

"No," Roniva conceded. And with the finality of a decision, a reprieve, she said, "No." Then she startled Alihahd by reaching out and holding her palm flat to Alihahd's chest as if she could read his heart through her hand. "But tell me, wherefore this mercy to one who would have seen thee dead?"

"No mercy," said Alihahd. "To let him live with himself? I am being unspeakably cruel, Fendi."

"Ah, thou knowest not our Ben-Tairre." She reclaimed her warrior by the speaking of his name. "Thou speakest not of him." She crossed her arms and moved toward her throne chamber.

Under the archway she stopped, looked over her shoulder,

onyx eyes glinting from the shadow of her brow. "So who dost thou know who draweth his every breath in pain?"

A silent ghost of the Aerie, his head and broad un-Itiri shoulders shrouded in a hermit's hooded black cloak, Ben moved through the halls like one without a soul, having no eyes for the world around him, his sight turned inward, lost and locked there, wrestling something dark. He was half citizen of the grave already. Cold followed in his wounded steps, lapped at his shredding spirit as he struggled, parts of himself gone, parts alien, all in chaos. He drifted, mute, bearded, and strange.

Arilla shaved his face to make him appear more an Itiri, and so that he might know himself when he met his own reflection. She did not call to him down in the well where *he* was. He would come out when he was ready, when he was healed. Or he would die. Or stay mad forever.

Alihahd passed through an arcade, his gaze chancing inside a stone vault where a shaft of sunlight fell from a single tall window across the hooded figure kneeling in meditation, a sword across his knees. Alihahd knew the shape and winding of the thick muscles in tense repose beneath the black pall of the concealing cloak, and was frightened by the sight. Not the sword, but the madness itself terrified. The vision of dreadful memory tearing the powerful apart loomed, called to him.

Alihahd shuddered and passed by.

IV.   The Opal Crown

The door to Serra's cave swung in with a swirl of icy air, and a shimmering apparition in black and gold extended a long black hand ringed and sparkling in starlight. The Fendi never came to Havenside, and all those within the cave, startled by the visitor, were at once on their feet with a kicking back of stools and falling over of cushions.

Gold pendants dangling on delicate chains from many rings

were sent into wild pendulum dancing with the slow waving of the beckoning hand that was for Alihahd. "Come know us," said Roniva.

Behind Alihahd, Montserrat turned over an hourglass, and Layla whispered to Alihahd as he stood motionless and puzzled, "It is the first of the Sword."

Amerika ran outside to look at the stars, and comprehension came to Alihahd. The Sword was the first sign in the Itiri calendar. The new year had arrived, the year of the Opal Crown.

Alihahd joined the dazzling Fendi on the Ledge Path underneath the glowing field of the Milky Way. Amerika seized his hand and pointed straight up at the sky with a small gasp of discovery at a familiar occultation, a sign of the vernal equinox; and from up on the sentinels' ridges came a crash of bronzes, and from all over the Aerie rose a squalling that made Alihahd think of a den of beasts trapped in fire. But the raucous sounds were the alien voice of celebration. Out of all the caves and arcades poured rivers of shrieking, bright beings; torchlight blossomed on every terrace; and Alihahd's senses were stunned by the sudden cataract of color after the muted days of restraint. All the ledges filled with the crush of celebrants, and on various levels the lively tap of wooden instruments started up different beats heedless of one another.

Roniva now appeared very sedate in her shimmering black robe and gold pendants, standing tall and stately above the mobs of ranga that thronged the paths of Havenside. Her thin fingers closed on Alihahd's upper arm. Her hand was hard but the grip was not tight. She spoke close to his ear to be heard without raising her voice. "There are no warrior cheela this year to make a clan of the opal crown. But there is a fire. Thou shalt see."

Thou *shalt,* the Fendi said. It was not invitation; it was mandate. Alihahd yielded to the pressure of her grip.

As he was drawn away with her, he looked back to Amerika, whose hand had slid from his. He was losing sight of the little girl as the crowd flowed like water into the widening gap between them. "Are you coming?" He had to shout.

Amerika hung back, her hands clasped in her full skirts, her round cheeks burning in red blush. He could not have heard her had she tried to yell. She motioned no, her head down to the side, and she was absorbed into a gaggle of jubilant ranga to festoon the arcades with flowers and ribbons. Alihahd was pulled in the opposite direction toward the bridge, and he had to turn and watch his own step when he began to cross, starting with his right foot and counting twelve steps.

In the tempest of sound and color and firelight and motion through which he was led, one impression pounded at Alihahd ever louder like a wind brass: inhuman. As he crossed the bridge from Havenside to Aerieside, from gabbling ranga to shrieking aghara, the alien dimorphism of the species hit Alihahd in a storm wave. On one side of the abyss crowded short, stocky cherubs, bubbling in an alien speech, their skin white in the night except those closest to the torchfires, who had turned half dark. The ranga were cheerful. On the other side, the aghara, the warrior-priests, celebrated with more imperative, a desperation of bottled, forbidden energy finding release. They were resplendent in their bright scarlet, emerald, and ultramarine, colors of fire and gemstones. But all impression of humanity they had ever given Alihahd jangled against what was jumping before his eyes and blaring in his ears. The feeling of familiarity and whatever he'd sensed they'd had in common dissolved into feral howling and dancing and wild array. Alihahd pulled into himself against the fevered activity, his nostrils narrowed in aversion. Everything, down to the smallest details, suddenly struck him very wrong—the warrior's nailless fingers, their long toes, their inhumanly lithe and alabaster white bodies, their neat white teeth without canines, their hairless limbs, their gem-green eyes, and the crimson burn scars on their smooth faces.

Roniva, as if sensing fear in the tensed muscles and crawling skin under her hand, firmed her grip and led her woodenly stiff guest beyond the Aerie to a place where a bonfire blazed in a great stone pit partly sheltered by a tall, undercut cliff which hung over it to form a shallow cave. The smoking, flaming firepit was circled by savages—or so Alihahd could but regard them—bright, dancing figures wielding naked blades, screeching wordless cries, and stamping the stony ground with bare feet. It would have surprised Alihahd not at all to have been thrown into the fiery pit as sacrifice to their sun god. But at the pit's edge, he found his arm released and he was free to fade back to the fringes of the crowd, out of the fire's intense heat, into deep shadow, until he backed into the granite wall of the overhanging cliff.

He felt dizzy, wanted to leave, wanted the cold, rough-crystalled rock to swallow him up. Whether from something in the smoke or the lateness of the hour—maybe a flashback—or his own imagination run riot, a feeling of unreality like being intoxicated was overtaking him.

He saw Roniva in flames. She was dancing. Other warrior-priests followed her into the pit, leaping with the flames, becoming one entity with the tongues of fire, and tearing the last common thread that bound the two species, theirs and Alihahd's. He closed his eyes and tried to breathe without smelling smoke, and to close his ears against the hideous sounds.

The riot became louder and closer. The dancers moved out of the fire and into the shadow of the cliff where Alihahd was cornered now by their turbulent congregation, his hiding place reddened with the licking light of firebrands.

At another edge of the throng within the grotto, Alihahd sighted Harrison Hall and Layla watching the revelry, and he made his way along the granite wall toward them, proceeding in starts, halting to avoid brushing the violently writhing bodies of the dancers, who clawed the air in vicious motions of tearing unseen beings.

At last he came to stand with Hall and Layla, and a cold sweat broke out over his body. He knew he was very pale by then, and hoped the flickering red light would mask it. He swallowed.

He gained some slight strength being with his fellow humans among the savages. The Nwerthan Layla was a little barbaric herself, dressed in skins and wearing a gold-fringed shawl tied around her waist and a chain of berinx teeth around her neck, but she was not swept into the ferocious tide of the dance. She was just watching, smiling gaily with crooked teeth, a shine on her freckled cheeks.

Hall was a tall pillar of swaggering dignity amidst the maelstrom, his worn, dusty brown redingote and rawhide boots a shadow in the bright colors. He clasped his hands loosely behind his back. The ruddy light played across the dynamic planes and hollows of his wedge-shaped face surveying the spectacle, interested but removed from it, a gentle curl on his lips at some secret jest, like the master of the show. His upswept eyes were lined at the corners in merriment.

He glanced aside at Alihahd. All the muscles in the captain's face were slack but for a twitch under one glazed blue eye. He was perfectly white.

"Are you unwell?" Layla's voice jarred some life into him, but he only turned his staring eyes toward her and could not speak.

"I didn't realize our captain was so tender-hearted," said Hall, his tone bantering and curious. "It seems we have shocked his finer sensibilities."

Alihahd's eyes darted away again, back to the warriors as order was appearing from the chaos, and bedlam resolved itself into a ring with Roniva in the center. Her robe was singed, and soot dulled her glossy skin. She circled around a level platform of stones that slowly and awfully took on the image of an altar.

Roniva's barking laugh reported above the rest, with no gaiety in it, only lust and cruelty. The sleeves of her robe were torn and hung in clawed ribbons from her elbows. Thin simian forearms and spidery fingers lashed out and tore anything within reach. Her laugh extended long and rose to a shrill scream, carrying a chorus of others up with it, so high it was not a scream but a siren catching the harmonics of the rock grotto and swelling toward a skull-splitting pitch. The sound peaked and shattered again into laughter.

Hall glanced again to Alihahd, who had backed against the granite wall and stiffened into the same face of horror he'd worn in the space station, breathing shallowly as if the air itself were poison. Blue eyes fluttered but remained open, inexorably drawn to behold through swirl of black smoke the descent into the midnight of a culture, the dark elemental side of all that was noble and spiritual in the Itiri.

They were neither warriors nor priests now, but animals, all trace of civilization—even alien civilization—rending with their cries.

Their voices became an ancient chant, and out of the ring two celebrants lugged onto the altar a spiny-hulled melon looking like a quilled creature big as a pig. The two drew back into the crowd, and the chant grew louder. A sword appeared in Roniva's hands. She screamed a rapish scream; tungsten-plastic flashed in a lightning strike onto the altar and split the melon in two. The pulp oozed out red as blood in a pool of sticky juice. Roniva dropped the sword and leapt onto the altar and plunged both spidery-fingered hands deep into the spiny victim and wrenched out the stringy dripping insides and held them up toward the sky, her head thrown back, baying like a wolf creature in primordial triumph, the red juice dripping on her face and down her arms.

Alihahd ran out.

He was alone on the windy mountainside, off of any beaten track, away from the noise, when finally he stopped. He hung over a boulder, panting, groped along the rocks to a rising bank to hold himself on his feet. He'd taken a gash on his shin through his trousers. He'd run headlong in the dark without heed for his step, as if pursued by wolves.

The predator that appeared in his tracks was Harrison Hall, stepping long in leisurely pursuit over the rising ground, Layla trotting after him, two steps to Hall's every one. Layla's impish face was soft in concern and genuine confusion. "What happened? Did it make you sick?"

Alihahd took a few stumbling steps along the embankment, still trying to get away, but they followed him. Hall was grinning. Others admired Alihahd's horror of violence.

But was it violence that horrified?

Hall moved in. He leaned his hand on the rocks by Alihahd's head. Alihahd turned his face away, one hand holding onto the rocks for balance, one arm circling his stomach.

"No," Hall said slowly and smiled. "That kind of moralistic outrage doesn't come from one who's never known carnage."

Alihahd turned completely around, hugging the rocks, his forehead against stone. Hall leaned in closer so Alihahd felt his breath on his cheek as Hall spoke. "Captain, you are much too civilized."

Alihahd moaned.

Hall seized his arms and forced him around to face him.

"Leave him alone!" said Layla.

"Everyone knows that gentleness is the mark of a five-star sadist."

Alihahd lunged free and fled over the rocks, cross-cutting all the twisting paths, making straight for the Aerie. Hall's heavy steps behind him made him quicken his labored flight.

He came over the last rise to the Aerie's amphitheater, and he ran along the Ledge Path to the bridge. Even in his panic he had to stop, begin his traversal carefully with his right foot and measure and count in shaking breaths twelve steps across—with Hall hounding his tracks, sounding a false count in his ear.

"One, two, three, four—"

"Thirteen, fourteen, five, six, seven—"

Was that ten or eleven? Alihahd became jittery because he was unsure now. Or was it twelve? It had to be an even number; he was on his left foot, but he hadn't reached the end of the bridge. But he was really too close for ten. There was a galloping in his stomach; his hands trembled on the guide ropes.

He ran. "Eleven, twelve." And Hall pursued him into the blackness of his own spartan, orderly cave.

Hall paused just inside, fists on his hips. He was in no hurry. He towered, a menacing blot in the doorway, until his eyes adjusted. Enough starshine spilled through the opening to allow him to see the quarry he'd run to ground cowering within. He could hear the ragged breathing.

"You've had blood in your mouth, Captain. And the horror is, it did *not* horrify."

A sound like a swallowed sob choked from the dark, and Alihahd tried to rush past Hall to the door, but Hall was everywhere in his path. "Tell me not. Tell me not. Look me in the eyes and tell me not." He backed Alihahd up against the wall, making a cage of his arms around Alihahd's head so Alihahd could look nowhere but at Hall. Silver-blue light from the glowing Milky Way washed all color from his face and paled his eyes, which were wide with echoes of horror.

It had not even been true savagery he had fled. In the Itiri's barbaric celebration there was no pain, no fear, not even of a stupid animal. Nothing tortured, nothing killed, the expression of viciousness was all without true pain. Alihahd had run from phantoms—the mere illusion of savagery. Brutality was not what was there; it was what Alihahd saw. He had brought it with him. Hall had seen a woman splitting a melon. Wide, glassy blue eyes saw else.

Hall touched his chin lest he look away. "Tell me not."

The eyes lowered and closed. Thin blond lashes quivered, then lifted again as Alihahd's face relaxed and left off its tense trembling. The face smoothed, iced over hard, and the eyes fully opened cold, cold, cold. His demeanor was controlled, unnatural, terrifying. For a moment, even Hall was touched by dread of what he had uncovered.

Resonant voice came from great depth and grew in power. "And so, Mr. Hall, what if you are right?"

"I am," said Hall, absolutely certain. When one set out to corner the devil one had best be prepared for when he turns around. "You tell me what of it."

Alihahd's face transformed again to a third, unexpected guise, one that was inaccessible, unruffled, and sly. Hall was surprised. Alihahd was many things, but of all traits glimpsed, hinted at, or suspected, cunning was nowhere among them. Alihahd gave a very cool approximation of a smile as if to say this game was over and all that had happened up till this moment was a charade. "I think you are mistaken this time." He ducked under Hall's arm and walked away, without urgency, without any feeling toward anything good or evil.

The perplexed hunter pulled in his carefully laid snares and looked for tears that were not there, and he wondered how his prey could possibly have slipped out. Hall sat on the balustrade of the arcade, one foot up, his back against a pillar, and he tugged at his mustache.

Ranga with flowers in their red hair were dancing to a gentler music here on Havenside. Simpleminded beings, they had no demons to purge this new year. A ranga woman running through the arcade paused to hug Hall, and ran on. She was hugging everyone.

Across the abyss, Hall spied the lonely figure of Arilla dressed in brown. The fire clan of the carnelian serpent had nothing to celebrate.

A flying bug buzzed at Hall's face, and he snatched at it. He felt nothing in his closed fist, though he could have sworn he'd caught it. Slowly he uncurled his fingers to look. The bug flew out.

I had him. Hall clicked his tongue against his teeth. Then realization dawned and he slammed one fist into his opposite palm. *I had him.*

He'd been made to believe his hand was empty and he'd let his quarry go.

I'll be damned.

Hall swung his leg down from the balustrade and stood up. He *had* been right. Just because Alihahd could find it within his resources to dissemble and take on a whole new facade in his extremity did not mean that the hunter had not found Alihahd's true face, the one that belonged to his name. Alihahd had never been clever. But Alihahd could suddenly *create* clever. He was a man easily underestimated, because his capacities were near limitless.

Hall was pacing. Discovery, an accelerated chase with an ever more interesting prey with a dwindling space in which to run spurred his movements.

So mild, so civilized, compassionate to a fault, Alihahd could be naught but a savage sickened and afraid of his own soul. The Itiri warrior-priests, as civilized as he, were not beyond recognizing themselves and acting out their own barbaric roots which every race must have; no species sprang perfect from the head of a god. The Itiri expressed their barbarism on melons. They could face their baser nature, let it out Dionysiac fashion. They knew what could happen when nature was refused. It could only be locked in a brittle cage for a time. And then the breaking was unspeakable.

So where had Alihahd met his secret soul and begun to run from it? Had it been something *seen* or something *done*? Hall felt he had *done* something. Alihahd was too contrite to have been a mere witness to a relished horror.

But Alihahd said he had never fought Na'id. He said he had run from Jerusalem.

It was Jerusalem then that turned him. Sacred duty uncovered what was unholy in him and he ran.

Then which of the three Gods had he deserted? He did not seem overly attached to any one of them—not when he'd claimed to be Baha'i. At first, Hall had been convinced he was a Jew. He was circumcised at least, and he had the attitude of a martyr. But now Hall was thinking Alihahd had to be a Christian. He was too forgiving to be a Jew, too indefinite to be a Moslem. And he had the self-destructive, ox-in-yoke, virtuous servitude of a repentant Christian sinner. He had to be a Christian.

Hall *wanted* him to be a Christian.

Because there was something else at Jerusalem he could be.

V. Enemies

Alihahd walked the Ledge Path, the thawing rocks popping and snapping around him. With the passing of the equinox, the mountain had not seen the last of the snows, but the warm spells were lasting longer each time they came.

Anything above freezing felt mild now, and Alihahd was back to wearing his tunic again. He could see white, pink, and lavender blossoms on the trees in the valley, and a green-yellow haze of new leaves on all the branches. Spring had come.

He viewed it darkly. His universe was closing in.

Something nudged at his heels. He glanced down and his heart skipped in the momentary shock of the unexpected—a big dark shape, furry and alive. In the following instant, he realized what it was and he relaxed in disgust. It was a marlq.

The marlqai had been living on the mountain since before Alihahd had come. They were alien guests of the Itiri, like Alihahd himself; but he and the marlqai had never crossed paths before this. Heretofore they had conspicuously avoided each other. Alihahd did not care to be near the marlqai, and the marlqai had good reason to keep their distance from humans.

Superficially the marlqai looked like big rabbits. The size of a small sow, they had long ears, round, soft eyes, and brown fur. Their ungainly paws were for locomotion only. A cluster of slender, hairless, prehensile tentacles, usually kept hidden in a furry protective pouch in their chests, emerged in a wormy mass to perform delicate work, such as writing or navigating starships. The marlqai had a starship here. But they did not use it to leave. They preferred to remain as guests of the Aerie. Freeloaders, some would call them.

The marlq at Alihahd's heels sniffed him, muttering to itself in the marlqine speech of clicks and whirrs.

Scents were important to the creatures. They had a highly

developed sense of smell, and could impart the sensation to other marlqai through their tentacles with perfect accuracy, bypassing the inadequate medium of speech.

The rabbity nose quivered and snuffled over Alihahd's leg. Alihahd ignored it, hoping it would go away.

Alihahd had never liked the marlqai, had in fact hated them. He felt nothing now but distaste and mistrust. They were belligerent, parasitic beasts, repulsive to him for their incongruous size and their unsightly tentacles. There was some obscenity in a rabbit that size, and in the naked tentacles coming out of a furred thing so that it looked to be infested with alien leeches eating out its chest.

The sapient beings were fellow refugees of Na'id persecution, yet the rebel runner Alihahd felt no kinship with them. He regarded the Na'id aggression against the marlqai the same way the Na'id did: as rodent control.

The marlqai had no homeworld anymore. The Na'id had eradicated them from the marlqine homeworld and driven them to near extinction during another of the undefeated General Shad Iliya's campaigns. However, the marlqai who had managed to escape the purge of their native planet had quickly replenished their numbers out in their spaceships— like rats— and spread like a plague to other worlds. There were at least two dozen of them now on the mountain, most of those born here.

Suddenly, an angry drumming in quick tattoo came, along with pressure like a vise closing around Alihahd's leg, the clacking of tooth on bone and a stab of pain. Alihahd looked down, nauseated more by the sight than the pain, which hadn't yet fully penetrated through his shock. The beast had wound its tentacles around his leg and was shredding his flesh with its teeth, sounding its loud, furious rattle, red froth foaming from its mouth.

All that blood was his.

Alihahd tried to shake the marlq off, but the weight was half his own, and everything weighed heavily on this planet. The monster held fast.

Alihahd bent over and pulled, hopped, staggered to the very edge of the Ledge Path, using his hands on the ground to help him, dragging the marlq with him. At the brink, he dropped to his left knee, gripped a granite outcrop with both hands—distantly aware of boundless depth and the far-below rush of wind in a great space—and with a grunt, he heaved his right leg and the grotesque thing over the edge.

Granite bit his palms, his hold slipping with the downward yank of the marlq's weight. Still the creature held, dangling into the chasm, still whirring and drumming and chewing. It coughed red bubbles.

Alihahd clawed the rock for a better grip, and he jerked his leg to kick the marlq loose. The tentacles tightened.

Rediscovering the strength of an old fury, Alihahd held tight to the rock spur, swung his leg out, and brought it back in hard. He heard the dull, sick crack of the creature's skull on stone, and he swung out again, his muscles searing, sweat streaming down his sides and beading on his contorted face, lips pulled back into an agonized snarl, and he beat the thing's head on the stone, again and again.

Finally the drumming stopped; the tentacles loosened. The creature slipped from his bloody leg and dropped into the abyss.

Alihahd collapsed, hugging the granite boulder. His tunic stuck to his sides; drops of sweat trickled down his scalp under his hair. His leg was an unfocused mass of pain. Then came other marlqai galloping over the summit of Havenside in answer to their comrade's drumfire. They stopped at the crest and looked for their relative; they found only blood and Alihahd. They charged down the path, their eyes all arage, seeing murder.

Alihahd lifted himself onto his left leg, staggered, stumbled, then finally crawled to the bridge in swimming pain.

As the angry marlqai reached the Ledge Path with bared teeth, Alihahd's shuddery hands grasped the bridgehook, and he wheeled, rising, throwing his back against a pillar of the arcade, holding the metal barbs out toward the charging animals.

The marlqai bunched to a halt five paces away, noses twitching, eyes wary and malevolent, watching Alihahd and the hook. Muscles beneath their soft brown pelts tensed, untensed; paws inched forward. They looked as if they might rush him. They smelled weakness. The Earthman looked easy.

Suddenly Alihahd brandished the hook. They flinched. Then they lowered their heads and inched their feet forward.

They were going to try it anyway.

In an instant, an Itiri warrior-priest was standing between them, having leapt down from the higher level to block the attack. The warrior waved the marlqai away with wide sweeps of both his arms. They shuffled back haltingly before him, furtively shifting their heads to either side, looking for a chance to get past. One tried, and the warrior caught it by the ears and backed it up with the others: not roughly.

Still gripping the hook in one hand, Alihahd bent down and tugged out a long splinter of bone from his shin. He swayed, dropped the hook, caught himself against the pillar, and slid down, fingers tripping over the stone, his eyes darkening.

Then he was lifted atop firm shoulders—he smelled Hall—with his head hanging upside down, and he was carried across the bridge swaying in the wind. The crevasse swirled askew in his wavering vision. A thin smear of blood on the rock where Alihahd had beaten the marlq's head wove into view, swam out of view. The world was spinning, the mile-deep abyss at the vortex. He started to retch.

A comfortingly familiar voice growled, and he felt its rumbling vibration beneath him. "You vomit on me, Captain, and I'll drop you." It *was* Hall.

Alihahd spit up, gagged on it. Hall did not drop him.

At the end of the endless, upside-down journey, Alihahd was laid down in the cave of the physician, who began to tap numbing needles into his pressure points to deaden the pain, but Alihahd saved him the trouble by losing consciousness.

When Alihahd awoke, he did not know where he was. He had seen this cave before, but he did not know it now. He heard Roniva's voice somewhere outside, but he did not know her. He did not know what planet he was on. There was pain in his leg. He did not know what it was from.

He rose to rest on his elbows, his head clearing. From the distance he heard marlqai drumming in response to something Roniva was saying. He remembered.

He looked down at his throbbing leg. There were stitches in it. Stitches. They had *sewn* him shut.

There are stitches *in my leg!*

It had never occurred to him to wonder how primitives closed a wound without pseudo-skin and adhesives. The stitches struck him as absurd. Then funny. It was the natural sequence to being attacked by a giant bunny-rabbit.

His leg hurt to look at. It was discolored purple-red and splashed with the orange stain of a healing herb. Some flesh was missing from his calf, and his shinbone dipped in where pieces had splintered off. His ravaged skin, held shut with zipper-tracks of sutures, was puffed up with outrage but not infection.

He still wore one boot. The other lay on the floor, shredded and caked with brown blood.

Alihahd sat up, swung his legs over the side of the cot, and rose to stand on his left foot, the ball of his bare right foot resting on the cold stone floor without weight on it. The deepest wound in his calf oozed a little. His head throbbed—or perhaps it was only echoes from his leg. Everything felt veiled in a haze of pain.

His mouth was dry and coated with a film; his throat burned acidic. He hopped to a clay storage jug filled with cool water and drank. Then he hobbled outside to the open terrace of the second level of Aerieside. The cold air cleared his senses and swept away some of the misty ache.

He heard Roniva's voice again.

Moving along the narrow path of enameled cobbles at a painful hop, he followed the sound, steadying himself with both hands on the mountain's south face .

He came to where the path turned in to the natural amphitheater between the twin crests, and he saw the marlqai, across the fissure on the first level of Havenside, being asked to leave.

Roniva was bedecked head to foot in gold, and she blazed in the meager sunlight. Her hair was twisted into an intricate crown. A cheela held her familiar, and two other warriors stood with her.

She did not address the marlqai directly. She did not even face them. She was angry.

No one had ever been asked to leave Iry.

It was not an unreasonable thing to ask. The marlqai owned a ship; they were able to leave at any time. They simply had not cared to go. They still did not want to. They wanted the Itiri to kill Alihahd instead.

Through the warrior-priest who was translating the alien clacks and mutters to Roniva, the marlqai insisted that Alihahd must have started the fight. Marlqai never attacked unprovoked, while humans, in contrast, had a history of wanton aggression against the marlqai.

But all witnesses had reported that the marlq in question had made the first hostile move.

The marlqai whuffled and chittered insinuatingly that all the witnesses were humanoid.

Roniva whirled on them before her interpreter could translate. She understood their language after all. Her teeth flashed white, and she spoke to the outsized rabbits directly. "Get out!"

The creatures hopped back in concert. Then they apologized for their blanket slander against humankind.

Roniva answered coldly through her intermediary, "Tell them I accept. Tell them also to leave."

The scene left Alihahd shaken rather than vindicated. The marlqai shot baleful glances at him across the rift as they prepared to go. What they saw in their turn, if they could read human faces, was madness in the staring blue eyes with white all around. Alihahd's facial muscles stiffened till they trembled.

An old specter loomed. Another break in utopia. Sanctuary was cracking and he could not hold it together.

Someone came to his side. He did not look, did not need to. He knew the pony-trot step. He could not face her.

You are not safe anywhere. No matter how far you go, how fast you run. Your furies will find you. There is nowhere to hide.

"They should have made me go," he said from deep in his chest. "I do not belong here."

Amerika's voice was all hurt disappointment. "You still hate it here."

Alihahd wrapped his hand in her hair and rested it at the nape of her neck in a fist, with great restraint and care, as if the alternative were to strangle her. "No,' he said softly, more to the mountain than to the girl. "I should like nothing better than to stay here forever."

Harrison White Fox Hall changed. As the dusk deepened into night, something that started as a gnawing thought grew inside and transformed him. Serra watched in alarm. Something boiled up to a level just short of open violence. She saw it through his eyes. Tiger's eyes. He terrified her.

But the dangerous eyes were not seeing her. They had turned to some inward vision and he paced, prowling in some place other than here.

When he brushed past her and his attention flickered momentarily to recognize her, he beheld her with startled impatience that seemed to demand, *What are you doing here?*

Finally, he stalked out and went to the isolated cave where he stayed when Serra bled.

A little while later, Serra ventured up to bring him some tea before she went to bed, but she turned back at the door.

He was just sitting there polishing his gun.

Hall hummed snatches of a battle tune, rubbed a soft mhoswool cloth once more over his gun, checked the sight, and holstered it. He felt a vigor he had almost forgotten in the months of tranquillity. The exhilaration of hatred.

The same puzzles had been running through his head over and over all day.

Marlqai do not attack unprovoked.

Marlqai have long memories.

Hall could read people well and had trouble admitting when he was wrong. His reluctance to back down had blinded him for too long. It was time to make amends.

At first, he'd had Alihahd figured as a onetime coward. He knew Alihahd was a man with a past to be made up for—so moral and self-effacing, with the righteousness of a reformed sinner. It was the kind of self-hatred borne by one who had been in battle and run.

But no. There had been something wrong with that idea from the beginning.

Alihahd had been *someone* before he was Alihahd. He was not just one of dozens of small cowards who ran at the moment of truth. There was fear in him, true enough. But there was also a streak of sturdier, crueler stuff. And there was blood on his hands, Hall knew that now despite the denial. The mistake had been in assuming that the man had either run or made war. Hall had forgotten that one could do both.

Alihahd had not run—not until *after* it was over.

That was his sin.

He had stayed and fought. And won.

*   *   *

Dawn's longest rays slanted through the door and cast a warm yellow patch on the cave wall by Alihahd's bed.

He sat up, sick to his stomach, and brushed the sleep from his eyes.

He checked his wound. It had scabbed over quickly and cleanly and hardly swelled. He put his fur-lined boot on over it and tried to stand.

If he did not flex his right ankle and foot at all, and did not put his full weight on it, he could manage to move around. He went outside, limped up the mountainside, and found a place to pass water, steam from it rising in the frigid morning air.

He took a walk at his awkward gait over the now familiar mountain, though it was painful, for he had a sense that this would be the last time.

Around him, spring was unfolding in earnest. Winter-born mhos cubs mewed in their burrows under budding thickets. A triller tried out its notes as the rising sun softened the brittle air. Underfoot, green shoots thrust up from the hard winter ground and peeked through the dead tatter of last year's brown grasses.

Alihahd sensed the gun at his back before he saw it. A voice sounded behind him. Hall's.

"Alihahd."

VI. Leopards

Alihahd stopped, rooted to the spot. Never had Hall called him by his false name, and the voice was ironic and deadly.

Slowly Alihahd turned. There was the gun, and it was Hall's. Tiger eyes loured behind the barrel. Alihahd returned the gaze with no emotion at all, only weariness. He turned his back again and limped without haste at his same painful, stumbling pace up the grassy scarp, and he walked away.

*   *   *

Hall lowered the gun. He'd had his sights on Alihahd, finger taut on the trigger, until he disappeared over the rise. Now Hall stared in disbelief at the empty space where he'd been. Did Alihahd think he was calling a bluff? Harrison White Fox Hall was not bluffing. He was about to march over the rise after the awkward figure and have it finished, but something was holding him back.

Instinct.

There was something confusing here. Hall could swear Alihahd comprehended the danger he was in. Hall had sensed some fear, seen tension in his shoulders and the muscles of his back braced and waiting for the shot. Alihahd did not disbelieve the death threat.

Yet he had remained so utterly unresponsive, offering no defense. Was that strategy? Did he think passivity would earn him pardon? No. Hall thought not. Alihahd was not so deluded. And then Hall realized the answer was right there.

The man wanted him to shoot.

The rains came, freezing at night into icy sheets that did not always melt in the days. Alihahd had not come back to his cave.

Alihahd had wandered far from the Aerie, slowly, lame and aimless. He did not take shelter, save to seek out the quiet airpockets where the winds would not beat him. He slept in the rain. Then the ceiling of the world lowered as the sun began to set; what was left of the clouds, after the long rain and high winds dissipated them, sank with the cooling air and settled themselves around the mountain peaks and wrapped everything in damp, blinding whiteness. Alihahd could not see past his hands; so he sat in a wet grotto and waited, chill seeping into his bones.

By nightfall, the mountain peaks surfaced free of brume, and the sky was cold and icy clear. All below him the sinking blanket of clouds looked like an arctic wasteland faintly sparkling in the starshine.

The wet ground began to freeze. Alihahd took a few steps into the open and slid a little on the slippery surface. He recognized no landmarks in the jagged black crags that loomed around him and wracked the horizon. He was alone but for a pair of moving lights—the eyes of a starving meeger aprowl at night.

The wind had stilled; the air was keen. Alihahd's breath drew in, sharp and cutting, feeling of ice crystals in the air. The temperature had dropped steeply since the cloudbank had sunk. It was too cold to stop moving, and dangerous to sleep, but that did not sound like a good enough reason not to. Alihahd did not care, caught in a powerdive that seemed, once begun, to have no lower limit.

Morning came gray. Another cloud layer had formed far above, and the mountaintops were isolated between the two, cut off from both ground and sky in some elsewhere place, a limbo.

The black-hooded warrior came upon the Earthman face down on the frozen ground.

Alihahd unstuck his eyelids, opened them a crack, and focused on the broad, scarred yellow feet next to his head. Painfully, he raised his head and looked up.

Ben's black-shrouded figure stood mapped against a bleak sky, at one with the mountains' stark gray solitude. Broad shoulders were slightly forward, his powerfully thewed arms crossed, his shadowed head bowed under the hood. It was said his mind was gone, that he'd nearly died. And still he hovered between life and death, retreated into hooded silence till something would decide things one way or the other.

Ben regarded the half-frozen Earthman curiously.

A bird cried in the raw air.

Ben uncrossed his arms and lowered his hood. "Should I summon a healer?" he said.

"Absolutely not," said Alihahd. He sat up on the ice and touched his numb fingers to his forehead gingerly, as if it might split.

A man with a piece missing, or parts that did not fit, Alihahd had too much conscience for his position, too much ability for his will. He lacked enough instinct for self-preservation, had too much for a man who wanted to die. If only he did not have a conscience he would be fine. He would also be the greatest monster the galaxy had ever seen. As it was he was merely close.

He sighed in sorrow. He was lost. "I really don't know what to do."

Black bangs fluttered over Ben's low forehead in the chill

breeze and brushed at the red scars on his cheeks. "Thou might try getting off the ice."

Alihahd held his blue fingernails out before him, frowned, nodded, all in slow motion. "Very practical," he said. When the long view was too overwhelming, look to the small and immediate. That much he could cope with.

With leaden slowness, he brushed off some of the crusty white snow that coated strands of his hair. His tunic was stuck to the ice. He pulled it free and rose stiffly. It was difficult to stand. His joints seemed solidified. He could not feel his toes, nor his ears. He ached, weary from shivering, but he could not stop. It would be so easy if he could die.

Then he realized he could arrange *that* very simply.

Sardonic laughter filled his thoughts. *This will be quick.* He would be too cold to feel the sword stroke. He faced Ben. "Do you know who I am?"

"Yes."

Belief drained away. Alihahd was dumbstruck. Yes? *Yes?* His neat and certain scheme fizzled out. How was this possible? "Since when?"

"Since first I saw thee," said Ben.

Alihahd remembered the murderous fury in the dark eyes. It had been recognition. *And yet I live?*

Alihahd shook his head. He stared at the young man. He should not be here. He should not be talking. Last time Alihahd had seen him he had been beyond retrieval. Yet here he was.

Ben had turned his back to the breezes and was looking at Alihahd over one massive shoulder. There was a mildness to his mood. Black eyes were neutral despite their fierce narrowness and the oblique angle of his brows and three angry red broken lines on his cheekbones. The ring of the carnelian serpent shone like a drop of blood on his finger. There came the thin sound of the kestrel's cry as it rode the winter air high overhead.

No longer angry; no longer mad; no longer even human. Ben had become truly alien.

Alihahd denied what he saw. There was an ancient expression. "Leopards cannot change their spots."

Ben considered this. He answered with quiet dogma, "Leopards do."

Alihahd echoed softly, "Leopards do." He gazed up at the sunless sky. "One would think there would be hope for me then, wouldn't one."

VII.   Colors of Treason

The hide cover over the cave mouth lifted aside with a gust of cold air, then dropped shut again. Harrison White Fox Hall, reclining shirtless and barefoot on his bed, looked up, his eyes heavy and narrow as a sated tiger's.

Alihahd stood in the entranceway.

The small cave was hot. The heat was an assault on Alihahd's eyes, which began to water and kept closing, wanting sleep. His nose thickened and began to run. Coming in from the outside glare, the cave was very dark; he could hardly see Hall, the faded walls, anything but the reddish-orange glow from the low hearth. His voice was deep in reluctance, underlaid with embarrassment. "Mr. Hall."

"Captain," said Hall from his bed, low and warm— physically warm if a sound could be so.

"I am cold," said Alihahd.

"Did you come for help or to be shot?"

"Shoot me."

Hall smiled, shook his head. He swung his long legs over the side of the bed and sat up with a grunt. "Come in." He stood, took a towel from his yellowwood chest, and crossed to Alihahd, who was not moving. Hall brushed some of the snow and water beads off his darkened blond hair. "Whistle."

"What?"

"Do it," Hall ordered.

Alihahd tried to round his rubbery purple lips. He

puffed out toneless rushes of air, then, barely, a discordant whistle.

Hall's languid eyelids raised slightly in surprise. "I am afraid I think you will live." He pressed the towel to Alihahd's wet hair without rubbing.

Alihahd closed his eyes, felt Hall's hot breath on his face that seemed very *fat*.

"Take your clothes off. Get in the bed." Hall unclasped Alihahd's belt with a tug and let it fall at his feet.

Teeth chattering, Alihahd pulled his ice-stiffened tunic over his head and limped to the bed. His fingers would not flex to unlace his boots, so he just sat, shaking. Hall put a heavy, coarse blanket around him, and took his boots off for him.

Alihahd's right leg from heel to knee was a solid bruise, but, protected by the thick fleecy boot, the wound was healing, even though lower down his toenails were blue.

Hall put more fuel on the hearthfire, then crawled into bed with Alihahd under a heap of blankets. Hall's hot, dark skin raised in gooseflesh at the touch of Alihahd's own clammy skin against him. He pulled the covers over Alihahd's head, which lay at his shoulder. It was like being in bed with a corpse—a very, very, cold corpse—one that would not stop shivering.

"Ever try to kill yourself before?" said Hall.

"Several times," came the murmur at his chest under the covers. "Have not gotten the hang of it yet."

"I guess not."

Hall dozed on and off over the hours. Alihahd kept moving, jolting him awake.

After a time Alihahd began to thaw and regain feeling. His toes itched fiercely. Clearing nostrils filled with the scent of straw in the mattress and scent of Hall.

Alihahd lifted the covers away, moved to the edge of the mattress, and shakily placed first one foot, then the other on the floor, and he stood. Hall seized his wrist. "Where do you think you're going?"

Alihahd mumbled—he didn't know where he was going—"This is not done where I come from."

"They eat people where you come from," said Hall.

After a dumb pause, the full significance hit Alihahd and

he yanked free of Hall's grip and searched for something to wear. He almost bolted out into the icy night naked, just to get away from Hall—no, not really Hall, from himself, the one person above all he could not bear to face.

But why else did I come? Alihahd thought with despair, one of those undeniable truths that shrank from the light.

I knew. I know him. He started to shake again.

He'd come to be destroyed.

He heard Hall's sardonic laughter echo off the close walls. "Nazi."

"You are saying that just to anger me," said Alihahd, trying his best to ignore him.

"Succeeding too," said Hall, and he sat up. "Hey, nazi, you looking for something to cover yourself?"

He didn't mean clothes. The tone was much too insinuating. Alihahd turned.

Hall held up Alihahd's container of melaninic pills. Alihahd hadn't seen them since he'd taken them from *Omonia* Station. He'd assumed that he'd misplaced them, but he should have known that he hadn't. He valued them much too much. He tried not to let his horror show; maybe Hall would put them down.

Hall pitched them one by one into the fire. The precious little pills sizzled with tiny sprays of orange sparks. Tawny eyes slid from the fire to Alihahd's stone face. "Oh, don't pretend you don't care." *Phhht* went another pill. "Here, do you want one?" He held one out, then let it drop in the hearth. *Phhht*. "I'm going to burn them all." *Phhht*. "So you may as well fight me for them."

Alihahd trembled. Blue eyes were wary, on the brink of their mad aspect, watching his hopes for brownness and normality go up in orange sparks.

Phhht.

Then Hall grew bored with his game and made to spill the whole bottle into the flames. Alihahd lunged.

The pills were in the fire as Alihahd grasped Hall's wrists. "Too late!" Hall laughed.

"Damn you," Alihahd said, quaking. "God damn you."

"Ah. Ah." Hall said tauntingly and opened his fist. There were three pills left. Alihahd snatched for them, and Hall snapped his hand shut. Alihahd tried to pry his fingers open, couldn't budge them, drew his mouth down and bit Hall's hand, hard enough to draw blood.

Hall roared and pushed his fist into Alihahd's face. Alihahd reeled back, blood on his lips. "Well, that's nothing new," said Hall, rubbing his hand. "Go on and lick it."

Alihahd spat in Hall's face. "Sadist."

Hall wiped the blood from his eyelids. "Not half so much as you are."

Alihahd's wan face paled.

"Yes," said Hall. "Come on, now. I have three pills left. You've killed before, what's stopping you now? I swear, as I live, I will burn these. Why don't you come get them, and have some enjoyment of it while you're at it?"

"I do not want to hurt you," said Alihahd. The twitch returned under his eye.

Hall drew a long switch, too green to be kindling, from the firewood pile, and he struck Alihahd across the face with it, raising a red weal on his cheek. Alihahd flinched back in pain and startlement.

"Why not?" said Hall. "You ought to." He hit him again. "Fight me. This gentle son of a bitch is not who you are." He lashed him again, and Alihahd cringed under the stinging whip, and edged, doubled over, toward the bed. When he was near enough, he suddenly uncurled and seized up Hall's gun—Hall had left it by the yellowwood table—and turned it on Hall, threatening. The blows stopped. Something shifted behind the blue eyes, some veil lifted; and there was an insane lucidity upon him, cold, and aware, alive, capable— and reveling in bloodthirst.

"Ah, there he is," said Hall. "The man I wanted to talk to."

And he called him by name.

The cold shattered and crumbled. Alihahd threw the gun away from him and screamed, in Na'id, "Ili! Ili!" *My God! My God!*

Hall dropped the remaining pills in the fire. "Well, hell," he said.

Alihahd woke, pushed away the covers. Alive. He was surprised.

He looked aside. Hall was awake, his eyes shut, resting

quietly. His foxhead pipe sat on the yellowwood table; both opal eyes were gone. Morning light lined the hide cover of the cave that was still warm and stuffy.

Alihahd cleared the phlegm from his throat, brushed fine salt from his eyelids, let go a sigh.

Hall gave him a tap that was a demand for comment.

Alihahd recited, "For I am a shining being who lives in light, who has been created from the limbs of God." A pause followed, then a derisive sound in his throat.

"That Na'id?" said Hall.

"Yes. How glorious humankind." He sat up. "Might I have something to wear?"

"Yeah," said Hall, reached over to a drawer, pulled out some things, and let them drop on Alihahd.

Alihahd rose unsteadily to his feet and dressed. He touched the welts on his face. "You bastard."

Hall gave a one-shoulder shrug.

Alihahd walked to the door, faced back. Hall lazed in the bed, not ready to stir yet. Alihahd said, "It would have been easier, Mr. Hall, if you had killed me. Then I would not be wondering what I am to do next."

Hall waved his hand idlly. "And put you out of your misery? What kind of avenger would I be then?"

Alihahd stepped outside to the bracing cold air that stung his sensitized skin and turned his breath to crystalline clouds.

He went to his own cave to wash, then to Serra's for tea. Serra put something herbal on his welts. She did not ask where he'd gotten them. Alihahd had never seen any marks on Serra. He'd seen bruises on Hall. Serra threw things.

Alihahd held the hot cup between his hands and let the steam unclog his nose. He felt soggy, like the muddy gray mass that was left after pouring water on a bonfire. At the same time he felt light, as if part of him had burned away, no longer weighing him down or giving off choking smoke and sparks.

He went to the door and gazed out, leaning forward with his left hand on the doorjamb, his arm straight, his weight off his bad leg. The tea warmed; the cold air revived. He took no long views, taking each instant as it came, looking no farther than his nose. That was the safe way to go. His furies had broken their leashes and attacked with all their merciless savagery, and now sat in a corner, all snarled out, unchained, but doing no more than glare at him, snuffling, not biting.

He had not changed his spots. He guessed he might as well claim them like bastard children.

After all, they are my spots.

An outcry of eagles drew him out of the cave. Others of the Aerie, ranga and warrior-priests, came out to the ledges and terraces to look at the sky. A roar on the horizon followed the flight of four low-flying starships, colored electric blue and vivid red, making a low recon pass over the valley.

The next pass would bring them directly over the Aerie.

Hall came out to the ledge and lifted his beam weapon and took aim along the predicted flight path and waited.

The four ships returned, blazing twin symbols of Galactic Dominion/Human Supremacy. As they pulled up over the mountain they showed their designations: X99, X37, and X24. Alihahd could not see the other but knew it was X48. He reached over and rested his hand on Hall's stabilizer. "Those are mine," he said. Then he clarified. "Alihahd's. I never thought they would come looking here."

"Thou must have been a great leader." The voice was Jinin-Ben-Tairre's. There was a question in his tone, and tentative respect for someone who just might be his better— for all his sins and weaknesses—and an unspoken *Shall I follow thee?*

Another admirer, one who had seen black depths and the darkest side of his own nature, this one, of all of them, knew what he was admiring. That kind could not be shaken. The rest of them worshiped a graven image.

"Some people were under that impression," said Alihahd.

He turned away and went back inside Serra's cave. Hall leaned in the doorway behind him, his arms crossed. "Well,

Captain, since you are alive, what *are* you going to do next?''

Alihahd picked up his cup where he'd left it. ''I am going to finish my tea.''

PART FIVE

JERUSALEM FIRE

I.   Rebel Ships

The four starships X99, X37, X24, and X48 had come to rest far from the Aerie on a high narrow plateau wedged between a mountain and the River Ocean. They were Alihahd's ships, but Alihahd was aware that it had not been rebels who had sighted him and the Itiri at *Omonia* Station. Na'id had seen him. It should have been Na'id who came looking here. And Alihahd could not be sure that it was *not* Na'id who had come. There was nothing to say that the four starships could not have changed hands in the past year. Alihahd would do well to identify the ships' personnel before going to them. Jinin-Ben-Tairre sent his familiar ahead to the plateau where the ships had landed and their crews had camped. The kestrel returned screaming.

"The bird sayeth they are Na'id," Ben told Alihahd.

Alihahd absorbed the news with little expression. "Even if they are mine, they are supposed to look like Na'id," he said.

"The bird is not bright," Ben conceded.

The bird squawked.

The only thing to do then was for Alihahd to go and see for himself.

On the far side of the mountain from the starships' encampment was an Itiri village on the inland plateau two kilometers up and twenty-five degrees Fahrenheit cooler than the coast. Here Jinin-Ben-Tairre brought Alihahd aboard a primitive airplane that would be beneath the notice of a starship's scanners. Layla, Harrison Hall, and Vaslav had come as well. They stepped out of the plane in sight of the Itiri village. Its low white buildings, washed golden in the light of the morning sun, were clustered closely along stepped streets, their rooftops mostly flat, as they would be in a place where it rarely rained, or domed mudbrick for lack of timber.

"It looks like Jerusalem," Alihahd murmured.

Vaslav spoke at his side, impressed and intrigued. "You've seen Jerusalem?"

Alihahd took a breath. "I saw it."

"Before or after the Fall?" said Vaslav.

"Both."

The boy paused, then proceeded cautiously, "You saw it twice?"

"No. Once."

Vaslav was in awe.

Alihahd spread his hands, conjuring a picture, his gaze far off. "This is like the Old City. The new city goes on and on over the hills. The slopes were choked with gray limestone blocks of apartment buildings, office skyscrapers, synagogues, churches, mosques, everything of all eras. The Old City was the part the Bel wanted untouched. The rest was expendable, if need be . . . they didn't know that. . . . She burned. All night." He stiffened with an involuntary shudder. "Men and women killing men, women, and children . . . they would not stop. . . .

"There were three armies. The 27th, the 9th, and the 34th." He pointed at the horizons around the village. "The 9th and the 34th had been there for years. The 27th was there to end it. . . ."

Vaslav whispered, "Where was Shad Iliya?"

"Mount of Olives," said Alihahd. "Small for a mountain. No olives. Many graves."

And he described the battle in detail, every tactic. It was a long tale, but no one interrupted. They did not notice the time passing. Alihahd continued, chillingly photographic, detached and impassioned at once, to the end.

His wide, gaunt shoulders slumped, and he broke from his near-trance. "Jews are the most tenacious people in the known universe," he said tiredly. "You can burn, flay, trample, enslave, outlaw, boil, and eat them, and they remain Jews. They bewilder and humble me.

"And Arabs. They died in droves and still they came—the

ones who did not turn and run at the first shot. Those who
stayed were the ones who died all night long. They would not
surrender.''

Vaslav was trying to pinpoint what was odd about Alihahd's
account. For the most part it had been a cold, harrowingly
factual replay of events. But what was wrong?

"I thought you said you never fought Na'id," said Vaslav.

"I did not."

And he had not said what *he* had done in the battle, Vaslav
realized. But obviously the man had been there, in the middle
of it.

And then Vaslav knew what was wrong with the story. It
was the point of view—where he must have been to have
seen the battle that way.

Mount of Olives.

Alihahd prepared for his hike down the mountain. He
would approach the ships' camp on foot to see who had come
looking for him before he made his presence known. Layla,
Hall, and Vaslav all insisted on accompanying him; they
would not be left behind on Iry. Jinin-Ben-Tairre was staying.
"I shall wait here for you three days," he told the humans.
"Then you are in the hands of your own kind."

But which kind are they? thought Alihahd.

His gaze locked briefly with Ben-Tairre's. Then the warrior lowered his eyes to his own rag-tied feet. A soft black
forelock fell across his brow, and Alihahd thought he suddenly looked very human. Alihahd felt he ought to do something, say something.

*We have the same soul, you and I. The blood-soaked
wretched of this war.* But neither of them was the demonstra-
tive breed. They let each other go without a word or gesture
to say there was ever any bond between them.

Alihahd and his companions started out. It was to be a
steep and brambly trek down. After the dry air of the mountains the moist lush forest of the windward slope was unbear-
able to them; and they needed to be on guard against a whole
different set of hazards in this lower country.

They had not gone far when Layla cried out, "Sail snake!"
And she pointed up.

Hall grabbed Vaslav and pulled him down; Alihahd and
Layla dropped; and the four of them crouched into the under-

brush as a long, undulating, leaf-green reptilian body glided through the treetops.

The snake passed by without noticing them. The humans stayed in hiding until the inevitable mate appeared and passed over as well.

Complete thy journey before nightfall, Alihahd had been advised. *Sail snakes see heat. In the dark, thou wilt not see them. Thou art too big to eat, but it may strike before it realizes thy size.*

Alihahd stood up. This would prove to be a very long walk.

"Why did they land the ships down there anyway?" said Hall, grumbling. The interior was much cooler and drier.

"Must be my people,". said Alihahd and pushed his way ahead through a thicket of willowy saplings. "Na'id plan better."

Alihahd lost his bearings. *How long has it been since I've had to deal with a tree?* His clothes were tough but breathable—sturdy trousers and a dolman-sleeved shirt with its drawstring waist and cuffs loosely tied—but still they stuck to him. The moisture that slicked his skin had nowhere to go.

A leafy branch slapped his face. He pushed it away and tried to find the sun through the verdant screen all around him. *Which way?*

Down. That much he knew, anyway.

He'd become separated from the others and was about to call out, when he heard shooting—fire and return fire—more than three.

He bounded through the underbrush with clumping leaps, favoring his right foot. He broke into a clearing—

—and came face to face with a Na'id lieutenant.

II.   Return of a Legend

Alihahd and the Na'id officer pointed guns at each other and did not shoot.

The dark young lieutenant gaped and slowly shook his head in disbelief and denial.

Alihahd knew what that look meant, and he felt sick.

The Na'id's expression hardened, and he took aim. Alihahd did not move; only stared up the barrel in helpless horror.

There was a shot.

The Na'id fell forward, the back of his blue uniform shirt purpled with blood; and behind him in the woods stood Harrison White Fox Hall.

Hall tramped out of the underbrush and came to Alihahd.

Alihahd swayed on his feet, leaned toward Hall, who grabbed him and steadied Alihahd against him.

Alihahd pushed away, staggered to the body, and fell to his knees. He turned the youth over, brushed black hair off the paled face and out of the open black eyes. He touched the chest that was warm but unmoving.

"Know him?" said Hall.

Alihahd shook his head. *He knew me.*

Hall lifted Alihahd bodily, and Alihahd did not resist this time. He stumbled away from the site, holding on to Hall. Alihahd did not talk. Couldn't.

In the forest, Vaslav was yelling for them. Harrison Hall sang out, then crouched down in the ferns, taking Alihahd with him, tawny eyes darting cautiously, gun ready for who-ever might answer.

A small, bewildered voice sounded at Hall's side. "Did I shoot?"

"No. I did."

"Didn't think I had," Alihahd mumbled. But he had not been certain. He only knew that he had been facing the young man with his gun. He could not remember shooting, but there had been a shot and it was the Na'id, not Alihahd, whose eyes glassed over and who fell facedown in the brush.

Vaslav came crashing out from the trees into the clearing and tripped over the Na'id body. He danced back and called shrilly, "Captain! Harry? Layla?"

Hall hissed, and Vaslav hied himself back to the cover of the wood. He saw Alihahd curled under Hall's arm. "Are you hurt?" said Vaslav.

Alihahd spoke weakly. "No." Then stronger: "No." He shook himself free of Hall and stood on his own feet. "Where is Layla?"

"Here," said Layla. She'd come to them quietly as a forest shadow.

"Let us go, then," said Alihahd. "Fast now."

The four moved quickly to put distance between themselves and the clearing.

When they paused for breath, Alihahd sat down, his heart pulsing in his wounded leg. He pulled Hall down to him by the arm so he could talk quietly. "How many did you kill?" He had not counted the shots.

"I bagged five," said Hall.

Alihahd did not like that number. "Vaslav?"

"None," said Vaslav.

"Layla?"

"One."

Alihahd relaxed a measure. Six was a good number. "That was probably the whole patrol. We might have an hour before someone becomes alarmed at their failure to report."

Someone. The Na'id base camp could not be far.

"Shall we turn back?" said Hall.

Alihahd bowed his head, chin on his chest. If those four ships were manned by Na'id, where were Alihahd's rebels? All two thousand of them. Alihahd lifted his head, level and grim. "You go back. I have to see."

"I can't let you go alone," said Hall.

"I do not need a nursemaid," said Alihahd.

"Yes, you do," said Hall.

From up the mountain—in the direction of the clearing which they had fled—came fighting snarls and yelps and growls. These would be wolf-hyenas at the bodies of the six Na'id patrollers.

"Yes, I do," said Alihahd, standing. "Shall we get this done?"

The sun was overhead. They would need to strain to reach the coast and climb back up through the forest and the mountain pass to the Itiri village where Jinin-Ben-Tairre waited for them by nightfall.

Alihahd's leg was failing, and he ended up leaning on Hall most of the way down, his arm slung around the taller man's neck.

He had fallen into a melancholy brooding. "They all come home to roost," he murmured. "It cannot be coincidence. Chance is not so vindictive. Must not someone be directing events?"

But Harrison Hall had demonstrated an amazing ability to defuse any such lofty conjectures. "It only *looks* as if someone is in control of all this. When you think of all the trillions of possible coincidences that *don't* happen, you see how random it all is. Odds are that some coincidences will happen—by chance—even if the odds against any one specific coincidence are a billion to one. It would be odd if there were no coincidences. That would be evidence of intervention. As it is, I see none. You're on your own, Captain."

"You're a cynic, Mr. Hall."

"But a realistic one."

Harrison Hall had both feet planted squarely in *this* universe and troubled not with the Great Beyond.

Hall looked aside at the fair head bent down near his shoulder. Alihahd was watching his step. Hall touched his hair, passed a lock of it between his fingers. He had never seen hair so fine even on a child. But there were strands of white among the blond. "You think too much," said Hall.

"Only when I'm sober," said Alihahd dryly.

The four spaceships rested on a level area long ago cleared of trees by a great fire. The carpet of new yellow grass was underlaid with vestigial black dust and coal; and still the dead, charred skeletons of once tall trees spiked the plain at far intervals.

Alihahd, Hall, Layla, and Vaslav stole up to the perimeter of the wide, burnt clearing and hid behind a mossy boulder at the very edge of the forest.

Alihahd peered out cautiously to the ships on the exposed plateau. Among the ships wandered men and women biding their time in the sweltering heat, finding it preferable to the cool confinement of their space vessels. Their sweat-patched Na'id uniforms were fleet red, not the army blue of the patrol Hall and Layla had killed.

A dozen crewmen, seeking the shade of the forest, ambled very near to the boulder where Alihahd hid. From the emotions that played across Alihahd's face as he viewed them, his three companions guessed the worst. But Alihahd exhaled heavily and stood. "Those are mine."

He gave Hall his taeben and he walked slowly and loudly into the open, his hands wide and empty.

Twelve guns turned and aimed.

Alihahd's rebels had always been quick to draw their guns. Alihahd had never let them use them.

"Put those down," bellowed the strangely dressed, white-skinned, blond man come limping from the forest.

The rebels jumped, stuttered, and stared. They knew the voice; the command was a ghost from the past. What they *saw* needed reconciling. The Alihahd they remembered was swarthy.

Still they knew him when he spoke again. "It is I."

At once the guns were put up, except for two of the most stunned, who were nudged by their comrades and hastily followed suit.

The thick silence broke. "Alihahd!" someone cried at last.

Exultant and dazed smiles flashed, and one crewman dashed to the ships, yelling, "Alihahd! Alihahd!" And all the rebels gathered around to see.

It was an awkward reunion, with enough excitement, some tears, but no embraces or backslapping, and the welcomes were clumsily expressed.

Then the throng parted for the approach of a stocky woman in Na'id commodore's uniform. Blue tribal tattoos around her lips broadened as she smiled, but with no more surprise or jubilation than on recovering a lost nose ring. *So there you are*, said the smile.

The commodore, Musa, took off her broad-brimmed hat, put it on Alihahd's fair head, and said, "What happened to you?" She meant his color, not his disappearance.

"As you see," said Alihahd. He had not smiled once.

Musa pressed her stout forefinger experimentally to his white cheek. "Is this real?"

Alihahd spoke tautly. "Do you honestly suppose anyone would look like this on purpose?"

"I guess not," said Musa. "Not unless you're trying to be the reincarnation of Shad Iliya."

Alihahd's smile was very thin.

A few grins around him slackened. A fierce, blue-eyed glare from Alihahd silenced any comment. Alihahd spoke to Musa. "You are aware that there are Na'id on this planet."

"Can't be," said Musa, as a whispering wave of consternation passed through the rebel troops.

A strong voice from the woods said, "Are."

That was Hall. And all the rebel guns raised and pointed at him.

"Are," said Alihahd, pushing down the nearest weapon. "But that is not one. Put those things away before you shoot each other."

And when all the weapons were holstered, Hall, Layla, and Vaslav came out of hiding.

Alihahd muttered aside to Musa while the rebels were distracted by the appearance of his companions, "Not battle-ready, Musa. Your ships should be arranged at dome points. Cannot do it now without attracting attention to ourselves."

"I didn't think it necessary in uncharted space," said Musa.

"You were followed."

Musa's broad brow creased. "Why would the Na'id follow us? As far as they know, we're a loyal squadron."

"Evidently you have been discovered. Appears they are tracking you to all your contacts and bases before they make their final strike."

Musa pouted contemplatively, assessing the dimensions of the disaster. "Shall we make a run for it?"

Alihahd looked up at the sky. There was nothing in it for the moment. "We have to assume they know where we are."

Musa nodded. "How did *you* know where we were?"

"A bird told me."

Musa knew better than to question Alihahd when he was being evasive. She let it slide and addressed the crisis at hand. "We're sitting ducks down here."

"We are worse if we take off," said Alihahd. Four ships slugging out of a thick atmosphere made a slow, concentrated target. On the ground, even if the Na'id located the ships, they could not be certain of where all the people were.

"I would feel much better in a spaceship," said Musa.

"So would most Na'id. I would not," said Alihahd. Harrison Hall had come to his side.

"But you're a brilliant spaceship strategist," said Musa.

"I am merely competent in the air," said Alihahd. "I am brilliant on the ground." He glanced to Hall. "I don't lose."

Musa turned with a shrug, clapped her hands, and shouted a command: "Ships on dome points! Now!"

The rebels hurried to obey, and they arranged the ships at optimum angles for their combined forcefields to raise a nearly impenetrable energy-shield dome.

"What have you on the scanners, Musa?" Alihahd asked while he waited.

"No ships." Musa opened her thick arms in bafflement. "You say there are Na'id; I don't know where they are."

"It is a metallic planet," Alihahd said.

Musa agreed. "They could hide anything here."

The engines of the repositioned ships were winding down. They were ready to raise the shield dome on Alihahd's command.

Alihahd held his breath. He was inviting direct confrontation if he raised a defensive dome now. If the Na'id were monitoring, they would see the dome on their scanners and they would know they had been detected. "Raise it," said Alihahd and waited for the repercussions. "Is there wine to be had?" he asked Musa.

"Y—"

"No," said Hall.

Musa looked quizzically to Alihahd.

"Never mind," said Alihahd.

Someone gestured skyward and sang out, "Here they come."

All eyes turned up.

Alihahd watched with sinking soul. Twelve ships appeared, not battleships of a space fleet, but troop transports of an army bearing twelve thousand infantry soldiers. The ominous silhouettes of delta-wing ships flew in the formation of three broken echelons matted against the twilight sky. It was a known pattern, the personal signature of a very special army.

Alihahd breathed, "This goes beyond chance and coincidence. This is destiny." *There is a God and He is vengeful.*

It was the 27th Army. The victors of Jerusalem.

III. Shad Iliya's Army

Alihahd motioned aside to Vaslav without looking at him. "Vaslav, man a transceiver."

The boy ran to the flagship as the delta-wing transports of the infamous 27th Army were touching down. They came to rest on the burn-cleared plateau a scant kilometer from the rebel camp and set up on defensive points so that their own energy dome nearly overlapped the rebels'. Then uniformed soldiers poured out of the dreadful ships like bottle-blue ants.

"Hm," Alihahd grunted, commenting to himself, noting something interesting.

Hall raised his eyebrows at him questioningly.

"The uniforms," said Alihahd. "They never used to wear those."

The bright metallic blue with red blazons told the galaxy who these soldiers were; the colors reinforced Na'id identity and pride in the Empire. Shad Iliya never used them, preferring less conspicuous battle-drab. But ever since losing Shad Iliya, the soldiers of the 27th Army felt increasing need to insist on who they were. They had lost battles since Jerusalem. The blue uniforms were a small signal of slipping morale.

Alihahd touched Musa's sleeve. "I want everyone into battle fatigues and assembled out here inside of four minutes."

"Assembled in what order?" said Musa.

"No particular order. Just so they take a position and hold it."

"Yes, sir."

If there was one thing Alihahd's people were trained to do, it was act as if they knew what they were doing in dangerous places where they had no business being and about which they knew nothing. They were an army of impostors and spies, not soldiers.

As the rebels drew ranks, the scanner technician came to

Alihahd to report that she had found where the Na'id had been hiding earlier. Their ships had come out of a deep canyon below sea level, between two metallic mountains, less than ten kilometers to the west. Like chameleons they had been easily overlooked until they moved. "If we'd taken off, we'd be dead now," said the tech. "It'd be a skeet shoot. You were right, sir."

Alihahd nodded without comfort. There was no pleasure in being right when it meant he had saved himself for a fate worse than death.

The Na'id were assembling by battalions, smart and orderly, each by its ship. They outnumbered the rebels six to one.

But for the soldiers of the 27th Army there was something unsettling in facing an enemy wearing Na'id uniforms—and the drab colors they themselves used to wear when they were still undefeated. The more sensitive of them were aware that hidden things were moving here.

Vaslav came from the flagship to report, "The Na'id opened communications. They demand surrender."

Alihahd's eyes never left the ranks across the plateau. "Refuse."

Vaslav ran back to the ship's transceiver to relay the message.

A rebel ship commander beside Alihahd took a quick breath for courage, then spoke. "Do you know what you're doing, sir?"

Alihahd was showing signs of fear. Sweat beaded his tall forehead; his mouth and eyes were lined in white.

"We're not an army," the commander reminded him.

"They do not know that," said Alihahd.

"They'll find out when they attack," said the commander, suppressed hysteria tinging his voice.

"If they attack."

The commander licked salt from his upper lip, then caved in to bald fear. "Captain, do you know who they are?" he blurted. "That's Shad Iliya's army. Those people took Jerusalem!"

Blue eyes and white face turned slowly. The voice was deep. "I know."

The commander's eyes grew huge, and he backed away, choking on a whimper.

Vaslav came bounding back from the flagship, his face bright red. "Sir, their general calls you a madman and demands that you personally reconfirm your answer. He also wants to know if you realize who they are."

Alihahd put a hand on the youth's hard, spare shoulder. "Confirm the refusal for me. And tell the general this verbatim—verbatim, can you?"

Vaslav nodded intently. His hands were furtively making gentle, nervous motions. Alihahd wanted to slap them.

"Tell the general that I am in the habit of studying thoroughly any opponent, knowing his habits, strengths, weaknesses, motives, and all facts available—pertinent and *impertinent*. Do you think you have that?"

Vaslav raised his chin and dashed away, his lips moving, reciting to himself.

"And Vaslav!"

The boy turned.

"Tell him I thought Alihahd was dead."

Vaslav's face blanked in puzzlement. "Sir?"

"Tell him."

Musa offered Alihahd her comlink so Vaslav would not need to keep shuttling back and forth. Alihahd shook his head. "Let him run. Let them wait."

A fresh sweat broke over his brow in the late heat of the westering sun. The day was never-ending. These kinds of days never did end. The second-worst day in his entire life. Or was it the worst? He closed his eyes, brushed away a buzzing yellow fly. *O God, O God*, he cried inside. And imagined he heard an ironic voice answer, *Yes?*

He opened his eyes, despairing.

Vaslav returned, unnerved. The boy had been prepared for anger from the Na'id general at the message, but he had not been ready for quite the violence of the reaction. There had been more to that message than was apparent. "Sir, the general is hopping mad. He turned that color." Vaslav pointed at Musa's scarlet fleet hat angled atop Alihahd's blond head. Except for Harrison Hall, Alihahd was the only rebel not in uniform. By now all the rebels, including Vaslav, were in battle gray.

"The general wants to know who you think you are," said Vaslav. "Because you're not the man you're pretending to be; no one ever was or will be. And all Alihahd's cowardly tricks can't change that." Vaslav's voice faltered. His Adam's apple bobbed. "He wants you to quit hiding your face and come to the transceiver and look him in the eyes, because he already knows that yours—your eyes—aren't . . . blue."

Alihahd nodded. His face was ashen. He slowly blinked his blue eyes. "Thank you."

"No message?"

"Not for the transceiver."

"Sir?" Vaslav began, bewildered. He was carrying every word that passed between the two leaders, yet he hadn't the least idea what was being said and why their words fell on each other so hard. And besides that, Alihahd's eyes *were* blue. "Who are you pretending to be?"

Alihahd sighed. "Not." He took off the broad-brimmed hat and gave it back to Musa. He limped forward from the ranks in the direction of the Na'id ships, hesitated, then continued out toward the perimeter of the shield dome. His skin tingled and hair pricked as he passed through the force field, his movements slowed, like walking through mud, till he was out of the dome.

The rebels gasped. "Is he mad? He'll be killed!"

Harrison Hall rocked back on his heels, amused. "A little mad, maybe. Killed? Not yet, I think."

He could see Alihahd's white skin even at a distance, and fancied he was even more pale than normal. Alihahd was horrified, and it was not fear of death. He wished he were dead. He could not have been more sickened and terrified walking into a fire and knowing his flesh would burn.

Nothing stirred during his slow progress out to stand between the two armies. Everyone was quiet, watching his painful advance. He forgot to breathe, then breathed too quickly, feeling the pressure of the air now, the effects of descending too far too fast.

I want a drink. He could have in all reality murdered Hall for making him go through this cold sober.

The Na'id did not shoot him. A murmur rolled back through their ranks. Alihahd dared not look at faces, and he kept his eyes strictly over their heads. Then, because he could no longer resist, he glanced down once. Their faces, the whole sea of them, read pure shock. Ice trickled through Alihahd's stomach, guts, groin, and into his jellied legs, and he stopped. This was far enough. At the next step he would fall.

He held his position there, midway, and let them stare. His mouth felt full of bitter pins; his heart wobbled high in his chest and the palms of his hands throbbed. He felt faint. *Not even God can help me*. He forced himself to untense his muscles. *As if God actually would*.

He swallowed, gathered his breath low, and found his voice. "Soldiers of the Empire!" he thundered. The voice carried over the plain and rebounded off the mountains, steady, loud, and resonant.

Alihahd prayed the voice would not break on him. It never had.

He was dying inside, everyone staring at him—those blank, horrified faces. If he looked at them again he would freeze. He heard their murmurs, the deadly secret spreading.

"Yes, I know who you are!" he shouted at them with a fury that was really fear. "*You are my enemy!*"

The murmurs silenced. Alihahd glanced down quickly at their glassy faces, every one of them unmoving, as if they were watching a special weapon of theirs—a big gun they once had—which had made them feel so powerful and invincible while it was theirs, till one day it turned around and they were looking up its barrel and feeling very small. *You are my enemy*.

He should not have looked. It was some moments before he could speak again. In the silence the Na'id fear mounted to near panic. Alihahd needed to be careful. Cornered beasts bit. *O God, if you get me out of this without a battle I will never presume to lead a body of your people ever again*.

The Na'id believed themselves cornered. Alihahd would show them an out and hope they ran for it without realizing he was all roar and no teeth.

"If there be a battle today, you will attack. I will not. The decision for bloodshed is yours entirely." He paused, watched their panic abate a degree. "*But*," he shouted, and they flinched. "Know it be me you fight, and you know better than anyone that I have never lost a battle."

Even the young soldiers who had never known him were stunned. His image was aboard every ship. The soldiers of the 27th visited his shrine before every mission. God had left and joined the other side.

The shift in morale could be felt across the plateau.

Both sides were astounded. Alihahd sensed his rebels behind him reeling at the shock, and he was sick again at the prospect of turning around and looking back. His stomach had gone from ice to water.

He saw movement in the Na'id ranks—a single person walking forward out of the camp toward midfield. Alihahd knew him—a broad, stolid bulk in general's uniform, older than Alihahd, with silvering black hair, not much changed from thirteen years ago when everything was normal and this man was his lieutenant commander.

Ra'im Mishari trudged out for conference with the enemy captain. His steps were tired, and a thick forefinger worried at the tight collar of his uniform in the damp heat. For all the years of Ra'im Mishari's service, the computer still could not fit a collar to the general's taurine neck. Even that had not changed.

General Ra'im Mishari came to Alihahd and stopped. He and Alihahd faced each other in silence, awkward as two former lovers.

Alihahd stood at his full height, his eyes turned down to his old second.

Ra'im Mishari's heavy brows contracted; his square jaw moved, grinding. His broad chest expanded. He started to say "General," but blurted out with a cry of pain, "Shadi!" and nothing to follow. Just his name. He felt like shedding tears, but a leader could not before two armies.

Alihahd waited, with no compulsion to say anything.

Ra'im snorted, opened his collar. He looked up. "I worshiped you."

"That was a serious mistake on your part," said Alihahd.

A cloud passed over the sinking sun. Ra'im Mishari glanced toward it in relief, then back to Alihahd to say matter-of-factly, "You realize you just shot our morale to hell."

"That was the idea."

"We wouldn't have a chance if we engaged you now."

Yes you would. Six to one? Come now, Ra'im, have you deified me? "I realize."

"You leave me no choice."

"That was also the idea."

A glimmer of a sad smile flickered at the corners of Ra'im's eyes. It sounded so familiar—the deft maneuvering, the sure simplicity, ever one step ahead. So it seemed to Ra'im. He frowned. "How could you desert?"

"What else does one do when one is born on the wrong side?" said Alihahd with profound tiredness, his blue eyes skyward and lost. "I do not know if what I did was right—I suspect not. But I did not know what else to do. Suicide, I suppose. But frankly I lacked the courage."

A tremor disturbed Ra'im's square, solid chin. The speech sounded exactly like the man Ra'im knew—and he remembered how distressed his general had been last time he saw him thirteen years ago.

Ra'im spoke low, nearly guttural, emotion-charged and personal. "You should've said something. The Bel would have done anything for you."

"I did not say anything? I thought I had," said Alihahd airily. "You all treated me as if I had gone mad."

As gently as he could, Ra'im said, "But you had."

Alihahd smiled, eyes shining at the sky. The thought had not occurred to him. He found it funny. "But even a madman does not like to be treated like one," he said.

Ra'im Mishari remained very grave. "Why did you hit those space stations?"

Ah. Omonia. They suppose that was I? Alihahd sobered. "I did not," he said without explanation, but clearly knowing more than he was offering.

Ra'im spoke slowly, trying to discount the other possibility. "Itiri warrior-priests are legends, of course."

"Of course," said Alihahd curtly and turned away before Ra'im could ask if the Itiri were allies of his. *Let him think. The size of this bluff was staggering.*

Alihahd faced his rebel camp, and he paled again. A moment's faintness passed over him, then he started his painful return, his back straight and stiff.

The rebels were silent. What had happened out there, who he was, was still sinking in.

Alihahd was accustomed to having all eyes on him, but he had never been looked at like this in his life. The stares were tearing his guts out.

When he reached the camp, someone jabbed a gun in his face.

The shock of even that kind of gesture had long ago worn off, and Alihahd did not even blink. He put his hand on the barrel, pushed it away, and announced in a husky growl,

"For anyone else contemplating assassination, I suggest you wait for a more advantageous time."

He scanned the sea of eyes, some still denying, some crying. No one moved against him. They may have hated him, but he was still the highest card in the deck, and they would not remove it from play when it was in their hand.

Vaslav was stricken; he was bawling. Only Musa and Harrison White Fox Hall were unaffected.

"Alihahd," Musa said to herself, her brows high. "He left."

"He certainly did," said Alihahd raggedly. He looked to Hall, who was enormously entertained, then Alihahd walked past and headed for the forest. Hall fell into step at his flank.

"Do not say anything, Mr. Hall," said Alihahd.

"Not a word," said Hall breezily.

Inside the woods, Alihahd let himself limp as badly as his wracked leg wanted to. He found a fallen tree trunk and sat heavily. His hands were quaking in aspen-leaf tremors. Lancing pains shot up and down his leg. His whole fiber sang in delayed reaction to horror. He cupped his hands over his nose and tried to stop hyperventilating.

In time, he became conscious again of Hall sitting beside him, trying to light his pipe full of soggy tobacco with a moist flint. His muttered imprecations were somehow soothing, and Alihahd gathered strength from his mocking presence.

Noises from the camp filtered into the woods where they were, as the rebels began to thaw from their frozen shock. Only now was their kicked anthill beginning to buzz and scurry and crawl in reaction. Alihahd let it settle itself without him. The rebels would be better by themselves for now, and Alihahd needed to be alone—except for Hall, who did not count.

The woods were shady, deep, and peaceful, cooling with the sun's setting. Alihahd let its damp quietude surround him. He watched a droplet fall from a wet leaf; a creature like a red ant tracked through the moss on the rotting log.

He whispered his own name. It had been so long since he owned it

"Shad Iliya."

IV. Shadow of Masada

Shad Iliya was born into a patrician house under the most auspicious circumstances, the second child of two war heroes. His mother was already carrying him at the battle of Antarctica, and it was said later that Shad Iliya had been winning battles before he was born.

Like most prominent Na'id citizens, his mother had made a point of being on Earth when her time came so that her child could be called a true native Earthling; and someday when he fought for the Empire to bring all of Earth under Na'id control, he could say he was reclaiming his homeland. He could not be called an invader.

He was bred from the cradle to be a leader, and proved to have a natural ability, but he faced a great struggle to advance to any significant position because of his unpatriotic color. His parents were a typical Na'id mix of racial traits, so their second son was a bewildering embarrassment. He learned guilt early. Even as a child he knew he was evil. He hated his color and all it meant.

So did his peers. He was lucky at least to be highborn and afforded the protection of his patrician heritage; no one dared destroy him. As it was they were merely unmerciful.

He tried to tan in the sun, but his fair skin only burned. He begged but was refused the use of melanin drugs, for they were deceitful. He was not trying to be deceitful—everyone knew what he was. They called him nazi. He just wanted to look like the others. But he could not.

So he would have to be great instead. Praiseworthy.

He sought refuge in the army, where he was good. He rose to the rank of major and dead-ended there. The rank was plenty high enough for someone who looked like him.

He would have died a major but that the most powerful individual in the Empire had taken a liking to him. The Bel felt for the despised and talented young man, and he married his niece to Shad Iliya.

Shad Iliya's superiors noticed right away that *some*one was letting the Bel's kin stagnate at his current rank.

But he was still an embarrassment to promote. They could not have a blond, blue-eyed *Aryan* leading battles against other humans. The symbolism was very bad. So they sent him to faraway alien lands, where he was simply a human being combating the nonhuman menace. Out of the public eye he could be quietly elevated as his merit dictated. And Shad Iliya advanced rapidly.

In semi-exile all those years, fighting on aiien soil, he never lost a battle, and his record grew so astonishing that it reached public view anyway and he became a hero. At long last his name could be spoken aloud. And he was fondly nicknamed the White Na'id, their brilliant oddity.

His victories helped to soothe the Empire's other defeats. His reports could be counted on for good morale. He never failed—still always alien wars. No one realized that keeping him out of sight also kept him blissfully blind.

He would never have run, never have wakened from his illusion of Right, had he not been turned against his own kind.

He could slaughter inhuman aliens till Doomsday without a blush of repentance, as he had slaughtered the marlqai—he *still* had no regrets about that. But the Empire needed its best to end the century-old battle for Jerusalem.

Shad Iliya did his duty, and Jerusalem fell to him.

And it came to him like a revelation. He held his hands to his face, the truth still blinding thirteen years later in the cool and shadowy Iry forest.

"We were wrong. We were dead wrong."

Gregorian Year 5843 C.E.

It was hilly country, the land around Jerusalem. The Na'id ships had been landing in the desert hills beyond the city for days until they formed a wide ring with which to raise an enormous energy-field dome over the top of the defenders' widest dome, cutting the city off from its millions of allies.

Defenders and attackers could not see each other yet for the distance and the hills, except atop one hill captured in a surprise thrust during the 27th Army's initial landing—the Mount of Olives. The arriving army set up headquarters there for their general, the new supreme commander of the Jerusalem campaign.

The Mount of Olives was an exposed promontory, but difficult for the defenders to fire upon, for it was actually within their first line of defense. They had lost an emplaced missile cannon on the crest of the mount. The cannon was a Na'id possession now, but it faced outward and it would have been an engineering feat to turn it around on the city, were the Na'id supreme commander of a mind to try. That no such attempt was made worried the defenders. They feared this new army might know how to fight a war.

Jerusalem was encased in energy shields, shells within shells of shields, which kept out electromagnetic radiation of frequencies higher than ultraviolet, as well as n-particles with wavelike properties. The city bristled with antiaircraft and bomb-intercept guns. Its only vulnerable points—so it was believed—were the windows created in the shield domes by the defenders through which to fire their guns. Previous attacking armies and fleets had flown over the city in their spaceships and hammered at those windows with little result.

Now the Na'id were bringing down their ships and ringing the city like a closing noose. An uneasy Jerusalem waited on guard against the new strategy.

Then arrived on the site the famous general, the thirty-four-year-old Shad Iliya. He stood in the open vehicle that shuttled him from his ship, across the Judean desert, toward his new headquarters on the Mount of Olives. The jeep moved fast. Shad Iliya liked the speed. He stood up to survey the land and to be seen. The dry desert wind stung his fair skin and sang in his ears.

At the western foot of the mount, the jeep turned sharply past its center of gravity and it flipped over and spilled its august passenger out to roll in the ancient dust.

The general's waiting aides and horrified driver scurried to pick him up. But Shad Iliya was young, and he was already on his feet by the time they reached him. He shook himself and slapped a yellow coating of dust from his drab gray-green uniform. He spat dust. He would remember the taste for a long time to come.

He looked to his aides easily, his pride only slightly muted, his spirits not at all. "Well. Where are we?"

They directed him up the Mount of Olives.

As he hiked up the slope with an energetic spring to his walk, his aide trotted alongside him, explaining, "There's a twenty-first-century Neo-Hellenistic chapel we've turned into a war office."

"You did not damage it, did you?" said Shad Iliya.

"*No*, sir!" said the aide with proper reverence for the work of human hands, as they reached the summit.

Over the top of the hill, Shad Iliya received his first view of Jerusalem, the golden city. He caught in his breath and felt his destiny whisper to him. The city looked like its pictures and holos, but here, present and living, its majesty spoke. The unmistakable golden Dome of the Rock stood in the foreground, the venerated ruin of the crumbling western wall beyond it, within the boundaries of the Old City. The Old City was the enemy prize to be captured, a flag of separation and a place rich in human history. The hearts of three major religions crowded that little space.

"So close," he murmured. "We are here."

"It went just as you said, sir," said one of his aides. "The Resistance didn't expect this line of attack at all. Here's what we're using as headquarters, sir."

The aide directed him to a handsome little chapel high on the eastern slope of the mount. There was nothing higher on the hill left intact after countless interfaith wars through centuries past.

Shad Iliya took a moment to admire the chapel's neat, graceful architecture with its blue tiles, white pillars, and painted entablature. One benefit of religion was that it had spurred humankind to great works of art during the childhood of the species when Man needed an anthropomorphic divine Father to protect him and tell him right from wrong. And Man built these lovely things for His sake. But the work was human; the achievement was human; the glory was human.

Farther down the mount's slope stood a charming Byzantine basilica with many-domed roof. Shad Iliya was enchanted. "Is that ours?"

"Nominally, sir," said an aide.

"Can I see it?"

"Not advisable, sir. It's too dangerous. That's Gethsemane. Our forcefield ends right there."

The young general nodded to the disappointing reality. He would have to wait. His blue-eyed gaze lighted on the elegant Dome of the Rock. He drew himself tall, extended a long arm to point, and announced in full voice, "Before the week is out I shall walk beneath that dome."

Swept along with his emotional tide, the general's knot of aides broke into spontaneous applause. Though the city had withstood an assault of a hundred years, if *their* Shad Iliya said one week, then the city would fall in one week. The faith of Shad Iliya's followers was absolute. Shad Iliya would not lose.

Shad Iliya smiled at them. He accepted adoration in those days. He actively sought it, and was sometimes given to theatrics.

Drawn by the sound of unrestrained applause, which could signal the arrival of only one person, Lieutenant Colonel Ra'im Mishari came out through the cluster of white pillars fronting the chapel to greet his general. Ra'im had supervised the taking of the hill as ordered. Shad Iliya could count on Ra'im to follow orders to the letter.

Silently behind Ra'im trailed the morose generals of the 9th and 34th armies, whose command Shad Iliya had assumed. He had met the generals earlier, on shipboard, to take the command baton from them. They greeted the young usurper sullenly. They regarded his initial success as minor and unpromising. They had been here for years. They knew the intractability of the city.

Shad Iliya returned their salutes, then addressed his lieutenant colonel, "Very good, Ra'im. Any problems?"

Ra'im pointed down the slope to Gethsemane. "The rebels have been trying to move a line of portable projectile artillery into the valley. We've been shelling them before they can set up—those are the craters there—but you can see it's a narrow target."

The craters ran between the wall of the Old City and the Byzantine basilica, both of which the Na'id wanted intact and unblemished. The shelling needed to be precise.

"Where is the Jericho Road?" said Shad Iliya, trying to orient himself.

"That line of craters."

"I see." The general turned to go into his headquarters but was distracted by the sight of an ugly black tarp spread over a wide lumpy area beside the pretty chapel. "What is that?"

"The dead in stasis, as ordered, sir."

Shad Iliya was given pause. "So many."

"Theirs, sir."

Theirs. He was not accustomed to the enemy dead being human. The fact that he was fighting humans hadn't taken on reality till that moment.

He went inside the chapel.

The place had been readied for him by his alien slave, Pony, and his personal orderly, a lad of thirteen years with the interminable name of Sinikarrabannashi. He was called Sinikar

The breeze that soughed through the chapel's windows was dry and surprisingly cool. The faded blue-and-white-tiled floor had been swept clean; the Na'id standard and the flag of the 27th Army flanked the doorway; and the blue-and-red Na'id seal hung on the wall.

The curly-haired boy Sinikar saluted his general and, at a nod from Ra'im, put a comlink into his hand. "What is this?" said Shad Iliya.

"It was delivered, sir," said Sinikar.

"It's a direct private link to the rebel commander," said Ra'im Mishari.

Shad Iliya looked to Ra'im. "Which?" There were three.

"The Jew," said Ra'im.

It was a Jew who had organized Jerusalem's defense. The command was titularly a three-headed monster composed of one Jew, one Moslem Arab, and one Christian. In reality, there was one acting genius at the helm, and two figureheads for pride's sake, supporting him. The people of Jerusalem had succeeded in the Na'id goal of uniting the impossible trio of Judaism, Christianity, and Islam against a common enemy.

Except that the common enemy was Shad Iliya.

The artificial differences of religions annoyed Shad Iliya—especially these three religions. They professed belief in the same God, the Creator; they all used the same book with the same prophets and angels. Fundamental differences were few. According to two of them, God was sexless but still called "He," while the third gave Him a queen and a son, which did not sit well with the other two, but it was not as if one premised a pantheon, one an Earth Mother, and one fire worship.

In the name of mercy, it's the same damned God!

All three religions were, to Shad Iliya, anachronisms. Born out of early Man's fear of death, they were throwbacks to civilization's early days of infamy, and they perpetuated its slavery, male dominance, superstitions, and intolerance of other creeds—while straight from the Koran came the affirmation: "Mankind were once one nation."

The 27th Army was here to guide these reprobates back to a unified fold.

Shad Iliya strolled back outside to the chapel steps, turning the comlink over in his hand. He stopped between two white pillars and clicked on the com. He spoke into it experimentally: "Hello?"

The response was immediate. "Ah, the mighty Philistine general!" The voice was cheerfully mocking and male. "At last. I thought you were sending your toadies to do your dirty work for you."

"No. I am here," said Shad Iliya. "As you can probably see." He took another step out from the pillars and scanned the city whose labyrinthine ways somewhere held the owner of the voice.

A pause preceded the answer. "I thought you people wore blue."

Shad Iliya snapped his heels together and inclined a courtly military bow to his unseen watcher. Then he said, "I detest blue." An absurd answer to an absurd question.

The Jew laughed.

Shad Iliya avoided the traditional blue out of practical considerations. The shiny metallic-blue uniforms were designed to be an instantly recognizable announcement of Na'id loyalty. Shad Iliya did not like his soldiers to be so highly visible to enemy gunners.

He glanced to the black tarp. He wanted to have this ordeal over, and to take control of the city with the fewest deaths. He had never fought a campaign like this—trying to preserve both sides. He felt certain of victory but was uncomfortable with these new tactics. It would help if he knew his enemy. And he was discovering quickly that he did *not* know his enemy this time. Strategically hyperopic, he found that distance made for clarity of vision. Aliens were easy to understand and, therefore, predictable. These people were not predictable in the least.

The inevitability of their defeat and a promise of clemency in surrender were not enough to make them give up their intransigent stand. They were bafflingly illogical.

The two veteran generals, who had joined Shad Iliya on the chapel steps, had reported the same observations many times in past years. They watched the new general grudgingly, waiting for him to fall on his face as they had.

He lifted the comlink again. "Are your Christian and Moslem colleagues with you?"

"They are listening," said the Jew.

"Have you informed them of the terms we offer for surrender, or was the decision to refuse unilaterally yours?" Shad Iliya knew that this was an uneasy alliance at best. If he preyed on the suspicion that the Jew was overstepping his bounds, Shad Iliya might drive a wedge into their fragile unity.

But his opponent was not unfamiliar with the methods of propaganda. "Such a bald ploy, Philistine," said the Jew. "My colleagues are not impotent and they can speak for themselves."

The comlink was passed, and the Christian leader, Cardinal Miriam, gave her answer in a florid and prolix diatribe. She spoke in paragraphs of prose.

Shad Iliya cut in, "Your Eminence, I know of only one person who regularly uses lofty rhetoric in private speech, and that is I. Since this is a closed circuit, please speak plainly to me now, human being to human being."

"As you will, General. Go to hell," said the cardinal.

Plain enough.

Just then, from the loudspeaker in the minaret of the nearest mosque erupted a deep ululant *Allaaaaaaaaaaaaaaah Akbaaaaaaaaaaaaaaaaar!*

Shad Iliya took a step back, clicked off the com, and looked to his aides. "What is *that?*"

"Muezzin, sir," said Ra'im Mishari. "Moslem prayer call. Five times a day."

"That hideous noise in the name of God?" said Shad Iliya and clicked on the com again. "Are you still there?"

"I am, Philistine." It was the Jew again. "But I fear our

Moslem colleague must delay giving you his fond wishes. He
goes to pray now.''

"Then I shall talk to you later," said Shad Iliya.

"Keep the link with you, Philistine."

"You will be right in my pocket the whole time, Zealot,"
said Shad Iliya and clicked off.

The prayer call droned on for some minutes more. The
crowded city began to crawl.

"Look, General."

Moslems flocked to the mosques, filled them to overflow-
ing, spilled out of the courtyards and bowed down in the
streets. Jews and Christians in that quarter walked around
them.

Shad Iliya marveled. Religious ardor reached fanatical heights
under siege. Yet the conflicting faiths and conflicting sects of
the faiths squeezed into the small area seemed to have put
their righteous hatred of each other aside for the moment.
"They cooperate rather well for avowed enemies," Shad
Iliya commented.

"Don't they realize that only proves the Na'id point!"
someone said.

"That end of it rather appears not to have entered into their
consideration," said Shad Iliya with equal incomprehension.
He beckoned Ra'im to his side. "I require one crack pilot for
a possible suicide run."

Twelve officers in and about the war office overheard the
quiet request and leapt to volunteer on the spot.

The two veteran generals were gravely disgruntled. This
kind of blind loyalty to a leader was an unhealthy symptom.

Shad Iliya chose the nearest volunteer and instructed her to
take an echelon of eight robot spy planes in a low pass over
Jerusalem. "As low as you can manage without burying
them."

"I'll wave up to the minarets as I go by, sir," she said.
"Purpose of mission, sir?"

"Your ships will be transmitting to this office a computer
plot of the trajectories of all enemy fire which you draw.
There will be a lot of it. So."

He left off there, the rest understood, and he waited for her
to retract her bid.

She saluted, accepting the assignment.

General Shad Iliya saluted, held it a moment longer, as he

did in the face of valor, then barked for a car to take the pilot
to her spy planes.

Two computers were activated in the war office to record
the planes' signals as they came in. "Don't garble this,"
Shad Iliya told the technician. "I shall not have this done
twice."

He did not expect to see his pilot again.

He stood out on the chapel steps to watch the pass.

The sleek black planes went into Jerusalem in the 27th
Army's characteristic broken echelon.

They came out in perforated echelon. The lead plane crashed
into Mount Scopus, failing to pull up steeply enough. Three
others fell to ground fire. The four survivors streaked into the
desert. The war office waited, hushed, to see if they came
back. No one knew which plane had carried the pilot.

"Long live Shad Iliya and the 27th!" crackled over the
transceiver.

"She made it!" a technician called out to the steps of the
chapel.

The tall white general nodded phlegmatically, with an air
of near-indifference. But none of his soldiers supposed Shad
Iliya indifferent.

He said nothing, did nothing, seemed to be admiring the
skyline, until Ra'im Mishari came to him with the tech's
report of the lowest angle managed by the defenders' emplaced guns.

Ra'im passed the verdict to him in silence.

Twenty degrees.

Shad Iliya thanked him. Their eyes met. No more words
passed. Both knew what the information meant. Ra'im guessed
what his general had in mind.

The veterans of the 9th and 34th armies had no idea. All
they saw was apparent catastrophe in the half-destroyed squadron of valuable spy planes.

"With the supreme commander's leave," said one. "We
told you their ceiling was covered."

Shad Iliya was unconcerned. "We shall not be going in
from the air."

Faces slackened. "How then?"

Shad Iliya became impatient. Blue eyes glittered ice-cold.
"Since we are not about to tunnel either, I leave it to you,
gentlemen."

Sinikar, the orderly, stepped out of the chapel to inform his general that the Jew was on the radio.

Shad Iliya sighed, expecting this. These taunts would be on an open frequency to advertise the invincible general's disastrous air pass to the populace.

Shad Iliya went inside to the transceiver. "Yes."

"Well, Philistine, give up?"

"No. I was just now telling my colleagues to start digging. We are tunneling in."

The Jew laughed, then said, "No, Shad Iliya. You just found an opening on the horizons. You're coming in with an infantry."

Bald expressions of shock ringed Shad Iliya in the war office. Shad Iliya nodded, accepting the fact that he would get no breaks from this man.

"Yes, Zealot, I am."

"Good. That's where we're strongest. Not those guns." That affirmation was spoken for the benefit of the people of Jerusalem.

"We too," said Shad Iliya. He turned off the transceiver, looked to the two veterans, of whom he was already thoroughly tired, and said curtly, "At least *some*one knows what he is about here. Pity he is on the other side."

The city immediately started bracing for a ground assault. Shad Iliya needed to move fast. The defenders would try to stall for time to redirect some of their guns to ground level— and to the Mount of Olives.

The time-consuming element for Shad Iliya was proper deployment of the weary and dispirited soldiers of the 9th and 34th armies who had been pounding at the gates of Jerusalem for years. And they needed to be accustomed to the idea of an assault without ships, on foot, carrying projectile weapons. Wars simply were not fought that way anymore.

Jerusalem had the superior numbers. But even had each and every person in the city been a soldier, they only had hand-held projectile weapons for a few—because wars were not fought this way anymore.

Shad Iliya also took care to make wise use of his dregs. In case there actually was a battle, it would be finished quickly and efficiently. He still did not believe it was going to happen.

While the preparations progressed, the general sent saboteurs into the city to disrupt the defensive measures, while he instructed his own people to challenge any unfamiliar person in their midst to give a password, which was "Shad Iliya is God," in hope that the defenders would be unable to say it even if they happened to learn it.

For himself, Shad Iliya spent the first night rereading the Bible. He sat on a spartan bed under an open window in a small chamber of his war office. He found words that struck him to the heart and that would come back to haunt him later:

If it be possible, let this cup pass from me.

The garden was down there at the foot of the mount.

He closed the book and stepped outside to the chill desert night, watched the lights of the city spread out at his feet. The dry air carried to him the scent of cypress planted around the chapel. He overheard the exchange of night sentries:

"What is it with these Jerusalemites?"

"They think they're God's chosen people."

"Oh yeah? Well, if God wants them, let's make sure God gets them." The slapping sound was a palm on a metal weapon butt. "Chosen people. I'll show them chosen people."

Shad Iliya left the temenos of the chapel and strolled over the mount in the dark.

The Mount of Olives was teeming with graves, millennia's worth, sleeping under the fig trees and the pink-flowering oleanders. One could not walk without tripping over the marble fragment of someone's marker.

Shad Iliya did trip and alarmed a sentry at the edge of a stand of pine trees. "Halt!" said the girl, and pointed her weapon.

Shad Iliya spoke before she could demand the password. "I shan't call myself God, so do not ask."

"Sir!" The sentry shouldered her gun posthaste and snapped to rigid attention. "Sorry, sir."

"No need. Very good"—he squinted at her uniform in the dark—"Sergeant. At ease."

The girl shifted her gun on her shoulder and bowed her head. "Was a hell of a lot easier when the enemy didn't look like us," she said wistfully.

Suddenly sad, Shad Iliya nodded and laid a hand on her close-shorn curls. "Yes, it was."

The muezzin's stentorian wail, distorted through the loudspeakers, split the night's peace, and Shad Iliya lifted his hands in dismay.

He had wondered why he hadn't counted five prayer calls during the day. Here was the fifth in the middle of the night. They were going to drive him mad.

Either they or the Jew.

Jerusalem's commander called on the comlink at intervals to harass his adversary. Unlike the muezzin, however, the link could be turned off. Shad Iliya never did, and realized only too late that he should have. It was the Jew's most powerful weapon.

In the morning Shad Iliya woke, itching from a bout with stinging nettles which he had walked into unawares the night before. The Jew's voice sounded cheerily on his pillow. "Good morning, Philistine."

Shad Iliya rolled to the comlink. "Good morning, Zealot." He cleared his gravelly throat. "Surrender?"

"Never."

Shad Iliya looked to his chronometer and calendar. "Today is my birthday."

"Happy birthday, Philistine."

"Thank you."

"You're welcome. Your sixtieth?"

"Thirty-fifth, villain."

"You will be here for your sixtieth."

"I think not."

"Your army has been rotting outside Jerusalem for a hundred years."

Shad Iliya sat up in bed. "Not *my* army, Zealot. Not *my* army."

"Your great alien-killers? You will fare no better than your predecessors."

"How can you even talk like that on a closed circuit? Do you not blush? I know you are lying and you know you are lying."

"Maybe God knows better than both of us, then."

"Oh no."

"I must say, though, yours is the most thoroughly brainwashed army ever to knock at our gates."

"You mean that your propaganda does not work on my soldiers."

"Exactly."

The propaganda did not work because it had been aimed at the wrong targets. It attempted to undercut the Empire, the Na'id tenets, the Bel. But the soldiers of the 27th Army were not fighting for any of that. They fought for love of Shad Iliya. And the sterling Shad Iliya had no vices for a propagandist to use.

"You will find my army immune to your quasi-religious unreason," said Shad Iliya. "So you may as well desist—if you can. Disseminating lies comes naturally to your ilk, does it not?"

"Such insults!" said the Jew. "But what shall I call Shad Iliya? I can say nothing about Shad Iliya. Shad Iliya is perfect."

Shad Iliya smiled. "You have been talking to my soldiers."

"What don't you confess, Philistine? You've no addictions. You drink but a little. You're loyal to your wife even in the field for months on end. You've no strange hobbies. No hobbies at all. You must be a monster. You terrify me."

Oh, but no, thought Shad Iliya. *We have hardly begun with terror.*

The noose of ships and soldiers tightened around Jerusalem's hills, still out of direct sight from the city. Among the Na'id artillery was a great dragon-carved cannon several stories high, an enormous, primitive-looking thing like the bow of a bronze-age warship.

The Jew acquired a picture of it from his recon team, broke into disbelieving giggles, and opened his comlink at once in high spirits. "I like your pet, Philistine. It's cute. What's its name?"

"Its name is Ba'al," said Shad Iliya wryly.

The Jew belittled it blithely. At first, Shad Iliya thought his adversary was fishing for confirmation of a suspicion, but as the derision continued, Shad Iliya realized that the Jew had made his first overconfident blunder.

The Jew thought that Shad Iliya was assuming Jerusalem's shields were weak at ground level in the same way the city's offensive guns were lacking at the ground, and that Shad Iliya was basing his attack on that erroneous belief. The Jew thought Ba'al was an n-cannon.

Shad Iliya's fate whispered to him again. No doubt now. No doubt.

You stupid Zealot, dragons breathe fire.

The weapon was actually as primitive as it looked—Man's oldest weapon after the rock.

Perhaps we could use those too, Shad Iliya thought ironically.

But fire was the one that had first given humankind supremacy over all life on Earth.

And Shad Iliya went to sleep with a burden on his chest, like something sitting on his heart, cursed with the knowledge that, as a certainty, he could not lose this battle.

The muezzin woke Shad Iliya on the third morning. He rose from bed, dressed quickly without his slave's help, threw open the door of the side chamber that had become his bedroom, and stomped out to the front steps of the war office, where the sentries stood.

"Take out that minaret."

Uncertainly, the sentry changed his grip on his gun. "Really, sir?"

"No." Shad Iliya reached his open hand to the side; his orderly knew the motion and put a cup of coffee into it.

Shad Iliya's brow furrowed with a headache. He had not slept well. He marched back to his room and found his alien slave, Pony, making the bed. He chased Pony out and sat on the cot, brooding. His fingers laced around his coffee cup.

God damn you, Jerusalem.

Of the defense, he worried most about the Jewish forces. There was something charming and endearing about the Arab disorder and disunity. He could sometimes count on them to blow up their own weapons because of an incurable tendency to ignore strict directions and maintenance.

But there was something inhuman about the Jewish unity, precision, and capability. This battle would be a horror. Shad Iliya still refused to believe it would take place. Something would happen to intervene. Surely the leaders would come to their senses. He had given them time to make a patriotic show of defiance. Now it was time to be reasonable.

He rolled onto his back and propped his head up on the pillow against the wall, which was frescoed with faded and chipped Easter lilies. He flipped out the comlink and waited for the inevitable "Good morning, Philistine."

Shad Iliya dispensed with being pleasant and lashed out at the commander for his adherence to and willingness to let a city die for an antiquated religion.

"Antiquated!" said the Zealot. "Old makes it wrong? No, Philistine, old makes it right. Do you think if God were to reveal Himself to Mankind He would wait until now? What of the generations who went before? If there is a Revelation, it is an old one."

"*If*," said Shad Iliya. "The operative word."

"*You* brought the charge of antiquated against us. Don't change emphasis now because I defeated you on that front, O Ye of the Heathen Name."

Shad Iliya sat up and threw his pillow across the room. "When will you leave off this precious conceit of supposing you have a monopoly on the Supreme Being!"

"When God ceases to be."

That meant never. Shad Iliya knew the Jew's thinking that much by now. "I shall hang you from a minaret and use you for target practice."

"Why haven't you attacked yet, General?" said the Jew, sounding still very congenial and tranquil—joyful, in fact. An alarm went off inside Shad Iliya, though he didn't know why. A balance had shifted.

"I shall when I am ready," he answered guardedly.

"You're ready," said the Jew, as elated as an unarmed soldier stumbling across a fully stocked weapons cache. "You've *been* ready."

A lump had risen in Shad Iliya's throat. His hands were trembling unaccountably. He was going to say he did not know what the Jew was talking about. But only the guilty used those words, and of course Shad Iliya was guilty of nothing.

Except that Shad Iliya was afraid to kill. The coming battle terrified him, and the Jew smelled it. And the battle began in earnest. The Jew gave up trying to undermine the faith of the army in its leader and he began to gnaw at the head of the serpent itself.

"It is up to you to stop this war, Shad Iliya. You are the attacker. It is in your hands. You give the word that this atrocity may not be."

"You surrender," Shad Iliya countered.

"It is on your head, Shad Iliya."

And the charge of stalling came home double when the general overheard his own soldiers wondering about the delay.

"Are we starving them out?" said one.

"No. Can't be," said another. "It's not our way."

The thought chilled Shad Iliya. Blockade, starvation, was a messy way to go. It spawned gross inhumanity—or else martyrdom. Either way it was a hideous contemplation.

But Shad Iliya doubted it could even be done here. Any longer delay would allow the defenders to break the blockade. Time was the ally of Jerusalem.

For what am I waiting, then? thought Shad Iliya, then, in anger, *I am not.* "Ra'im!" he roared.

"Sir!"

"Twenty-four hours."

"Yes, sir."

All day long the Jew wielded his long knives, and Shad Iliya listened with dread, no longer able to turn off the voice of damnation. The Jew pulled out all holds. But one.

Throughout the campaign, the Jew never called the pale, blue-eyed general a nazi. It was the most obvious shot, and the Jew did not use it, for which Shad Iliya was both grateful and unnerved. Was it mercy?

He doubted it. For when Shad Iliya said, "I shan't glory in destroying your people," the Jew replied, "I shan't glory in destroying you."

You, said the Jew. Singular. Personal. He was not claiming victory. He was claiming destruction of Shad Iliya himself.

Sundown came, the eve of the battle. Jerusalem's guns were not ready despite the borrowed time. The defenders had no chance.

They seem to know. Shad Iliya watched the Arab men flood into their mosques, the women drape their heads and go through their motions outside.

The Na'id soldiers within earshot chanted with the muezzin playfully. They knew too.

A less certain Ra'im Mishari passed a scan scope to his general and directed his attention to a Jewish station in the new city. Shad Iliya lifted the scope and zoomed in on the group of soldiers. Some of them wore light-benders, which would make them invisible once activated, but that was not what was alarming Ra'im. It was their attitude.

Some lounged in groups, joking, passing around their dwindling supply of cigarettes, while others were dancing their circle dances of old—around a fire.

Shad Iliya shuddered and lowered the scope.

"Why are they so confident?" said Ra'im worriedly.

"They are not," said Shad Iliya. "They know."

"I don't understand."

"I do not understand either," said Shad Iliya with a hand on Ra'im's shoulder. "I only know it is so."

Before retiring for the night, Shad Iliya made a last desperate effort to avert the coming massacre. The Na'id supreme commander as a rule never initiated contact on the link. He did so now and asked privately for a surrender.

"Of course not," was the answer.

"What say your Christian and Moslem colleagues?" said Shad Iliya.

"We are in accord," said the Jew.

"*Ask* them!" Shad Iliya cried in obvious agony.

The Jew agreed to consult the other two members of the triumvirate, and he relayed their answers an hour later. "The Christian says that the Holy Land is not for the godless. The Moslem says Jihad."

"Shit."

"What means this word 'shit,' Philistine?"

"It is an Anglo-Saxon word meaning excrement, also synonymous with Jihad—so says Shad Iliya."

"Strange. Cardinal Miriam is forever saying that hell is the Anglo-Saxon word for war. Or war is hell. I forget which."

"God *damn* your flippancy! If you change your mind, this link will be open all night."

"It is a morning assault then, General?"

"Good night, Zealot."

The defenders were not to spend a peaceful night. Shad Iliya told his own soldiers to get some sleep—real sleep. He bid only a few night officers to keep Jerusalem awake till dawn in readiness. At the places where the guns were being lowered, he ordered heavy salvos and robot flyovers at 0213 hours, and again at 0400 and 0415. "And the moment the muezzin opens his mouth for the 0300 prayer call. Everyone else to bed."

Then he hiked down the far side of the Mount of Olives to his ship for a proper bath. His alien slave, Pony, came along to assist him. The pretty palomino-colored humanoid knew his master's routine and was never too much in the way.

Pony was an androgynous, lithe-bodied, doe-eyed creature

with white mane and horsetail. Shad Iliya had named the
slave; Shad Iliya was one of those people who called a
spotted dog Spot and a red horse Red. Pony's real name had a
click in it, and Shad Iliya was not about to torture himself
learning to speak clicks in order to pronounce his alien slave's
name. Pony was a useful thing, a pretty piece of furniture,
better than a robot. Pony would do anything for him.

Shad Iliya pulled Pony's mane and closed both fists in the
long, silvery hair, hardly aware of the creature in his hands,
his fierce thoughts elsewhere. *By heaven, you cannot fight a
war with human beings. Are we not one family?*

Pony waited meekly with bowed head, trying not to wince.

Shad Iliya swallowed hard. *Life goes from my limbs and
they sink, and my mouth is sere and dry; a trembling over-
comes my body . . . my mind is whirling and wandering. And
I see forebodings of evil, Krishna. I cannot foresee any glory
if I kill my own kinsmen in the sacrifice of battle. These I do
not wish to slay, even if I myself am slain. Shall we not, who
see the evil of destruction, shall we not refrain from this
terrible deed?*

He released his slave and returned to his room in the chapel
on the mount. Pony had already remade the bed and set out
his nightclothes and some drinking water. And a shot of
whiskey.

Good old Pony.

He lay down, the comlink on the marble-topped nightstand. He lifted his hand to it, wanting to call. But he could
not. He had nothing new to say. He would sound very weak
and frightened.

The Zealot called in the middle of the night. Shad Iliya
rolled to the nightstand and lunged for the com with shaking
hands. *Will he surrender and avert this bloodbath?*

No. He said he was lonely.

Shad Iliya was stunned. "So you call *me?*"

"You are the only man in the galaxy who can possibly be
as lonely as I."

Shad Iliya fell back on the bed, his eyes directed up at the
painted ceiling in the dim light.

Truth.

Cricket sounds and cypress scent drifted through the window. The night was starry.

Shad Iliya checked his chronometer. It was nearly time for the next missile strike.

"You are probably worse off," said the Jew. "Because you are wrong and know it."

"*Please*."

"Beg with me, Shad Iliya?"

"You know you will be slaughtered."

"I know that?"

"Are you waiting for a miracle?" Shad Iliya rasped savagely.

The Jewish commander was grim. "No. There will be no miracles today."

Shad Iliya closed his eyes tightly.

O gods, there truly will be a battle! The realization sickened him. *That is it. That is it.*

He tried to encourage himself with scriptures:

To forgo this fight for righteousness is to forgo thy duty and honor.

Fighting is obligatory, much as you dislike it.

The latter law the Na'id had taken from the Koran. And, realizing that, Shad Iliya fell deeper into despair. With both sides equally unbending, there was no way out. None at all.

Shad Iliya rose before dawn and bawled for Pony to bring his dress uniform from the ship. Pony obeyed and helped him dress, including a bullet plate. Shad Iliya activated the radiation screen in his belt and drank the radiation medicine Pony brought as an extra precaution.

General Shad Iliya appeared on the steps of the war office in high temper, his eyes ringed angry red, his uniform blazing metallic blue. Everyone else was in battle drab.

He marched over the crest of the Mount of Olives to address his troops. A holo transceiver carried his image to his soldiers on all sides of the city. His fury channeled to fervor, and he stirred in them a patriotic spirit he did not feel. Then, more to encourage himself than them, he read from scripture in a sonorous voice:

" 'No one can bring to an end the Spirit which is everlasting. Therefore, great warrior, carry on thy fight. If any one thinks he slays, and if another thinks he is slain, neither knows the ways of truth. The Eternal in thee cannot kill; the Eternal in thee cannot die. Weapons cannot hurt the spirit and fire can never burn it. The Spirit that is in all beings is immortal in them all. For the death of what cannot die, cease thou to sorrow. Think thou also of thy duty and do not waver. There is no greater good for a warrior than to fight in a righteous war.' ''

He closed, and the army erupted into cheers that resolved into a chant—not the Bel's name, or any of the Empire's catchwords, but his name, Shad Iliya.

There remained ten minutes until dawn. Shad Iliya gave the order to mobilize. He climbed back to his observation post on the chapel steps.

The city was quiet. The defenders were in hiding. They would have to be hunted down in the narrow streets and closed buildings, each a kind of fortress in itself with many traps.

The sun rose golden on the ancient town.

O God, save your city.

There were no crickets, no birdsongs this dawn. The muezzin's morning prayer call went unanswered.

I am going to take Jerusalem, and even the God of three peoples cannot stop it.

Not even I can stop it.

The Na'id army appeared on the horizon on all sides at once, a black shroud of soldiers and transport ships and guns drawing in on the city.

A cry rose out of Jerusalem as if the city itself had a voice.

Be frightened, Jerusalem. Be frightened and live.

The tall Na'id standard crested the Mount of Olives behind Shad Iliya and cast a long shadow across the entire city, old and new. Shad Iliya found himself in its shadow.

He scared himself with the sight he had created. He was struck by a strong premonition of death.

Across from him, on the far horizon, the great dragon cannon Ba'al loomed, its mouth gaping at the new city.

This is an abomination. What have I done?

He spoke into the command circuit. "Anthem."

The inciting military music sounded through the tiny speakers each Na'id soldier carried, and the Na'id army charged and opened fire with great din. Shad Iliya covered his ears with his hands.

Ra'im shouted at his side, "Sir, is all that racket necessary?"

The general nodded. "For the Arabs. If they cannot hear it, they think it will not hurt them."

They were an emotion-led people. Their wailing war cries

curdled the blood. Both sides of this conflict were acquainted with the great power of sound.

The defenders had a few surprises. Shad Iliya had anticipated that there would be some. One was a portable scatter-dart cannon that swiveled and felled Na'id ranks on the north side of the city.

Shad Iliya was on the command circuit quickly. "The scatter cannon," he said sharply. "Take that out. Whatever we have to use."

A cluster of twenty-four smart missiles were launched at it en masse. One got through, and Shad Iliya relaxed a measure. The expenditure of precious hardware did not bother him. What else was it for?

He wished it could all be done with robots. As the battle progressed he watched, sickened, as each contingency which he had hoped to avoid arose, and blood flowed in answer to it. The soldiers of both sides were heroes all, the best fighters on Earth—the people of Jerusalem fighting for their God, the Na'id fighting for Shad Iliya.

And my people can see me, Zealot. Your God is painfully absent here.

A beam ricocheted off his personal n-screen. He wheeled and fired toward the source with a bullet gun.

A child carrying a beam gun reeled back with a high-pitched grunt and died. It was a barefoot, runny-nosed gamin someone had taken in.

The body was spirited away by Na'id soldiers with hurried, embarrassed apologies.

Shad Iliya was left agitated and ill. The shock was not at the child's tender age—to Shad Iliya human beings did not gain or lose value with age—but that the child was human. Shad Iliya had never killed a human being with his own hand. It was too easy. There ought to have been more to it.

He swallowed down a rising gorge, lifted his scanner scope to his eyes, and watched the battle.

An hour passed. He contacted Ra'im, whom he had sent to supervise the western front. "Pull out of the west quadrant. Stand by with Ba'al."

"General, do you think—?" Ra'im started, stopped, re-started. "Sir, we're holding our own."

Questioning orders was unlike Ra'im. This battle was affecting him too. "This will go on all day," said Shad Iliya.

"At this rate, the city will fight to the last infant." He needed to break the back of the defense. Now.

"Yes, sir," said Ra'im, and he initiated the controlled retreat.

Shad Iliya withdrew into the war office and waited out the evacuation. An officer came to him to report, "We have a prisoner, sir."

"The Jew?" said Shad Iliya. He had ordered only one specific person taken alive.

"His wife," said the officer, and motioned for the woman to be brought in.

She was young—Shad Iliya's age—with long black hair, a dirt-smudged face, and blistered hands. Her wrists were bound behind her back and her ankles were shackled to restrict her steps to an abbreviated stride.

She knew the White Na'id at once. As she faced him, she whisked her long ponytail over her shoulder with an imperious toss of her head and spoke coldly in a rough, throaty voice. "Your wife is said to be the most beautiful woman in the galaxy. What do you want with me, General?"

Shad Iliya was angry. "You are a prisoner of war, not the booty of some pirate raid, so let us not play at that. And yes, my wife is beautiful. Myself, I would let you go."

"That would be a mistake," she said.

"I fear so."

Jewish women were not gentle things.

"Your soldiers are on the run," she said.

Shad Iliya nodded. His people were efficient in carrying out orders. Ra'im had them evacuating from the cannon's path.

The woman frowned, sensing from his calm something sinisterly easy in the Na'id retreat.

The general's young orderly, Sinikar, came into the room carrying a staple gun and ID with which to tag the prisoner's ear. The woman stiffened like a rod as the boy drew near.

"No," said Shad Iliya. He motioned Sinikar aside, and he removed the gold earrings from the woman's right ear and slipped them into her hip pocket. She stood rigid at his grazing touch. He took the ID tag from Sinikar and gently laced it through the woman's earring holes.

Her eyes slid to the side as if trying to see her own earlobe. "What does it say?" A slight quaver betrayed apprehension.

"It says you are dangerous," he said, then to his aides, "Get her out of here."

They walked her as far as the door, then she suddenly broke away and ran stiff-legged back to him, yanking at her shackles. "General!" she cried, frightened.

"Yes."

"Am I to be killed?"

"No."

She breathed in relief. But she was unsure if in reality she was better off.

A shout sounded from the portico over a descending-pitched whistle. "Incoming!"

"Get down!"

Shad Iliya dropped to the floor, taking the Jewish woman with him, covered his head and hers, since her hands were bound, as the shells exploded around the building in thunderclaps and clods of upheaved dirt clattered down on the roof in a dark hailstorm. One shell blasted very near and rang the chapel like a drum, sending down a rain of plaster on their heads and strewing white dust across the time-faded colors of the patterned floor.

Shad Iliya lifted his head, coughed in the dusty, thick, burned air. He checked the woman and then his curly-haired child orderly, Sinikar, for injuries. They were unhurt. He looked up at the ceiling. The centuries-old frescoes of his pretty chapel crumbled around his ears.

Suddenly furious, he dragged himself up and outside. The shelling had stopped. He glared at the city in a rage.

He went inside the office and punched on the command circuit. It was still operative. "Are we clear, Ra'im?"

"Yes, sir," Ra'im answered over the circuit. "We are. But a lot of noncombatants have moved into the west quadrant."

"Commence firing."

Ra'im paused. "You don't mean Ba'al, sir?"

"Yes, I mean exactly that!" Shad Iliya cried and punched off the circuit. *Am I speaking Swahili? Is everyone suddenly become deaf?*

He stalked out to the portico.

Jerusalem's layers of radiation shields were impenetrable to any of the empire's sophisticated death rays of a frequency higher than ultraviolet. But simple, primitive fire could pass through as unimpeded as visible light.

The ominous, dragon-faced tower of Ba'al came to life with a roar of flames and sent a long river of fire arching into the new city.

A shudder ran through Shad Iliya with the streaming flames and the long scream of his Jewish captive in the doorway behind him. Tears from some unknown emotion threatened his eyes. He inhaled unevenly, his shoulders, back, and neck taut. The scream from the city reached him even here. He shuddered again.

People flooded out of the western city, fleeing to the unburned part. They crowded toward the Old City. The Na'id would not destroy that part. There the fighting would be hand-to-hand.

A wall of thick, flickering orange-black fire was West Jerusalem. Its gutted buildings belched up more hell-hued billows. Shad Iliya watched, wild-eyed, as if mad.

He felt as if this were the first time he had ever really fought a battle. His enemies, dying before his onslaught, were people. Part of him felt sick, part . . .

His self sickened him.

In extremity, the veneer of humanity was wont to disintegrate, till one was left facing his essential self and nothing else. And seldom answered in times of rationality was the question of what happens when one cannot live with what he finds.

The great flames roared and billowed and snapped like a flag in the wind.

So unfurl our standard and fly our true colors. Flame and death.

The Jew's wife, several paces behind him, cried a contralto wail over her beloved, city, a pure emotion he could never find in himself. Shad Iliya never could act what he felt, and was never sure quite what or if he was feeling.

He beheld the city with his rounded, white-circled eyes, sweat on his brow, a lump risen in his throat. This felt like emotion. And the city burned.

The woman ran to his side with her shortened steps. "Stop it! Stop! I see you loathe it too! You are dying before my eyes!"

He gestured for her to be taken inside.

A girl soldier came to his shoulder, looked aside at her staring general, then followed his gaze to the burning city. "Terrible, isn't it," she said.

Shad Iliya couldn't speak. *Terrible*.

He saw the defenders braving the flames. Their heroism never failed. It was not simple martyrdom—there was that too—but these people wanted to *live*. Their energy, their spirit, their *life* could not be snuffed out. It put Shad Iliya to shame.

A black cloud drifted over the city and toward the Mount of Olives. Shad Iliya watched it come with detached disbelief. It was on him before he thought to go for a mask, and he was suddenly blinded, choking, and unable to breathe.

Someone groped to his side and pressed a mask to his face. It was the girl soldier, giving her general her own mask; then she staggered off blindly for another.

Shad Iliya retreated inside the chapel and shut all the windows. He tore off the mask. The air inside was hot and close and hung with floating soot.

The comlink sounded. Shad Iliya grabbed it out of his pocket in surprise.

A cold voice said, "You are brutal, Philistine."

"Did you think you had a monopoly on that as well?" said Shad Iliya.

"I did. No. Not a monopoly. A supremacy. We can be ruthless when we need."

"I am aware." He replaced the link in his pocket and turned his eyes to the Jew's wife, crouched in one corner of the war office. He and she were alone in the room.

Why didn't I let them talk?

He knew why. He wanted her. He was alone and he did not want her to have someone else, least of all the Jew.

He had never wanted a woman so strongly as he suddenly wanted this one. He could not say why. *Because she is here? Because she is his?*

"Stop staring at me," she said.

"I like you," he said.

Her back straightened against the wall. "May I say, General, that you revolt me?"

Shad Iliya was stung. He replied wearily, without rancor. "Why not? You Jews say what you like; to hell with 'may' or 'may not' anyway."

He checked the computer monitors at his station. One was dark. The Na'id fire had taken out one of their own monitors.

He tried to brush soot from his uniform, then gave up. He was very dirty. Only his watery blue eyes were undulled.

"Shad Iliya?"

It was the woman, crouched in the corner.

He turned, mute.

"I didn't mean that," she said.

He shook his head to say it was nothing.

"I had to say that," She stood. "You are my enemy."

"I am only a man," he said, very tired.

She shook her head, her mouth spread into what would have been a smile were it not so sad. "That is a Na'id view. I don't see that way. I am not Na'id."

He crossed to her and seized her shoulders in his big hands, beseeching and insistent. "You are *human*."

"I am Jewish," she said, helpless before the impasse. She was not immune to the syndrome of loving her captor, but she could remind herself that she was a Jew and this poor monster was not.

She did love him. She knew its cause, knew it to be false, but felt it burn regardless, impervious to logic. She was surprised that it had come over her so fast. But that was what came of living at the brink. The law of mayflies and fireflies; if you have but one day to live, you live your whole life in one day, and brightly.

Shad Iliya still held her shoulders. He heard her breath deepen, and on impulse he drew her in to him and kissed her. Her mouth rose and opened to his in startling passion. Inflamed, he put his arms around her, held her, ran his hands over her hard waist and her moving hips that pressed against his groin. Her grasping hands bound behind her back raked red weals into his hands as they stroked her body. He buried his face in her long hair falling loose from its tie, and a deep, sultry voice in his ear said, "Take me."

Shad Iliya laughed weakly. "I can't. Not now. Later."

"I won't want you later," she said. "I need you now."

He covered her mouth with his, and they sank together to their knees as the flames blazed over her city and an all-consuming dark cloud engulfed the landscape and blackened the windows of the chapel.

Armageddon raged outside—the last great battle between good and evil. Except that there was no good and no evil.

Just us. And both of them were terrified beyond what the human body and spirit were meant to bear. They pressed together and licked and bit and sucked and groaned in animal abandon—the rest outside was madness and this the only sane thing being done in the world.

His passion-clumsied fingers had only begun to fumble at the closings of their clothes when one of his aides cried from outside, "General!"

Shad Iliya scrambled to his feet and ran to the door, forgetting his mask. But the slight wind over Jerusalem had shifted and the air outside was clearing.

The lifting cloud revealed a new scene.

A black-robed troop of Moslem soldiers had moved into the valley at the foot of the mount under cover of the black smoke.

Now revealed, they stormed up the slope with a hideous outcry, dying by the tens and twenties with every step as Shad Iliya's guards cut them down in rows, and still they came with warbling shrieks. The Arabs used the most modern weapons—beams—which reflected off the modern Na'id screens. They themselves fell to simple old-fashioned bullets, their useless radiation screens aglitter, and still they charged in a torrent as if there were immunity to death in their blood-fierce wails.

Shad Iliya took up a machine gun and mowed them down, row on row as they came at him, right up to his very feet.

When they were all dead, he took a staggering step backward. His hands shook; his eyes stared.

People. These were human. There were hundreds of them. Their blood was spattered on him. He licked sweat from his lips—tasted blood.

Dizzy, he dropped the gun, dead Arabs all around him, some staring glassily back at him, a ghastly mirror. This was what he saw inside Shad Iliya.

Shad Iliya clenched his fists.

It was their own fault they lay all down the slope in heaps. He wanted to scream at them. *Stupid! Stupid!* They carried the best weapons. But the best weapons did not work here. *Rocks* would have worked better.

Jerusalem, you are stupid!

Idolatry is worse than carnage—so said the Koran. How was the Empire to absorb such a people? They were oblivious to their human kinship. One could only kill them.

Shad Iliya went back inside the chapel to find the Jewish woman. She was dead—without wound, fallen to a beam shot. She was the only person on the mount downed by the Arab attack.

Shad Iliya knelt with a groan. She appeared to be sleeping, her face relaxed into rough-cut prettiness. He did not touch her because he was covered with blood. *Wake up, woman. I need you.*

He tore himself away from her side and stood.

Who is killing whom and why—does anyone know? Do I?

At length, in the evening, the first faction of the defenders surrendered. The Christians were far and away the most reasonable of the three. Racially they were the most Na'id-like, a mixture. They knew suicide when they saw it. Not that they hadn't martyrs. Every people had its share of martyrs, thought Shad Iliya, except the Jews, who were made up of nothing but martyrs as far as he could tell.

Once the Na'id forces occupied the Christian quarter, the Moslem resistance collapsed into confusion and left the Jews outflanked.

Shad Iliya climbed to the summit of the mount at day's end. It was a bloody sunset, the sky aflame with tortured hues. The sun's long light cast a red wash over the burning city.

I warned you, Jerusalem. Did you not believe me? You are my city. What did all your blood gain you?

He stood immobile, a tall, angular silhouette against the flames, his straight arms held a little out from his sides, his feet planted wide on the ground, his head thrown back. The wind fluttered his clothes. He tensed and trembled as if in great pain.

This is yours, Shad Iliya.

The recorders, standing ready to immortalize this moment, caught the victorious general so, surveying his conquest; and this was the scene that would go over the Net.

Down below, Na'id soldiers poured into all parts of the city. An aide came to his general's side.

Shad Iliya's voice was deep. "Inform the Bel: The city is ours."

The veterans of the 9th and 34th armies ran amok in the streets, wreaking their personal vengeance on the city that had spat at them for so long. They killed, raped, and maimed, out of control.

"There will be charges filed in cases of excessive violence," Shad Iliya ordered over the command circuit. It was a threat only. He did not intend to carry it out. "I want this rampage stopped. And I want the Jewish Zealot. Alive."

Then he secured his personal screen, holstered a handgun, and descended into the city on foot, stepping carefully down the slope cluttered with the bodies of Arabs he had killed. He waded through the garden of Gethsemane, muddy with blood of the faithful, and his boots squished an arrhythmic baseline to the raw chorus of gathering crows and keening eastern women.

The Lion Gate opened for him, and the supreme commander entered the Old City. Blood flowed down the Via Dolorosa, where the fighting had been close-in with bayonets and scimitars.

Shad Iliya turned into a darkened side street, illuminated his lantern, and proceeded slowly down the crooked way. Moldering walls hugged close the avenue strewn with sand and debris, smelling of spice and vegetables and urine. He heard rustling and he halted, lifting his lantern high, expecting snipers.

A herd of mangy goats gazed down at him from a rooftop.

A clothesline stretched across a third-floor balcony, its sooted wash waving in the night wind.

A black kid ran bleating across his path in the stepped, zigzag street, and skirted behind a boarded-up kiosk beside a rickety wooden table on which sat the aluminum keg and three dirty glasses of the water seller. The street's single videophone lay smashed on the concrete.

A jeep whined, careened round the corner, flashing blue and red lights. It jounced to a stop and an aide jumped up. "Sir!"

"Yes."

"The Jewish commander, sir. We have him located."

Located, he said. Not *We have him*. "What do you mean, 'located'? Is he dead?"

"No, sir. He's holed up in an alley. He has a weapon and we can't get near. We're afraid to try stun. He's critically wounded. Should we move an armored tank in, sir?"

"No. Take me to him," said Shad Iliya and climbed into the jeep.

The vehicle swerved through the crooked streets, scattering flocks of geese and chickens before its path and avoiding bodies of the dead and groups of prisoners corralled by the occupation force.

They arrived at the entrance to a cul-de-sac where was amassed a broad array of firepower and soldiers hiding behind either corner. Trapped inside the dead-ended alley was one man.

"What kind of weapon has he got in there?" said Shad Iliya, dismounting the jeep and reviewing the assemblage of arms and artillery that held the Jew at bay. "An atom bomb?"

"No, sir. A pistol, sir. And a knife, we think," said the captain.

"A pistol and a knife," Shad Iliya muttered. "We think." He drifted toward the alley.

The captain gasped and seized his general's shoulders as he wandered too close to the alley's opening. "Stay out of the firing line, sir. He shoots at all comers. He killed our medic."

Shad Iliya shook the captain off and stepped toward the alley.

"Sir, he's a madman!"

"I know that," said Shad Iliya. He walked out into the open and threw his own gun aside.

At the far wall of the cul-de-sac lay the solitary man of about fifty years, short and muscular but not big, his scanty black hair graying. his legs sprawled at odd angles as if his back was broken and he partially paralyzed. He was hardly an impressive figure, and Shad Iliya wondered if this was indeed his adversary. Not that he expected more. He simply realized that he did not know what his Zealot looked like now that he was unarmed and within this man's range. His gesture had been very rash. *Have I a death wish?*

The wounded man lifted his balding head and saw the white Na'id at the mouth of the alleyway, and he smiled as if actually happy to see him. "Ah. Philistine."

Shad Iliya let his hands drop loosely to his sides. He spoke, emotion-choked. "Zealot."

The Jew let him approach. Shad Iliya knelt, lifted the Zealot's head and shoulders off the pavement, and cradled him in his arms. The Zealot let his gun slip from his hand.

Suddenly Na'id soldiers rushed into the alley, but Shad Iliya held up his hand to stay them, and they all froze. "Out," he said.

"But sir—" the captain started.

"It is not my custom to repeat orders!" Shad Iliya roared, still holding his fallen enemy, and the soldiers hastily backed out of the alley.

The Jew shut his eyes, a faint smile on his lips. "Damn, I could've used a voice like that," he murmured. He was very badly hurt, Shad Iliya could see now, some of his bones crushed, his lower organs probably damaged and slow-bleeding. He was dying.

"Our medical technology is better than yours," said Shad Iliya. "You can be revived if you will allow—"

"I'll cut my throat," said the Jew quickly and gripped the hilt of a knife sheathed at his belt.

"Very well." Shad Iliya had expected that answer. "You are going to die then."

The Jew winced in pain, but accepted it, his imminent death.

Shad Iliya suddenly could not. He realized that he did not want the man to die. It frightened him unreasonably.

"If I asked you to live?" said Shad Iliya.

"Why?" said the Jew. "For you?"

"If I ask as a man?"

"Which is to say, 'as a Na'id.' No, Philistine. I like you well, but the life of a man is not at stake here."

"Then tell me what is, and do not say your damned God!"

Brown eyes opened and gazed up at him. The eyes were large, long-lashed and beguiling, the eyes of someone who enjoyed life, lived it very hard and loved many women. "Do you know what freedom means?"

Shad Iliya sighed. "No. I guess I do not. I don't understand."

"Go to Masada, Shad Iliya, if you would understand Jews."

Brown eyes closed. He was not a big man, Shad Iliya noticed; then why was he so heavy in his arms?

"Tricks, Philistine," the Jew spoke again, reproaching, his eyes still shut. "You resorted to tricks. I was foolish not to recognize that flamethrower. Who would have thought it? In this century."

"I had to," Shad Iliya said apologetically. "Your soldiers were better than mine."

"They fight like demons—yours. They do all right for not being Jews and having nothing of substance to believe in." He grimaced with a spasm; relaxed again. "Do they really believe so strongly in that Na'id drivel and doubletalk? What makes them go?"

"They believe in me."

The Jew opened his eyes. "You don't worship a heathen god; you *are* one."

"I begin to think so," said Shad Iliya softly.

The Jew's eyes flitted up and down him, to his sooty hair, dirty face, soiled uniform, and red-brown crusted fingernails. "You're a bloody mess. So how does it feel to kill your fellow humans?"

"What?"

"No *what*, Shad Iliya. This is your day of glory."

"I don't understand," he said, afraid that he actually did.

The Jew moved in for the kill. "Did ever an overwhelming emotion ripple your flat existence before they sent you to kill real men and women?"

Shad Iliya needed quickly to interrupt and shift this line of talk. "And what about you?" he protested.

"No," said the Jew placidly. "I am part of something larger. Something I believed in and still do. You—yours is up in flames." He gestured up to the ash-smeared sky with his eyes. "See there the family of humankind blots out the stars. It's splattered on your face."

An explosion somewhere in the city punctuated the accusation.

"Shad Iliya, I am in a great deal of pain already. Please don't squeeze my ribs so tight."

Shad Iliya loosened his hold mechanically, hardly hearing him with his conscious mind, all the pitiless words driving straight to his heart and into his guts. He stared without real sight.

"Oh, Shad Iliya, you loved it. You were never so alive in your life. The rest is tasteless. You don't even like sex. This is your lust."

Shad Iliya uttered a groaning growl of fury under snapping rein. "You are calling me a pervert."

"You are. The worst kind."

"I fucked your wife."

"No, you didn't," said the Jew as if he really knew. "Here is your ultimate act of love." He slipped his dagger into Shad Iliya's hand. "And you never loved anyone more than me."

Incensed, Shad Iliya took the knife from the Zealot and stabbed into his chest. He did not know how many times.

Warm blood on his hands, Shad Iliya lowered the body to the ground—or pushed it off his lap. He did not know exactly what he did. And he got up on wobbly legs to stand alone in the alley, not certain who had more thoroughly destroyed whom. The Jew was dead. *But what am I?*

Shad Iliya had only killed the Jew. What the Jew had done to Shad Iliya he did not yet know. The Jew had done something—irreversible and final as death. He was the last human being Shad Iliya ever killed.

The young general emerged from the alley badly shaken.

His officers brought to him another prize with which they thought he would be pleased—Her Eminence Cardinal Miriam.

Plodding slowly with swollen ankles, not to be hurried on any account, the stout, white-haired woman let herself be led, sedate and unresisting, but still righteously proud.

Brought before the general, she glanced at him once. "Your hands need washing." And that was all she had to say regarding Shad Iliya.

She had blue eyes.

Two officers assisted the cardinal into a jeep to take her to the prison ship.

Shad Iliya wandered away with aimless, stumbling steps, his aides following uncertainly at a good distance.

The crowded buildings opened to a wide way where the dead bestrewed the street, twisted in the shapes of a violent end, fallen over each other, spreading sticky pools.

Shad Iliya stared with unholy awe; there was an obscene beauty in the stillness. He walked softly among the tortured corpses, unblinking.

Black-faced crows sailed out of the night sky and settled on the bodies.

Shad Iliya reached for his gun; did not have it; seized

someone else's—one of his aides'—out of its holster and shot at the birds.

The flock of them rose with a riot of hoarse squawking.

Shad Iliya screamed an order. "Get those things off our dead!"

"Those aren't ours—"

"Keep them off!" He ran up the gradient bricks of a ruined wall and fired at the crows from the top. "Get them off!"

His aides rushed to see the command carried out. "Yes, sir!"

From his vantage atop the wall, Shad Iliya could see the red glow from the western city, and caught glimpses of his soldiers rounding up prisoners in various sectors. Sporadic gunfire marked the clearing out of remaining pockets of resistance.

He climbed down from the wall. He had a vow to keep. He mounted a jeep and ordered the driver take him to the Dome of the Rock.

His orderly, Sinikar, offered him a gas mask at the door of the mosque. He did not take it.

He wished he had. Inside was a grisly scene of slaughter, and the fetor of mortification hit him in a suffocating wave. He held his breath. His eyes watered and throat constricted, trying to gag.

It was the same in all the mosques and churches and synagogues. The people had taken refuge in the houses of their God as if He would save them. He hadn't. They died so easily. And He did not strike down Shad Iliya.

Allah had told His people: *Fight for the sake of Allah those that fight against you.*

They had.

Kill them where you find them. Drive them out of the places from which they drove you. Do not fight them in the precinct of the Holy Mosque unless they attack you there; if they attack you, put them to the sword.

The colorful walls of the holy mosque were smeared with blood, the floor piled with bodies wrapped in their prayer rugs because someone had tried to make it neat for him. The air was cooling with nightfall, but the place was still thick with a miasma of rot and rigor from bodies cooking in the ninety-degree heat of day.

Of a sudden, from above, the loud deep prayer call erupted in its changeless refrain. It was a recording. A dead voice calling dead Moslems to pray to an indifferent God.

Is anyone left to answer that?

Shad Iliya beheld all the prostrate bodies, a travesty of adoration in the reeking air. The voice blared and reverberated insensate. Shad Iliya shook.

It's dead! It's dead! It has been dead all along!

He ran outside and put a bullet through the loudspeaker.

His aides came to him, worried. He bent over, hands on his knees, gulping air, his sides heaving. He tried to chase the foulness from his nostrils, his mouth, his throat, but even out here the sticky-sweet, sickening odor of burning human flesh permeated the city.

In weary, croaking voice, he asked, "Do we have anything that will put out the magnesium fire?"

"Yes, sir, but—"

"Then put it out," he said, lifting his head.

In the distance he heard the sound of human voices, many, chanting in unison.

His aide was speaking. "But sir, it will burn itself out by morning."

"*Put it out!*" he shrilled.

The voices in the distance gathered strength and volume. He could make out the words. His name.

"Shad Il-i-ya! Shad Il-i-ya!"

He rubbed his hands against the sides of his uniform, but there was not a part of him clean of blood.

He remembered what the Jew had said—*It is on your head, Shad Iliya.* In the aftermath, he felt it.

"Shad Il-i-ya! Shad-Il-i-ya!"

It is on your head, Shad Iliya

He knew it was. There was nothing he could do to change it.

He could only keep silent and wish his station would allow him to cry.

Upon taking the city, Shad Iliya was immediately relieved of supreme command of the combined armed forces at Jerusalem. Someone else was put in charge of normalization. It would not do to have a nazi lord over the city. And Shad Iliya was grateful not to linger over the kill. Later the honors and decorations would be heaped high to bury the intimated slight.

Shad Iliya was uninterested, totally oblivious to the state of his honor. He roamed his ship listlessly. He was bathed and dressed in a fresh uniform of olive drab, his blond hair stripped so clean it drifted up in untamed oilless wisps. Everything around him was scoured and spotless. His bare feet collected no dust on the pristine deck. His fingernails were cut very short, smooth, white, and immaculate. It had taken hours to steam the feel and stench of death from his pores

Some orderly or officer was always there to wait on his every order and whim. He said, staring, "When you stab someone more than once it means you are deranged, does it not?"

"Oh, the Zealot, Abram," said the adjutant. Shad Iliya really had made a mess of him. "Don't worry, sir. That part didn't get out to the news Net."

That was hardly the point. Shad Iliya walked away from the adjutant.

He was still in shock, still bewildered. "I don't understand," he murmured. "I don't understand Jews."

Go to Masada, Shad Iliya, if you would understand Jews.

Birds sailed through the canyon, small and swift and smooth, black with dull orange atop their wings. Shad Iliya looked down at them from the top of the massif, a height that was dizzying for its steepness rather than actual elevation.

Desert. All pale brown and white earth surrounded the fortress. No growth but a bare touch of sparse, dull scrub winding along the dried-up wadi far below. Silent but for the wind. Utter silence broken by high lonely cries of the birds sailing through.

Zealot, you are mocking me with this.

He wandered among the ruins alone; sat on a step of a building that was long gone. Bewildered.

Masada was a desolate tell among several other eroded desert mesas banded in brown and lighter brown strata. Piles of scree slipped down the cliff faces and lay in fans at their bases. The air was very dry, making details clear, flattening everything to cartoon unreality.

Shad Iliya brushed away a fly.

This is me, not you, you stupid Jew.

Magnificent, wind-blown waste.

Hard shadows. Sky blue above. Dusty, pale horizons.

On the other side of the tell were more cartoon-stark canyons and the turquoise Dead Sea.

Why must everything be dead?

He had come here for an answer, and there *was* something here. He wished someone would explain.

The sun rose higher; shadows shrank. The jagged, sharp shadow of the massif drew in toward its western face in the advancing daylight and became something ominous and awesome in Shad Iliya's sight.

The shadow of Masada. It did not talk.

I don't understand Jews at all.

The Bel invited Shad Iliya to a fête in his honor at the palace on Mat Tanatti. Shad Iliya requested time to recover, so the Bel sent him to a villa on the coast of the Levant, a beautiful, relaxing place, and sent Shad Iliya's older brother there personally to ensure his comfort. The hero who brought the hundred-year battle to an end could ask for anything and it would have been granted. He wanted nothing.

One of his aides, a lieutenant, worried that his general was despondent, but he was not of a rank to say so and be heard.

Shad Iliya prowled the halls of the villa, not to be consoled by anyone. Neither did Na'id philosophy soothe: *Time destroys all. If you had not fought them, still they would have died.*

Because it was not the carnage that haunted him. It was the liking it. He mentioned it in an unguarded moment to his brother.

"Oh bosh, Shadi; you're the gentlest, most philanthropic person I know."

Shad Iliya whirled on him, eyes ablaze, teeth bared. His brother exited quickly because he knew Shad Iliya meant to kill him.

He boarded a ship for Mat Tanatti, deciding Shad Iliya needed a few days in relative solitude. His famous brother was simply distraught from the battle and his herculean efforts. And the incident did not merit repeating

*   *   *

Shad Iliya sat drinking at a painted wrought-iron table and chair set out for him on the beach. His aides stayed apart but to replace the bottle and to bring to the table a receiver which would pick up the Bel's speech when it was broadcast over the Net.

This is the hour of humankind's greatest victory. . . .

The air above the water shimmered in the summer heat. Shad Iliya's head lolled onto his shoulder. He poured another glass of cognac—poured twice as much as made it into the glass. No matter. The bottle was always full.

. . . a new nation in which we are all brothers and sisters. And no human being calls anyone Master. . . .

The words shimmered with the air, as if he could see the sound. It was coming from all sides. No. It was inside his head.

. . . Babel refounded. We are one people once more. United we stand and even God shall not sunder us ever again.

Before him the glittering Mediterranean lapped at the brilliant strand. He was hot. His blond hair felt as straw tinder to the touch of his hand.

The water lured. He gravitated toward it.

The beach was soft and difficult to walk; his feet kept sinking in the burning white-gold sand, making his steps more staggering.

At last he slipped into the warm water. Either it was warm or he was drunk; probably drunk, he concluded, because he had taken his glass with him. He was perplexed to find salt water in it instead of cognac when he took a drink.

He swam. His thoughts and perceptions ran clear—seemed to. The world was incandescent, the late sun bright upon the water.

Waves rolled in, lifted him, and he rode up with them. The bigger ones swelled over his head and made him sputter and blink.

He saw where the waves were flattened, and he made his way there to the darker water.

Next the world was dark and gritty without sun as he was drawn with a wave that sucked him down and under.

Strengthless against the current, he tumbled like a rag doll in the turgid water. He saw himself, as if outside himself, in a dream-vision: his bloodless, pasty, blue-white body flopping backward heels over head on a flexuous spine, slack limbs floating and twining in the roiling water, doughy-fleshed and dead.

He blundered into a mass of weeds at the murky bottom, pushed feebly against their slimy leaves, and found his arms tangled in a woven rope net that was pulling him up.

His head broke the surface next to a wooden boat, and he inhaled with a huge gasp.

A voice sounded above him, female and perturbed. "You have torn my net."

"I am sorry." He wiped seaweed from his face. There was no wind. The small fishing boat's single pointed sail hung slack in the still air.

"Hold on to the side of the boat," said the woman. "I will row you ashore."

He grasped the wooden gunwale slick with a thin film of green algae and let himself be towed. It was marvelous to be breathing and to see the setting sun.

The woman put up her oars, several meters out from shore. "Can you make it from here?" she said.

"Yes."

He let go the side of the boat and swam in toward the beach.

He gained footing in the shallows and dragged himself out of the water, then dropped to his knees in the deep sand, exhausted.

Suddenly his aides were swarming around him in alarm—in sheer panic—helping him to his feet, staring into his face, and lifting his eyelids with their thumbs.

What is wrong with them?

"Where were you?" they cried. "We thought you were gone for good!"

"Just a swim," he slurred. *Jushaschwim*, he'd said, belched, apologized thickly.

And they told him he had gone down and did not come up.

"The woman in the boat," said Shad Iliya, turning back to the water.

There was no woman. No boat. Just red sun on water. He blinked. He turned back to his aides, concerned now. "Did you not see her? Sinikar?"

The young orderly shook his head. Someone else said, "He's drunk."

"I am not drunk!" he bellowed, staggered back, retreating from them. Their faces were full of doubt.

"I *am* drunk," he admitted in lower tone. "I am not *that* drunk."

A dry blanket was placed over his shoulders. A condescending voice said, "Come with us, sir."

A groan rose in his closed throat, opened to a roar. "No!" He threw off the blanket and stumbled in the sinking sand to the water's edge. He raised his puckered hands to his brow and scanned the empty horizon. *Where is she?*

He kept tripping along the waterline in search, only to be cut off and surrounded by coaxing, patronizing voices and reaching hands that closed in on him.

Like wild game cornered by hounds, he roared and snapped to keep his aides away from him. He drew himself up in drunken magnificence and proclaimed himself lucid and them all idiots.

They were embarrassed for him. They wanted to clean him off, get dry clothes on him, and put him to bed. He was weak and drunk and tired, and eventually they managed to take him back to his pleasant-scented, airy room in the spacious villa and coerce him, babbling and objecting, in between the crisp fresh sheets.

Pony brought him some tea with honey, lemon, and whiskey.

A lieutenant slapped Pony's golden hands. "No whiskey!"

Shad Iliya sat up in the bed. "Don't hit my slave!"

An aide pushed him back down.

"Where is the woman?" he said. "A Jew. I bet she was a Jew." He ordered she be brought to him.

"We'll look for her, sir."

They were lying to him. He knew they would not look.

"Pony, find her."

Pony was crying. Why was Pony crying? Stupid alien.

In supreme frustration, he closed his eyes and slept for a while, simply to escape the jackasses around him.

He woke in the middle of the night, alone, still drunk. His aides were sleeping in another part of the villa. Pony was out on the beach, looking.

Shad Iliya rose from bed and gazed out the window. The moon was very bright and cast a cold, eerie light on the landscape.

Out on the sand dunes a flock of hooded crows stood, all facing one direction. They were Moslem crows. Facing Mecca.

Shad Iliya turned inside the room. He found a knife and slashed his wrists. He was going to slash more but lost courage.

That was asinine.

He searched for a wrap. He spurted blood all over the room ransacking it for a closure, overturning his nightstand, pulling out drawers and throwing things aside. Finally he summoned a medirobot, which entered via the service chute and sealed his wounds.

Then Shad Iliya set the machine on a self-destruct sequence, furiously jealous of its mindless ability to destroy itself when he could not. And jealous of its mindlessness.

Before the medirobot could explode, Shad Iliya emptied it of its supply of melaninic. He had always wanted to be dark. Then he climbed out the window—his aides had locked the doors—and just wandered away, leaving behind what looked like murder.

Harrison Hall's whisper called him back. "Captain."

Alihahd sensed strain in the voice, but could not answer, staring far away, caught between past and present, wondering what Harrison White Fox Hall was doing on the Mediterranean beach when he hadn't even met him yet.

"You're crushing my hand."

Normality returned to Alihahd's eyes. He released Hall's hand all of a sudden; he could not recall having taken it. Hall's skin stayed whitened a few seconds where he had squeezed it.

It was fully night in the Iry forest. The air was cool and moist, redolent of damp soil, wood, and lush foliage—and the smoky musk of Hall sitting beside him on the rotten log.

From beyond the trees came the subdued sounds of the rebel camp, waiting in stand-off with the mighty Na'id 27th Army.

The past had caught up with him. He had always known it must. Something this big could not stay hidden. The universe was not wide enough. And he had not exactly been avoiding the Na'id these past thirteen years. He had walked in their very midst—as if he wanted to be caught. It seemed he most wanted that which he most dreaded. And what he most dreaded had found him.

This was Jerusalem all over again—a great Na'id force facing a hopelessly doomed and cornered resistance—except that he was on the doomed side this time. Cosmic justice? He had made his last possible play, his only chance, to bluff his way out of the impending battle; he had shown his face.

The Na'id were frightened, for certain; but had it been enough? They had not retreated. They should have done so by now if they were going to. They were still out there on the plateau as if deep down they suspected that the rebel force was only a paper tiger with a clay general.

Prospects looked bleak. They had to run. They had to. There was no other hope.

Alihahd reflected on the events that had brought him to this pass. He could not have done anything differently. All decisions were forced by Fate, despair, ignorance, and cowardice. Had things been different, he could have done differently. But the past was fixed, and hypothetical extrapolations of alternate conditions were futile.

He spoke hypnotically, gazing back at the dream as it faded. "You doggedly execute your duty even though you know you are wrong. You dull your brain with wine to fog the edges of a reality that is too harsh to bear in full light, and still your thoughts will not shut off. There were no choices. It was this or death. And I lacked the courage for an honorable self-execution."

He had spent the two years following the fall of Jerusalem in alcoholic oblivion in the alleys of Cairo, a city that could swallow anyone without a trace. At length he had dared to wake and ask what date it was, and for the first time took a fearful peek over his shoulder to see what he'd been hiding from for two years. It was still there. He was still the man who had taken Jerusalem. And now he was also a deserter from the Na'id army. His name was revered. And in all the universe only he knew it for a lie.

He still could not find nerve to kill himself. So he had to figure out how to live.

Henceforth he was *Alihahd*, and never completely sober, though seldom as drunk as in a Cairo street.

He had tried to make amends with his conscience and do only what he thought right. But that meant assessing first what was right and wrong, what was the measure, and who was the final authority. His ultimate authority used to be the Bel. When he had thrown off the authority of the Bel by deserting, he had kicked the base of his whole life out from under him. The universe was suddenly without direction, confused and terrifying.

In an almost sober moment he'd taken level stock of his situation and asked of his Furies: *Who is in charge here now*? And came the horrifying answer: *You are*.

He had no recourse, even to God. He did not believe in God—not often. And even if he had, he had made war on God's people. He could not call to God.

He was alone in the universe. Most people had someone to answer to—God, parent, country, leader, law.

I have nothing. He was without country, without law, without God. *And I am the leader.*

And now, thirteen years later, the base had collapsed again and the universe was on its ear once more. The ultimate authority was wrong again. Alihahd was revealed as a fraud. So was the legendary Shad Iliya. He was running circles on an eternal battlefield, Hero, Rebel, Traitor, thrice a legend on both sides of the same war.

V. Noblesse Oblige

In the early-morning hours, a messenger ship rolled out of one of the 27th's twelve huge transports, rose from the Na'id camp, and left planet, burning a red streak across the sky. The troubled rebel camp bustled and droned, wondering what the move could portend. Alihahd/Shad Iliya would know. Vaslav was elected to approach him and ask; but no one could find Vaslav. So the rebels drafted another youth to go instead.

The girl came upon the infamous general in the dark of the forest, sitting on a log, talking quietly, human. The girl didn't know what she had expected of Shad Iliya—a man-eat-

ing cyclops perhaps. But despite the horrible white face and
eerie blue eyes, he had not lost the calm demeanor and
personal qualities that made him Alihahd; and the girl dared
come near and ask what he thought the Na'id might be doing
by sending out the small ship.

Alihahd brushed a bug from his sleeve. He had seen the
blazing track overhead, and knew it for a robot ship making
deadly haste to Mat Tanatti. "They are sending to the Bel for
advice. They do not want to use the Net, not even in code."

The girl chewed on her peeling lower lip. "What should
we do?"

"I would say that until the ship returns with instructions
from the Bel, the Na'id will do nothing. So why don't you go
to bed?"

The girl smiled nervously. "Really? We're that safe?"

"For the moment."

The girl cast him a grateful look and ran from the forest.

When she was gone, Hall leaned forward to rest his elbows
on his knees, turned his head to face Alihahd, and said,
"What *does* it mean?"

"It means they are not running," said Alihahd. He tossed
a strip of bark away from him. "It means we are dead."

Nocturnal beasts chittered, hooted, and peeped. Insects sang.
Trees rustled. In the distance the ocean rushed. They were
all lowland sounds, strange to Alihahd's ears, attuned now to
the mountains.

At length, Alihahd rose, exhaled a voiceless sigh. "I suppose it is my turn now." He quit the forest without further
explanation and went to the rebel flagship. Moments later, a
second robot messenger ship took off and painted a red trail
across the stars—this ship from the rebel camp, bound to
where with what message only Alihahd knew.

When Alihahd reemerged from the flagship he found Layla
sitting cross-legged on the ground at the bottom of the ramp,
waiting for him. She had stripped off her shirt; her chest was
beaded with sweat in the sweltering, thick air that did not
cool much with the night as it had on the mountain. She hung
her head. Wilted stray hairs come unbound from atop her
head stuck to her neck. She moved only to swat at the flying
bloodsuckers that lighted on her damp skin.

As Alihahd reached the bottom of the ramp, she looked up
at him for a long time, and finally he questioned it. "Layla?"

"You are a traitor?" she said. Her question was not a question—merely incredulity seeking confirmation.

"It seems I am," said Alihahd.

He was surprised to see Layla looking so ill. He beckoned. "Come inside. This ship can readjust your blood. You will feel better."

She reflected on the offer, then reached up her tiny hand to him. He took it in his own big, gnarled hand and pulled her to her feet.

As she followed him up the ramp, she said, "Do you really think it is a tottering tower of cards?"

"What is?" he said.

"The Na'id Empire."

He had said that once, hadn't he? The woman had a good memory. "Yes," he said. "I am afraid it is."

Layla was reviving when Alihahd was summoned away by one of his rebels shouting from outside, "Captain! Come quick!"

Alihahd descended the ship's ramp at a long-legged trot to find the situation outside radically altered.

Across the plateau, the Na'id had mobilized. Their troops were assembling in the battle order along the perimeter of their defensive energy dome.

Even in the dark, Alihahd could see that their ranks numbered short. At least a quarter of them were missing—presumably wearing activated light-benders and moving God knew where. Alihahd grabbed one of his subordinate commanders by her upper arm. "Tia, get a scanner and find those ghost soldiers. You are looking for maybe three thousand people. Go." As the young woman ran, Alihahd turned to his second. "Musa, what happened?"

"I don't know. They just decided to move," said Musa. "I've ordered all our people into their ships."

Alihahd nodded, watching the massing enemy troops across the field. With his own people inside their ships, the Na'id could not see how frightened and disordered they really were.

"Message for the Na'id?" Musa asked.

"None," said Alihahd.

"Orders?"

"None."

Musa stopped herself from asking, "Do you have a plan at

all?'' Instead, she withdrew to crouch underneath the flagship and activated her personal radiation screen.

Alihahd walked a few steps away from the ships to stand isolated on the wide plain beneath the black sky. This side of the plateau was silent and empty. A moist wind brushed over his skin, rustled his shirtsleeves. Across the way, like a band of clustered stars, was the enemy's twinkling row of lights and screens, nothing to bar their attack.

Alihahd spoke softly into the empty space around him. ''Well, Ra'im?'' The humidity seemed to mute the sound.

Any one of the Na'id viewing him through a scope could have read no feeling, no fear on his face or in his loose stance. And perhaps that was what was giving them pause. They did not advance.

Alihahd heard sauntering footsteps on the charcoal-underlaid grass. They came to a stop behind him. Alihahd did not turn, keeping his eyes on the army that would not attack. ''Delay and delay,' he said in quiet disapproval. ''Like Jerusalem.''

Harrison Hall's ears pricked. *Like Jerusalem.* It was not the first parallel to be noticed.

Was all this intentional? Harrison Hall thought, *We are trapped here under the direction of a guilt-ridden, suicidal Na'id general on the wrong side of the battle of Jerusalem.*

There was a plan after all.

Hall took a backstep. ''Been nice knowing you, Captain.''

Alihahd remained as he was. ''Goodbye, Mr. Hall.''

At his own little camp in the forest, Hall gathered up his things—his pipe, a few packages of foodstuff and a water purifier pirated from the rebel ships stores, a bio scanner, a tinder, and the disparate devices salvaged from his own space-ship, *Nemo,* by the mandesairi—and he fitted them all into a small pack. He stamped out the campfire he'd made for himself, bound back his long graying hair, tied his russet bandanna across his brow, slung his pack over his shoulder, tucked his gun in his belt, and hiked up through the trees.

He had not gone far up the densely forested slope when Layla came running after him, her form sparkling with a radiation screen, a taeben slung from one shoulder. She closed her hands on the retreating man's coat and pulled him to a stop. ''Where are you going?''

"Anywhere else," said Hall. He tugged free of her and took long strides up the mountain incline.

Layla ran alongside him, two steps for his every one. "There is going to be a battle!" she cried.

"Is that right?" said Hall.

"You are needed!" Layla blazed.

Hall faced her. "Not so."

Layla demanded explanation with a freckled scowl.

Hall let his pack slide down his arm to the ground at his side. "He can kill himself without me." Layla started to object, but Hall cut her off. "It's Jerusalem, Layla. This time he's on the side he thought was right the first time around—the side that got butchered. Jerusalem never had a prayer, and neither do we. He doesn't intend to win this one. He doesn't want to. This is a setup for a hopeless battle. History repeats itself—especially when the same person is calling the shots."

Layla turned away. She tilted her face up, blinking quickly with gathering pools in her eyes, trying to deny what she heard

"Vaslav left a long time ago," said Hall. "It's time we did too. If we stay here the possibilities are limited—and survival is not among them. He may run away himself."

Layla wheeled with clenched fists. "No!"

"It would not be out of character." He took Layla's small, callused hand, and uncurled her fingers. "He never deserved the kind of loyalty he commands. Come with me. I need you."

Layla pulled her hand away and threw her head back. "I will stay. And if it is to death, I die."

Hall lifted his pack again and started away backward, still facing Layla for his parting. "He hasn't fought in thirteen years. Unlike some of us, he doesn't even remember *how* to win."

A ship roared overhead, entering Iry's atmosphere. It was another Na'id troop transport bearing reinforcements.

"Sounds like it's starting." said Hall. "You'll be late." He turned and quickened his pace.

Layla ran down the mountain as the ship came to land.

VI. Ends of a Circle

Layla reached the forest edge, dashed across the exposed stretch of plateau, and dived underneath the rebel flagship, where Alihahd and Musa were. No shots had been fired yet. The rebels stayed hidden inside their ships; and the Na'id army still held its position as another Na'id transport ship, the *Dayyanu*, came to land on the Na'id side of the field.

"Reinforcements?" said Layla breathlessly, elbowing her way to crouch between Alihahd and Musa.

"Of a sort," said Alihahd.

Layla lifted the scope of her taeben to watch the debarkation of the new company. Layla was night-sighted and could see well without an infrared filter. "They're all brass and police," she said. "And a general." She quickly groped the ground beside her with a blind hand, keeping her eyes on the scope. "Give me a bolt rifle. I think I can pick him off from here."

"No, Layla." Alihahd stayed her eager hand. "Wait."

Layla straightened and blinked. "Then we are to kidnap him?"

"Wait. Just wait."

Musa pointed. "They're breaking up."

It was true. The Na'id troops had begun to drop back from battle positions along the edge of the shield dome.

"It came over the Net while you were gone," Alihahd told Layla. "A stop order from the *Dayyanu*. The 27th did not believe it until now. They thought it was a trick of ours." He smiled. "Of mine."

"Why would the *Dayyanu* tell the 27th not to attack us?" said Layla. Layla thought in black and white; this did not fit her template.

"There are other ways of winning," said Alihahd. He borrowed Layla's taeben to look at the new general.

Across the plateau, in a small glowtorch-lit ceremony, an

honor guard of the dispirited 27th Army relinquished its standard from the flagship *Nashparu*, sometimes known as *Courier*, to the *Dayyanu*; and General Ra'im Mishari passed the command baton to the new general, an older man unfamiliar to Alihahd on sight.

Damn you, Ra'im. Why did you not run? What an overblown mess this has become.

Ra'im had always been a good soldier. He was not a good leader.

Why did you not stay a lieutenant commander? thought Alihahd. Then, mournfully, *Why did I not stay a general?*

"I can still hit him," Layla insisted.

"Don't hit him," said Alihahd, lacing his long, knobby fingers together. "Where is Mr. Hall?"

"Deserted," said Layla.

Alihahd nodded. "You go too."

"It is my battle!" Layla cried.

"No battle," said Alihahd. "It is a surrender."

"No," said Layla.

"It has to end somewhere—the blood," said Alihahd.

Layla chewed on her lip, brown eyes welling with tears. Suddenly, she seized his arm and pulled. "Then you come back to Aerie with me and Harry. Let *them* fight if you cannot. You are not of them anymore. Or them." She threw her hands toward both the Na'id and the rebels.

"Run?" said Alihahd, his brows elevated into his long, unkempt bangs. "That has to end as well." His voice dropped very low, emotion-suffused. "I am Na'id. I have never stopped being a Na'id."

Layla started to speak.

"Do not fight me, Layla. If I have ever made a harder decision, I do not remember." He passed his hand over his eyelids. His eyes hurt. "My army is not an army. They are a mob. They have no training, no discipline, no experience—and little enough luck, it appears. Half of them don't trust me, and, fact is, neither do I. We never had a prayer here; I do not know what possessed Ra'im to make him think we did. Musa, have you delusions of surviving an armed encounter with the 27th Army?"

Musa expelled her breath and admitted realistically, "No." She crossed her thick arms, still doubting the preferability of

surrender. "What kind of terms do you think you'll get?"
She harbored visions of torture and prison and execution.

"What I *have* are: no investigation or prosecution for past
crimes against the Empire; no reprisals against any of my
rebels for this current action; citizenship for those who do not
resist; no questions."

"How in Creation did you get those?" said Musa.

"Those are the terms I offered to the Bel—take or leave.
He appears to have taken." He indicated the Na'id army
dissolving its battlefront.

"How can you trust the Bel, though?" said Musa.

"The Bel is the only person in this galaxy that I actually do
trust," said Alihahd. "If he gives his word to a thing, then it
is so. You will all be conscripted, of course, as able Na'id
citizens are. But you could fall to a worse army than the 27th.
It is not an agreeable prospect, nor even tolerable perhaps.
But the alternatives are unthinkable. There really are none."

"What about you? What happens to you?" said Musa.

"Me, they will eat." He turned curtly to Layla. "Be off
quickly now before they become greedy. I did not surrender
my allies. Watch for patrols. They will be combing the
woods for deserters. And take Vaslav."

"Vaslav is not here," said Layla.

Alihahd frowned. "Where is he?"

"Gone. He must have run away."

The frown deepened. Alihahd hoped the boy knew what
decisions he could live with. Alihahd was not worried about
Harrison Hall.

A rebel officer called to Alihahd from inside the flagship,
"Captain, there's a message for you from the new commander of the 27th Army. He'll talk only to you."

Alihahd started to rise. He spoke to Layla. "Go now. The
surrender will be at first light." It would take till then to ease
the news to his troops.

At sunrise, the rebels came out of their ships, weaponless,
and deactivated their shield dome.

The 27th Army rushed in.

The sudden charge of soldiers terrified. Their ferocious
speed made it seem they would strike down the unarmed
rebels, under truce or no. But the Na'id only sought to take

control before someone could balk, take out a concealed weapon and start shooting.

There was some brutality, but the old soldiers soon quashed it. Shad Iliya's army still had a tradition of decency.

A group of young military police grabbed Alihahd roughly and placed him under arrest. No veterans of the 27th Army had volunteered for that task; these MPs were from the *Dayyanu*. The new company with its new leadership was disgusted with the 27th Army for its total lack of initiative in this affair. It became rapidly apparent that this rabble band of rebel malcontents in Na'id dress was not an army at all. The Empire had been *had*. But there was no turning back on the Bel's word. And that knowledge made the Na'id furious.

One man spoke and a whole mighty army had turned into a litter of whimpering cubs. Neither did the one man look like much—spindly, limping, worn, on the downhill slope of middle age; the seventy-year-old Bel looked better. And the Na'id scorn mounted. The great general Shad Iliya's incredible record, seen in this new light, was attributed not to genius but to the machinations of a con artist.

They handled him with more force than they needed—he was not resisting—but not half so much as they wanted.

Alihahd endured the abuse—which was mostly verbal, with some hard shoves and spits—and even welcomed it. It was a thing due. He'd been running from it for years and now felt a perverse relief that it had caught up with him at long last.

And the battle had not happened. He'd escaped that trap, the awful circle, with no blood shed but his own. He had revisited Jerusalem and said *This shall not be*.

Someone slapped his face. He tried not to smile or cry.

The MPs chained his hands behind him, then looped the chains around a charred tree, where he was to stand for hours while his rebels were searched, corralled, identified, and their criminal records deleted, to the increased grumbling of the loyal Na'id. And periodically, young soldiers filed by to gawk at the Traitor with mutters and torment.

The veterans of the 27th Army avoided him.

Even his rebels, feeling sold, called him Traitor.

The sun beat down on the windless plateau. The dead tree offered no shade, and Alihahd languished in the stifling air.

The afternoon wore on; he felt his skin burn, his joints

ache, his muscles cramp with dehydration in the suffocating heat, and he gloried in the pain. *Some kind of deviate you are.*

His perception split onto two levels, one aware in bright detail of the burning ache in his limbs, the itch of his clothes stuck to his wet skin, the fly that kept returning to his twitching cheek. On the other level his mind was detached, and he felt surprisingly well. And he was aware that his sense of well-being was symptomatic of serious trouble. But since there was precious little he could do about it and no one around him who could possibly care, he ignored the hazard and enjoyed the alertness.

He recovered some sense of *self*—or found it; he was not sure he'd ever had it to begin with.

After a long while, an MP strutted a slow circuit around the prisoner's tree, his wide chest thrust forward, his fleshy buttocks thrust back. He stopped before Alihahd. Bulging eyes looked down a wide nose. Thick sensual lips formed a sneer. "What's the matter, nazi? Too good for us with your pretty blue eyes and your yellow hair?"

Alihahd gave no answer. There had been no real question.

Another MP circled in from behind, the same curl on her lips. She plucked at Alihahd's loose, rough-weave shirt, inspecting the unfamiliar fabric between her stubby fingers. "What kind of costume is that?" she said.

"Doesn't match your eyes," the man commented on the side.

Alihahd sighed and answered civilly, "It is the dress of the people of Iry."

The woman sniffed disdainfully. "There are no people of Iry."

Alihahd wondered how he could have let that slip his mind. *I have changed. This place has truly done something to me.*

The fleshy man made another remark about his pretty blue eyes.

Alihahd lost patience. He snapped his head around and shot at him, "I think you like my pretty blue eyes."

Thick lips twisted into amazing shapes of outrage. The pulpy face beetled huge in Alihahd's field of vision, breath smelled sickly sweet, and suddenly his knee smashed up into

Alihahd's groin with an explosion of pain and nausea. Alihahd folded over, unable to breathe—and he knew the man enjoyed that too. He should not have invited it, he thought dimly as he sank down the tree to which he was bound, drawing air in a ragged gasp.

A party of officers marched to the site and dismissed the MPs.

The ranking officer, a lieutenant of the new company, merely stood over him for some moments, watching him retch and gasp at the foot of the blackened tree trunk. Then she pulled him to his feet by his hair and stepped back. She regarded the hand with which she'd grasped his hair curiously and remarked to one of her companions, "Hot."

Alihahd panted, his weight pitched back against the chained post, trying not to pass out, then wondering why he bothered to try. The revilement started up again, of slightly more literate and vastly more pretentious bent than what the MPs served him. The neat and pretty little lieutenant with the blindingly shiny buttons had a big voice and an advanced education, the better with which to recite her creed at him. For her and the young officers this was a chance to lambaste a general with impunity. One even drew a blade and set it against Alihahd's throat. "You will suffer all the torments of hell for what you've done, Traitor."

Alihahd had recovered his breath. "Unless hell is peopled with fools such as you reciting their everlasting twaddle, I would gladly go this very moment, if any of you is willing to send me without an order from your betters." He spat the last word at them, and his eyes flashed down toward the blade at his neck, daring them.

He could almost hear Harrison Hall chuckling at *that* speech.

The officers were taken aback. The blade was sheathed. "Be too merciful," one mumbled.

"Then you may stop your threats and posturing and you may shut up. I am not impressed or frightened. I am, however, annoyed."

"You would do well to be fright—"

"Am I then to be killed with the jaw of an ass?" Alihahd roared to the sky. "The glory of the Na'id Empire is its unparalleled ability to vomit back cant."

And all six officers at once contested that charge hotly.

Deliverance came at last, painfully, in the form of a veteran officer who had walked over to them, attracted by the noise, and observed, quietly appalled. He called it off, then stood looking at his former general in shame, shook his balding head, and walked away.

Alihahd was sorry. He could have taken the empty heckling all day, but that one silent look of shame undid him. His head slumped on his chest; his eyes closed. He listened to the distant tide; it would be going out now. Tides were wonderfully predictable without moons, but not very powerful. He focused on the sound of far-off water, let it rush through his head, until the crunch of a single set of footsteps came very near along with the oscillating beep of a medikit.

Alihahd lifted his head, finding it strange that someone should be interested in his state of health.

Not this man. The medic set the kit down brusquely and dutifully took a sounding of the captive, without one ounce of personal care. He was a coarse, common man wanting to do his job and be done. "Where've you been?" the medic said gruffly, confounded by the reading. He took of his hat and mussed his already disheveled hair.

"That machine ought to tell you," said Alihahd.

The medic clicked off the scanner dubiously. "A mountain?"

Alihahd nodded, his throat too dry for many more words.

"Your heart is bigger."

"Is that a fact," said Alihahd faintly.

"Strictly literal, sir," said the medic and rummaged through his kit for a diadermic injector, which he brought to Alihahd's chest.

"Poison?" said Alihahd.

"If it was up to me," said the medic. He gave the injection, and Alihahd immediately felt a few degrees cooler and more comfortable. He was surprised.

"Who ordered this?"

"Supreme Commander General Işşurish," said the medic testily, putting his kit back together. "You've been summoned to his presence." The man snapped his lips shut, reconsidered, and rephrased under strain, "Invited. I'm to *ask* you."

"Well," said Alihahd lightly, feeling buoyant on his borrowed time. "If it will get me out of the sun, lead on." He shrugged in his chains.

The medic grumbled, let slip a curse, then said, "You won't tell on me, will you, sir?"

Evidently he had orders to be polite. "No," said Alihahd.

The medic grunted, took up his kit, and tramped away to send back a six-person escort-guard to collect and deliver the supreme commander's guest.

VII. Jerusalem Stands

The cabin inside the Na'id flagship *Dayyanu* was blessedly cool and air-controlled. It took Alihahd's eyes a moment to adjust to the softer light.

The supreme commander, General Işşurish, waved away the six enormous guards in the unhurried way of gentry, leaving him alone with the captive. The general did not worry that his prize prisoner might bolt or attack him. Alihahd's hands were still bound. That precaution was more than sufficient. Işşurish was a big man, if not nearly as tall as Alihahd.

The general was a patrician, full of manners and breeding— one of Alihahd's own kind.

"Shad Iliya," said Işşurish in greeting, swiveling his chair to face him. "And Alihahd also, I believe."

Alihahd stood mute. His silence convicted him.

"You are two men I've always wanted to meet." The general had a long-standing admiration and sense of professional rivalry with the great Shad Iliya; and an obsession with bringing the infamous Alihahd to justice. But since both had been reported dead, Işşurish never dreamed he would actually meet them—and not in the same person.

At first the idea of the two being the same was incomprehensible. How could such an illustrious proponent of the Na'id ideology turn about-face and become such a trenchant foe? But it made more and more sense as he thought about it, and Işşurish began to nod.

Zealots did not come from nothing. Işşurish remembered the story of the Christian zealot St. Paul, who had been no unknown, apathetic unbeliever before his conversion, but rather a notorious, active, fanatical Christian-killer. To Işşurish there was nothing at all miraculous about a zealot's becoming a zealot. Goals may change. People did not. Great hate could become great love, or love hate. The degree was constant. If Shad Iliya were to transgress, he would transgress hugely— nothing furtive and measly about it.

That Shad Iliya was Alihahd made all the sense in the world.

Işşurish did not expect to understand Shad Iliya's *reasons* for betrayal, and he was not going to berate him. The prisoner was his honored enemy.

Işşurish had never met a legend before. Strange, he looked like a man—a battered, outspent one at that—dirty, ragged, tough-knit, and too lean, nothing at all soft but those liquid eyes. There was something very human in his worn, bedraggled features. And something else, the elusive quality of an immortal leader. It could not be pinned down, but it was definite in its existence.

"I wish we could have met on the battlefield," said Işşurish. He wanted to do battle with a legend and see who won.

Alihahd did not. There was no more romance in war against his own kind. He had already had his time to match wits and strengths with a great adversary in a battle to live through the ages. He had his undying fame; and all he could see was a hillside littered with human dead.

It was not to be explained. And this man would not understand, even had he been there.

"Your army is a disappointment," said Işşurish. "The 27th."

The brilliance of the 27th Army under Shad Iliya had been that each member worked well in his or her singular capacity. Ra'im Mishari was a perfect second-in-command, and everyone else was perfect in place. But after Shad Iliya had gone, they had all been promoted to positions in which they did not belong, and perfection had fallen apart.

"The victories must have been yours, not theirs," Işşurish said. "Such a loss." He shook his head. "You present a sensitive problem, General. I'm not sure yet what I'm going to do with you." Then, as if suddenly realizing that he was remiss as a host, the patrician sat forward and solicitously swept his arm toward a chair. "Sit. Water? Are you hungry?"

Still standing and making no move toward the offered seat, Alihahd spoke for the first time, in a flat tone of injured pride and rebuke. "I have not been given leave to piss since I surrendered."

Işşurish was alarmed at his oversight as only aristocracy could be. There were still manners in the field.

Alihahd's bonds were removed, and he was permitted to go unguarded to the commander's facility. He had, after all, come to them of his own accord.

When he returned to Işşurish, he sat in the chair, his weight to one side, elbow on one chair arm, his feet flat on the deck and spaced wide, relaxed, yet alert and commanding, even as a prisoner. His presence seemed to take over whatever sphere he came into.

"Do you want a change from those barbarous clothes?" said Işşurish.

"These are fine," said Alihahd. He knew he must smell gamy by now, but he had become attached to this alien garb, and the supreme commander could just endure the stink. Alihahd was not feeling as magnanimous as his host.

"Your funeral was very inspiring," said Işşurish, wending his way leisurely to the point of this meeting. "I was profoundly stirred."

Alihahd said quietly, "I saw it."

It had been broadcast over the Net to all parts of Na'id-controlled space, a ceremony of great pomp and solemnity. There had been a long procession with horses and foot soldiers and drums. The Na'id standard had bowed to Shad Iliya's family crest; and flags were lowered to half-mast throughout the Empire.

He remembered now that his daughter, Nikalmati, had been crying.

His beautiful widow, Libbya, had not. She stood, tragic and cold, with her lover standing a few paces in the background. It was a small scandal when she remarried before the official mourning period was done. Alihahd thought it a wise move on her part not to be called Shad Iliya's widow for long.

There was erected a cenotaph, and a shrine in his honor—not as a god, but as a hero. And he had his day of the year when a rite was performed for him. Respect for great men and women did not end at death for the Na'id.

To discover that they had been revering a live traitor for the past thirteen years would be a major scandal.

It was too late to execute him quietly and pretend he had never surfaced. Too many people already knew.

"It is in the terms of surrender that your life is forfeit," said Işşurish. "But I'm not sure if the Bel wants me to execute you here or if I'm to bring you back for public trial. He signed it rather peremptorily. He did not elaborate on his orders. He was quite upset." He watched Alihahd's face for reaction, saw little that he could read. "He left it up to my discretion—which means I'm to read his mind and do what he wants." Işşurish was talking confidentially to someone who also knew the Bel intimately. "You know how he is."

Alihahd motioned affirmative with a close of his eyes. He knew.

"I would like to be able to tell you exactly what you are in for," Issurish continued. "I have no desire to make this too bad for you. It will be suitably bad enough as it is. But I have not yet decided. I am not a mind reader."

"The Bel sent you here to dispose of me for him," said Alihahd. "Of course, he will hold it against you when you return to Mat Tanatti, but it is what he wants. He cannot tell you outright because he needs you to take responsibility for the action."

The general nodded. It sounded in keeping with the Bel's sometimes split character. The Bel's words, thoughts, and actions were not always outwardly in synch. The curse of the Bel's preeminent position was that he was seldom free to speak his mind or heart.

Işşurish was afraid that Shad Iliya was right. Işşurish would bear the brunt of this debacle. The Bel would be furious if he reported Shad Iliya dead, furious if he brought him home.

But in time, the Bel would forgive and reward those who made hard and ugly decisions for him and saved him from public grief.

Yes, Shad Iliya knew the Bel very well.

Işşurish had not actually been asking for help from his prisoner. He was informing him of his status. For the rest, Işşurish had been thinking aloud to someone he knew could appreciate his predicament, talking calmly of deadly concerns, as if they were strolling in one's ornamental garden admiring the blooms and bragging about their children. It was the patrician way—artificial and comical to most, but it was a way Alihahd was bred to, knew, and was at home with, civilized to the last.

"Morning too early for you?" said Işşurish.

He meant the firing squad.

"Fine," said Alihahd and rose.

Işşurish stood also and paged his orderly. In a sudden surge of bottled-up disappointment, he said, "You never struck me as the venal type, Shad Iliya."

"I was not bought," said Alihahd.

"I was hard put to think so," said Işşurish quietly. "The Bel loved you."

A pang of sadness struck through Alihahd's veil of apathy. It had been a long time since he let himself think about whom he caused pain when first he ran away. "I love the Bel."

"Present tense, sir?"

"Present tense."

Işşurish paused. "Shall I tell him?"

"You may." He had not meant it as a message. It was a statement of fact.

Işşurish's orderly appeared and was given orders to take the prisoner to his quarters.

Alihahd was to spend the night aboard the flagship. The sergeant escorted him to secure quarters inconvenient to any exit. He waved the key, and the doorway's opaque energy barrier disappeared.

The orderly was a reluctant sort, like the medic, unhappy in his present duty of serving an archcriminal of the Empire. But he was not above talking to him. "How long have you been on this steamy rock?" He referred to the planet Iry.

"Best part of a year," said Alihahd, preceding his escort into the cabin.

"Oh. Then you weren't in it." The orderly turned on the light. "Guess you were real happy, though. When we lost Jerusalem again."

Alihahd's limping step hitched midstride. "What?"

The orderly grew uneasy. He licked his lips. "Just how isolated is it out here?"

"Exceedingly," Alihahd growled, turning. "What are you

saying?'' He stalked back toward the sergeant with demanding steps.

The sergeant drew his weapon. ''Don't. Just stay right there,'' he said, poking the air with his weapon for emphasis. ''I meant what I said. We lost Jerusalem. You didn't know? Now you know. We lost a lot of good Na'id too. Makes you happy?''

''No,'' said Alihahd. ''I am not happy.''

The orderly snarled, ''Then what the hell do you want?'' He backed out the doorway and reactivated the barrier, cursing.

Alihahd stood motionless in the middle of the cabin, lost in shock.

Jerusalem was free again. What did it mean? What did any of it mean? The historic battle—all the lives—it had been for nothing.

Why did we fight? Why did we fight? Jerusalem stands.

He let his head drop back and he gazed at the ceiling, chiding himself for trying to make sense of a senseless battle. All human battles were senseless and gainless, given time. It was one of the reasons—one of the good ones—why he could not do it anymore.

He broke from his marbled pose in weariness and sat on the cot.

The quarters were spartan, but luxurious next to the Aerie. It was odd to have all the conveniences again. He could easily become soft in conditions such as these, and he realized why he had almost died on first coming to the mountain.

He was to spend his last hours in comfort. Here was controlled air temperature, pressure, and humidity; soft bed; a pillow; water on tap; and even the extravagance of a bath and hot water.

And a vial of posion on the nightstand. Very thoughtful.

Alihahd bathed and dressed. He was loathe to get into his soiled clothes again, but did so out of defiance. He had already turned down the offer of a change and did not want to reverse his word now. Not that there was anyone to see.

Then he had a visitor.

Alihahd did not look at the young officer when he came in and would not have recognized him on sight anyway, for he was now a captain and twice as old as he had been at Jerusalem. Neither did Alihahd know the voice since it had dropped and become a man's. Alihahd only knew that the visitor was one of his own from the question: "Why, sir?"

Why indeed?

The young captain could tell that his former general heard him, though Alihahd did not acknowledge. Alihahd was not quite ignoring him. He was simply *elsewhere*.

"It wasn't that woman-in-the-boat business, was it?" The curly-haired youth hadn't taken the miracle seriously at the time. He worried now that Shad Iliya had.

"No, it was not that," said Alihahd. Even he was not certain that the incident had really happened now for all the time between. After a very long pause, he said, "Sinikar-rabannashi."

"Yes, sir," said his former orderly.

"You were at Jerusalem," said Alihahd like an answer.

"Was that it?" said Sinikar.

There was silence. A sigh. "Dead Arabs," said Alihahd.

Sinikar's eyes flickered left and right, searching for a connection—something to make the words make sense. His general was as bewildering as he had been on that last day. "Sir?"

Alihahd turned, his face graven, his stare frightening. "Dead Arabs," he said.

Sinikar backed to the door and fled.

The land outside would still be in sunlight. Time yet was left before nightfall. And before sunrise. Alihahd lay lightly drowsing on the bed, dreaming.

He dreamed that he wakened. It was fifteen years ago; he was in bed aboard his own flagship, *Courier*. His slave, Pony, had drawn his bath for him and stood next to the bed, white tail swishing, brown doe eyes gazing attentively down to him.

Soft voice said, "It is 0600, sir." And Pony recited the day's itinerary and asked if he wanted coffee or tea.

He ordered coffee, rose from the bed, thanked Pony, and stepped into the bath. He did not feel water.

At that point, he realized that he was actually still in bed dreaming.

He also realized that someone really was in his compartment.

He opened his eyes. It was Pony.

The little slave sat on a stool, agitated, blushing, near tears, his hands clasped between his knees, bright eyes fastened on his old master.

It was to be expected, but it had never occurred to Alihahd that Pony would still be attached to the 27th Army.

Alihahd sat up. His muscles had stiffened and shortened during his brief sleep, and he ached all over. He knew he was awake this time, and Pony was truly here.

Pony looked older in the texture of his skin. Fine lines fanned from the corners of his eyes. But his form, face, and musculature were still boyish; his eyes were still innocent—but that was because he was a stupid animal, thought Alihahd. A slavishly devoted slave, Pony had always adored him.

But Alihahd was not prepared to find Pony devoted still.

Sweet alto said, "I was sent to see if there was anything you require."

Alihahd shook his head. Muscles at the base of his neck knotted and pulled. "No, Pony. Nothing."

Pony was disappointed—devastated. He stood to go.

As Pony turned away, Alihahd caught sight of a heavy white scar on the left side of Pony's slender golden neck. His throat had been cut.

Alihahd jumped up, seized Pony's narrow wrist before he could reach the door, and pulled Pony around to face him. "What happened?"

Pony shrank, frightened by his demanding tone and rough hands.

Alihahd pushed Pony's head aside to the right, brushed away the long snowy hairs of his crested mane, and inspected the deep knife-edge scar.

The first thing that came to mind was that sometimes slaves were killed as grave gifts to their masters. But Alihahd had seen his own funeral, and no slaves' throats had been cut at his cenotaph. And if Pony *had* been intended as a gift, Pony would be dead; nobody botched a public sacrifice.

Alihahd took Pony's face in one hand, thumb and fingers on his cheekbones, and brought the enormous eyes around to face him straight. "Who did that to you?" he said, keeping hold lest the eyes avoid.

Small hesitant voice sounded muffled into his big palm, "When I thought you died . . ." He faltered.

He had done it himself, Alihahd realized in amazement.

The little fool didn't realize he had been gashing the wrong place. The human jugular vein was on the left; Pony's was up the back. He'd tried to kill himself.

Alihahd beheld his inhuman slave, mystified. *You did that for me, Pony?*

Alihahd loosed his hold from Pony's face. Reddened prints rose on gold cheeks where his fingers had pressed.

Naturally Pony had not been allowed to take his own life simply because he wished it. He was too valuable a property for that privilege.

Alihahd then noticed for the first time that the pretty eyes were sick to death of life. It had gone overlooked initially, briefly outshone by Pony's excitement at meeting his beloved master again.

Velvet soft lower lip quivered. "Sir, will they make you die again?" said Pony, and his eyes flooded tears.

Alihahd's impulse to comfort him was checked by an old awkwardness. Alihahd could not bring himself to take the weeping creature in his arms. He would feel odd and clumsy.

So he gave a command. "Help me to bed, Pony."

Pony's tears stopped at the reassuring sound of order and normality, even if it was all mirage. Pony wanted nothing more than to be allowed to do his job and forget that tomorrow must come. He laid out nightclothes for his master and helped him undress.

And Alihahd wondered, *Was I always fussed over like this?* He guessed he had been, because Pony was unchanged.

Pony even remembered to bring him a shot of whiskey. Alihahd hesitated—as if Mr. Hall would appear out of vacant air and hit him. Then he swallowed it, felt it warm him, and he gave the glass back to Pony. Pony dimmed the lights and withdrew.

Alone in the almost-dark, Alihahd lay back on the bed. He turned his head on the pillow and looked over to the poison on the nightstand.

General Işşurish came to the prisoner's quarters in the morning.

Alihahd lay stretched out on the bed, the covers thrown off, his arm draped loosely over the pillow.

He was alive.

Blue eyes opened.

"I'm disappointed," said Işşurish.

"So am I, actually," said Alihahd.

He could not do it. Never could. *If I could, it would never have come to this. There would have been a body for my funeral.*

The supreme commander's jaw tightened. *You lost your nerve.* "Well then. Come on." He left and sent Shad Iliya's slave in.

Pony laid out Shad Iliya's dress uniform and all his decorations. Alihahd knew what it meant.

"O gods, are we to go through all that?"

This was ugly business. He should have taken the poison.

Pony placed all the ribbons and medals and braids in order—Alihahd did not remember where all the damn things went—and Pony combed his wayward blond hair. "I should trim it," said Pony, trying to make the wisps lie down.

"No, you shouldn't," said Alihahd. "Just put on the hat and have done with this."

Shad Iliya always wore his hat dead square regulation, no matter which way the winds of unofficial military fashion blew: slouched, pushed back, or cocked to either side. Pony centered the hat just so, and stepped back. "You look grand, sir."

Alihahd checked in the mirror. He cut a trim figure, appearing not so gaunt as imposingly tall. The uniform could make anyone look good, and it *felt* right, after all this time, a dark cobalt blue with epaulets on his wide, angular shoulders, and clean-fitted lines down to knee-high black boots.

Pony, can you not guess what I am in for because of this?

Pony did not guess, and Alihahd did not tell him so as not to see his bright admiration fade.

The guards came to fetch him.

"Time, sir."

Shad Iliya was marched out, his hands unbound, in front of the entire assembly of Na'id personnel and the captive rebels as well. It was a long walk, but he did not limp; the uniform, the moment, his name constrained dignity. He saw his destination—a dead tree that had been trimmed to a tall, neat post. Alihahd wondered if the proceedings were being recorded.

At the post, he turned smartly to face the multitude. The guards dropped back, and Işşurish stepped up, being the only person of sufficient rank to perform this duty. His face was not that of the genial host on the flagship, but of a severe and efficient officer of the Empire, angry at having to do this. He stripped Shad Iliya of his rank, medals, and all the Na'id insignia with which he had just been decorated. It seemed ludicrous. But it hurt. Alihahd was surprised how much it truly hurt.

Işşurish finished by ripping the twin symbol of Galactic Dominion/Human Supremacy from Shad Iliya's hat and tossing the hat to the ground as trash. The insignia he placed grudgingly in his own breast pocket, a deep frown fissuring his jowls. He spun and marched away.

Left bareheaded, Alihahd felt the pleasant morning air on his scalp. The sun was rising to a clear sky. The day would be brilliant.

No longer called *sir*, but *you*, Alihahd was backed up to the post and chained there. A firing squad of twenty-one filed into position. The first markswoman asked him ritually if he forgave his executioners.

"Yes," he said.

The butcher waited nearby with a skinning knife with which to carve up the remains into pieces that the ships' food preparers were programmed to handle. The man looked like the kind who enjoyed his work. Alihahd hoped he was not one of those who kept souvenirs—not that Alihahd would know who did what with which part of his carcass, but it bothered him to think that the fleshy MP might come into possession of one of his blue eyes, or whatever else he might want to step on.

The row of marksmen dropped to one knee so as not to obstruct the view of the legion.

Alihahd could look into faces, and he saw more awe than hatred. None of them had a blood score with him. He had never taken a Na'id life.

The strained stillness to them transcended mere military attention. It was an awareness that they witnessed more than a death. The legend had only begun.

A breeze stirred on the plain with the warming air.

Ah. Eaninala.

Smell of charcoal and yellow grasses.

He was offered a blindfold; refused it. He felt the sun on his face; looked up at the bright sky. *I want to live very much.* He thought of all that was beautiful as the marksmen took aim.

The sun and Amerika.

VIII. Thunder on the Right

The order to fire hung unspoken, gnawing at the silence like the final resolving note of a melody, which was natural and expected, that did not come. Alihahd waited for it, became impatient, then alarmed. He lowered his gaze from the sky. The sea of faces before him had all blanched—even those of the firing squad—and all eyes stared past Alihahd, gaping at some horrible vision beyond him, threatening to break ranks. Someone cried, "Marauder!"

Alihahd cranked his head around to see behind his post to what they saw.

The ghostly image of a sailing ship. The derelict brigantine coalesced from shimmering air. It raised the hairs on the back of his neck, and he shivered in the heat. Something elemental in the rag sails and rotting timbers never lost power to affect him.

And suddenly all the spaceships imploded—all of them—with a resounding crack and thunder roll as the great engines consumed themselves. Astounded, Alihad's thoughts flashed like lightning, his heart leapt, and he roared, "Hall!"

Na'id troops cried out and scattered everywhere, trying to stop what had already happened.

And the rebel captives all bolted.

The melee that ensued covered the plateau, spread into the forest as rebels fled or mobbed their guards and seized their weapons. Shots were fired. The unarmed fought with their hands, with rocks, with anything within reach.

Alihahd was in the midst of it, tied to the stake, ignored. He was not going anywhere. He could not even duck.

The fighting moved away into the jungle. It was not a battle. It was a brawl. The Na'id were torn between chasing their stampeding prisoners and fighting the fires around their ruined ships. The ships won the most attention, though there was nothing left to save. Properly rigged, a Na'id ship could destruct with extreme efficiency.

This was a Na'id nightmare—to be stranded on an uncharted alien world. Alihahd felt a pang of compassion for the panicked troops, knew their terror.

He heard cries in the jungle, "Get the Marauder! The Marauder has a ship!"

The Marauder does not. It is on the bottom of the ocean, thought Alihahd. All that was left of it was "just a gadget" —the fearful specter still loomed over the plain—and a few implosion detonators, it would seem.

Alone and neglected, chained to the stake, Alihahd watched the grass fires switch with the fickle winds, and he wondered vaguely if they would come to him.

The fighting moved farther and farther away, until the soldiers were only voices to Alihahd. He still heard their distant shouts among the trees.

Then someone came out of the forest and ran toward him with a drawn dagger. It was Layla. She tried to saw at his metal chains.

"Layla, I surrendered," said Alihahd.

"I did not," said Layla. She looked for a catch, a spring, something to release the chains. "Damn!"

Soldiers were returning. Layla yanked at the chains, gave a grunt of frustration, and scurried back to the jungle at the last possible moment, elusive as an Itiri.

Lost-looking soldiers began to reassemble on the plateau, without orders, without a camp, directionless. At least the ghost image of the *Flying Dutchman* had ceased to menace over the plain by then. Someone else came to Alihahd's stake: Pony. The slender little slave sat at his master's feet, rested his white-maned head against the post to wait until someone came to get him.

Alihahd was thirsty. There was no fresh water. He saw frightened faces among the troops licking their lips and trembling with dehydration on the dusty plateau. Pony was wilted at the bottom of the post.

General Işşurish returned to the plateau, and some small confidence and hope revived in the lost men and women of the Na'id army. Işşurish wiped his brow, hot, thirsty, and tired, but not frightened. He moved like a leader who knew what he was about. Like Musa, he was difficult to rattle, even in catastrophe. He organized a few patrols and sent them out in search of water. He sent others to deal with the grass fires, which had almost burned themselves out by then, but it gave the soldiers something to do.

From the jungle, a band of ten soldiers brought a thrashing prisoner, hogtied and gagged with his own bandanna. They dropped him at General Işşurish's feet and gave the general a plastic black box they had found on the prisoner's person; it was a projector. Işşurish turned it on. The dim outlines of a brigantine ship began to shimmer over the trees. Işşurish turned it off. "Well," said Işşurish and looked down at Harrison White Fox Hall, who was trussed and double-trussed. "Is all this necessary?" Işşurish asked his soldiers, his voice dripping with tried patience.

"Yes sir," said the black-and-blue sergeant with teeth marks on his arms.

Işşurish looked down again. Orange eyes slid up slyly, not the least bit frightened or remorseful. Işşurish drew his gun and pointed it at the handsome, wedge-shaped head.

The captive did not blink. Işşurish guessed that his pulse hadn't even quickened. Işşurish holstered his gun. He could see the man was dangerous—confirming all that the black box implied. The kind with ice in the veins, and no heart, not to be trifled with—Işşurish would not even bother trying to intimidate him. Vain gestures were a waste of his time. "Where is your ship?" said Işşurish.

Hall snorted a laugh behind his gag.

Işşurish nodded. He'd expected that response. Torture was yet a possibility, though Işşurish had his doubts even to the efficacy of that. He ordered an organized search begun for the Marauder ship. Hall was sniggering at the general's feet.

"Don't look so smug, Marauder," said Işşurish calmly. "I am aware that you have the only working spaceship in the world. And while I would very much like to lay hands on it, it is not imperative. Someone will come looking for us eventually, or we will find your ship for ourselves, and your life and your smug secret will be worth sadly little then." He watched the orange eyes for a reaction.

How could anyone smirk so while gagged?

Işşurish turned away and gave orders to the soldiers who had brought him. "Put him with Shad Iliya. Guard them both closely. And take off that imbecilic gag."

"He bites, sir."

"Take him away."

The guards chained Harrison Hall to the same black, charred post as Alihahd. The two exchanged looks. They'd last seen each other to say farewell. "Captain."

"Mr. Hall."

"Be quiet," said a guard. She chased the little slave Pony away. Pony skittered off a few yards, then hovered at a respectful distance, tail switching, watching for an opportunity to come back.

The Na'id army had given up trying to recapture their other rebel prisoners. They hadn't the means to keep two thousand people captive. And they turned their energies to survival without prepared food, without pure water, without modern equipment. They couldn't even make Harrison Hall divulge his secrets without the devices and drugs from their ships.

Hall was pleased with himself. He was satisfied with the smoking piles of melted metal that were the Na'id ships. "I like my plan better than yours," he said to Alihahd.

"You have made a liar of me again," said Alihahd. "Caused a melee, stranded all of us on this planet, possibly incited an interstellar purge, and signaled the destruction of this world."

"And I robbed you of your neat and heroic little suicide," said Hall, cutting to the real source of his vexation. "I told you I wanted you alive and stinging."

"You are a devil."

"No. Angel. Who ever heard of an avenging devil?"

"Damn you! Damn you! Damn you!"

"Nothing more eloquent than that for me?"

"*No.*"

"Oh, but I first met you in a spate of elegant fury, Captain." He still remembered Alihahd exquisitely angry: *For myself, by you or by them, I will be equally dead. I don't very much care. So please either to shoot, talk, or go away. Or you may go to hell, where I am bound with or without you. Do you want me to repeat any of that?* "Do you know your buddy talks just like you do?" He meant Işşurish

He received only an exasperated roll of blue eyes from Alihahd.

Hall grinned. "You're glad to see me." He curled two fingers around Alihahd's wrist behind his back.

"Will you shut up!" a guard snarled.

Time passed slowly. Alihahd and Hall both slid down the post to sit on the ground, still chained. As evening came on, the Na'id were settling. They set up guards against sniping rebels and wild animals from the jungle. They'd built campfires and brought hundreds of animal carcasses to be skinned, gutted, and cooked. They boiled stream water and tested the palatability of jungle fruits on their remaining slaves such as Pony. Once they organized, time was on their side. Eventually, eventually, someone would come looking. The Empire simply did not lose its most famous army, a reinforcement company, and two generals, and not come investigating in time.

"We need allies," Hall mumbled aside to Alihahd.

Alihahd knew of whom he spoke. "It is not their battle," he said.

They both gazed up at the sky, attracted by the sight of an eagle soaring over the mountain.

Their minds ran parallel. Alihahd addressed Hall's unspoken thought: "It would go against conscience."

"Not *mine*," said Hall.

The two guards, who were bragging to each other about their marksmanship, turned back to their captives. "I thought I told you to shut up," said one. She was a tight-lipped, razor-lean sergeant with pock-scarred face, hatchet features, and a slight curve to her spine. She walked with her shoulders hunched forward, her pelvis tucked under, her sharp hipbones prominent against the fabric of trousers that were too loose on her. She sneered a lot.

The other guard was a beefy young man with peppercorn hair and a walk like a turkey cock. He snarled at the captives and returned his attention to his comrade's high claims regarding her sharpshooting.

Hall said loudly, "I was just saying: Odds say you can't hit that eagle."

Alihahd was horrified. "No!"

The sergeant turned her head back to them and gave a thin-lipped sneer. "Sure I can." She lifted her gun and took aim at the distant soaring shape.

"They are sapient beings!" Alihahd cried.

The Na'id sergeant looked up from her gunsight and regarded him queerly. It had been a nonsensical thing to say. "Alien's an alien," she said and returned her sights to her target. She took careful aim and fired.

The majestic eagle folded in midair and came fluttering down into the mountain jungle.

Alihahd was stunned. He rasped at Hall, "You *don't* have conscience."

"Absolutely none." Hall smiled. "Captain, you surprise me. I didn't think you considered aliens to be on a level with human beings."

"I changed my mind!"

The guard swaggered to Hall and looked down at him with a smirk. "Any more dumb bets?"

"None, ma'am," said Hall.

And from the sky came a clear, thin cry.

Ki ki ki ki.

IX. Legacy of the Red Geese

Directly overhead the kestrel hovered, suspended on a twilight breeze, while in the distance droned the engines of rapidly approaching aircraft.

"What's that?" Na'id cried, and Na'id guns pointed toward the sky.

Işşurish prowled the wide plateau, bellowing at his thousands of soldiers, "For gods' sake, if it's a working vehicle, don't shoot at it!"

And the Itiri came.

The ships landed in the jungle, and in a short time the warrior-priests appeared from the trees, twelve tall alabaster godlings with sunlight hair and eyes of brilliant green. From their midst advanced a midnight figure cradling a great limp feathered body in her wiry arms, its blood seeping onto her tunic and trousers. She stepped to the center of the plain and spoke with a voice like brass. "This is my brother. Who hath done this? This is my battle."

She turned slowly, a complete circuit, then stooped and gently laid the dead eagle on the yellow grass.

The kestrel was hovering above the charred post where Alihahd and Hall were bound. Roniva crossed to them. The two guards moved away at her advance, and the kestrel moved with the sergeant. Roniva stopped, looked at Hall and Alihahd in chains, looked at the kestrel, looked at the thin, snarling sergeant, whose shoulders hunched defensively as she hugged her gun, her tiny eyes darting. "Thou?" said Roniva.

The sergeant's thin upper lip moved in spasms; she was not answerable to this *alien*. "What the hell are you?" she sneered.

General Işşurish intervened. To Roniva he said, "Madame, if you have some problem with my soldiers, you will address it to me."

Onyx eyes shifted to him, to his general's insignia. "Thy soldier or thy head," said Roniva.

Işşurish's attitude immediately changed. "Is that a threat, you alien bitch?"

"No decision?" said Roniva curtly, without patience. "I decide." Faster than the eye could follow, Roniva had drawn her sword and slashed the sneering sergeant's throat open.

All at once, those Na'id soldiers with a clear shot aimed their weapons at the alien warriors, but in that same instant the Itiri had each seized the nearest Na'id soldier as a shield, and no one dared shoot. Roniva herself had caught Işşurish by the back of his hair and by one thick wrist, which she twisted behind his back. Twice her bulk, he could not move. "Thou hast come to my home like a great ape," said Roniva. "I will have thee and thy kind gone from here." She had looped his long hair once around the hilt of her sword, and she yanked on it for emphasis. Işşurish ground his teeth in silence.

Roniva took his handgun from him, then unwound her sword hilt from his hair, still keeping hold of his wrist behind his back. She glanced aside at the dead sergeant crumpled in a pool of blood like the eagle. Then she looked to Hall and Alihahd chained to the post. She looked away as if uninterested, then suddenly screamed, swung her tungsten-plastic blade, and slashed down at the post, severing the prisoners' chains in a single stroke. She hadn't let go of Işşurish.

Işşurish nodded, nothing daunted. "We will go. We will destroy your world."

Alihahd, chains hanging from his wrists, came to Roniva's side. "They can, Fendi."

Roniva lifted her chin. "Destroy it," she said.

A deep, groaning rumble and an unfirmness to the ground way down deep like the beginnings of an earthquake unsettled the field; and a great dark mass rising from the horizon slowly eclipsed the setting sun—a leviathan rising out of the River Ocean, spilling water from its crevices—and it kept rising like a continent taking flight.

"What is that?" said Işşurish. It was still rising.

"An intergalactic ship—what does it look like?" said Roniva. She was starting to sound like Harrison Hall. "Destroy that," she said.

Her snowy owl blinked in above her head and alighted on her hard shoulder. It batted Işşurish's head as it folded its broad white wings, and it squealed.

Roniva spoke sharply to Alihahd. "Now. Say to this one." She twisted Işşurish's wrist. "Say to him: 'Thy Bel hath been notified. Thy people are to be picked up and leave this planet. Not to look back. A ship of the rebel kind will come to collect the fugitives littering my forest. Be gone and continue your fight far away from here.' Am I understood?"

"Have you no concept of justice?" said Işşurish.

"Oh yes, justice," said Roniva. "Tell him we do not worship that god here."

"I demand—"

"Thou so stupid, take what I give thee or I shall give thee ash!" Roniva cried. "Another Dark Age for thy kind! A long one! Two thousand years was not enough!"

She threw Işşurish away from her. To Alihahd she said, "Stay close to me, in case they shoot."

Alihahd and Hall both drew closer. "You have a shield?" said Alihahd.

"This creature"—she stroked her owl's wing—"can absorb a great deal of energy. Come. I wish to be away from these beings.''

Alihahd and Hall followed her into the jungle. None of the Na'id tried to stop them, or fired on any of the warrior-priests. The intergalactic ship had risen its full bulk from the River Ocean and now dominated the darkening sky like a moon.

It occurred to Alihahd that Roniva could have summoned a rescue for him anytime she wanted—had she wanted to lead outsiders to Aerie. As if reading his thoughts, she said in perfect, modern Universal, "I do not like your people."

Alihahd glared at Hall. "At this point neither do I." As he walked, he nearly tripped over the cut chains which dangled from his wrists. Roniva noticed his difficulty, and she cut the chains off for him and Harrison Hall, leaving them with the metal cuffs.

"And to which side belongest thou?" she said to Alihahd. She already knew Hall's.

"I believe they both want to kill me, Fendi," said Alihahd.

"I will give thee a ship of thine own," she said.

Alihahd was too surprised even to thank her. Recent events still had him numbed, and consequences were still rolling into his brain. His stare kept returning to the gargantuan, impossible ship in the sky. Its details were difficult to distinguish. If he stared too closely at a point, he could no longer see it, like trying to focus on a single star, and he wondered of what it was made—light?

The thing's existence struck at the very foundation of the Na'id Empire. It represented a superior technology—superior to anything that had ever been known to humankind. The Empire was founded on the belief that God had created humankind in God's own image to rule over all of lesser Creation. Human Supremacy and Galactic Dominion had become a mockery.

Layla appeared from somewhere and pulled on Alihahd's sleeve. "It *is* tottering, is it not? The Empire?"

"It's falling," said Alihahd.

He supposed the clues had been there for any of them to see all along—the Itiri's tungsten-plastic swords, the disappearing familiars, and constellations that had been given names so long ago they would have to antedate Earth's first infant civilization—why hadn't that struck him as curious? Thousands of years ago, when men and women were nothing *but* great apes, someone had been here naming the constellations, naming them after swords, ships—and a Gateway.

He shook his head, feeling blind and stupid. He wondered aloud how the powerful Itiri could have allowed the deluded Na'id to strut and bawl like young bullies for so long, over-running the galaxy and calling themselves supreme.

Hall's tawny eyes assumed their wicked hunter's gleam. "Yes, how can such an aggressive people bear to watch and do nothing?"

"Aggressive?" said Alihahd.

"The Itiri?" said Layla. "They speak of nothing but peace."

"Ever listen to their music? It's not peaceful," said Hall. "You saw the New Year's celebration." He took a zircon and a turquoise from his pocket and juggled them. "Constant repetition of humbleness and serenity isn't the mark of a peaceful people. What is the need for the constant repetition if they are in fact so tranquil?"

Alihahd looked to Roniva. She was not angry. She smiled like a master criminal caught by a master detective. "Very astute, Harrison White Fox Hall." She turned to Alihahd. "You wonder at our constant readiness for war and wonder who is the enemy for whom we prepare. Only ourselves."

"But you seem to have the aggressive tendencies con-quered," said Alihahd.

Roniva put her spidery hand over his knobby one. "And so do you seem."

Alihahd smiled in rue and irony. They were as savage as he. So they could forgive him, forgive Ben, forgive the Na'id. The guilty did not presume to mete out justice.

"An ancient shame," said Alihahd.

Roniva raised her chin, affirmatively. "That ship"—she pointed at the monster from the sea "is not the one in which we—our forebears—came. Our ancestors were abandoned here with nothing. That ship was built with redeveloped technology after a long, long time in exile here. And when it was finally built—still a very long time ago—we sank it. We decided we did not want it; we did not want to be what we were, what brought us to this exile in the beginning. We wished to abandon that past and become someone else. You understand, Captain Alihahd? You see, we did not come here by choice, we were not pilgrims, we did not even flee here.

This is a penal colony. We do not even know where home is—some place where red birds fly like geese. It could be that we came from another time as well as another galaxy. Once we passed through the Gateway our ancestors could not know what date it was back home. They could have been millions of years in the passing. That was what our judges intended. They sent us so far even our familiars could not find the way back.''

"But do you know what your ancestors did to deserve this?" said Alihahd.

"*I* know," said the Fendi. Most Itiri did not know. "We conquered our galaxy. We the aghara are natural leaders; our ranga are a natural army of unquestioning followers. We ruled the *universe*, we thought. Eventually we were overthrown and driven out. Now we teach ourselves to own nothing, want nothing, to keep our superiority to ourselves. Humbleness we still have not. Judge, we must not. It is not for us to check, conquer, punish the Na'id. We *are* the Na'id. See you now why we must not take up this sword?" She looked to Alihahd and Hall.

"I see," said Hall.

"Then will you please to shut up?"

Alihahd laughed sadly. *I know these people*. He was suddenly very fond of Roniva.

The ship Roniva gave him was the *Topaz*. He was free to leave whenever he willed. He chose to wait until the rescue ships came to collect both the rebels and the Na'id, so that neither side would see his ascent and would not know to go hunting for him in space. The wait would not be much longer. He could abide awhile yet.

Night had fallen. Creatures of the darkness were calling within the jungle. Alihahd climbed up to the top of his ship and sat there underneath a wide break in the fringed canopy of tree boughs open to the heavens. He looked at the sky.

Low on the eastern horizon, the Red Geese were rising.

X. The Fallen Tower

The rebels' rescue ships came first. Layla and Harrison White Fox Hall left planet with them. The Na'id ships came later. Mustering the means to airlift twelve thousand soldiers on such short notice had been difficult. The humiliation of the mighty human army rocked the Empire. Alihahd wondered how the Bel was dealing with the incredible developments.

Then, before the Na'id ships ascended, a message for Shad Iliya from the Bel was delivered to Alihahd in the jungle. Pony brought it; the Na'id themselves were afraid to go into the night forest.

Alihahd accepted the capsule from Pony's golden hands, and he stared at it a long time before opening it. Something thickened in his throat. He could not face the contents.

In that moment, he remembered his youth as a pale oddity in a brown family, a suspected bastard. He remembered that as long as he thought he was a bastard he might as well dream that this man was his real father. Not that the Bel had any more Caucasian traits than his legal father did, but the Bel treated him more like a son than his legal father ever did.

Alihahd opened the message capsule and could not speak. Whatever he might have said was lost when he read the Bel's single question: *Was it the people?*

Alihahd looked up—lest the tears that were welling in his eyes fall. Second perhaps to Roniva, the Bel was the most powerful individual in the galaxy and close to the wisest; why was Alihahd surprised that he knew? *Was it the people?* All those dead at Jerusalem, humans dead at human hands.

Yes, it was the people. Why did you send me there?

Pony was waiting for a return message, his silvery tail swishing away the winged bugs that plagued him, his great brown eyes timorously scanning the treetops for sail snakes or for those enormous eagles, which terrified him.

Alihahd snapped the capsule shut and buried it in his pocket. Swiftly he sought out Roniva, while Pony faithfully dogged his footsteps.

He found her in deep jungle shade, seated on a moss-covered boulder, her tunic and trousers stiff with dried blood. Her long hair, hanging from its topknot, shone glossy blue-black in the winking lights from her nearby airship.

"A going-away present, Fendi," Alihahd announced. He took the startled Pony by his shoulders and presented the little alien to Roniva. "My slave."

Onyx eyes blinked slowly within the frame of the crimson scars on her high, sharp cheekbones. "We keep no slaves," said Roniva.

"You tell him," said Alihahd, and ran to the *Topaz*.

Pony turned his huge eyes diffidently to his new mistress. Roniva curled her forefinger on her lips. She did not know what she was going to do with him. She would think of something.

After the Na'id ships were gone, the *Topaz* took flight. Alihahd was soon in infinite space, free. He had the means to travel anywhere. The autopilot was asking him where he wanted to go.

He'd been flying aimlessly for quite some time before he told it:

Mat Tanatti.

The blue-green world was so familiar that the sight of it hurt. Once in orbit, the starship *Topaz* was challenged for ID and intent by ground control.

Alihahd transmitted an Absolute Priority signal. His message would go straight to the Bel. But when the channel opened for him, he could not turn on his audiovisual transmitter. He could not trust his voice anymore, and he could not face the Bel's image. He could imagine the benign, elderly face with fatherly eyes full of pain and betrayal. He could hear the Bel speaking: "You hurt me, Shad. You have embarrassed me, stabbed me in the back, damaged my Empire beyond repair. What would you have me do now? What would you have me do?" The image in Alihahd's mind was talking quietly, reasonably, as the Bel did when extremely angry, as Alihahd did; Alihahd had gotten the mannerism from him. He could not talk to the man face to face. So he encoded his message, requesting permission to land.

Who asks? came the coded reply.

Alihahd had many aliases under which to hide. He answered: *Shad Iliya*.

An eternity passed waiting for the response. It could be anything, a missile, a refusal, a fleet of police ships, or a cold, cold "Who?" He waited. He died a thousand times. The answer came, the only thing to be said; the rest they could discuss tomorrow.

Come home.

The Ring

Signs (Months) of the Year

                                   Equinox
1. The Sword
2. The Ship
3. The Crown
4. The Red Geese
                                   Solstice
5. The Twins
6. The Hexagon
7. The Gateway
8. The Flower
                                   Equinox
9. The Beacon
10. The Serpent
11. The Cross
12. The Triquetra
                                   Solstice
13. The River
14. The Wellspring   Shandee
15. The Veil
16. The Mountain

A sign lasts 10.74 days.

Shandee blows from the second of the River to the seventh of the Veil. The new year begins with the vernal equinox on the Aerie (Northern hemisphere).

Years are named in order for a sign of the Ring. Hexadecades are named in order for a gem in the Gem Cycle, which runs as follows: Topaz, Carnelian, Opal, Jade, Beryl, Onyx, Diamond, Tourmaline, Turquoise, Amethyst, Lapis, Garnet, Zircon, Adularia, Corundum, and Jet.

The present action of this story takes place from the sign of the Red Geese in the Year of the Opal Ship until the sign of the Sword in the Year of the Opal Crown.

THE NUMBERS

Number	Itiri Name	Universal Translation of Name
1	Enna	Sword
2	Shauul	Ship
3	Niaha	Crown
4	Shanwel	Red Geese
5	Bibi	Twins
6	Sorii	Hexagon
7	Dalanai	Gateway
8	Sianasad	Flower
9	Saufer	Beacon
A(10)	Elebanar	Serpent
B(11)	Yxa	Cross
C(12)	Jentas	Triquetra
D(13)	Mandas	River
E(14)	Maeus	Wellspring
F(15)	Ovron	Veil
10(16)	Lodee	Mountain

After sixteen the numbers are named in combinations of the
above; for example, seventeen is *endee*—"sixteen and one."
And so it goes: *shaudee, niadee, shandee,* etc.

The Hours

First watch	Hour of the bells	Sunset
	Hour of madiyal (the wind from the crevasse)	
Second watch	Hour of the winged mice (Bats)	
	Hour of the stars	Midnight
Third watch	Hour of the meteors	
	Hour of the berinxes	
Fourth watch	Hour of the sentinels	
	Hour of the dewcatchers	
Fifth watch	Hour of the sun	Sunrise
	Hour of the eagles (Talassairi)	
Sixth watch	Hour of the waning shadows	
	Hour of the killing light	Midday
Seventh watch	Hour of the lizards	
	Hour of the tide lilies	
Eighth watch	Hour of the waxing shadows	
	Hour of the swifts	

About the Author

Rebecca M. Meluch graduated from the University of North Carolina at Greensboro with a B.A. in drama. She also has an M.A. in ancient history from the University of Pennsylvania and a black belt in *tae kwon do*. She has worked as everything from a control clerk and keypunch operator to an assistant in the Classics department at Greensboro, and she has been active in nonprofessional theater. Her other novels, *Sovereign*, *Wind Dancers* and *Wind Child*, are also available in Signet editions. Miss Meluch lives in Westlake, Ohio.

THE WILD SHORE

Kim Stanley Robinson

'Simply one of our best writers'
Gene Wolfe

'A powerful new talent'
Damon Knight

2047: for 60 years America has been quarantined
after a devastating nuclear attack. For the small
community of San Onofre on the West Coast, life is
a matter of survival: living simply on what the sea
and land can provide, preserving what knowledge
and skills they can in a society without mass
communications. Until the men from San Diego
arrive, riding the rails of flatbed trucks and bringing
news of the new American Resistance. And Hank
Fletcher and his friends are drawn into an
adventure that marks the end of childhood . . .

A stunning debut by a powerful new talent.

'There's a fresh wind blowing in THE WILD
SHORE . . . welcome, Kim Stanley Robinson'
Ursula K Le Guin

'Beautifully written . . . with a vivid depth rarely
encountered in science fiction'
Washington Post Book World

Futura Publications
Science Fiction/An Orbit Book
0 7088 8147 5

WORLDS

Joe Haldeman

At last, man has reached the high frontier. Out in the orbiting Worlds the colonists live in full view of the stars yet still preserve their links with the home world.

But the Earth is tearing itself apart and soon the colonists must face the Universe alone.

WORLDS, the Hugo and Nebula winner, a brilliant vision of mankind's future by the author of THE FOREVER WAR.

'A future you can accept without question, full of casual reality which makes for high drama when the pieces start to come apart . . . as they do in a way you cannot doubt might happen in just this way.'
FRANK HERBERT

'Joe Haldeman's writing has never been better . . . there are scenes in WORLDS I will remember forever.'
STEPHEN KING

Futura Publications/An Orbit Book
Science Fiction
0 7088 8090 8

All Futura Books are available at your bookshop or
newsagent, or can be ordered from the following address:
Futura Books, Cash Sales Department,
P.O. Box 11, Falmouth, Cornwall.

Please send cheque or postal order (no currency), and
allow 55p for postage and packing for the first book
plus 22p for the second book and 14p for each additional
book ordered up to a maximum charge of £1.75 in U.K.

Customers in Eire and B.F.P.O. please allow 55p for
the first book, 22p for the second book plus 14p per
copy for the next 7 books, thereafter 8p per book.

Overseas customers please allow £1 for postage and
packing for the first book and 25p per copy for each
additional book.

interzone

SCIENCE FICTION AND FANTASY

Quarterly £1.50

- *Interzone* is the only British magazine specializing in SF and new fantastic writing. We have published:

BRIAN ALDISS	M. JOHN HARRISON
J.G. BALLARD	GARRY KILWORTH
BARRINGTON BAYLEY	MICHAEL MOORCOCK
MICHAEL BISHOP	KEITH ROBERTS
ANGELA CARTER	GEOFF RYMAN
RICHARD COWPER	JOSEPHINE SAXTON
JOHN CROWLEY	JOHN SLADEK
PHILIP K. DICK	BRUCE STERLING
THOMAS M. DISCH	IAN WATSON
MARY GENTLE	CHERRY WILDER
WILLIAM GIBSON	GENE WOLFE

- *Interzone* has also published many excellent new writers; graphics by **JIM BURNS, ROGER DEAN, IAN MILLER** and others; book reviews, news, etc.

- *Interzone* is available from specialist SF shops, or by subscription. For four issues, send £6 (outside UK, £7) to: **124 Osborne Road, Brighton BN1 6LU, UK.** Single copies: £1.75 inc p&p.

- American subscribers may send $10 ($13 if you want delivery by air mail) to our British address, above. All cheques should be made payable to *Interzone*.

- "No other magazine in Britain is publishing science fiction at all, let alone fiction of this quality." *Times Literary Supplement*

- -

To: **interzone** 124 Osborne Road, Brighton, BN1 6LU, UK.

Please send me four issues of *Interzone,* beginning with the current issue. I enclose a cheque/p.o. for £6 (outside UK, £7; US subscribers, $10 or $13 air), made payable to *Interzone*.

Name _____

Address _____

_____